Shojo Beat

Skip·Beat!

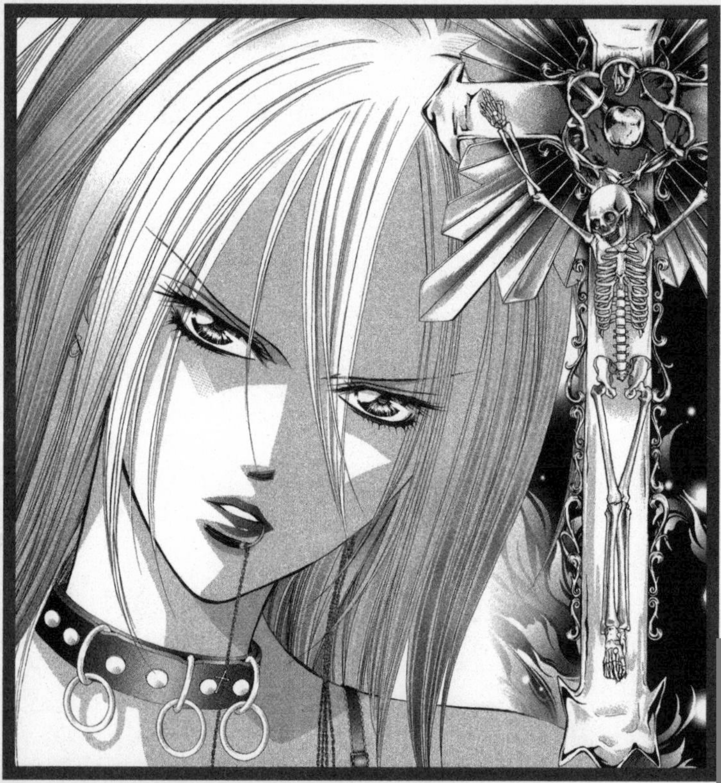

Skip·Beat!

Volume 29

CONTENTS

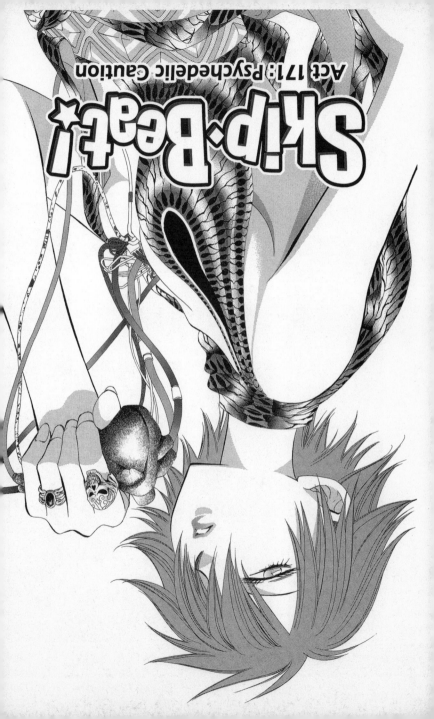

Act 171: Psychedelic Caution

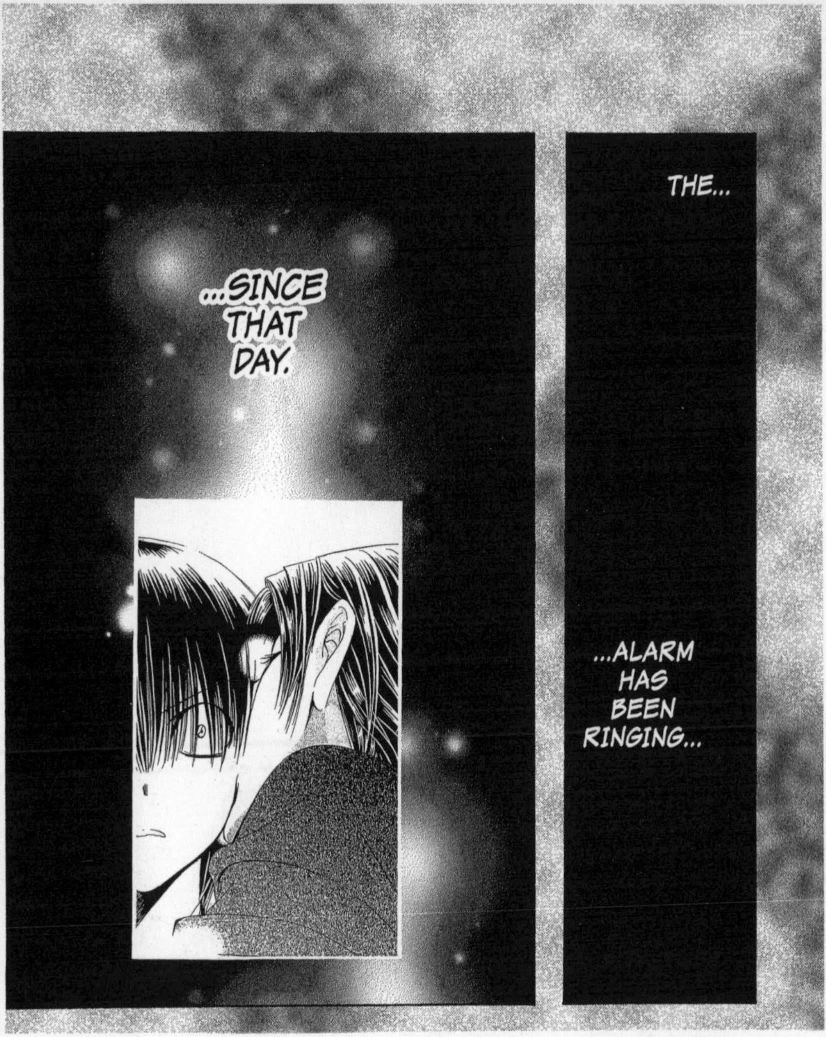
THE...
...ALARM HAS BEEN RINGING...
...SINCE THAT DAY.
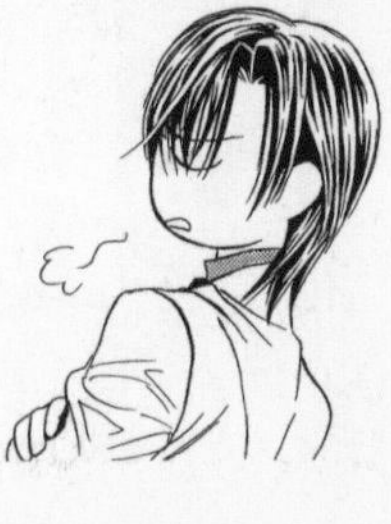

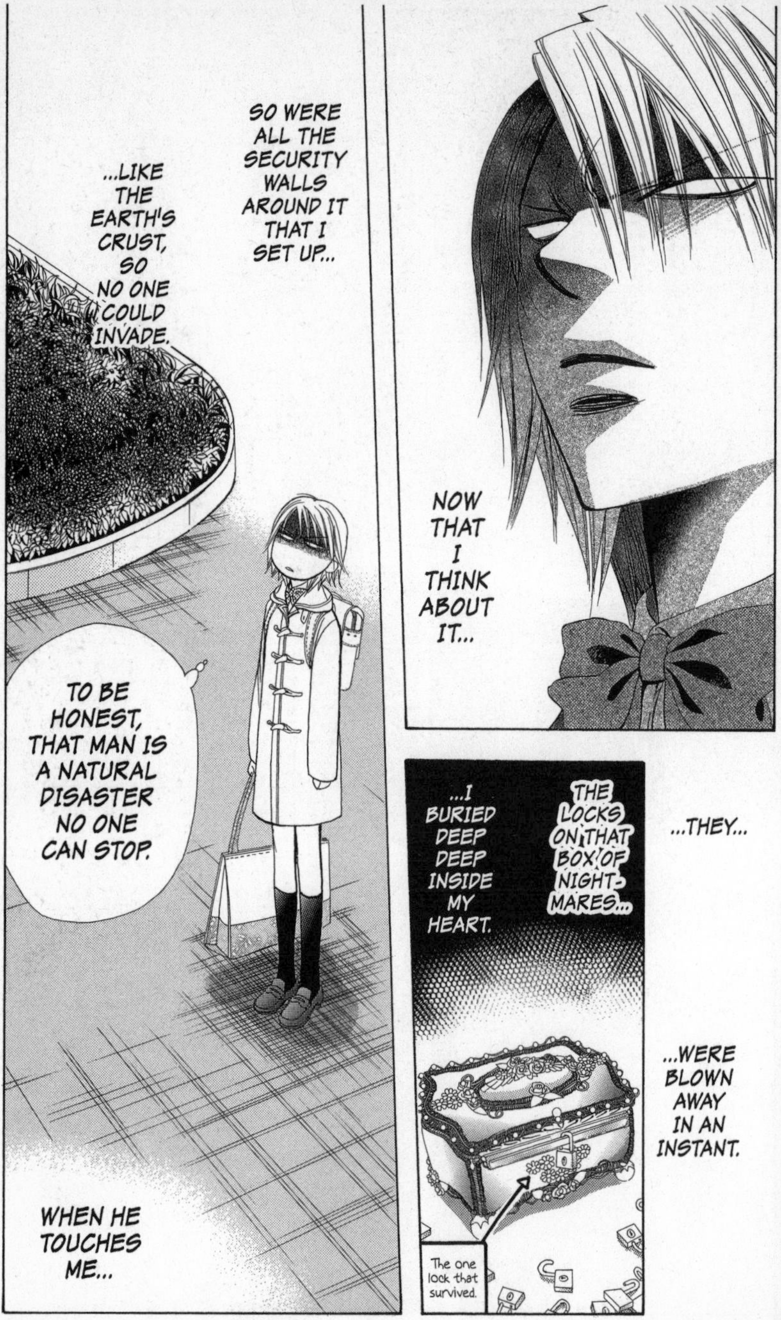
NOW THAT I THINK ABOUT IT...
...THEY...
THE LOCKS ON THAT BOX OF NIGHTMARES...
...I BURIED DEEP DEEP INSIDE MY HEART.
...WERE BLOWN AWAY IN AN INSTANT.
The one lock that survived.
SO WERE ALL THE SECURITY WALLS AROUND IT THAT I SET UP...
...LIKE THE EARTH'S CRUST, SO NO ONE COULD INVADE.
TO BE HONEST, THAT MAN IS A NATURAL DISASTER NO ONE CAN STOP.
WHEN HE TOUCHES ME...

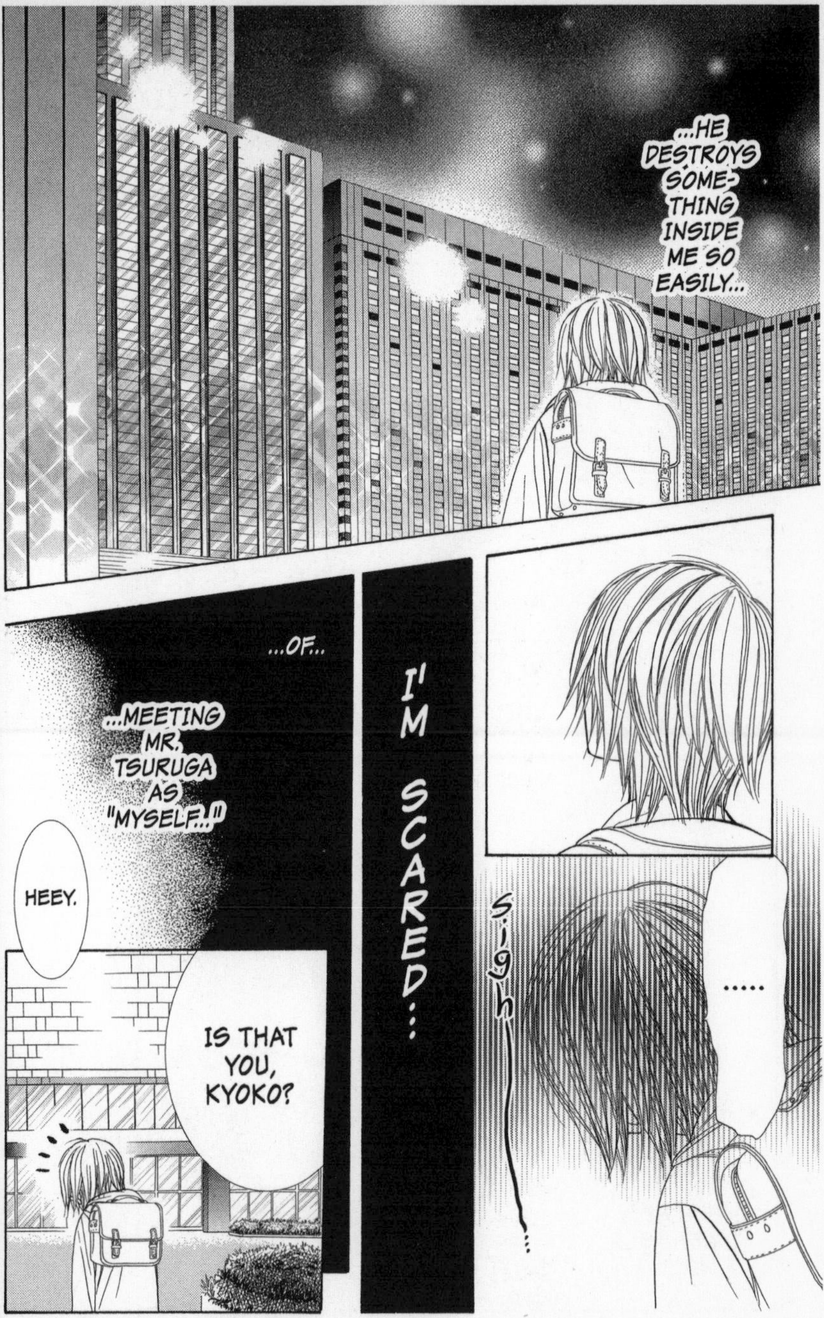
...HE DESTROYS SOME-THING INSIDE ME SO EASILY...
.....
Sigh...
I'M SCARED...
...OF...
...MEETING MR. TSURUGA AS "MYSELF..."
HEEY.
IS THAT YOU, KYOKO?

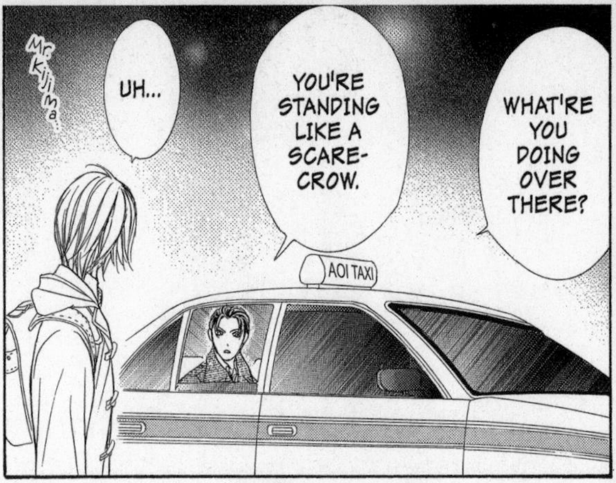
WHAT'RE YOU DOING OVER THERE?
YOU'RE STANDING LIKE A SCARE-CROW.
AOI TAXI
UH...
Mr. Kijima...
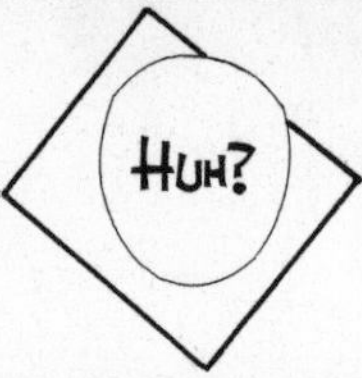
HUH?
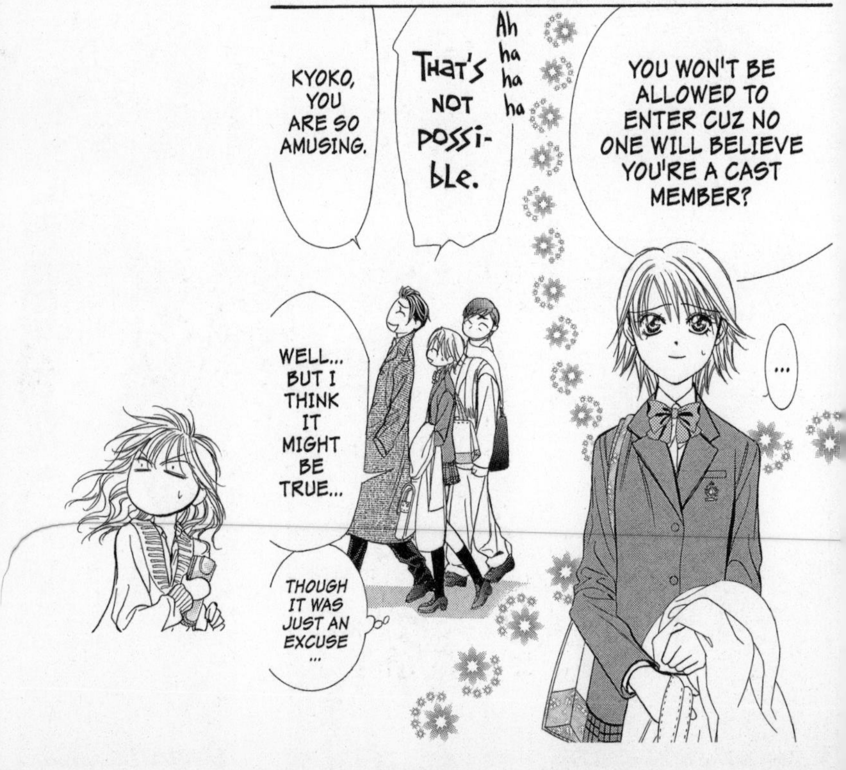
YOU WON'T BE ALLOWED TO ENTER CUZ NO ONE WILL BELIEVE YOU'RE A CAST MEMBER?
...
Ah ha ha ha
THAT'S NOT POSSI-BLE.
KYOKO, YOU ARE SO AMUSING.
WELL... BUT I THINK IT MIGHT BE TRUE...
THOUGH IT WAS JUST AN EXCUSE ...

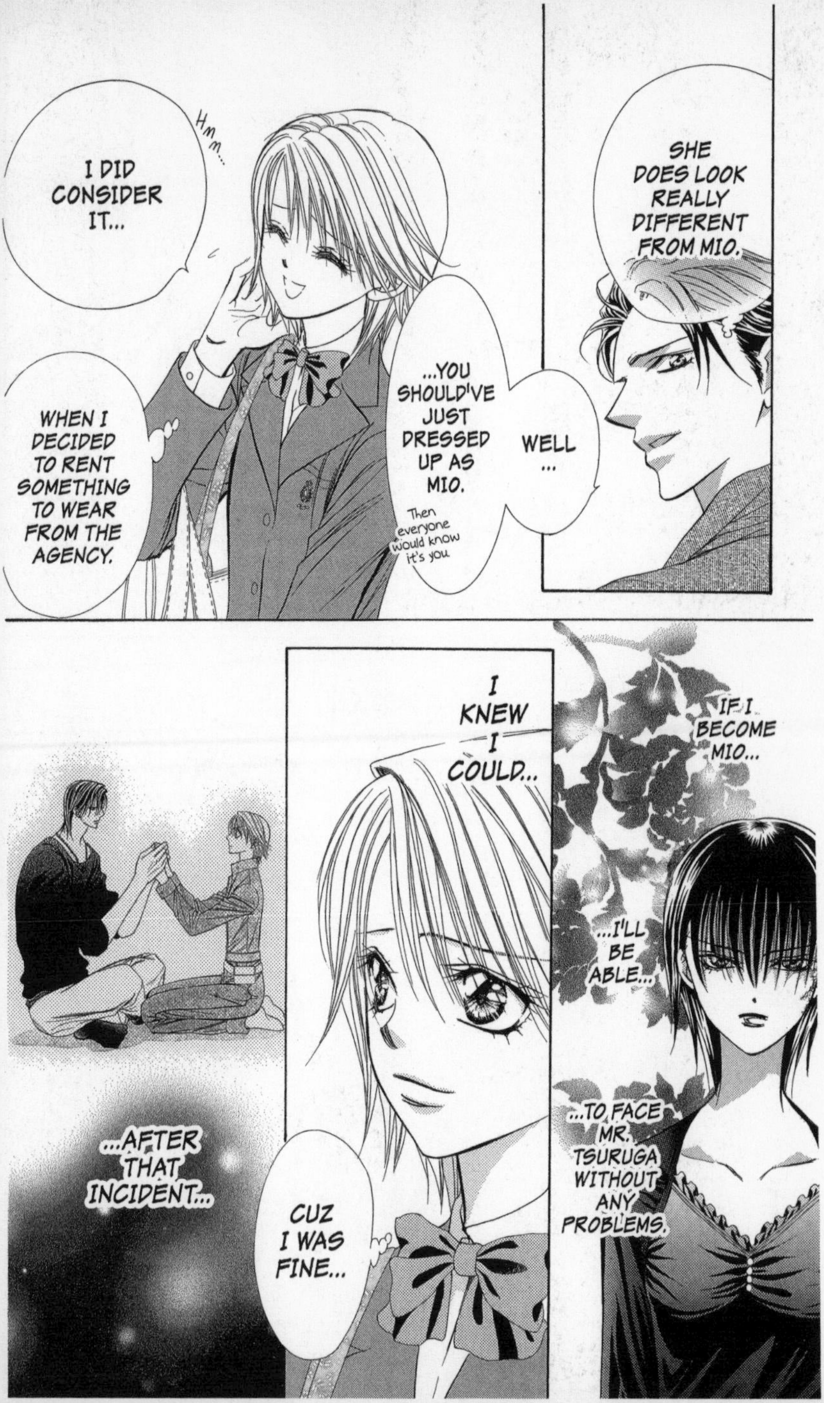
SHE DOES LOOK REALLY DIFFERENT FROM MIO.
WELL ...
...YOU SHOULD'VE JUST DRESSED UP AS MIO.
Then everyone would know it's you
Hmm...
I DID CONSIDER IT...
WHEN I DECIDED TO RENT SOMETHING TO WEAR FROM THE AGENCY.
IF I BECOME MIO...
...I'LL BE ABLE...
...TO FACE MR. TSURUGA WITHOUT ANY PROBLEMS.
I KNEW I COULD...
CUZ I WAS FINE...
...AFTER THAT INCIDENT...

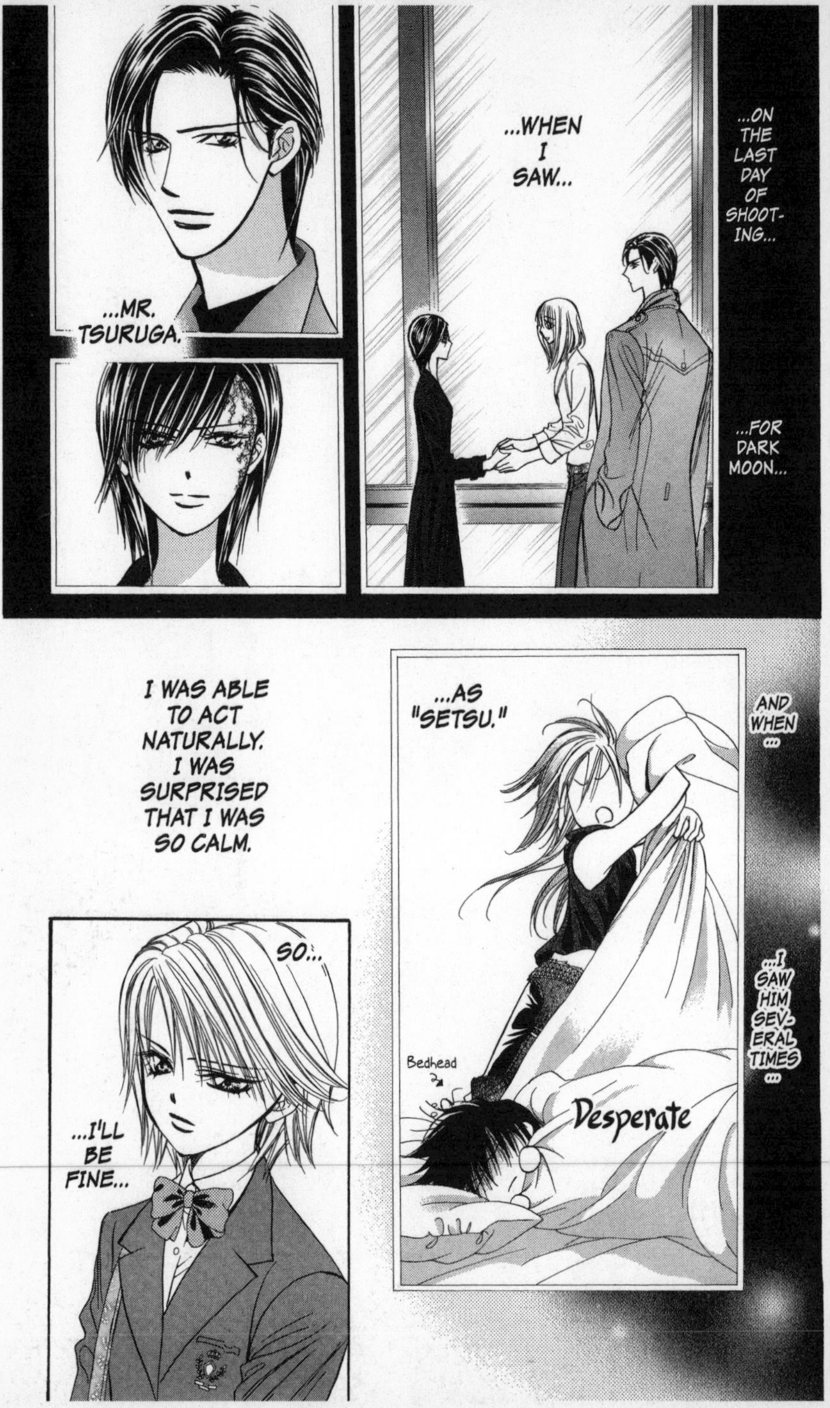
...ON THE LAST DAY OF SHOOTING...
...FOR DARK MOON...
...WHEN I SAW...
...MR. TSURUGA.
AND WHEN...
...I SAW HIM SEVERAL TIMES...
...AS "SETSU."
Desperate
Bedhead
I WAS ABLE TO ACT NATURALLY. I WAS SURPRISED THAT I WAS SO CALM.
SO...
...I'LL BE FINE...

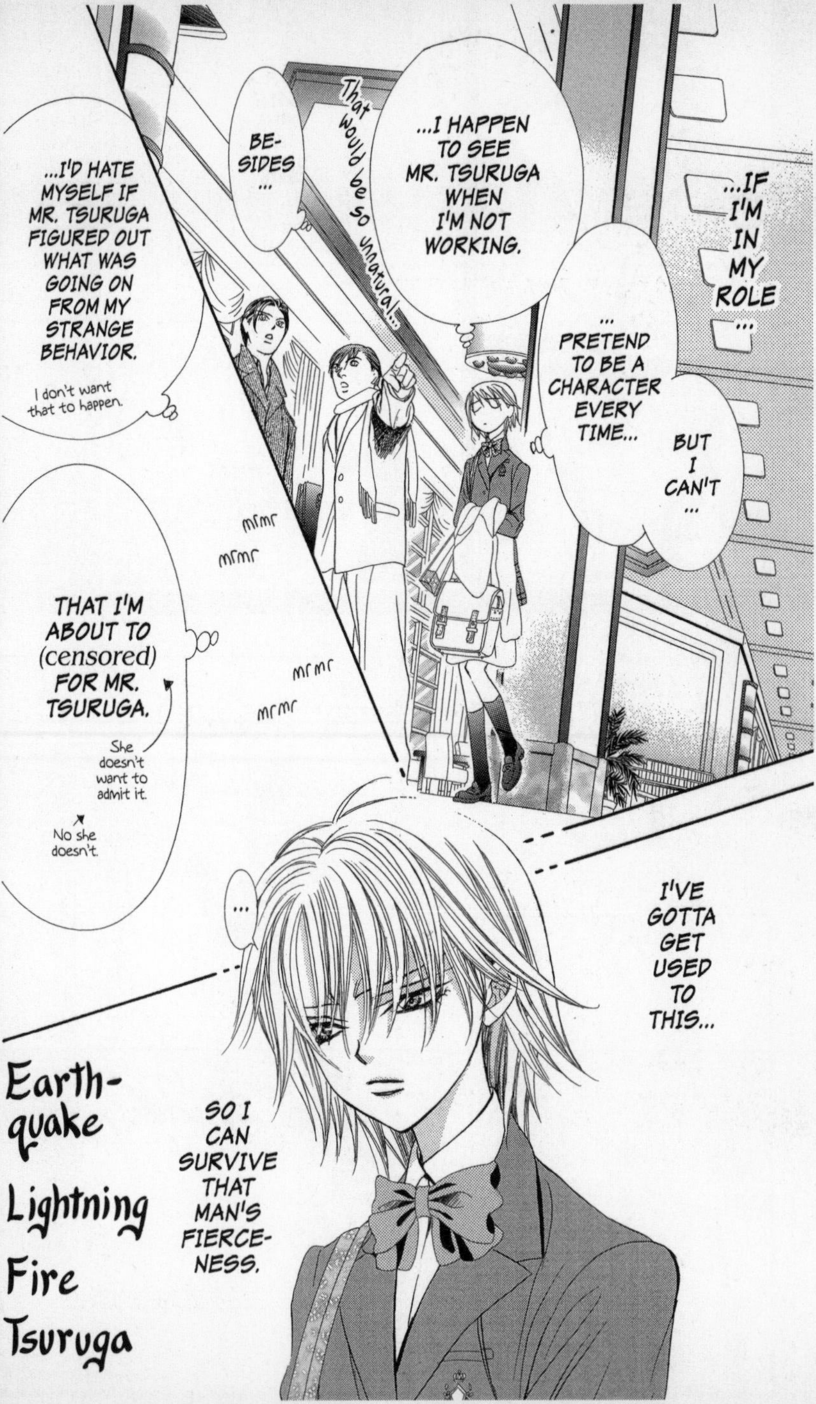
...IF I'M IN MY ROLE ...
... PRETEND TO BE A CHARACTER EVERY TIME...
BUT I CAN'T ...
...I HAPPEN TO SEE MR. TSURUGA WHEN I'M NOT WORKING.
That would be so unnatural...
BE-SIDES ...
...I'D HATE MYSELF IF MR. TSURUGA FIGURED OUT WHAT WAS GOING ON FROM MY STRANGE BEHAVIOR.
I don't want that to happen.
mrmr
mrmr
mrmr
mrmr
THAT I'M ABOUT TO (censored) FOR MR. TSURUGA.
She doesn't want to admit it.
No she doesn't.
I'VE GOTTA GET USED TO THIS...
...
SO I CAN SURVIVE THAT MAN'S FIERCE-NESS.
Earth-quake
Lightning
Fire
Tsuruga

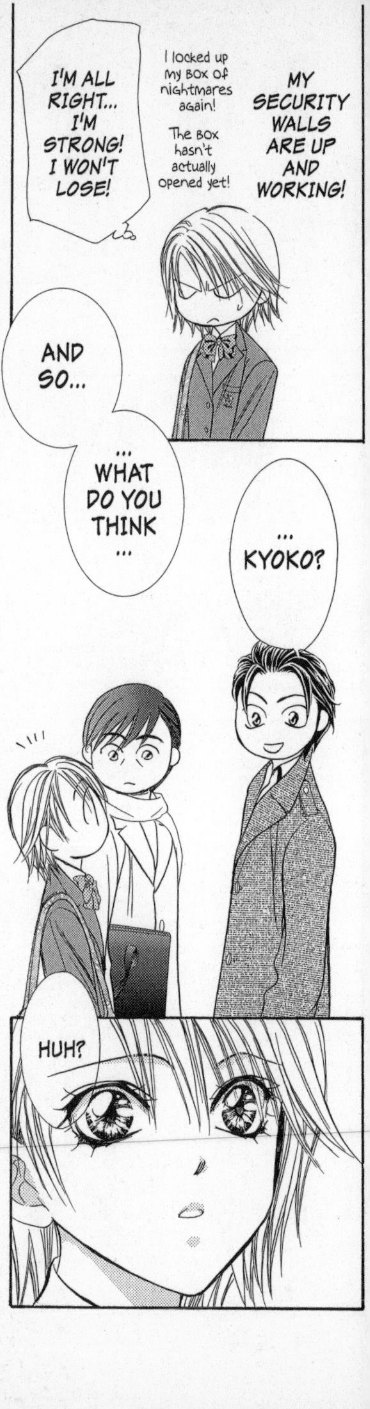
MY SECURITY WALLS ARE UP AND WORKING!
I locked up my box of nightmares again!
The box hasn't actually opened yet!
I'M ALL RIGHT... I'M STRONG! I WON'T LOSE!
AND SO...
... WHAT DO YOU THINK ...
... KYOKO?
HUH?

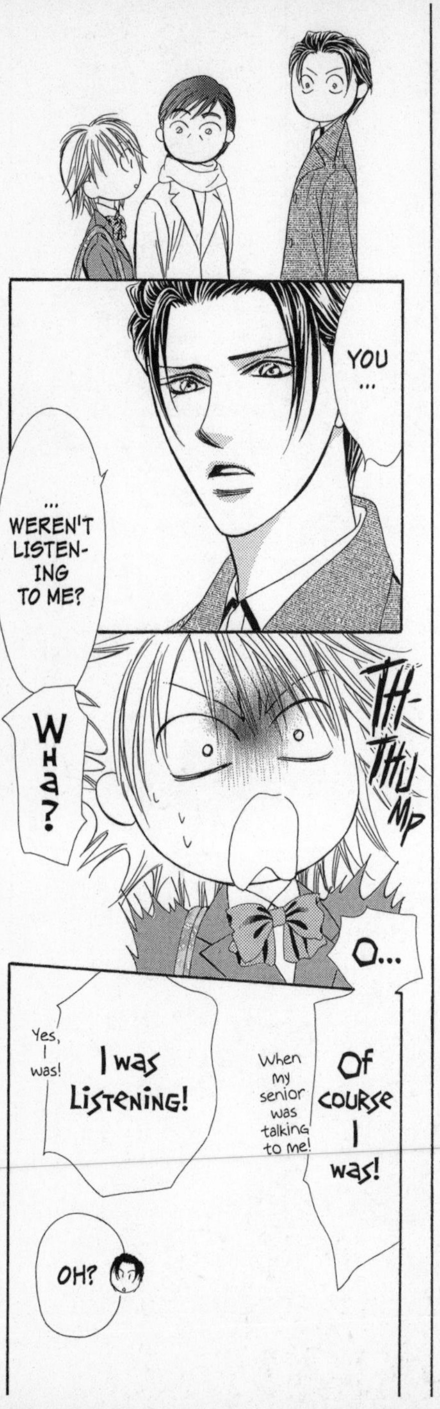
YOU ...
... WEREN'T LISTEN-ING TO ME?
TH-THUMP
WHA?
O...
Of course I was!
When my senior was talking to me!
I was Listening!
Yes, I was!
OH?

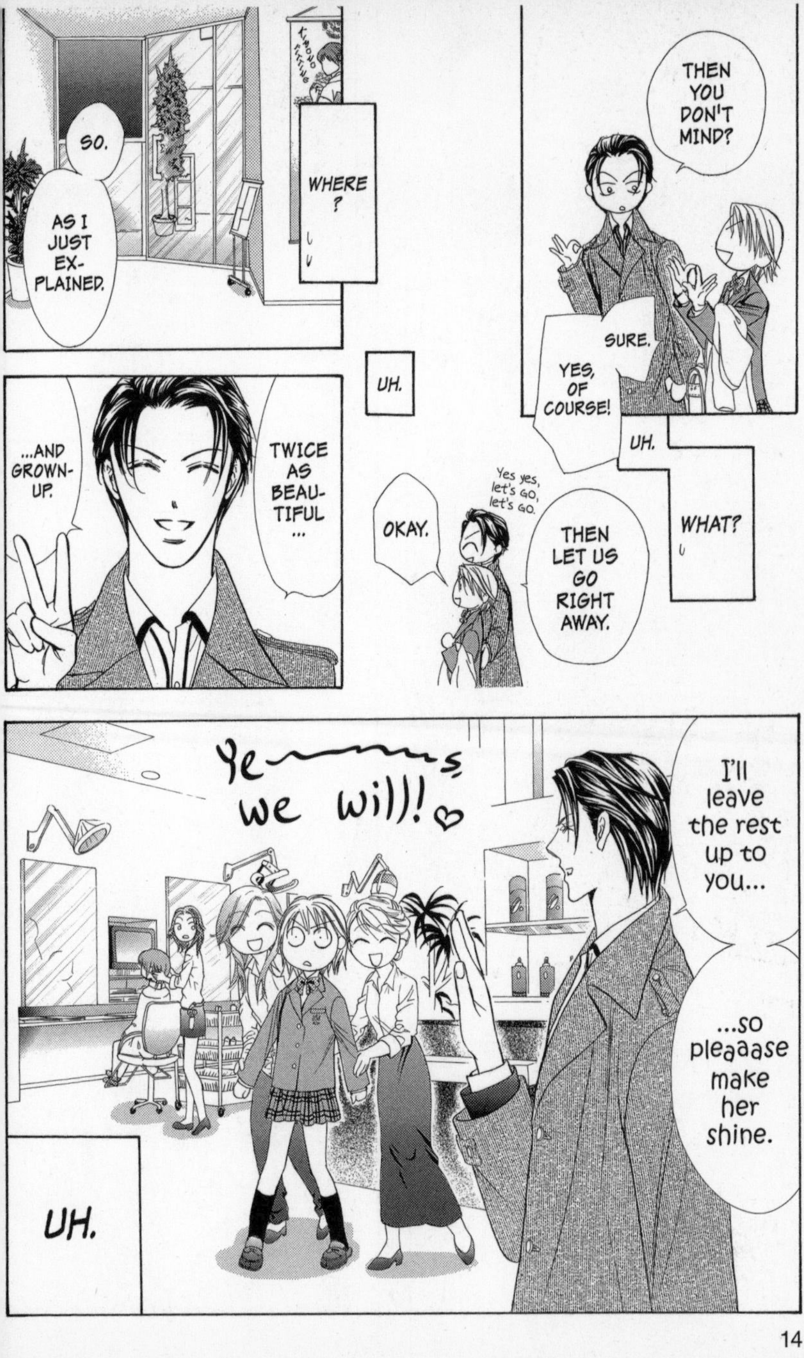
THEN YOU DON'T MIND?
SURE.
YES, OF COURSE!
UH.
WHAT?
THEN LET US GO RIGHT AWAY.
Yes yes, let's go, let's go.
OKAY.
WHERE?
SO.
AS I JUST EX-PLAINED.
UH.
TWICE AS BEAU-TIFUL...
...AND GROWN-UP.
I'll leave the rest up to you...
...so pleaaase make her shine.
Ye~~s we will!
UH.

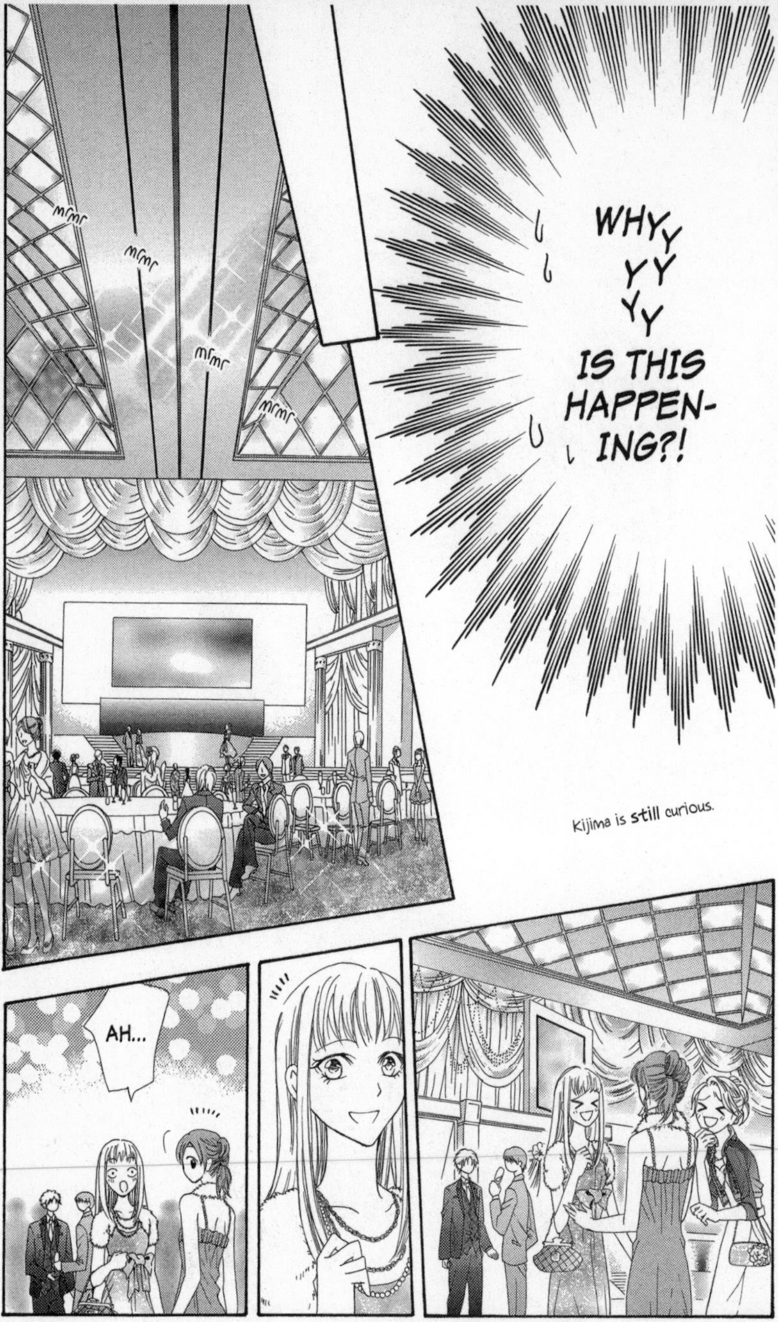
WHYYYYYY IS THIS HAPPEN-ING?!
Kijima is still curious.
mrmr
mrmr
mrmr
mrmr
AH...

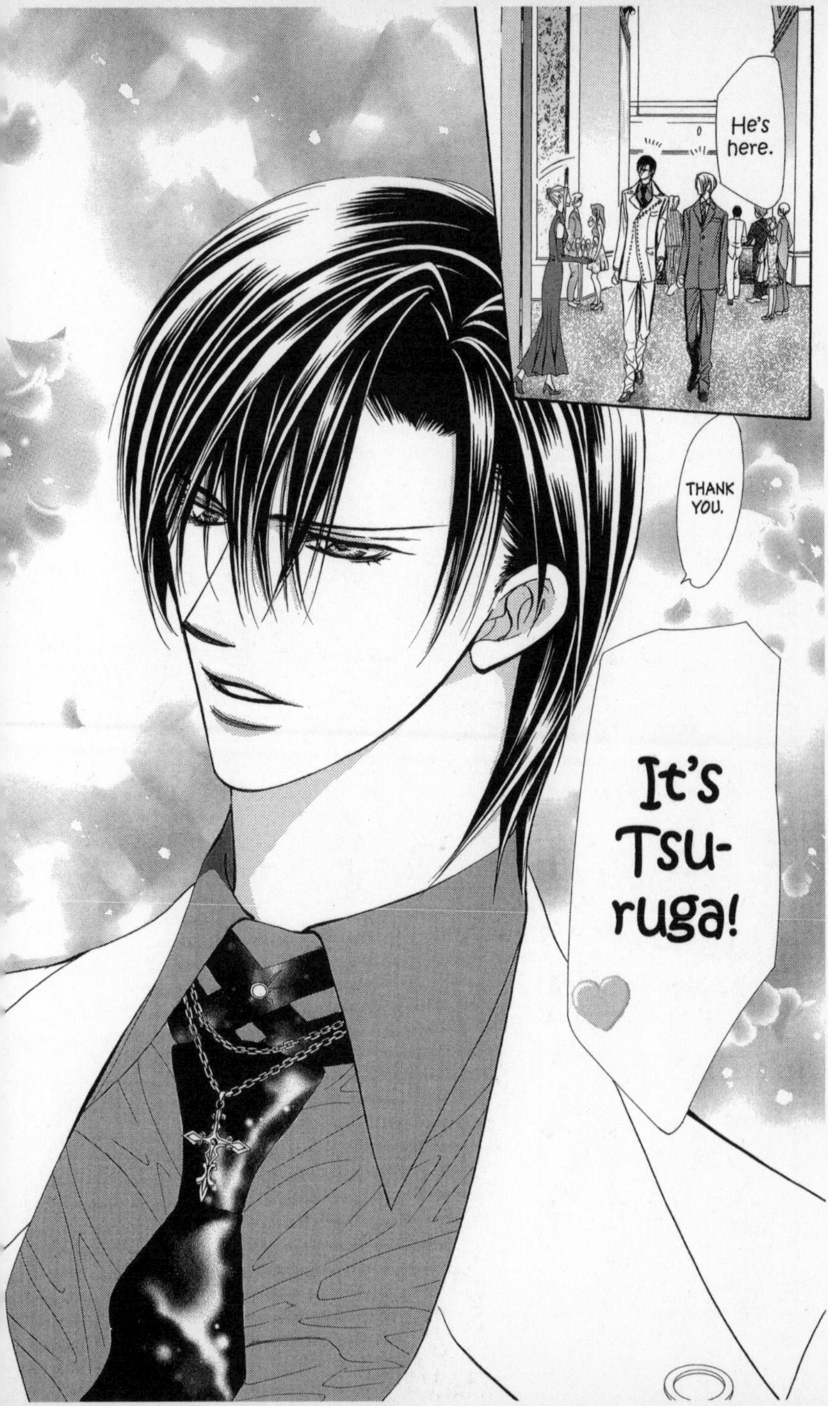
He's here.
THANK YOU.
It's Tsu-ruga!

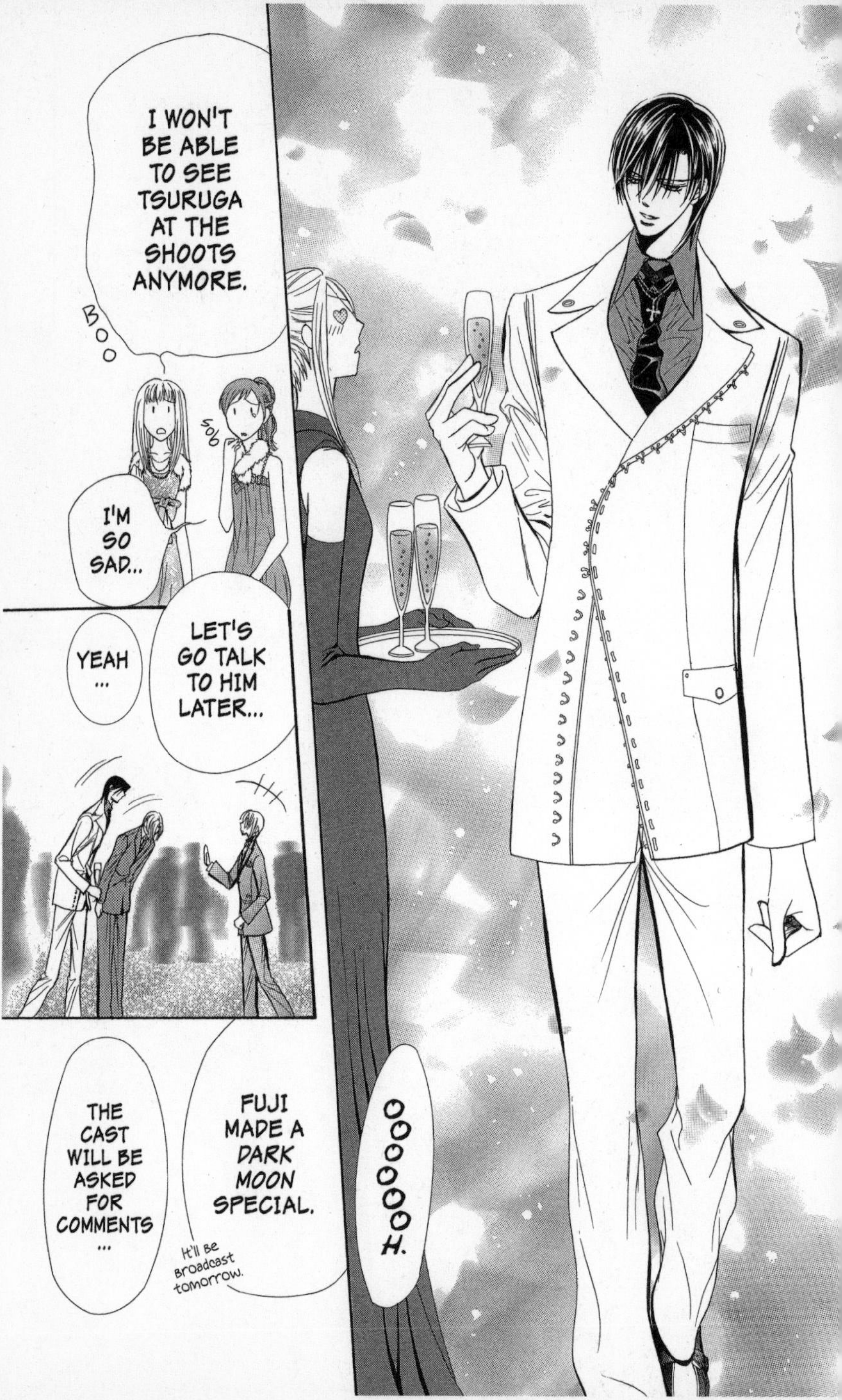
OOOOOOH.
I WON'T BE ABLE TO SEE TSURUGA AT THE SHOOTS ANYMORE.
BOO
sob
I'M SO SAD...
LET'S GO TALK TO HIM LATER...
YEAH ...
FUJI MADE A DARK MOON SPECIAL.
It'll be broadcast tomorrow.
THE CAST WILL BE ASKED FOR COMMENTS ...

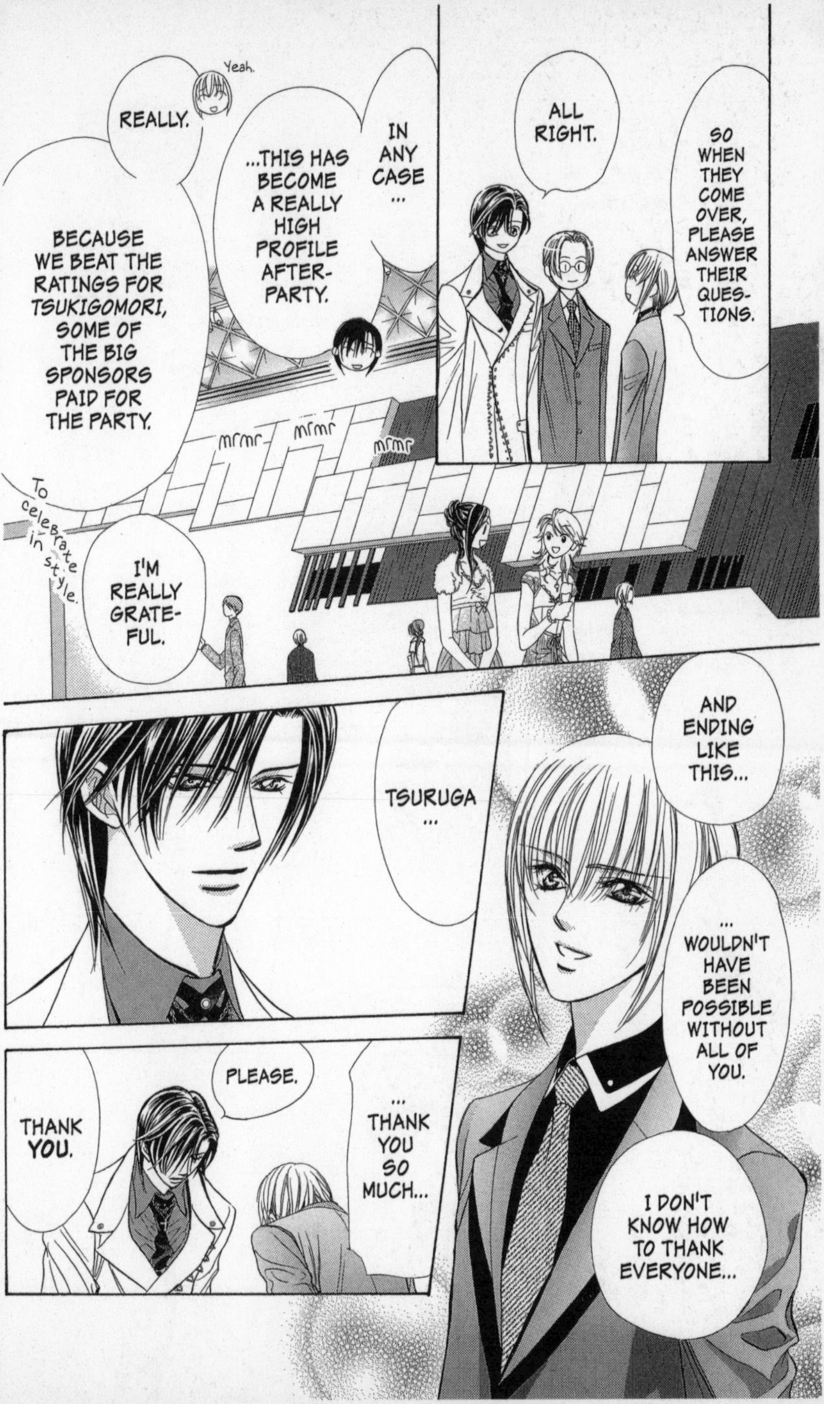
SO WHEN THEY COME OVER, PLEASE ANSWER THEIR QUES-TIONS.
ALL RIGHT.
IN ANY CASE ...
...THIS HAS BECOME A REALLY HIGH PROFILE AFTER-PARTY.
REALLY.
Yeah.
BECAUSE WE BEAT THE RATINGS FOR TSUKIGOMORI, SOME OF THE BIG SPONSORS PAID FOR THE PARTY.
mrmr
mrmr
mrmr
To celebrate in style.
I'M REALLY GRATE-FUL.
AND ENDING LIKE THIS...
... WOULDN'T HAVE BEEN POSSIBLE WITHOUT ALL OF YOU.
TSURUGA ...
I DON'T KNOW HOW TO THANK EVERYONE...
... THANK YOU SO MUCH...
PLEASE.
THANK YOU.

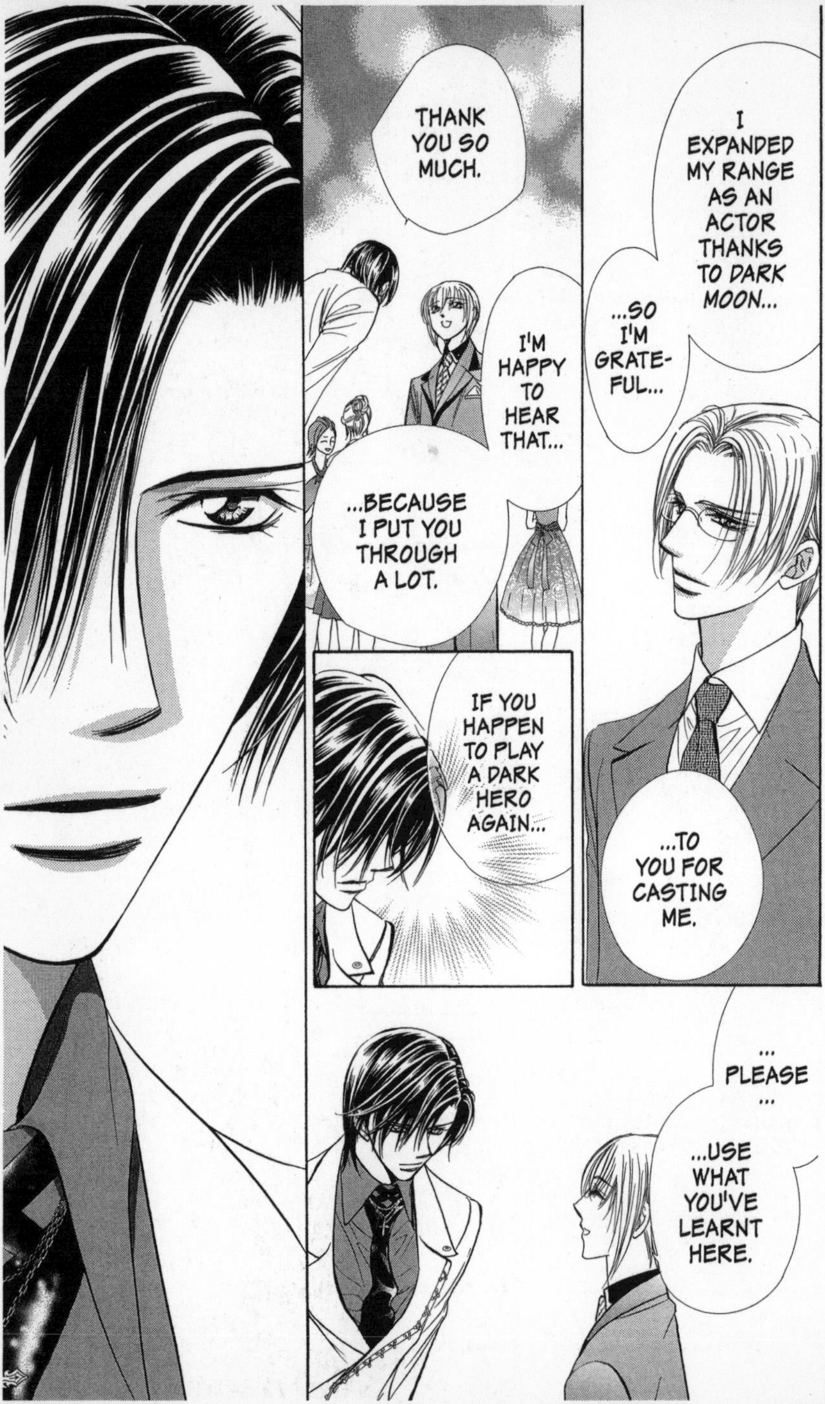
I EXPANDED MY RANGE AS AN ACTOR THANKS TO DARK MOON...
...SO I'M GRATE-FUL...
...TO YOU FOR CASTING ME.
THANK YOU SO MUCH.
I'M HAPPY TO HEAR THAT...
...BECAUSE I PUT YOU THROUGH A LOT.
IF YOU HAPPEN TO PLAY A DARK HERO AGAIN...
...PLEASE...
...USE WHAT YOU'VE LEARNT HERE.

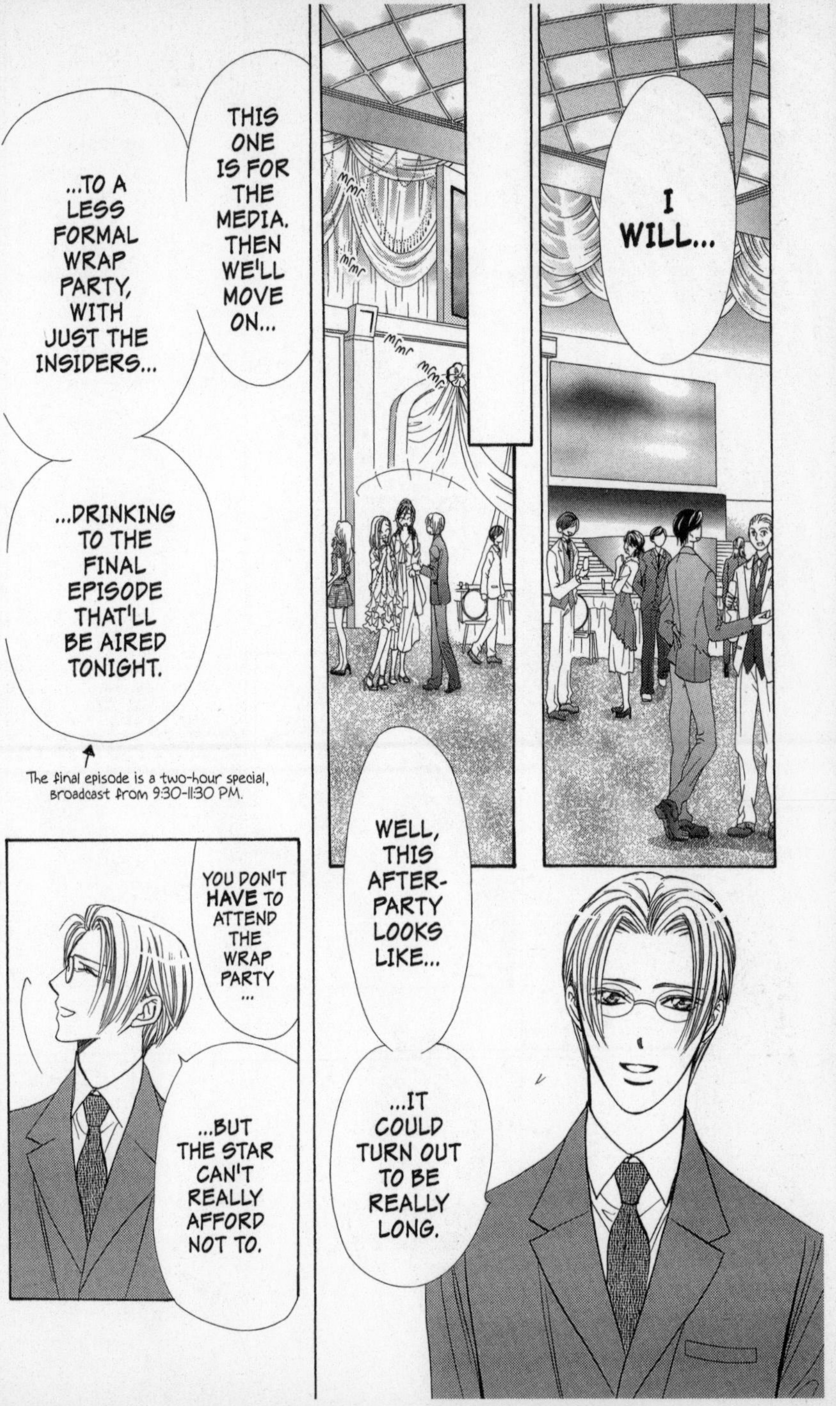
I WILL...
THIS ONE IS FOR THE MEDIA. THEN WE'LL MOVE ON...
...TO A LESS FORMAL WRAP PARTY, WITH JUST THE INSIDERS...
...DRINKING TO THE FINAL EPISODE THAT'LL BE AIRED TONIGHT.
The final episode is a two-hour special, broadcast from 9:30-11:30 PM.
WELL, THIS AFTER-PARTY LOOKS LIKE...
...IT COULD TURN OUT TO BE REALLY LONG.
YOU DON'T HAVE TO ATTEND THE WRAP PARTY...
...BUT THE STAR CAN'T REALLY AFFORD NOT TO.

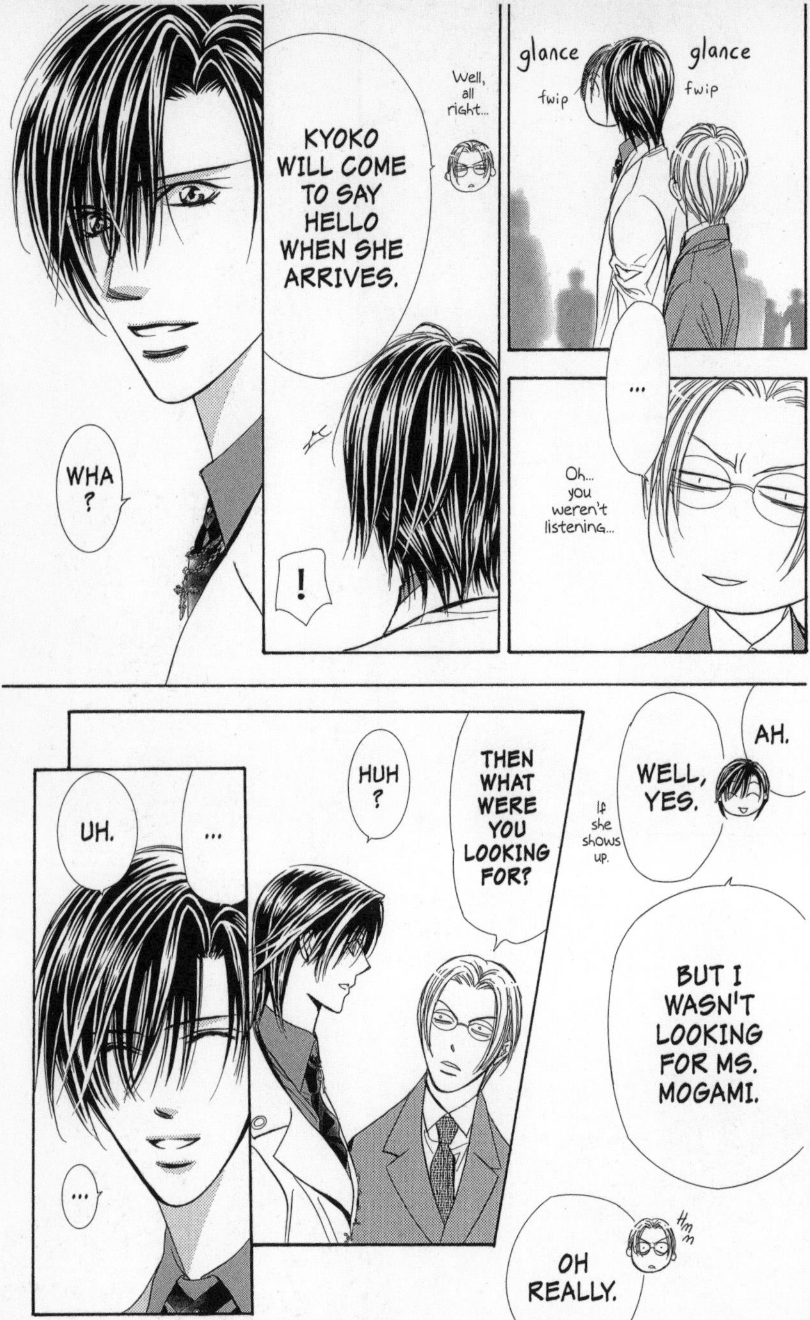
glance
fwip
glance
fwip
...
Oh... you weren't listening...
Well, all right...
KYOKO WILL COME TO SAY HELLO WHEN SHE ARRIVES.
!
WHA?
AH.
WELL, YES.
If she shows up.
BUT I WASN'T LOOKING FOR MS. MOGAMI.
Hmm
OH REALLY.
THEN WHAT WERE YOU LOOKING FOR?
HUH?
...
UH.
...

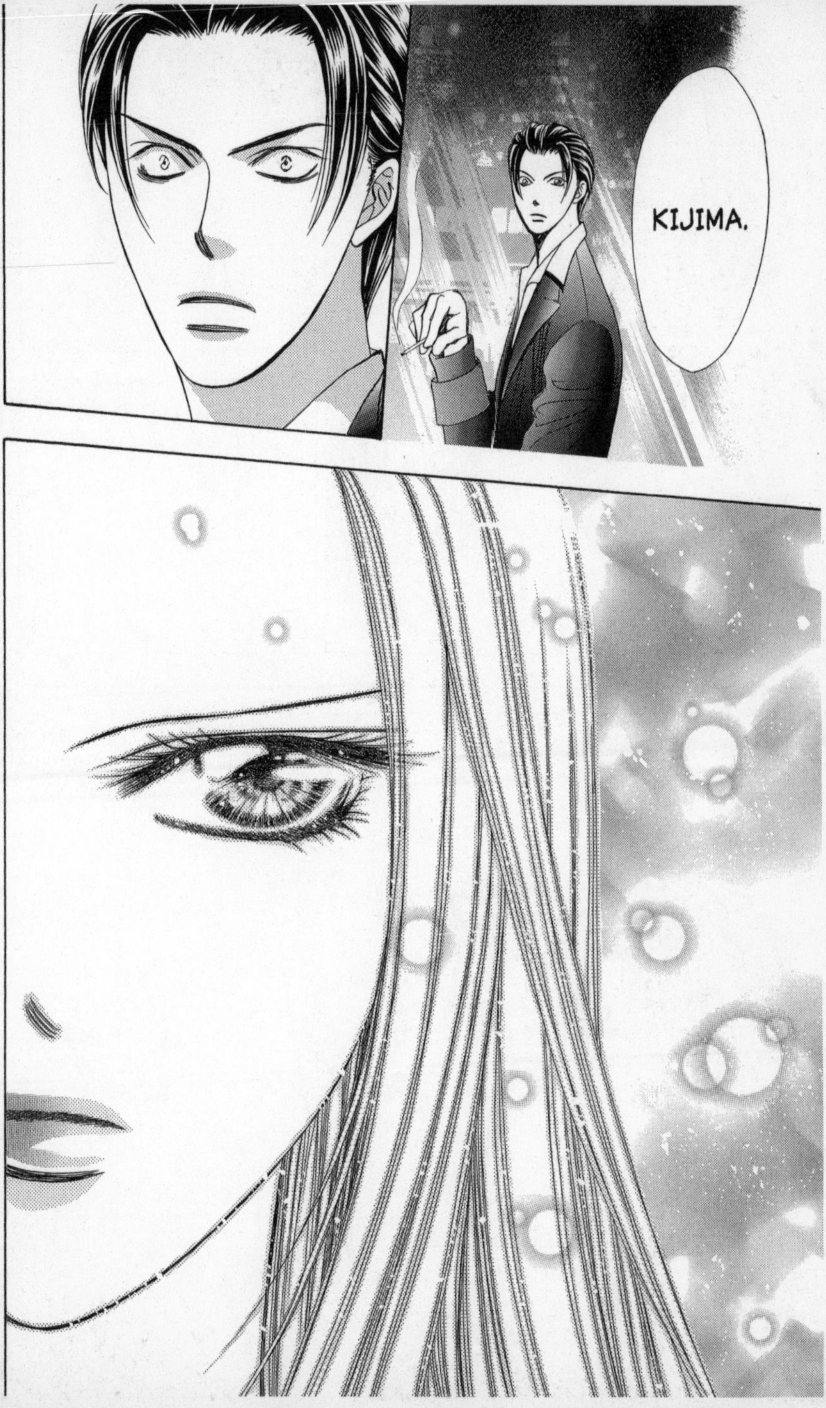
KIJIMA.

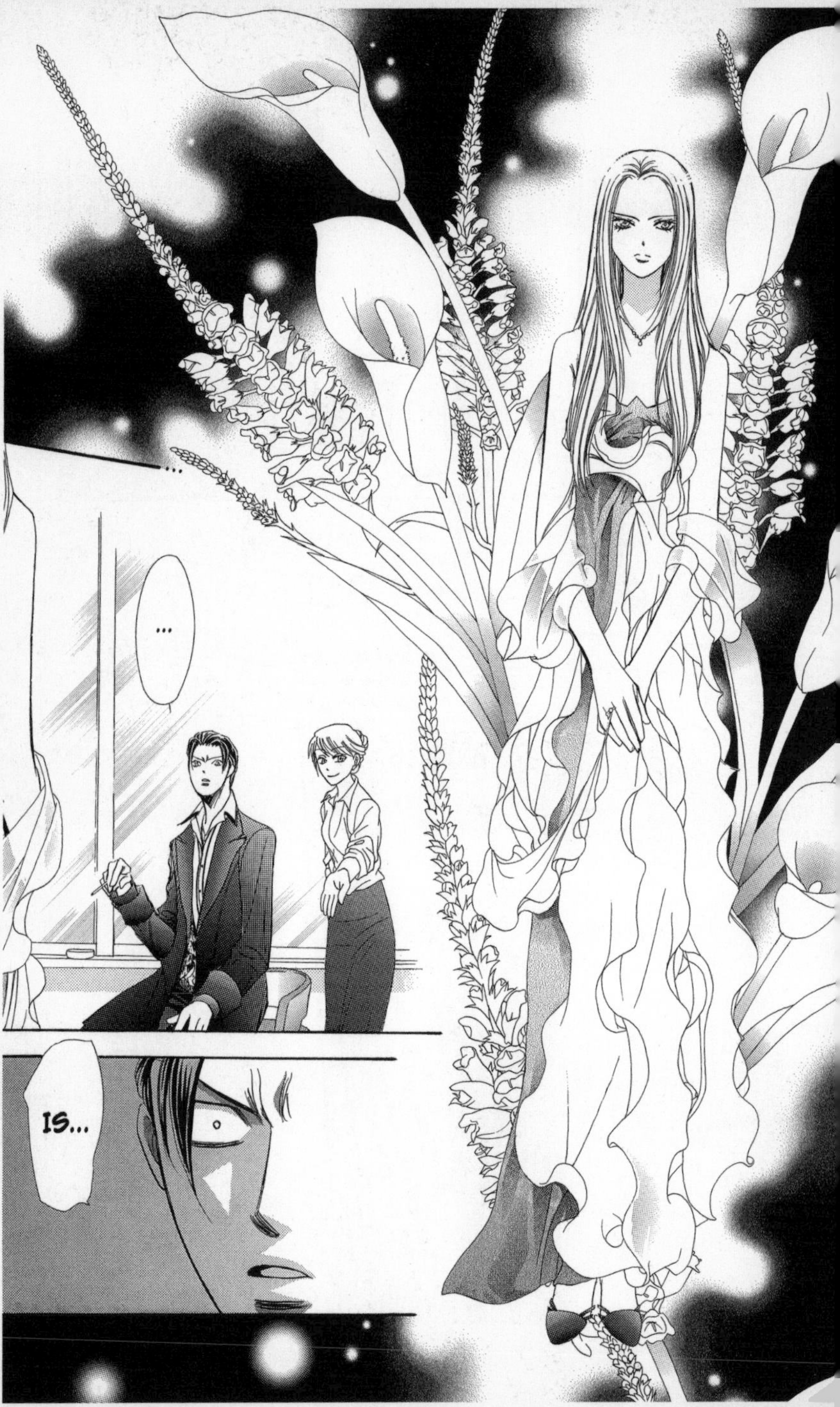
...
...
IS...

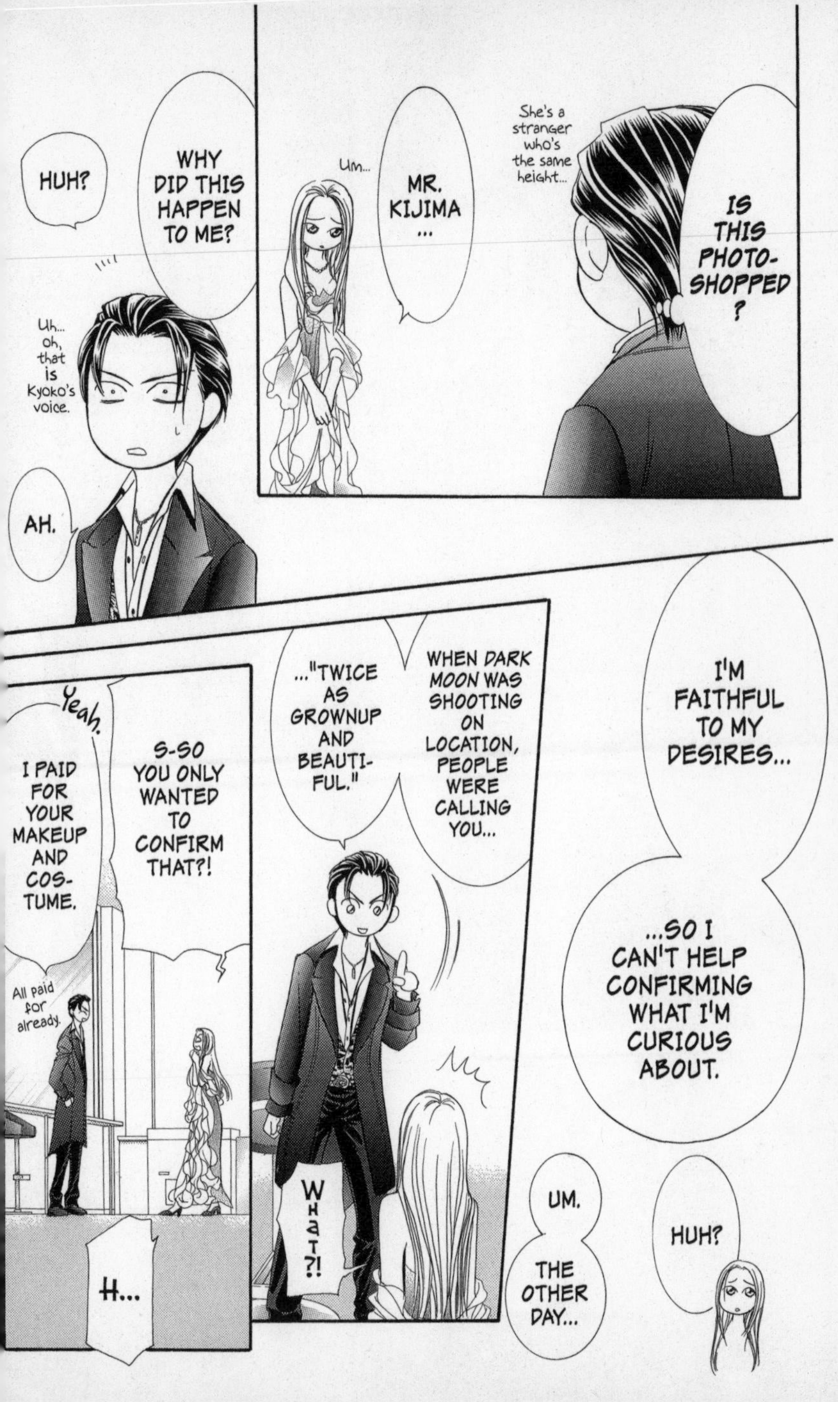
IS THIS PHOTO-SHOPPED?
She's a stranger who's the same height...
MR. KIJIMA...
Um...
WHY DID THIS HAPPEN TO ME?
HUH?
Uh... oh, that is Kyoko's voice.
AH.
I'M FAITHFUL TO MY DESIRES...
...SO I CAN'T HELP CONFIRMING WHAT I'M CURIOUS ABOUT.
WHEN DARK MOON WAS SHOOTING ON LOCATION, PEOPLE WERE CALLING YOU...
..."TWICE AS GROWNUP AND BEAUTI-FUL."
What?!
S-SO YOU ONLY WANTED TO CONFIRM THAT?!
Yeah.
I PAID FOR YOUR MAKEUP AND COS-TUME.
All paid for already.
H...
HUH?
UM.
THE OTHER DAY...

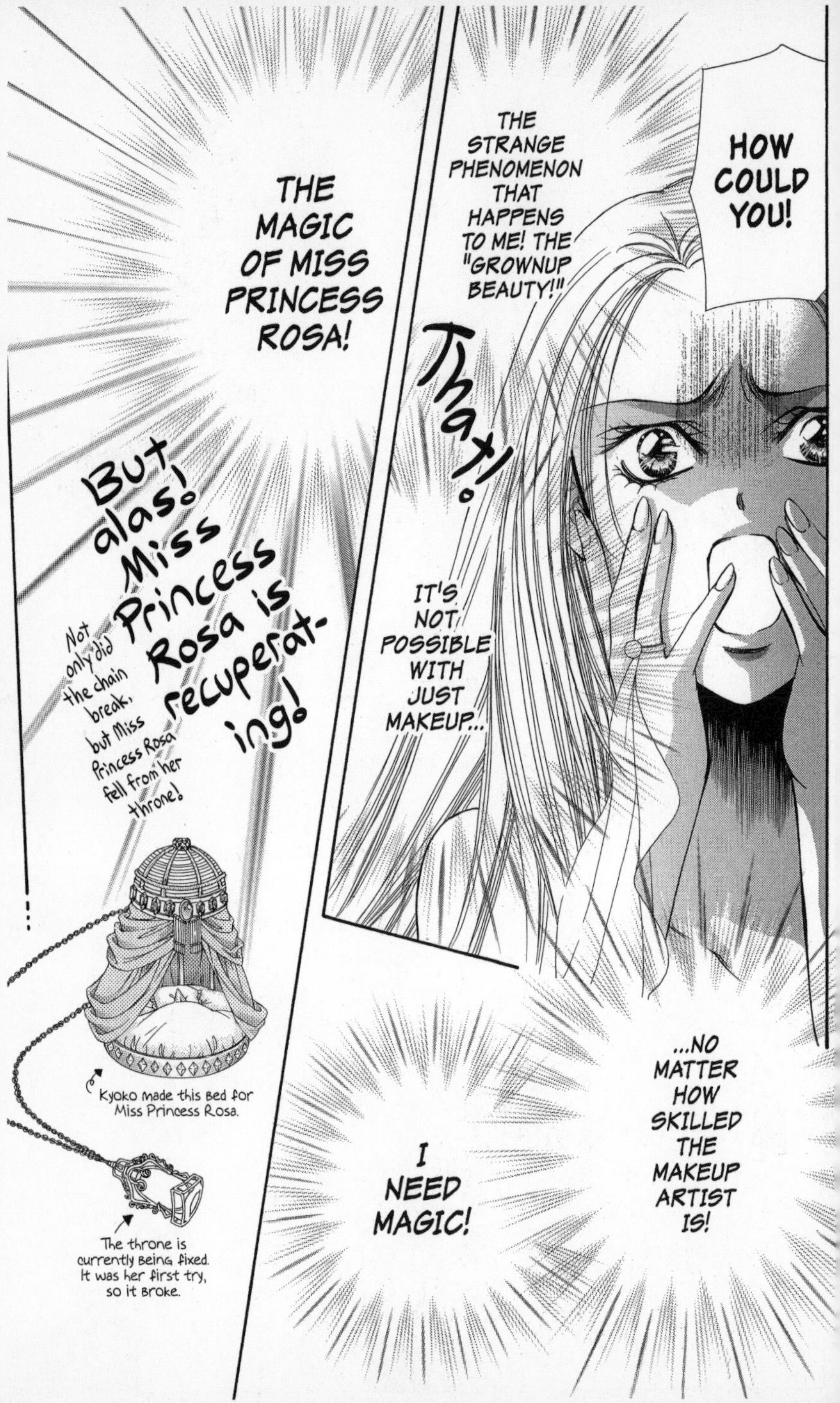
HOW COULD YOU!
THE STRANGE PHENOMENON THAT HAPPENS TO ME! THE "GROWNUP BEAUTY!!"
That!
IT'S NOT POSSIBLE WITH JUST MAKEUP...
...NO MATTER HOW SKILLED THE MAKEUP ARTIST IS!
I NEED MAGIC!
THE MAGIC OF MISS PRINCESS ROSA!
But alas! Miss Princess Rosa is recuperating!
Not only did the chain break, but Miss Princess Rosa fell from her throne!
Kyoko made this bed for Miss Princess Rosa.
The throne is currently being fixed. It was her first try, so it broke.

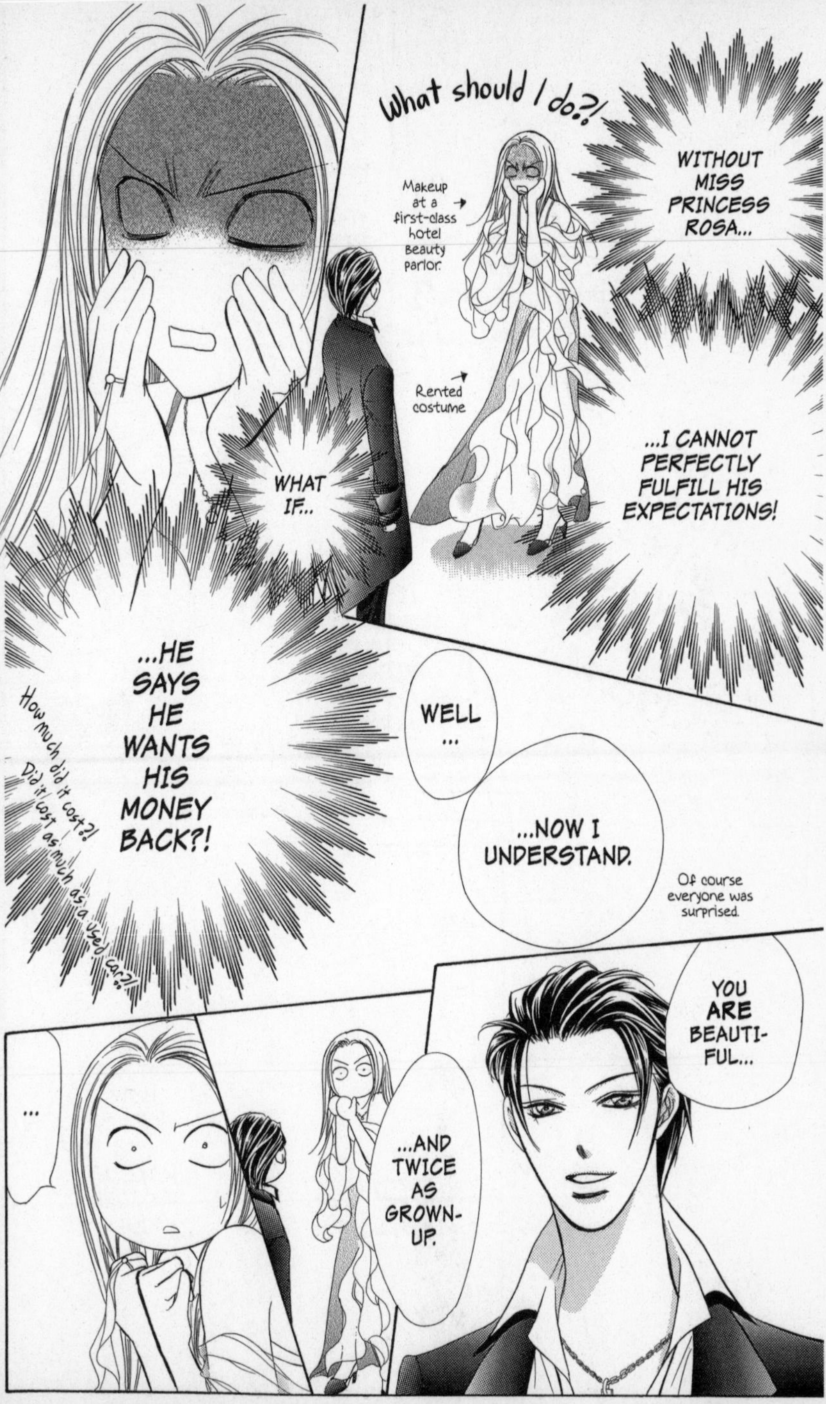
What should I do?!
WITHOUT MISS PRINCESS ROSA...
Makeup at a first-class hotel Beauty parlor.
Rented costume
...I CANNOT PERFECTLY FULFILL HIS EXPECTATIONS!
WHAT IF...
...HE SAYS HE WANTS HIS MONEY BACK?!
How much did it cost?! Did it cost as much as a used car?!
WELL...
...NOW I UNDERSTAND.
Of course everyone was surprised.
YOU ARE BEAUTI-FUL...
...AND TWICE AS GROWN-UP.
...

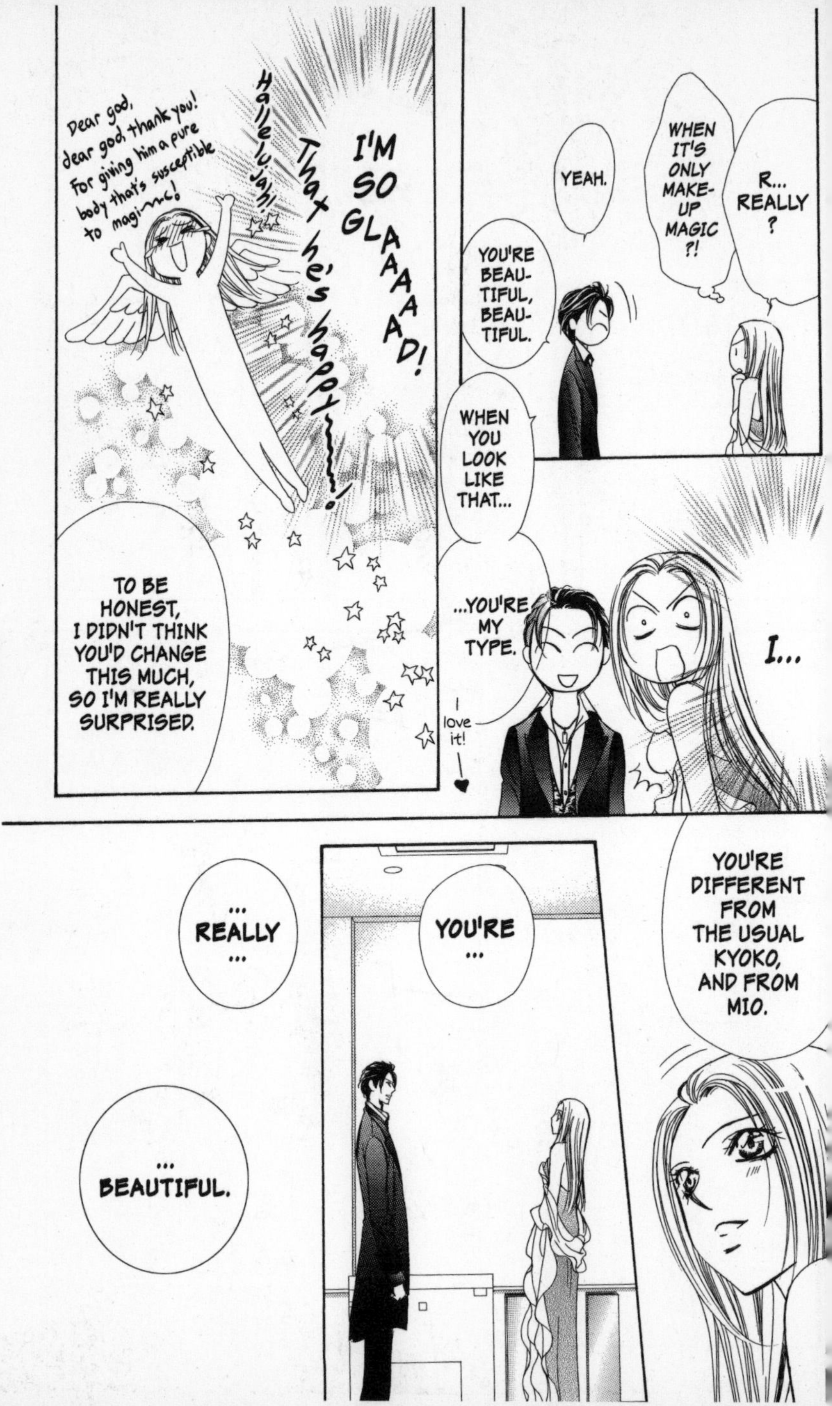
R... REALLY?
WHEN IT'S ONLY MAKE-UP MAGIC?!
YEAH.
YOU'RE BEAUTIFUL, BEAUTIFUL.
WHEN YOU LOOK LIKE THAT...
...YOU'RE MY TYPE.
I love it!
I...
I'M SO GLAAAAAD!
That he's happy~~~!
Hallelujah!
Dear god, dear god, thank you! For giving him a pure body that's susceptible to magi~c!
TO BE HONEST, I DIDN'T THINK YOU'D CHANGE THIS MUCH, SO I'M REALLY SURPRISED.
YOU'RE DIFFERENT FROM THE USUAL KYOKO, AND FROM MIO.
YOU'RE ...
... REALLY ...
... BEAUTIFUL.

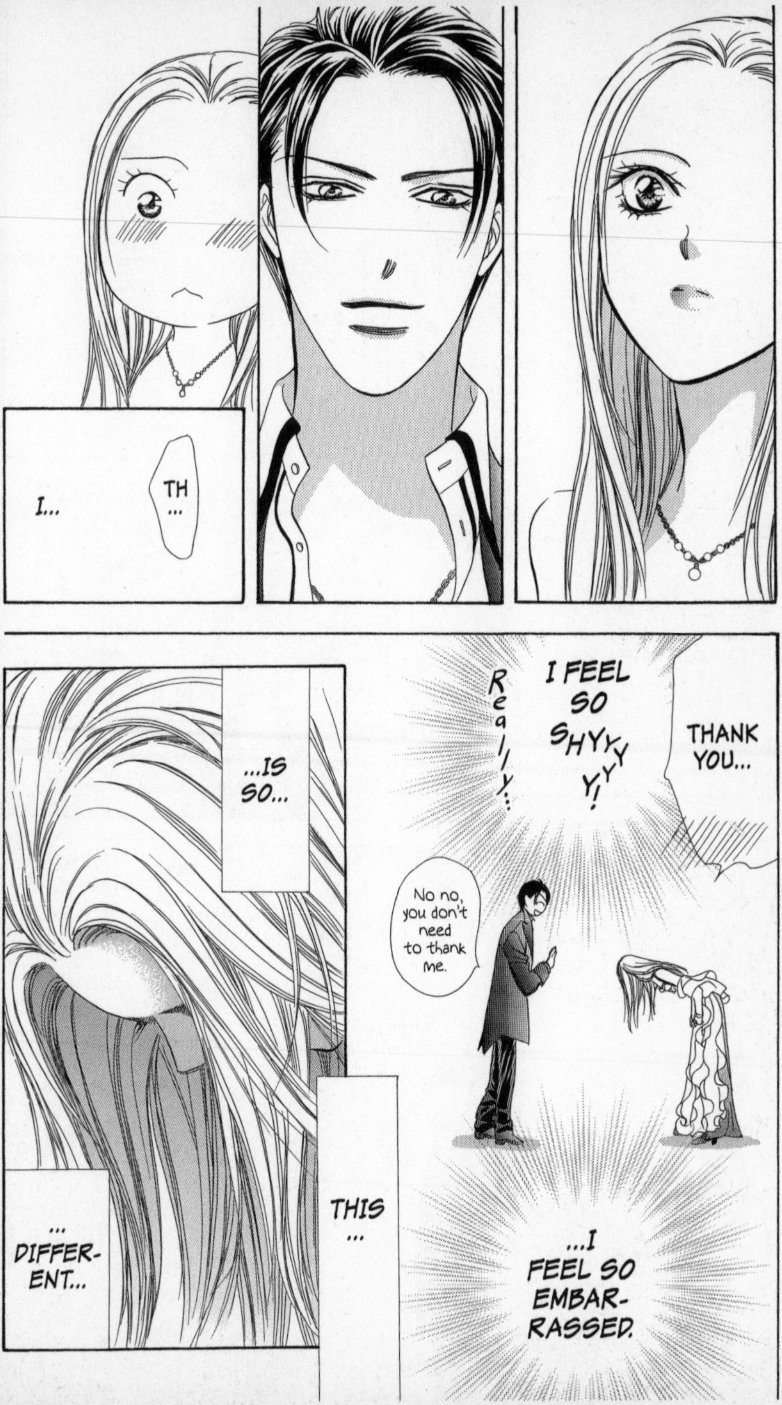
TH...
I...
THANK YOU...
I FEEL SO SHYYYYY!
Really...
No no, you don't need to thank me.
...I FEEL SO EMBARRASSED.
THIS...
...IS SO...
...DIFFERENT...

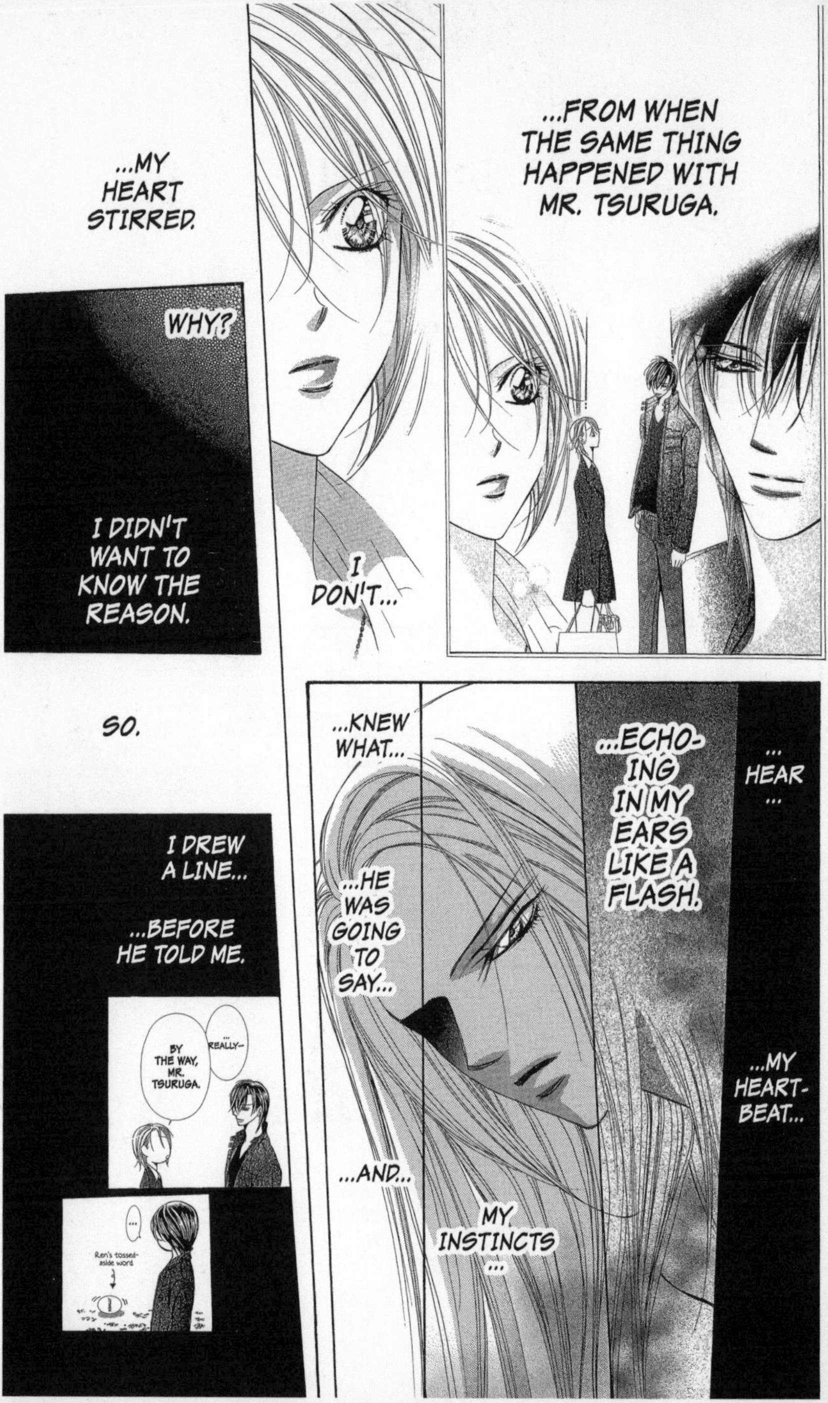
...FROM WHEN THE SAME THING HAPPENED WITH MR. TSURUGA.
...MY HEART STIRRED.
I DON'T...
WHY?
I DIDN'T WANT TO KNOW THE REASON.
SO.
... HEAR ...
...ECHOING IN MY EARS LIKE A FLASH.
...MY HEART-BEAT...
...KNEW WHAT...
...HE WAS GOING TO SAY...
...AND...
MY INSTINCTS ...
I DREW A LINE...
...BEFORE HE TOLD ME.
BY THE WAY, MR. TSURUGA.
... REALLY—
...
Ren's tossed-aside word

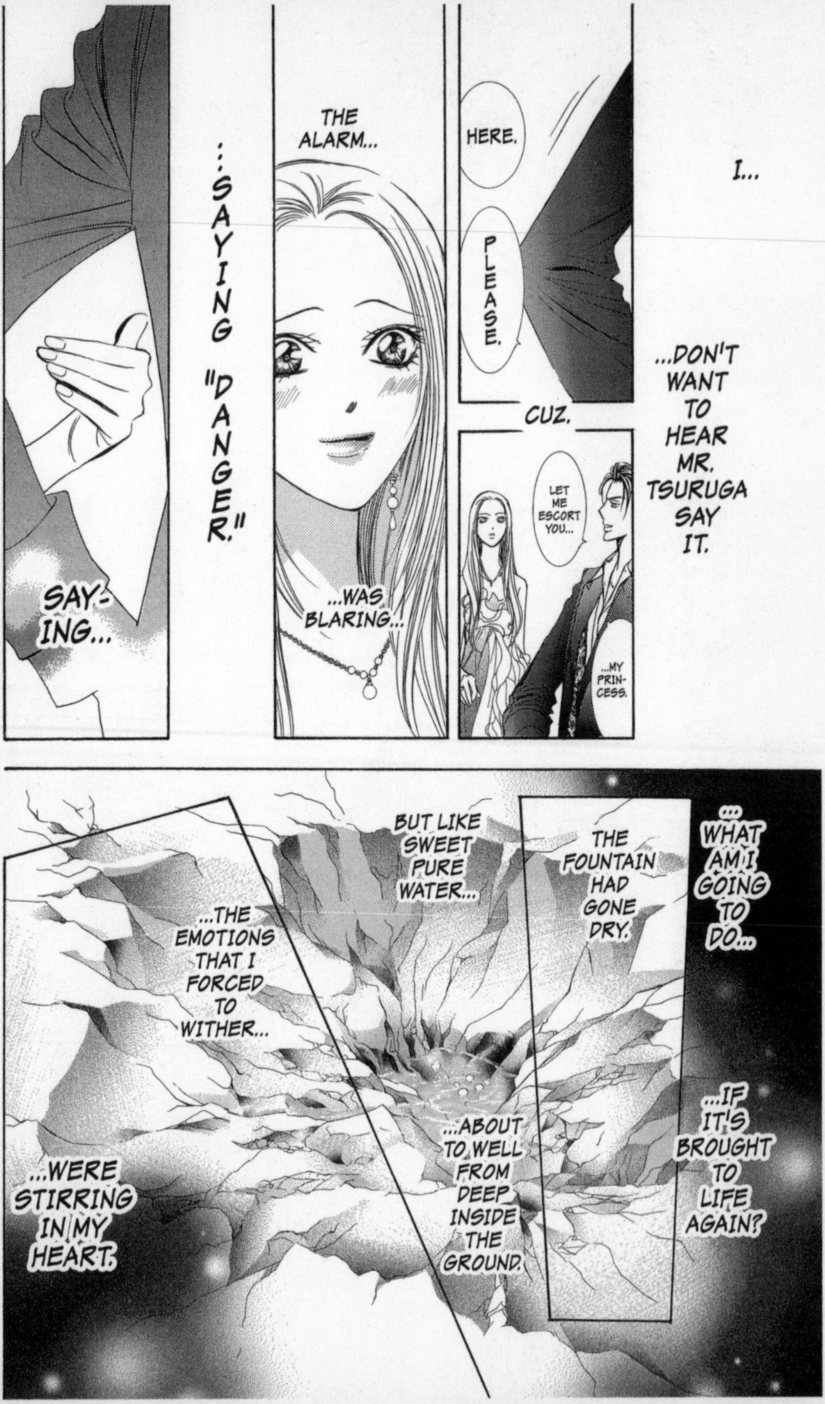
I...
...DON'T WANT TO HEAR MR. TSURUGA SAY IT.
HERE.
PLEASE.
CUZ.
LET ME ESCORT YOU...
...MY PRINCESS.
THE ALARM...
...WAS BLARING...
...SAYING "DANGER."
SAYING...
...WHAT AM I GOING TO DO...
...IF IT'S BROUGHT TO LIFE AGAIN?
THE FOUNTAIN HAD GONE DRY.
BUT LIKE SWEET PURE WATER...
...ABOUT TO WELL FROM DEEP INSIDE THE GROUND.
...THE EMOTIONS THAT I FORCED TO WITHER...
...WERE STIRRING IN MY HEART.

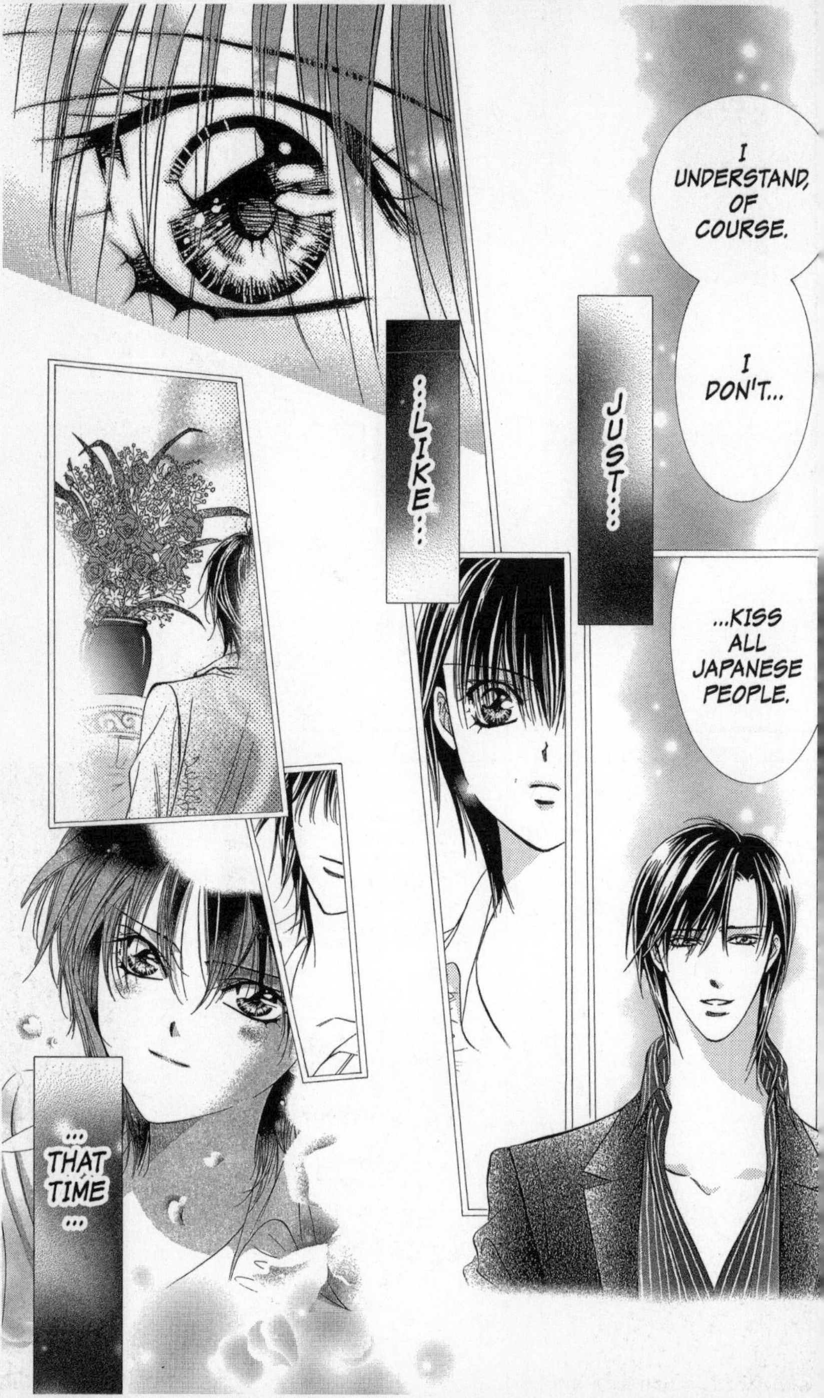
I UNDERSTAND, OF COURSE.
I DON'T...
...KISS ALL JAPANESE PEOPLE.
JUST...
...LIKE...
...THAT TIME...

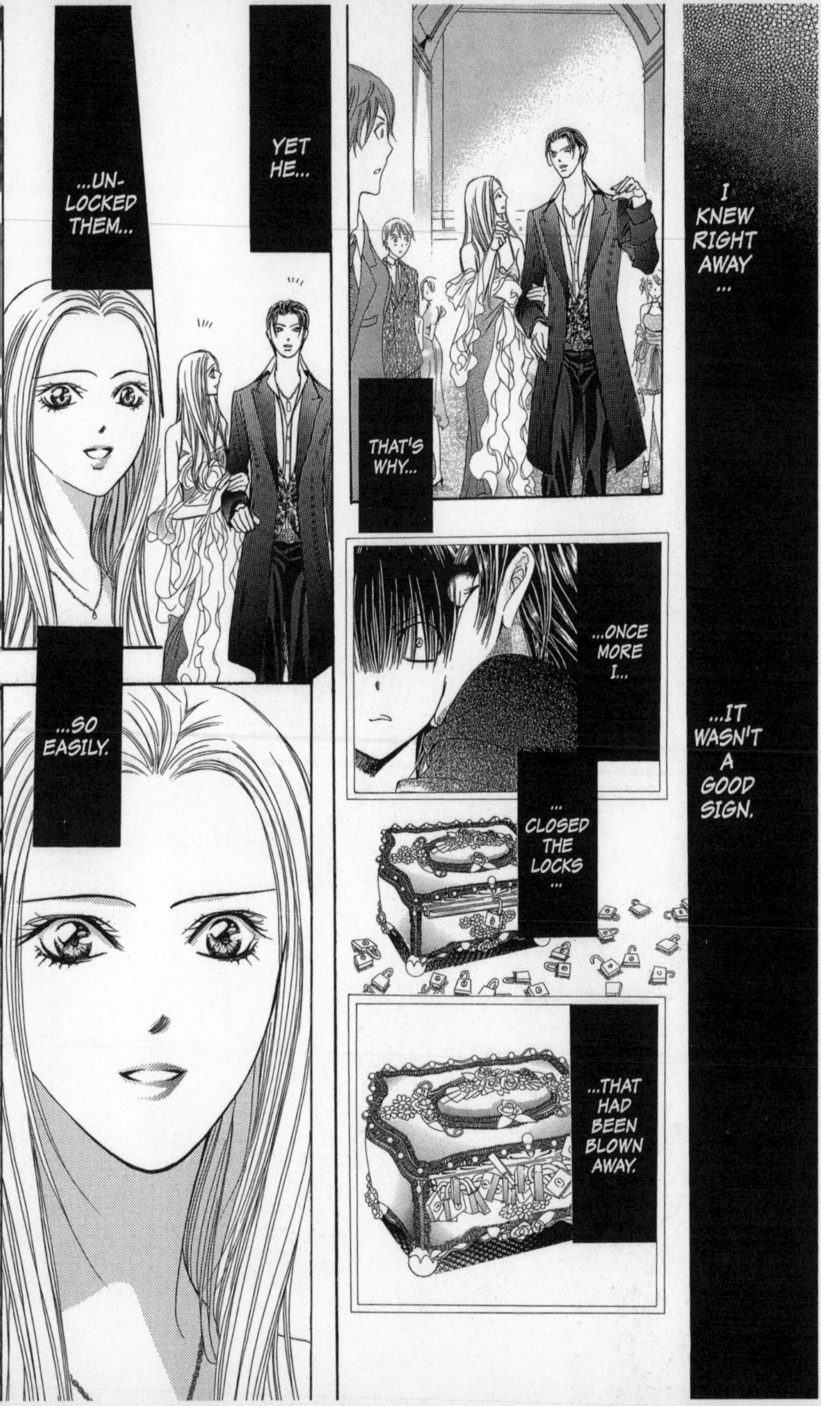
I KNEW RIGHT AWAY ...
...IT WASN'T A GOOD SIGN.
THAT'S WHY...
...ONCE MORE I...
... CLOSED THE LOCKS ...
...THAT HAD BEEN BLOWN AWAY.
YET HE...
...UN-LOCKED THEM...
...SO EASILY.

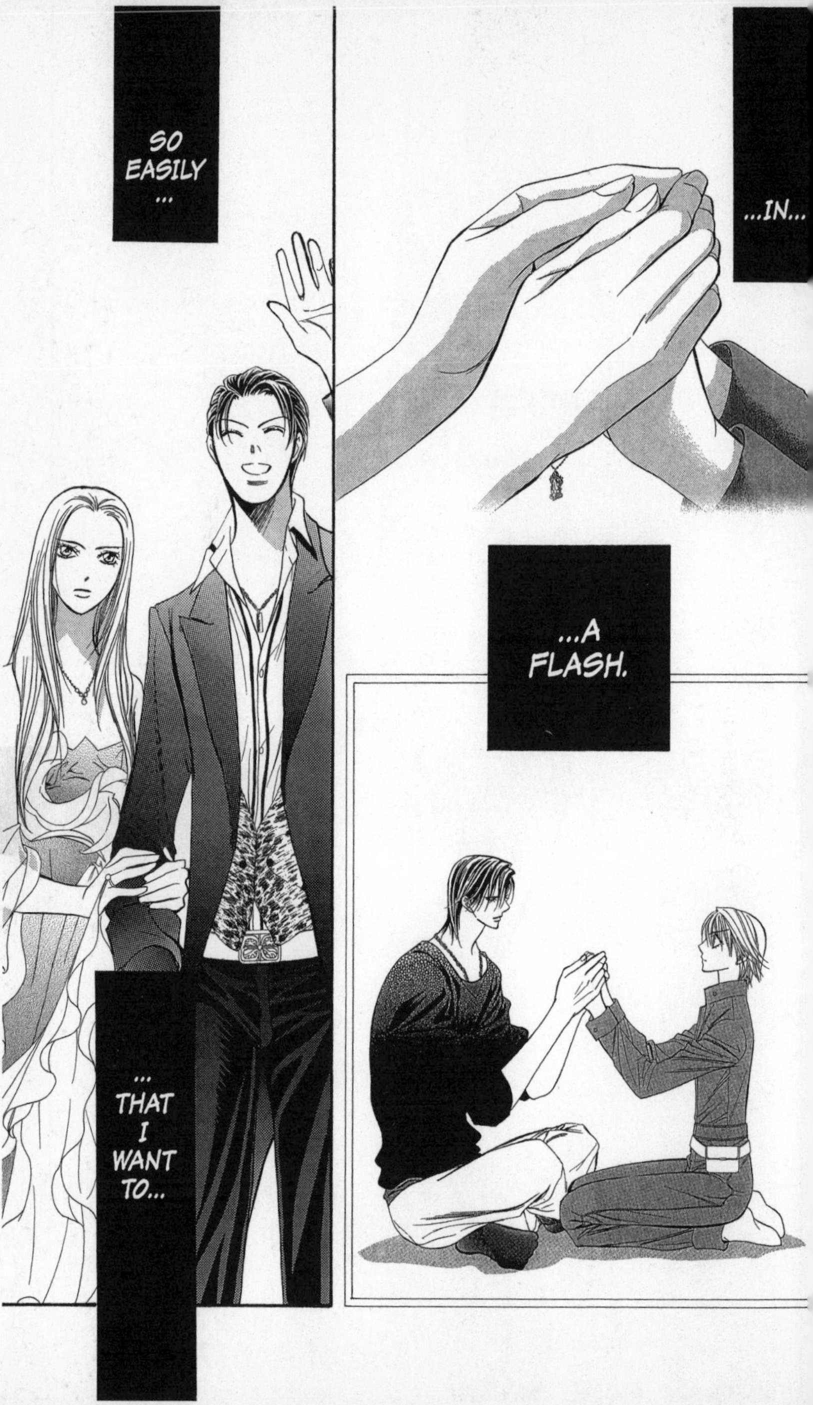
...IN...
...A FLASH.
SO EASILY ...
... THAT I WANT TO...

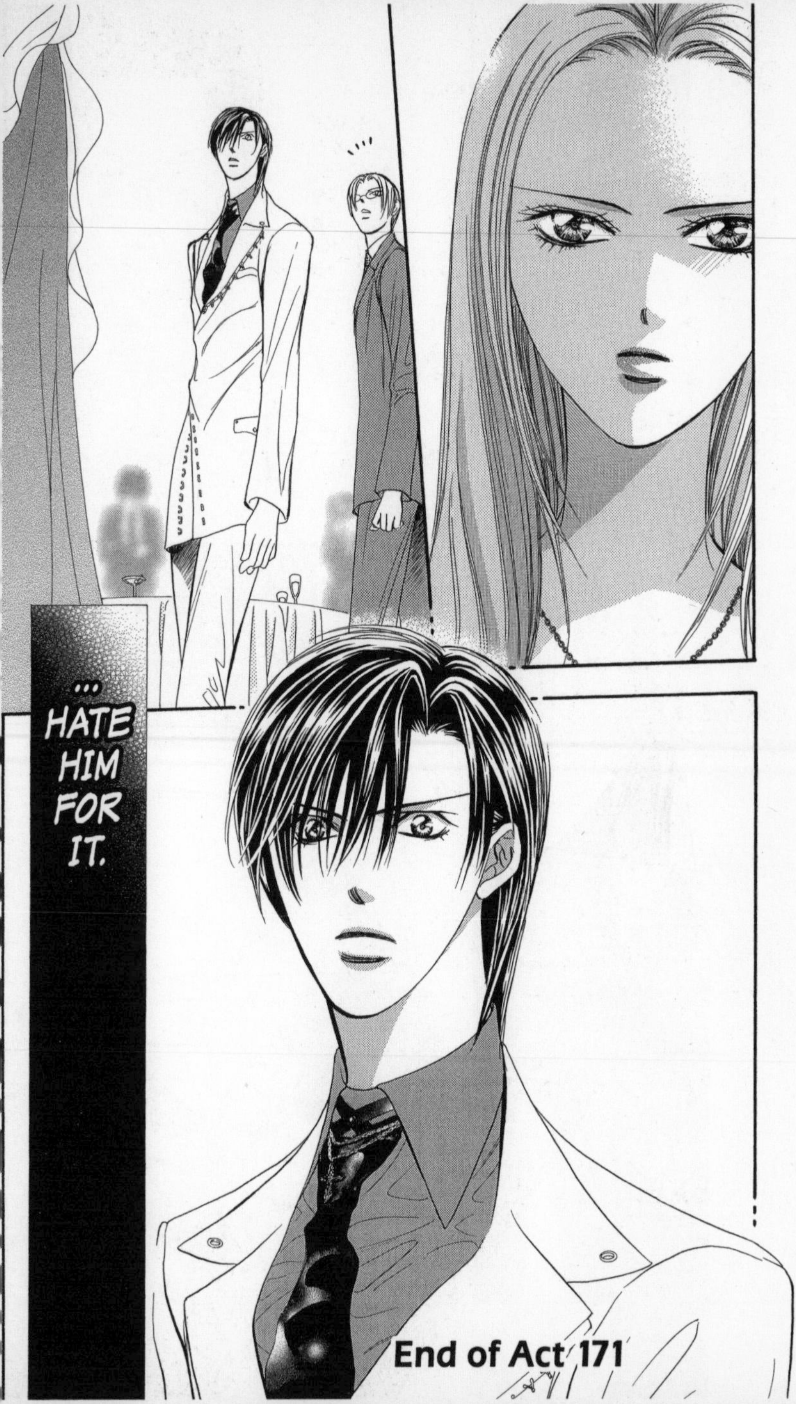
...HATE HIM FOR IT.
End of Act 171

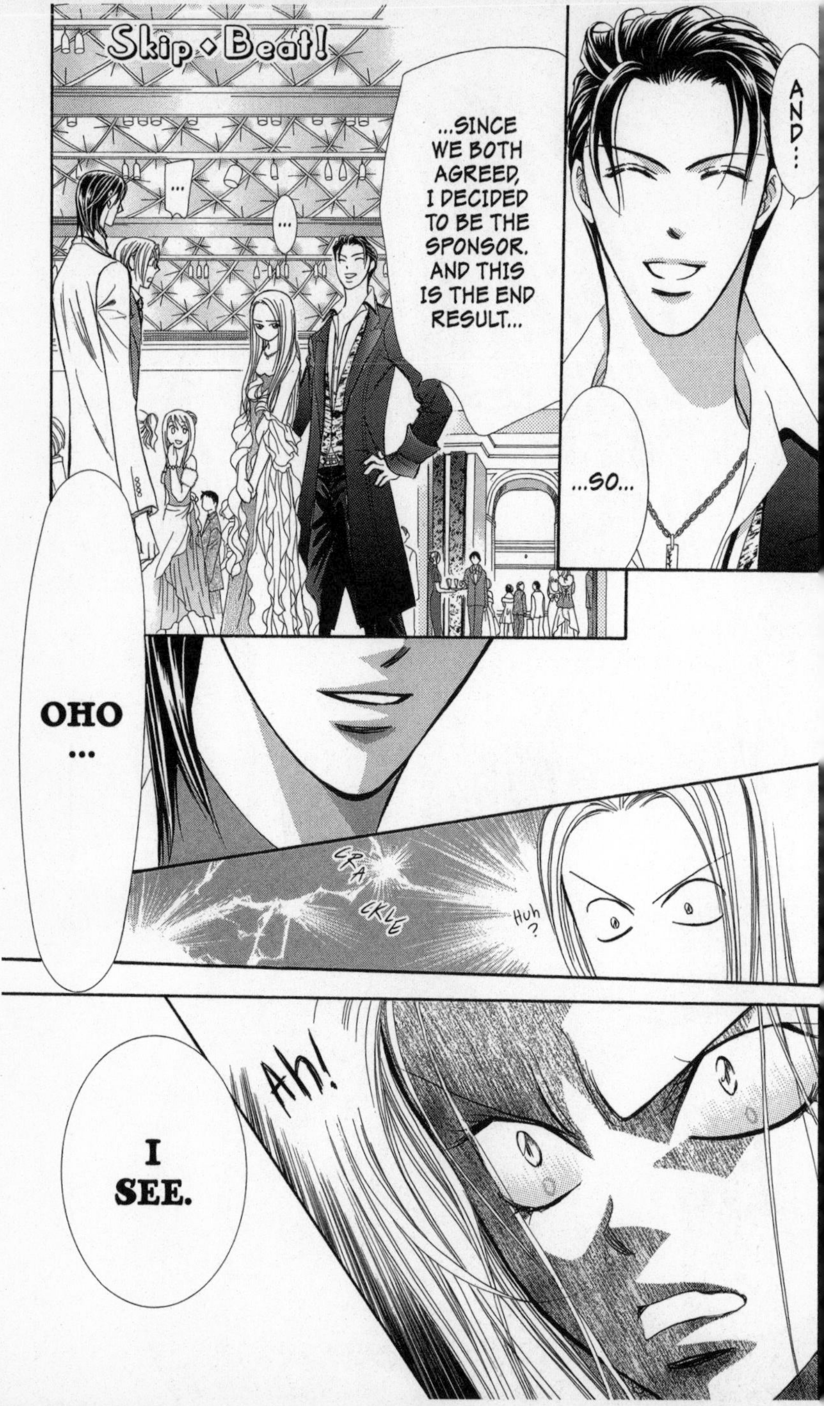
AND...
...SO...
Skip・Beat!
...SINCE WE BOTH AGREED, I DECIDED TO BE THE SPONSOR. AND THIS IS THE END RESULT...
...
...
OHO ...
CRACKLE
Huh?
Ah!
I SEE.

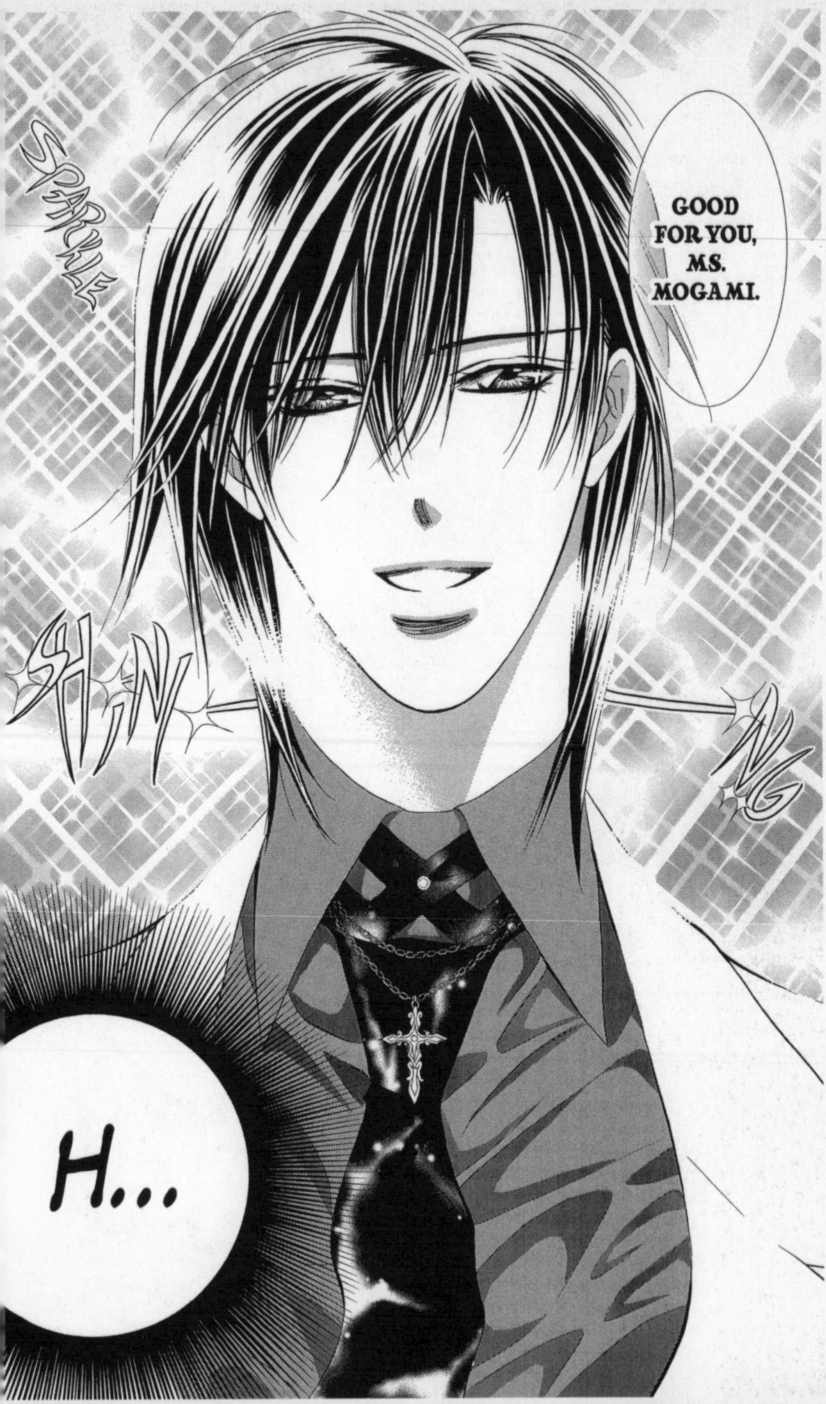
GOOD FOR YOU, MS. MOGAMI.
SPARKLE
SHINNG
H...

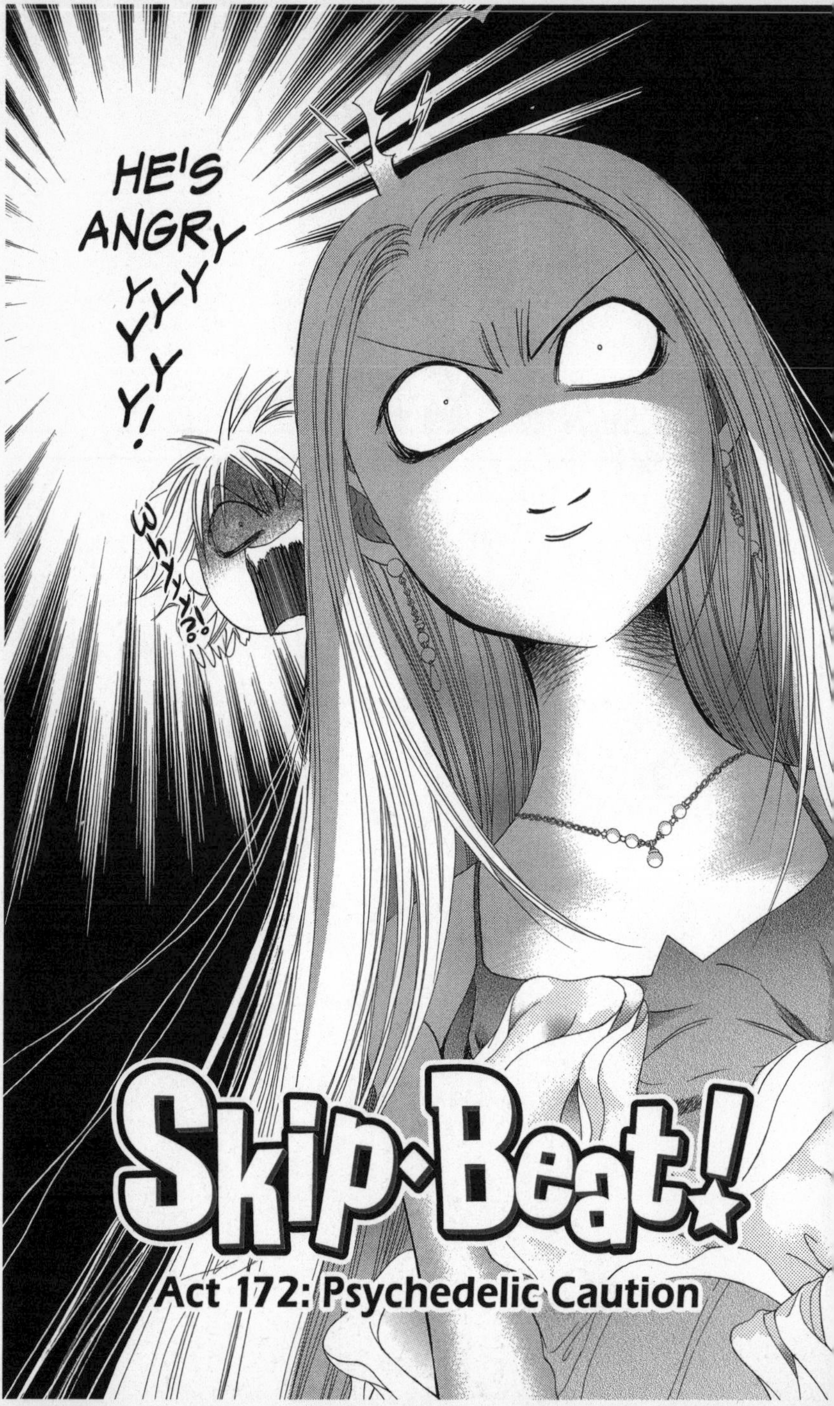
HE'S ANGRYYYYYYY!
WHYYY?!
Skip·Beat!
Act 172: Psychedelic Caution

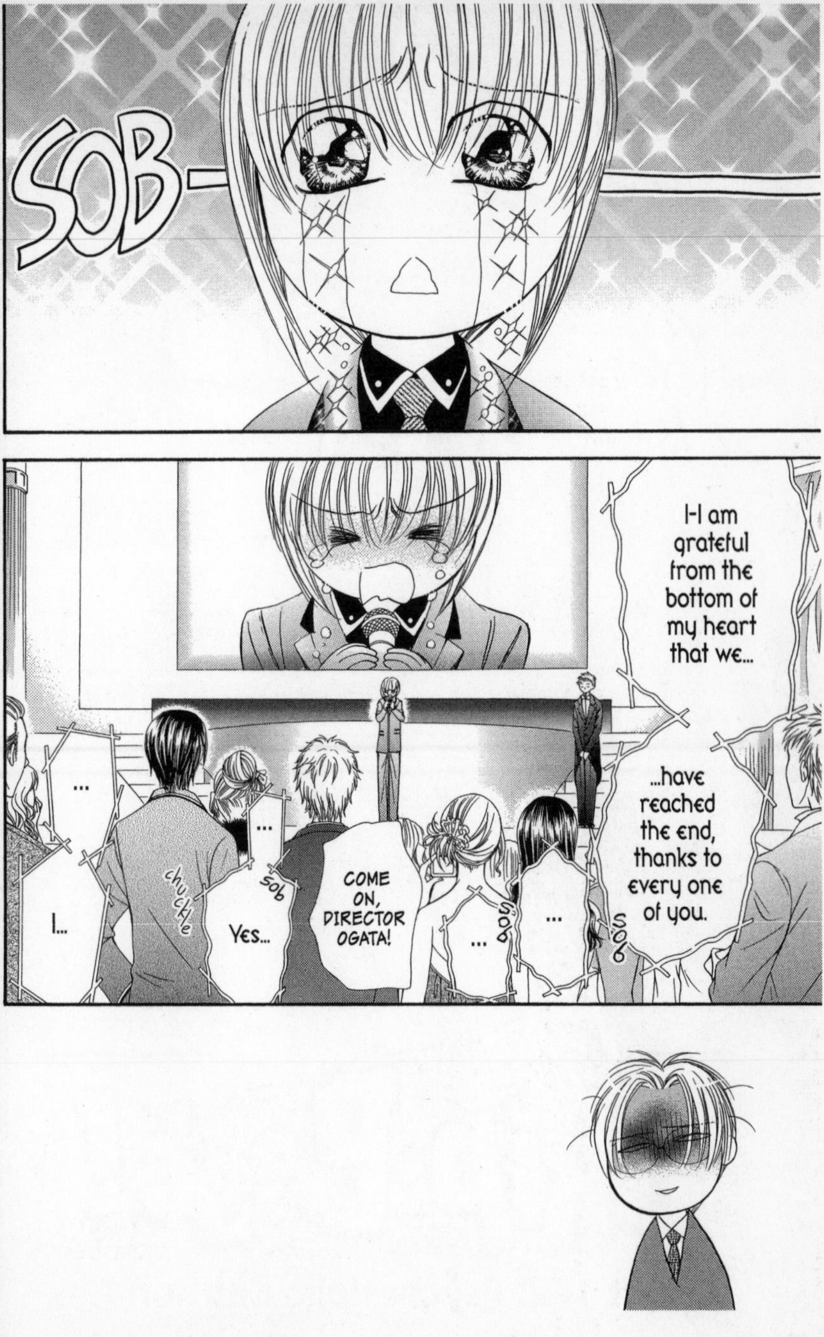
SOB-
I-I am grateful from the bottom of my heart that we...
...have reached the end, thanks to every one of you.
sob
...
sob
...
COME ON, DIRECTOR OGATA!
...
sob
Yes...
chuckle
...
I...

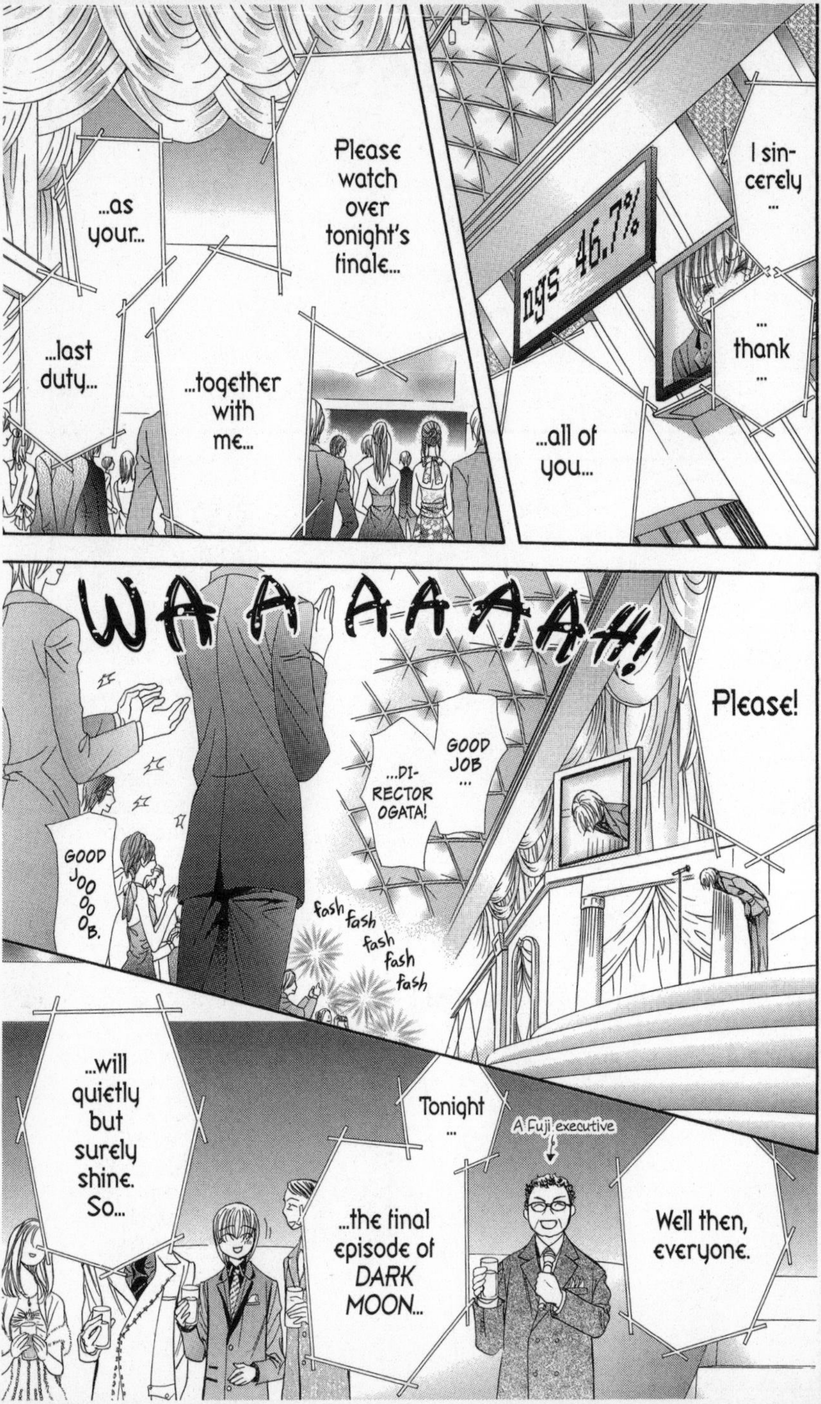
I sin-cerely...
...thank...
...all of you...
ngs 46.7%
Please watch over tonight's finale...
...as your...
...last duty...
...together with me...
Please!
WAAAAAAH!
GOOD JOB...
...DI-RECTOR OGATA!
fash fash fash fash fash
GOOD JOOOOOOB.
Well then, everyone.
A Fuji executive
Tonight...
...the final episode of DARK MOON...
...will quietly but surely shine. So...

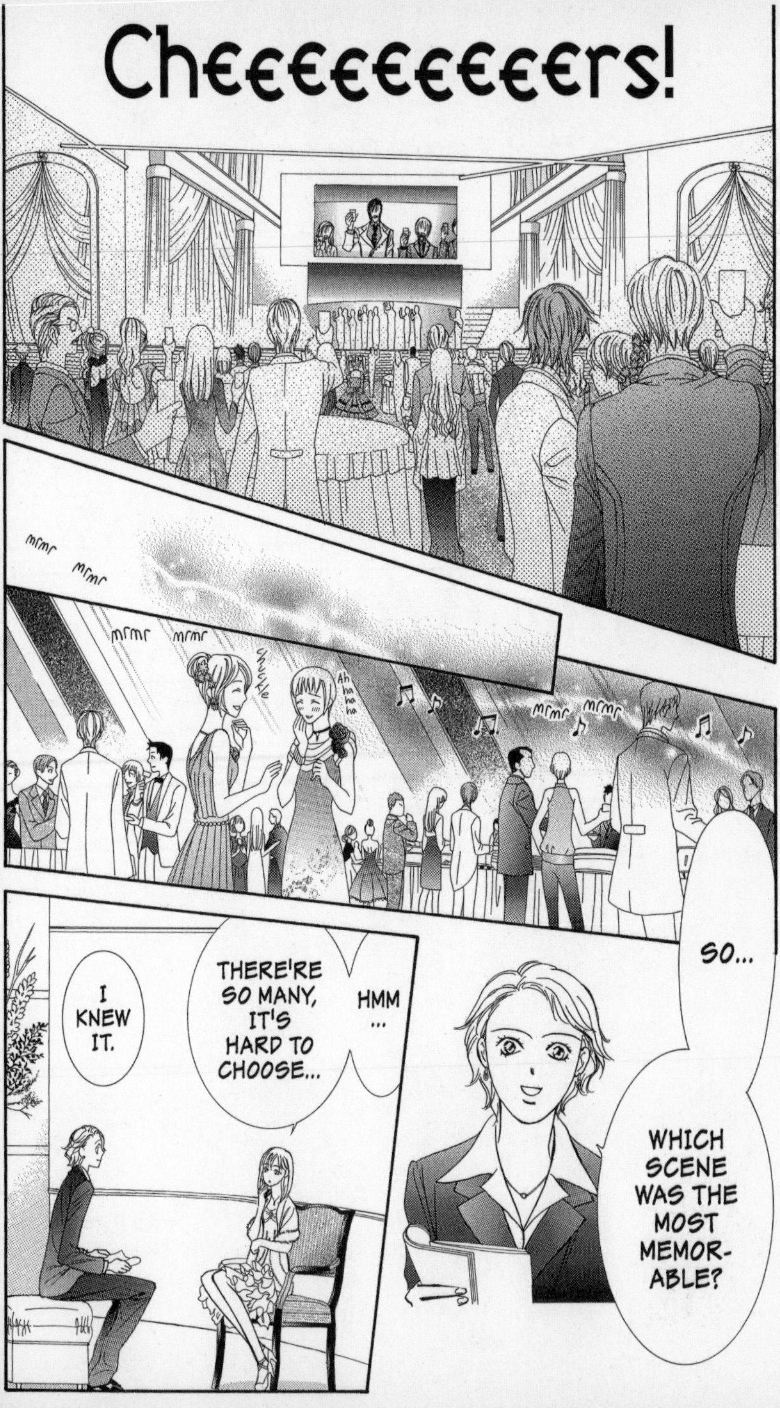
Cheeeeeeeeeers!
mrmr
mrmr
mrmr
mrmr
chuckle
Ahhahaha
mrmr
mrmr
SO...
WHICH SCENE WAS THE MOST MEMOR-ABLE?
HMM...
THERE'RE SO MANY, IT'S HARD TO CHOOSE...
I KNEW IT.

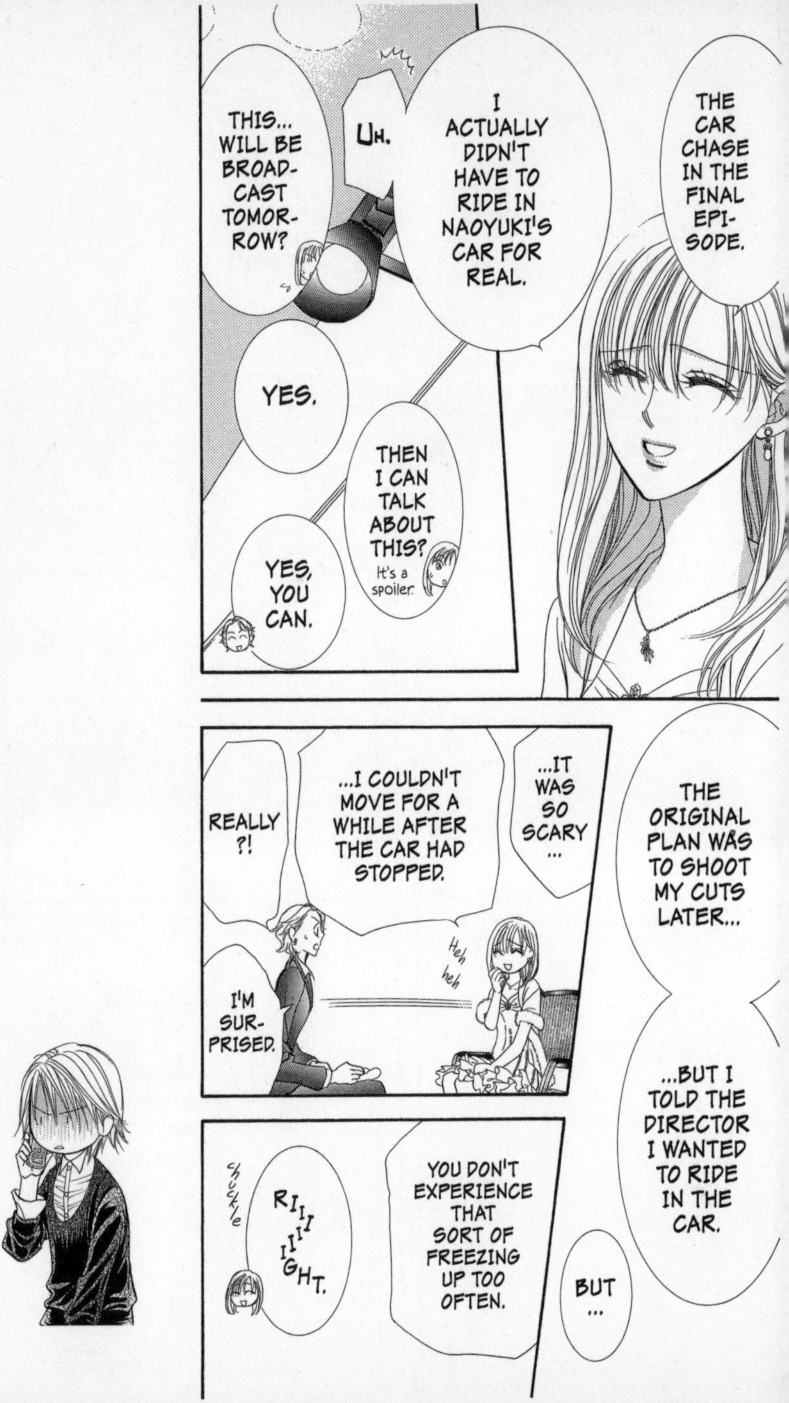
THE CAR CHASE IN THE FINAL EPI- SODE.
I ACTUALLY DIDN'T HAVE TO RIDE IN NAOYUKI'S CAR FOR REAL.
UH.
THIS... WILL BE BROAD- CAST TOMOR- ROW?
YES.
THEN I CAN TALK ABOUT THIS?
It's a spoiler.
YES, YOU CAN.
THE ORIGINAL PLAN WAS TO SHOOT MY CUTS LATER...
...BUT I TOLD THE DIRECTOR I WANTED TO RIDE IN THE CAR.
...IT WAS SO SCARY ...
...I COULDN'T MOVE FOR A WHILE AFTER THE CAR HAD STOPPED.
REALLY ?!
Heh heh
I'M SUR- PRISED.
BUT ...
YOU DON'T EXPERIENCE THAT SORT OF FREEZING UP TOO OFTEN.
chuckle
RIIIIIIGHT.

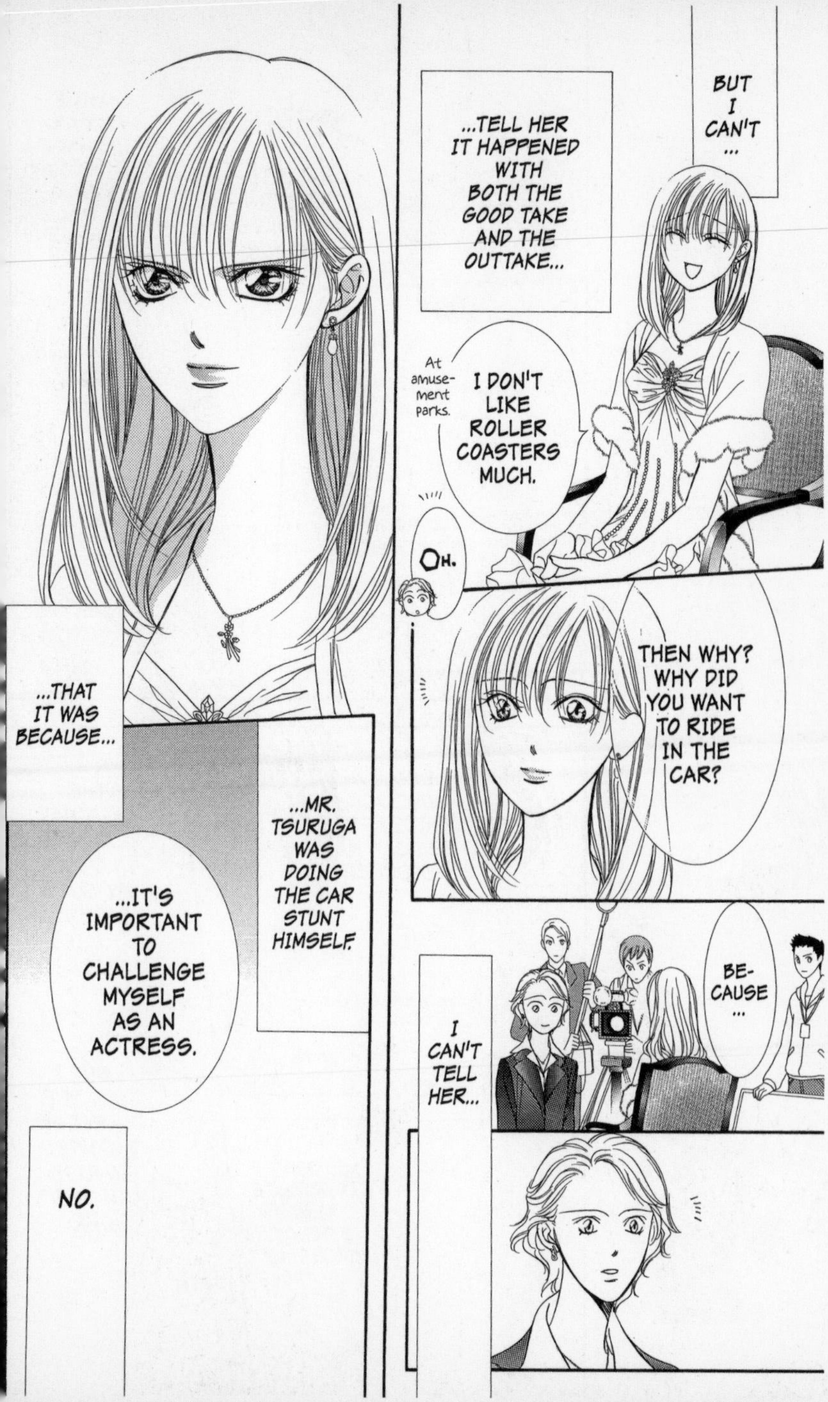
BUT I CAN'T ...
...TELL HER IT HAPPENED WITH BOTH THE GOOD TAKE AND THE OUTTAKE...
I DON'T LIKE ROLLER COASTERS MUCH.
At amusement parks.
OH.
THEN WHY? WHY DID YOU WANT TO RIDE IN THE CAR?
BE-CAUSE ...
I CAN'T TELL HER...
...THAT IT WAS BECAUSE...
...MR. TSURUGA WAS DOING THE CAR STUNT HIMSELF.
...IT'S IMPORTANT TO CHALLENGE MYSELF AS AN ACTRESS.
NO.

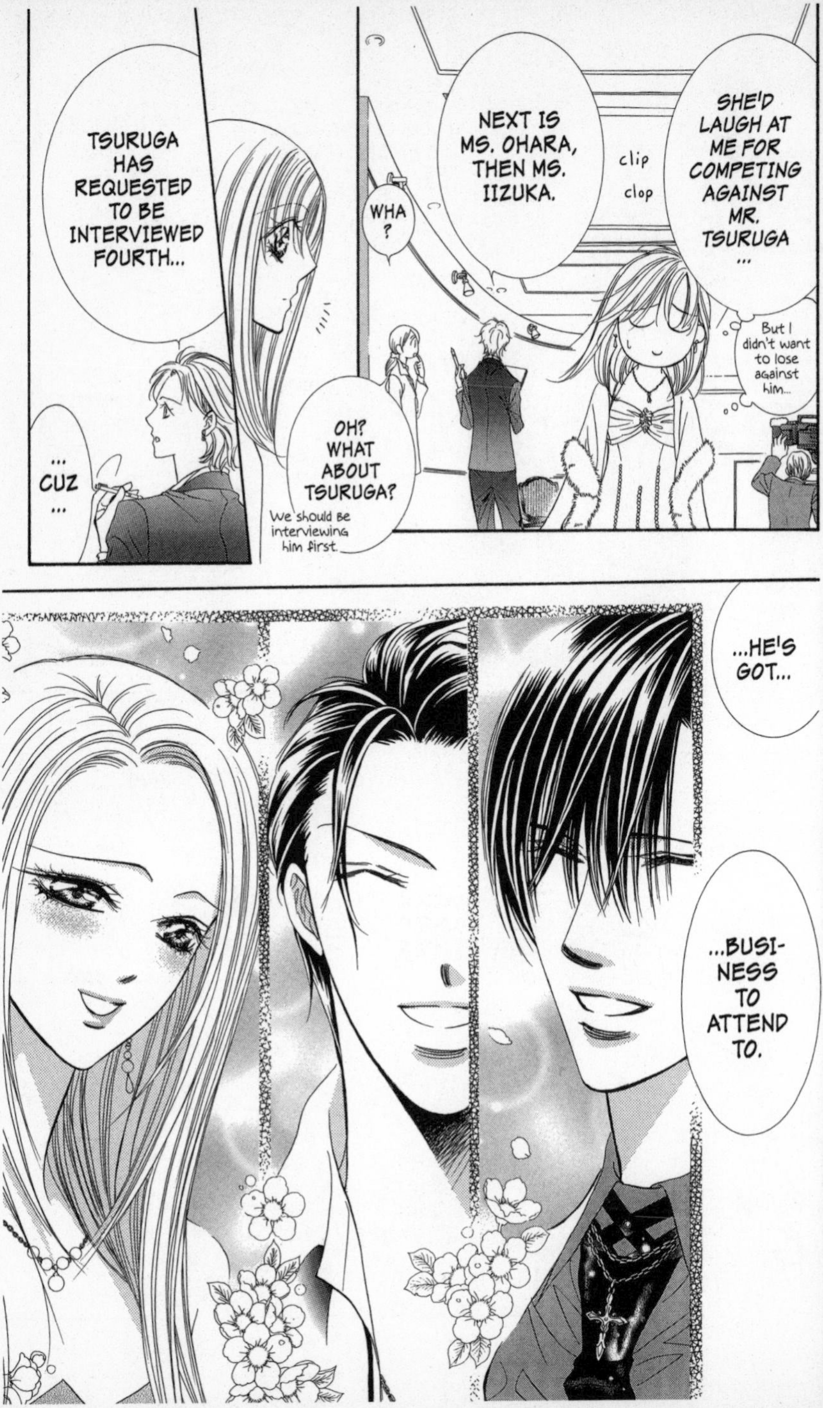
SHE'D LAUGH AT ME FOR COMPETING AGAINST MR. TSURUGA ...
But I didn't want to lose against him...
clip
clop
NEXT IS MS. OHARA, THEN MS. IIZUKA.
WHA ?
OH? WHAT ABOUT TSURUGA?
We should be interviewing him first.
TSURUGA HAS REQUESTED TO BE INTERVIEWED FOURTH...
... CUZ ...
...HE'S GOT...
...BUSI-NESS TO ATTEND TO.

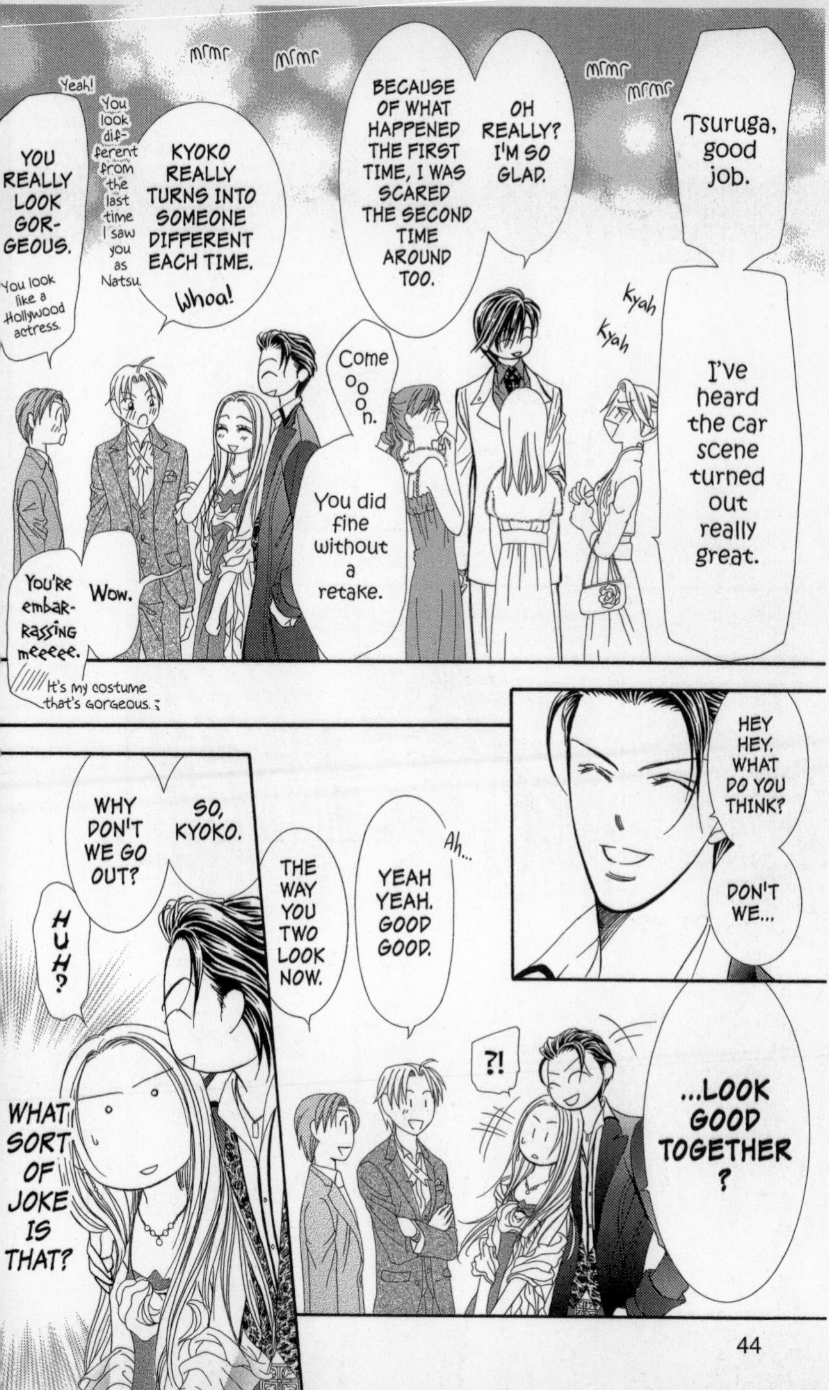
Tsuruga, good job.
I've heard the car scene turned out really great.
Kyah
Kyah
mrmr
mrmr
OH REALLY? I'M SO GLAD.
BECAUSE OF WHAT HAPPENED THE FIRST TIME, I WAS SCARED THE SECOND TIME AROUND TOO.
Come ooon.
You did fine without a retake.
mrmr
mrmr
KYOKO REALLY TURNS INTO SOMEONE DIFFERENT EACH TIME.
Whoa!
You look different from the last time I saw you as Natsu.
Yeah!
YOU REALLY LOOK GORGEOUS.
You look like a Hollywood actress.
Wow.
You're embarrassing meeeee.
It's my costume that's gorgeous.
HEY HEY. WHAT DO YOU THINK?
DON'T WE...
SO, KYOKO.
WHY DON'T WE GO OUT?
YEAH YEAH. GOOD GOOD.
Ah...
THE WAY YOU TWO LOOK NOW.
HUH?
...LOOK GOOD TOGETHER?
?!
WHAT SORT OF JOKE IS THAT?

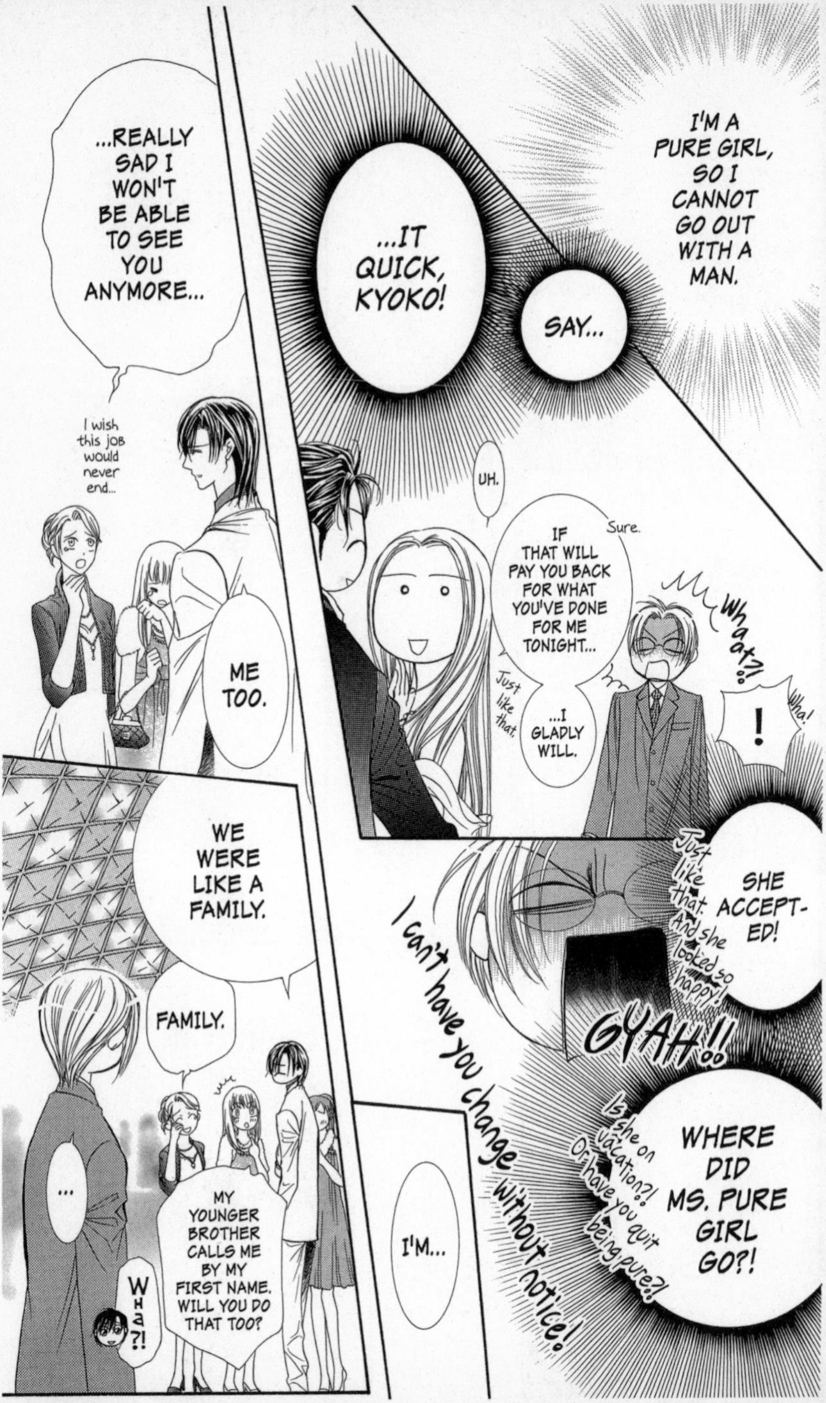
I'M A PURE GIRL, SO I CANNOT GO OUT WITH A MAN.
SAY...
...IT QUICK, KYOKO!
UH.
IF THAT WILL PAY YOU BACK FOR WHAT YOU'VE DONE FOR ME TONIGHT...
Sure.
...I GLADLY WILL.
Just like that.
Whaat?!
Wha!
!
SHE ACCEPTED!
Just like that. And she looked so happy!
GYAH!!
WHERE DID MS. PURE GIRL GO?!
Is she on vacation?! Or have you quit being pure?!
I can't have you change without notice!
I'M...
...REALLY SAD I WON'T BE ABLE TO SEE YOU ANYMORE...
I wish this job would never end...
ME TOO.
WE WERE LIKE A FAMILY.
FAMILY.
...
MY YOUNGER BROTHER CALLS ME BY MY FIRST NAME. WILL YOU DO THAT TOO?
What?!

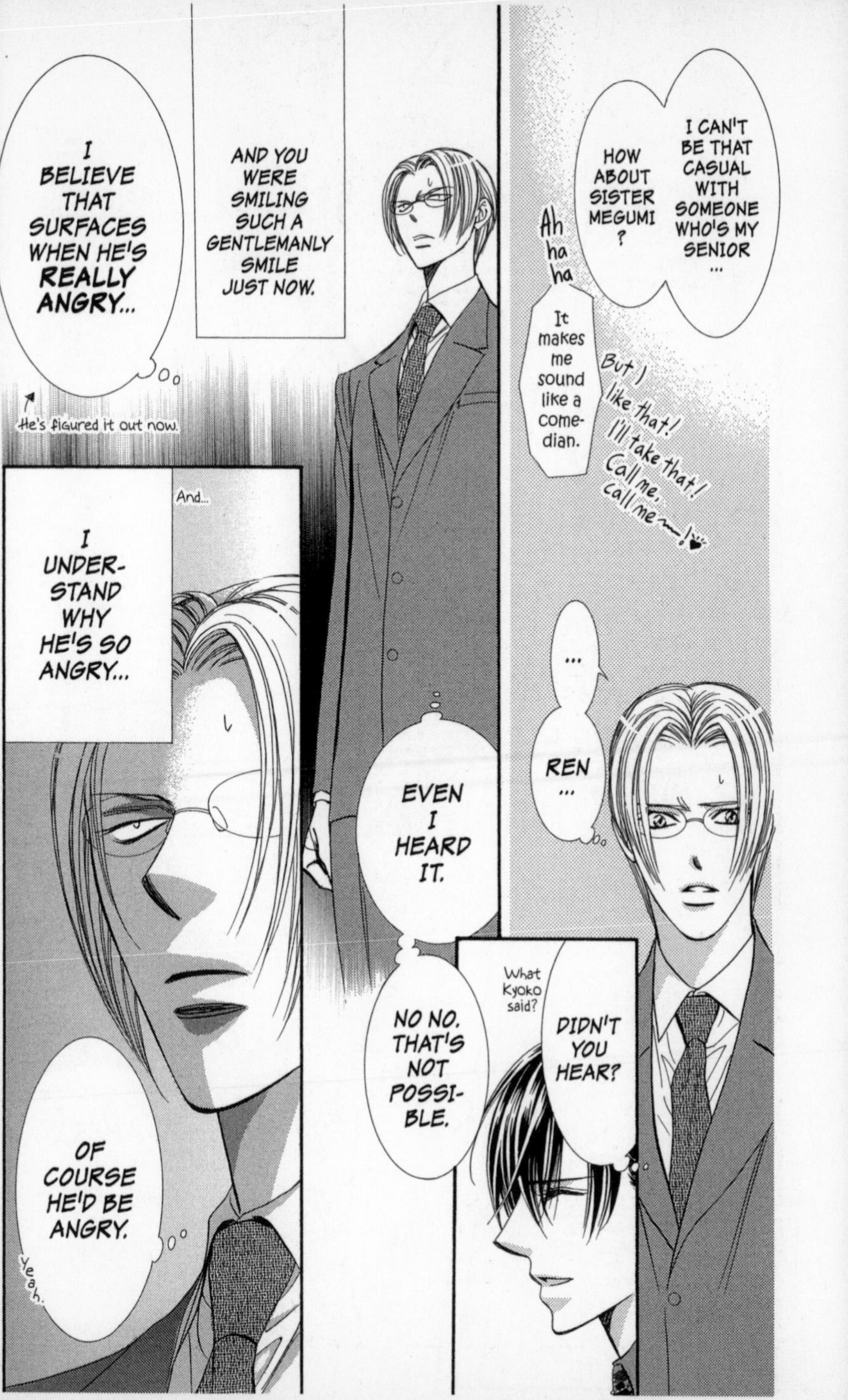
I CAN'T BE THAT CASUAL WITH SOMEONE WHO'S MY SENIOR ...
HOW ABOUT SISTER MEGUMI ?
Ah ha ha
It makes me sound like a come-dian.
But I like that! I'll take that! Call me, call me~!
...
REN ...
What Kyoko said?
DIDN'T YOU HEAR?
NO NO. THAT'S NOT POSSI-BLE.
EVEN I HEARD IT.
AND YOU WERE SMILING SUCH A GENTLEMANLY SMILE JUST NOW.
I BELIEVE THAT SURFACES WHEN HE'S REALLY ANGRY...
He's figured it out now.
And...
I UNDER-STAND WHY HE'S SO ANGRY...
OF COURSE HE'D BE ANGRY.
Yeah.

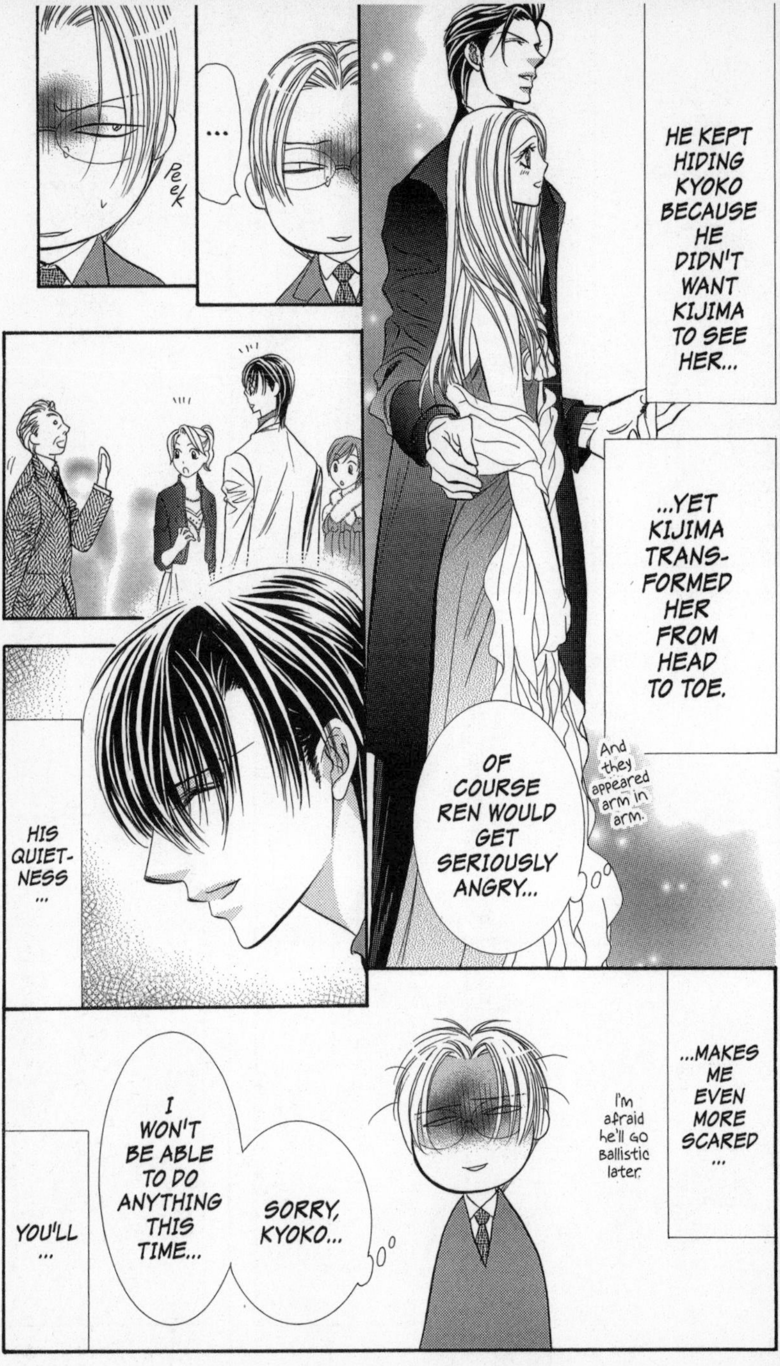
HE KEPT HIDING KYOKO BECAUSE HE DIDN'T WANT KIJIMA TO SEE HER...
...YET KIJIMA TRANS-FORMED HER FROM HEAD TO TOE.
And they appeared arm in arm.
OF COURSE REN WOULD GET SERIOUSLY ANGRY...
...
Peek
HIS QUIET-NESS...
...MAKES ME EVEN MORE SCARED...
I'm afraid he'll GO Ballistic later.
SORRY, KYOKO...
I WON'T BE ABLE TO DO ANYTHING THIS TIME...
YOU'LL...

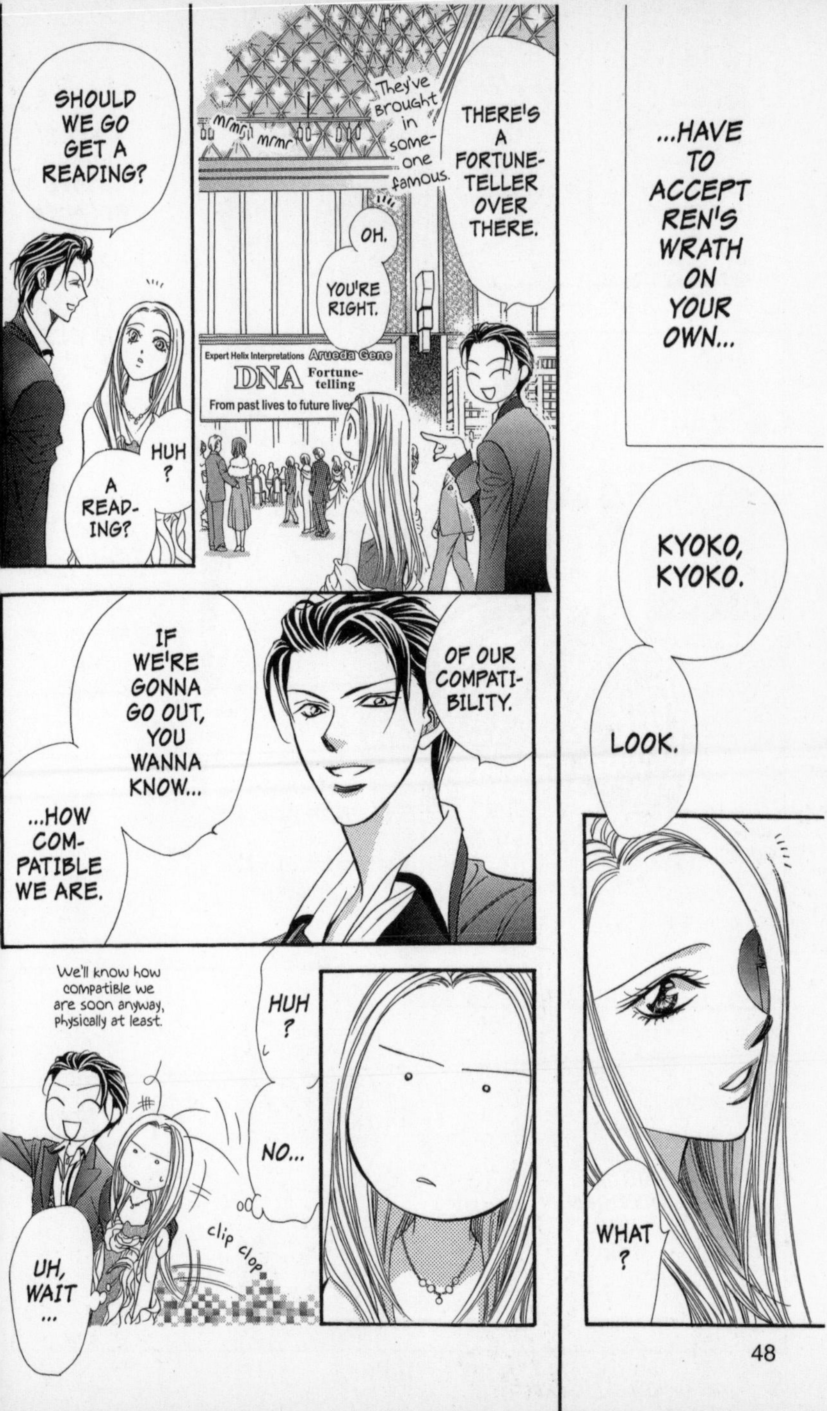
...HAVE TO ACCEPT REN'S WRATH ON YOUR OWN...
KYOKO, KYOKO.
LOOK.
WHAT?
THERE'S A FORTUNE-TELLER OVER THERE.
They've brought in someone famous.
mrmr mrmr
OH.
YOU'RE RIGHT.
Expert Helix Interpretations Arueda Gene
DNA Fortune-telling
From past lives to future live
SHOULD WE GO GET A READING?
HUH?
A READING?
OF OUR COMPATIBILITY.
IF WE'RE GONNA GO OUT, YOU WANNA KNOW...
...HOW COMPATIBLE WE ARE.
HUH?
NO...
We'll know how compatible we are soon anyway, physically at least.
clip clop
UH, WAIT...

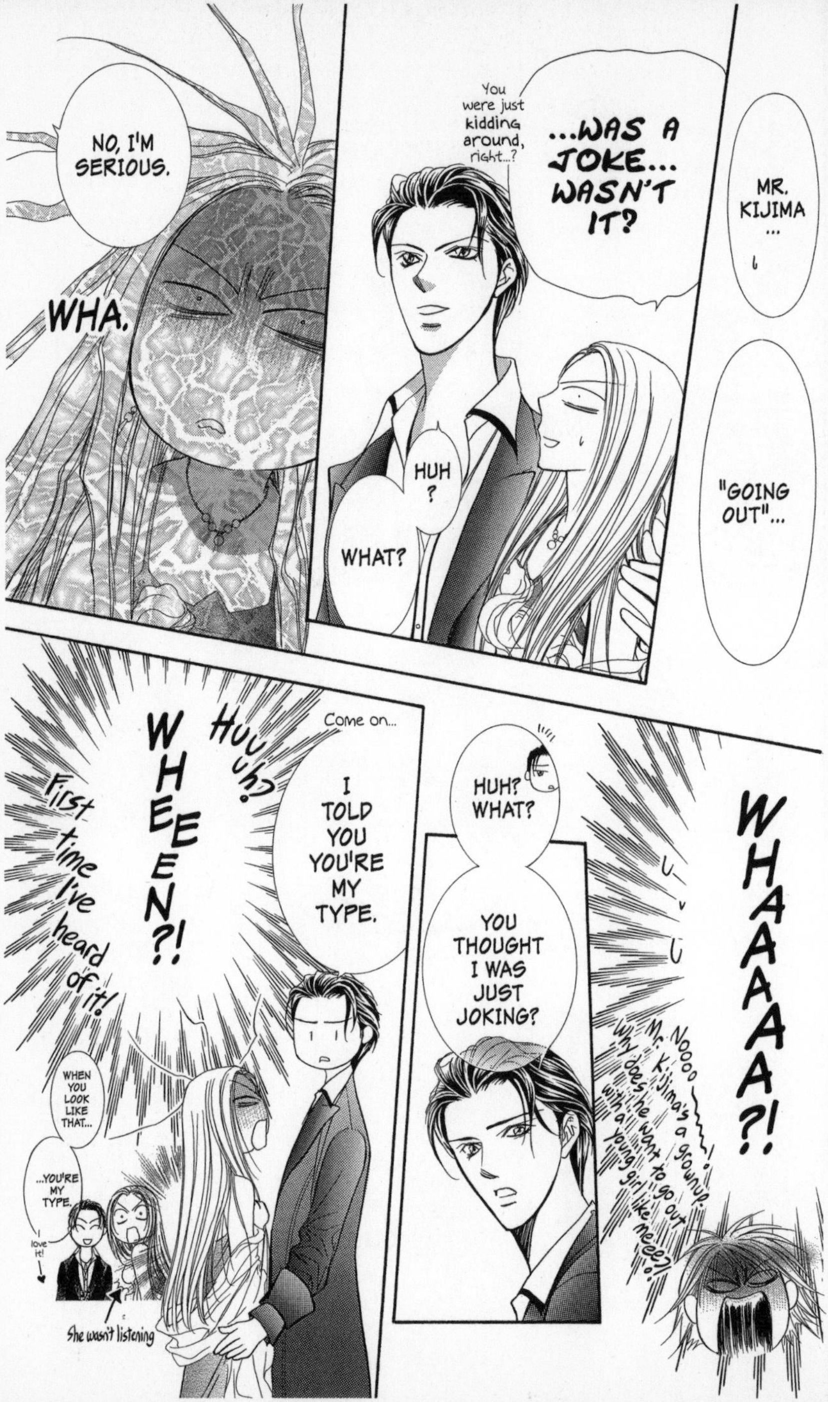
MR. KIJIMA ...
"GOING OUT"...
...WAS A JOKE... WASN'T IT?
You were just kidding around, right...?
HUH ?
WHAT?
NO, I'M SERIOUS.
WHA.
HUH? WHAT?
YOU THOUGHT I WAS JUST JOKING?
WHAAAAA?!
Mr. Kijima's a grownup. Noooo!
Why does he want to go out with a young girl like meee?!
Come on...
I TOLD YOU YOU'RE MY TYPE.
HUUuh?
WHEEEN?!
First time I've heard of it!
WHEN YOU LOOK LIKE THAT...
...YOU'RE MY TYPE.
I love it!
She wasn't listening

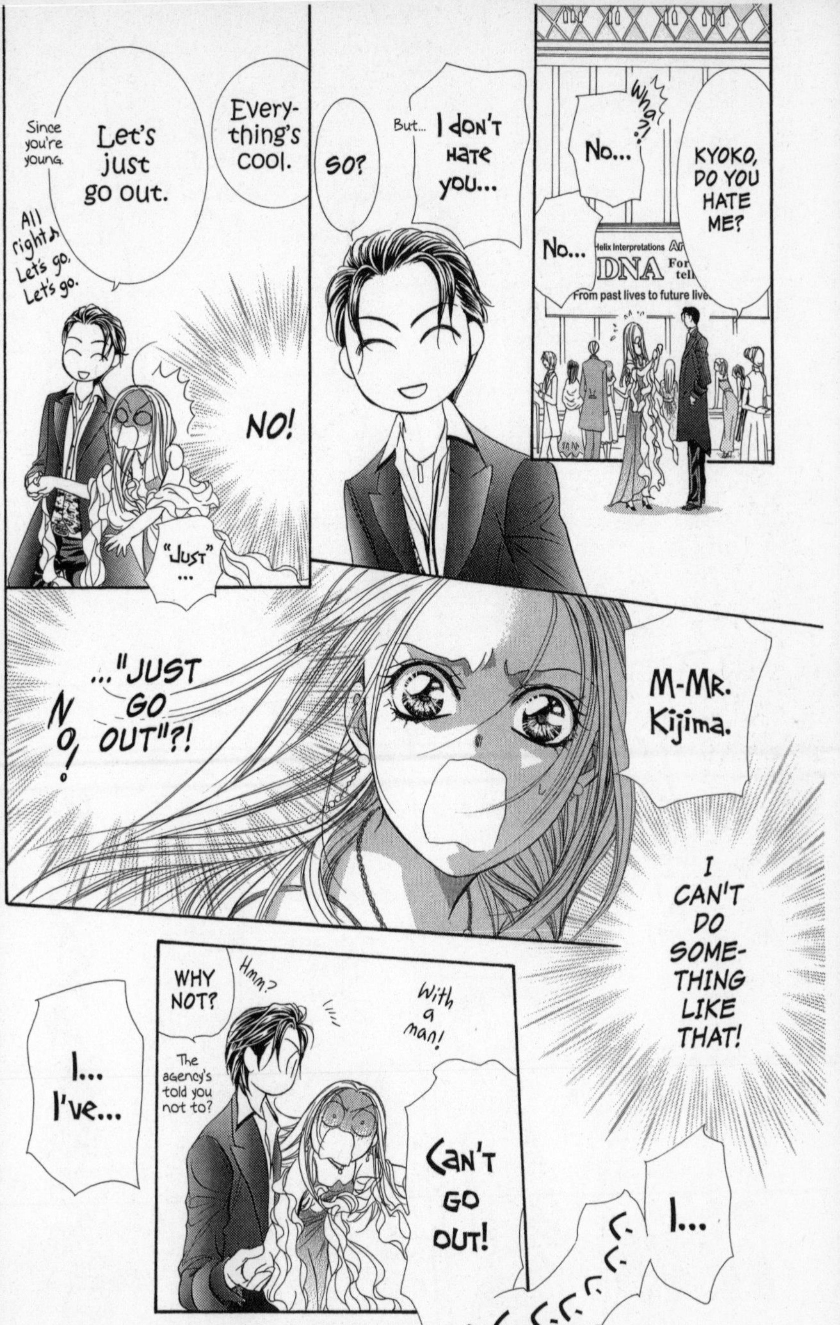
KYOKO, DO YOU HATE ME?
Wha?!
No...
No...
Helix Interpretations
DNA
From past lives to future live
But... I don't hate you...
SO?
Every-thing's cool.
Since you're young.
Let's just go out.
All right♪ Let's go, Let's go.
NO!
"Just" ...
M-Mr. Kijima.
..."JUST GO OUT"?!
No, no!
I CAN'T DO SOME-THING LIKE THAT!
Hmm?
WHY NOT?
With a man!
The agency's told you not to?
Can't go out!
I... I've...
I...
C-C-C-C-C-C...

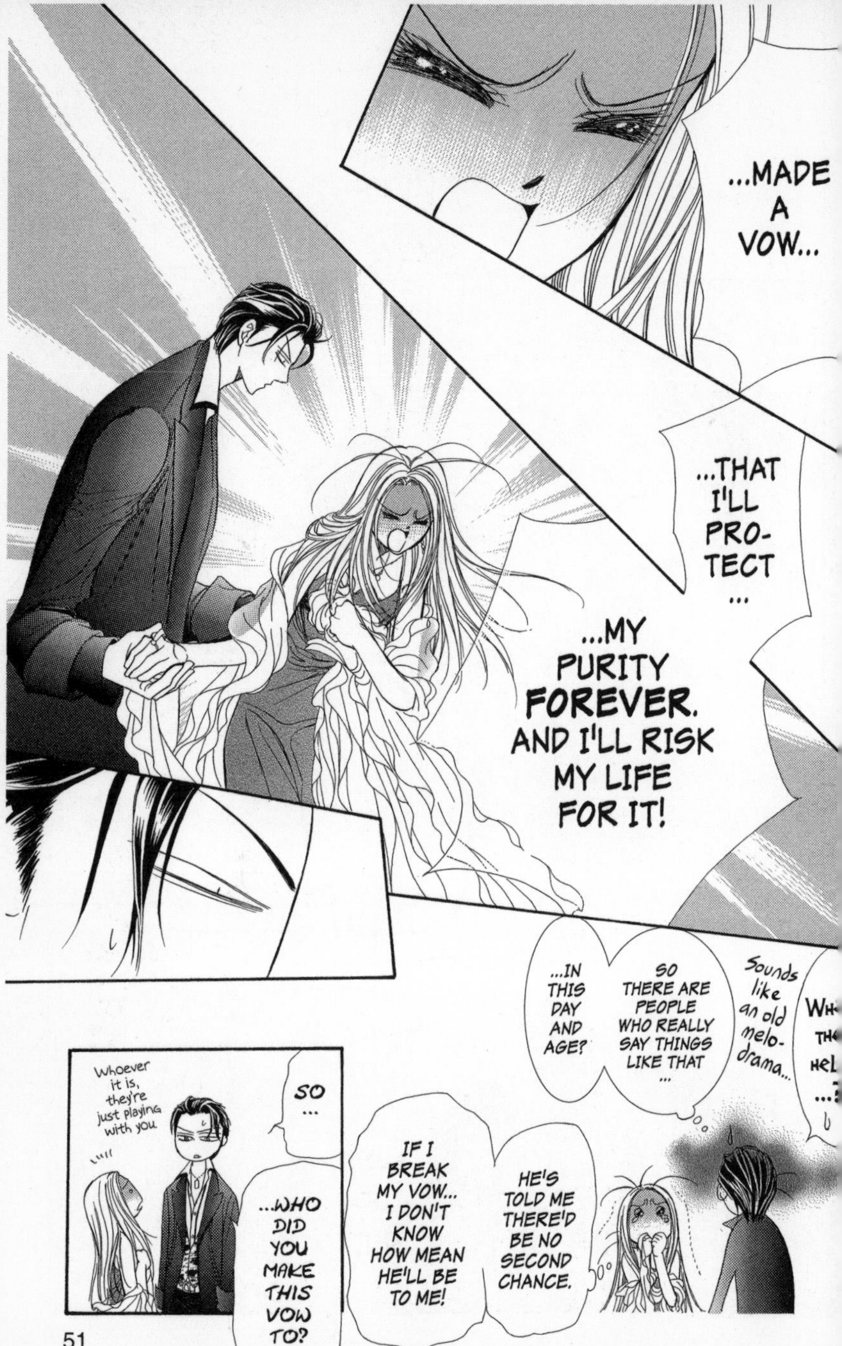
...MADE A VOW...
...THAT I'LL PRO-TECT ...
...MY PURITY FOREVER. AND I'LL RISK MY LIFE FOR IT!
Sounds like an old melo-drama...
SO THERE ARE PEOPLE WHO REALLY SAY THINGS LIKE THAT ...
...IN THIS DAY AND AGE?
SO ...
Whoever it is, they're just playing with you.
...WHO DID YOU MAKE THIS VOW TO?
IF I BREAK MY VOW... I DON'T KNOW HOW MEAN HE'LL BE TO ME!
HE'S TOLD ME THERE'D BE NO SECOND CHANCE.

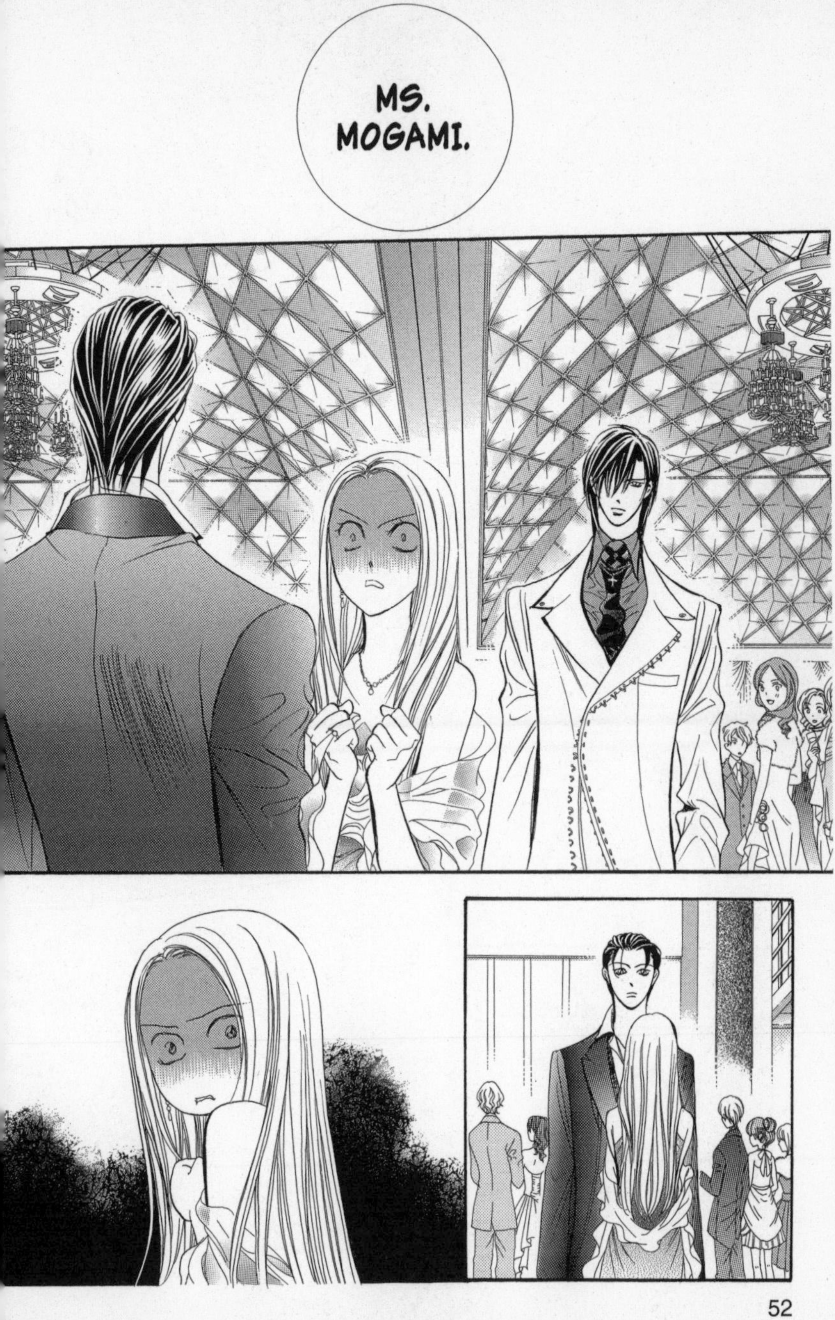
MS.
MOGAMI.

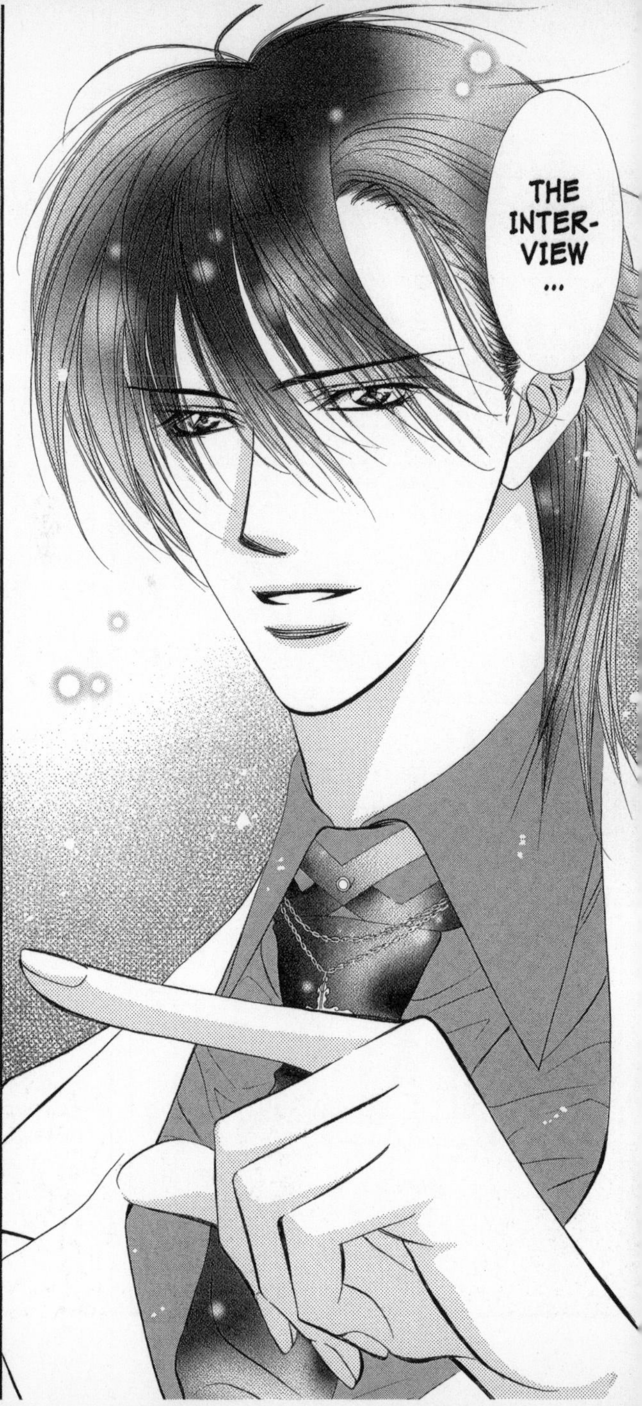
THE INTER-VIEW ...
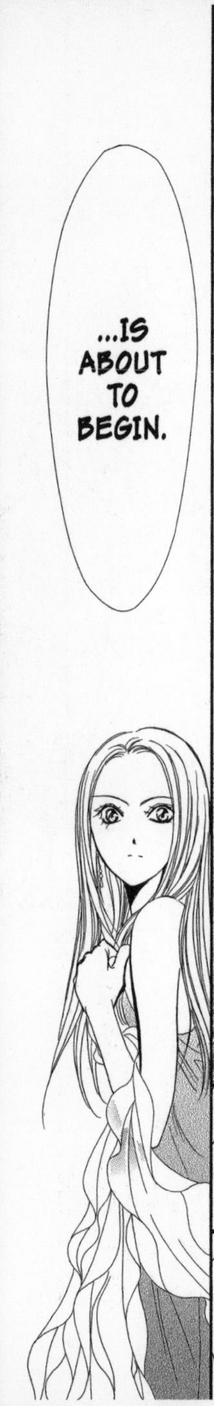
...IS ABOUT TO BEGIN.

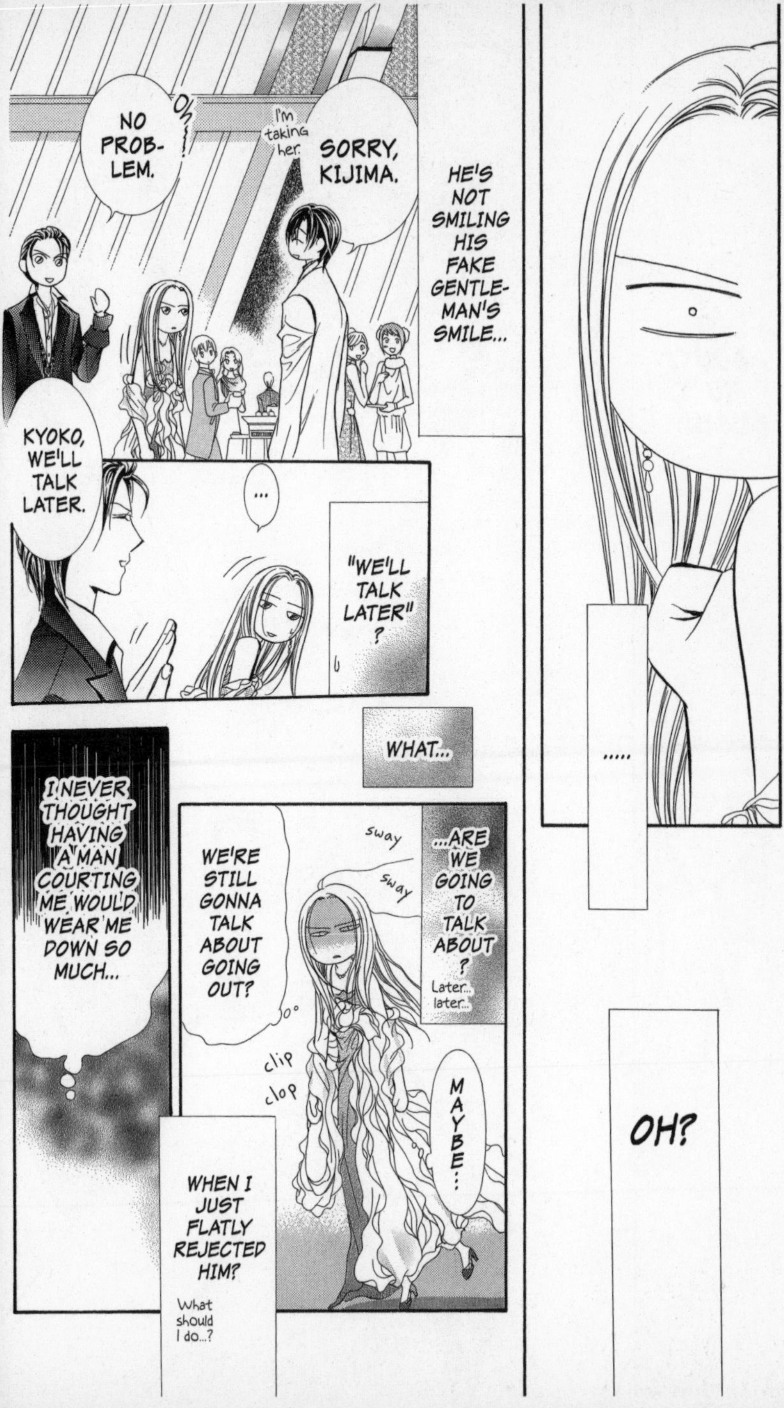
.....
OH?
HE'S NOT SMILING HIS FAKE GENTLEMAN'S SMILE...
SORRY, KIJIMA.
I'm taking her.
Oh—!
NO PROBLEM.
KYOKO, WE'LL TALK LATER.
"WE'LL TALK LATER"?
...
WHAT...
...ARE WE GOING TO TALK ABOUT?
Later... later...
sway
sway
WE'RE STILL GONNA TALK ABOUT GOING OUT?
MAYBE...
clip
clop
I NEVER THOUGHT HAVING A MAN COURTING ME WOULD WEAR ME DOWN SO MUCH...
WHEN I JUST FLATLY REJECTED HIM?
What should I do...?

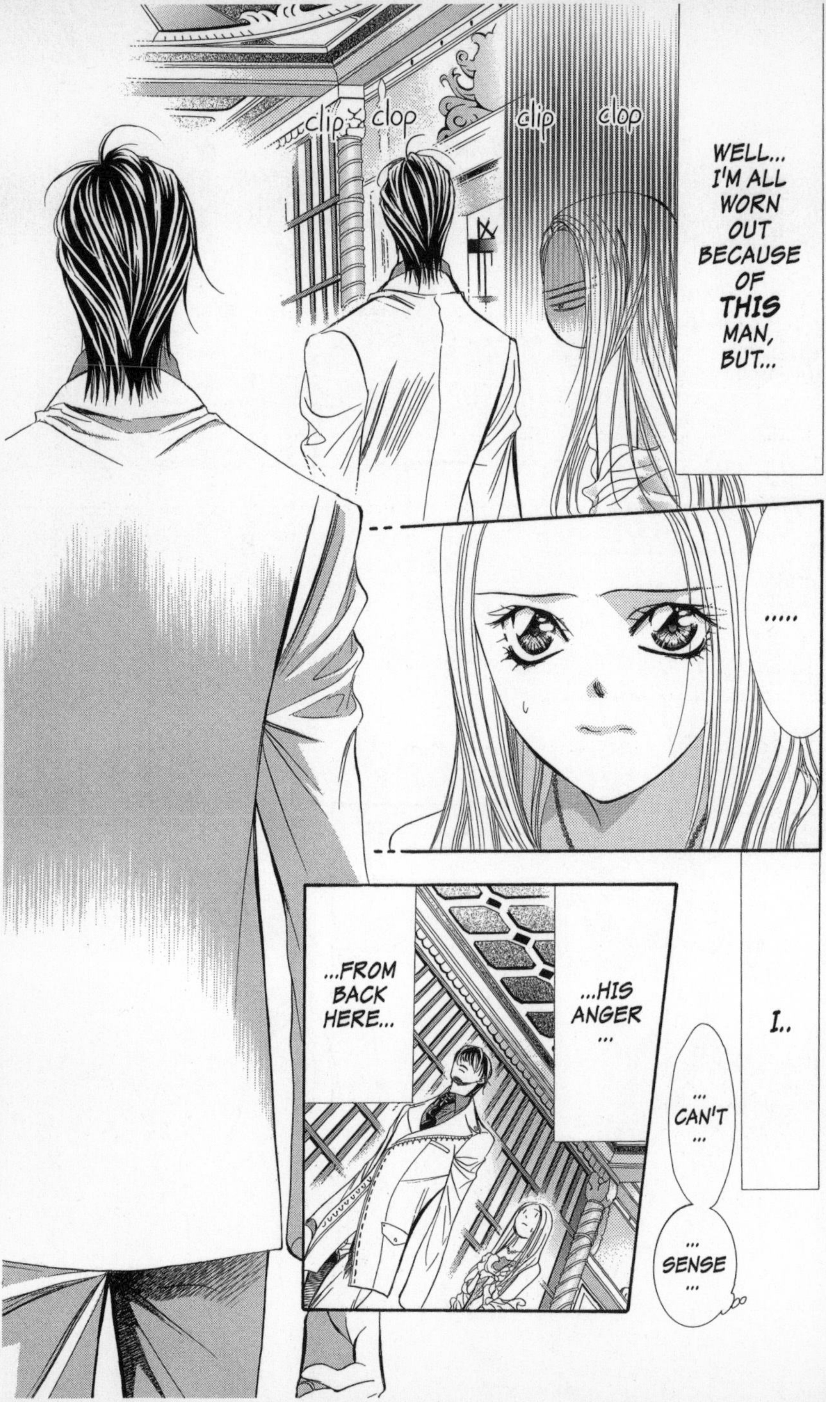
WELL... I'M ALL WORN OUT BECAUSE OF THIS MAN, BUT...
clip clop
clip clop
.....
I..
...CAN'T...
...SENSE...
...HIS ANGER...
...FROM BACK HERE...

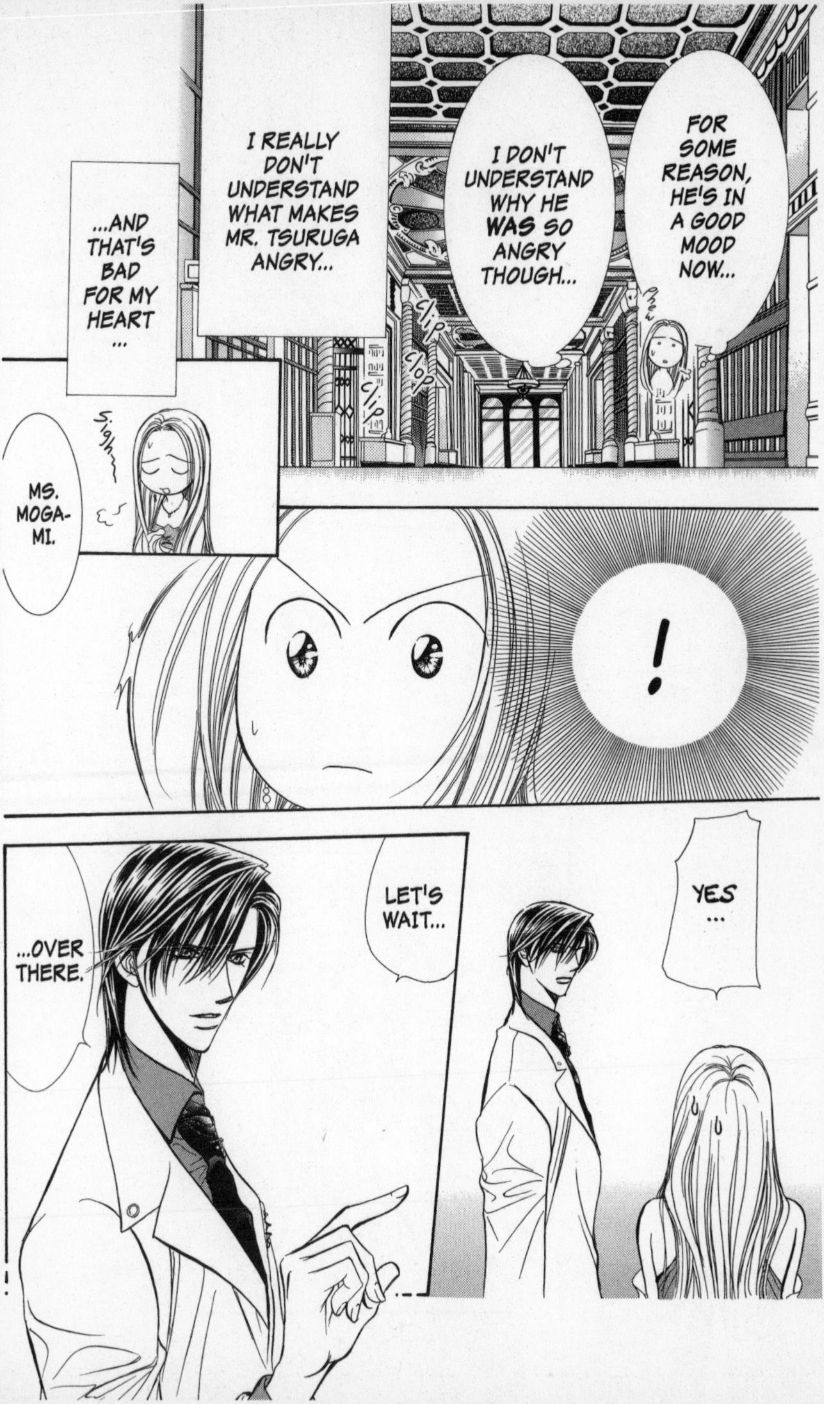
FOR SOME REASON, HE'S IN A GOOD MOOD NOW...
Phew
I DON'T UNDERSTAND WHY HE WAS SO ANGRY THOUGH...
clip clop clip
I REALLY DON'T UNDERSTAND WHAT MAKES MR. TSURUGA ANGRY...
...AND THAT'S BAD FOR MY HEART ...
Sigh
MS. MOGA-MI.
!
YES ...
LET'S WAIT...
...OVER THERE.

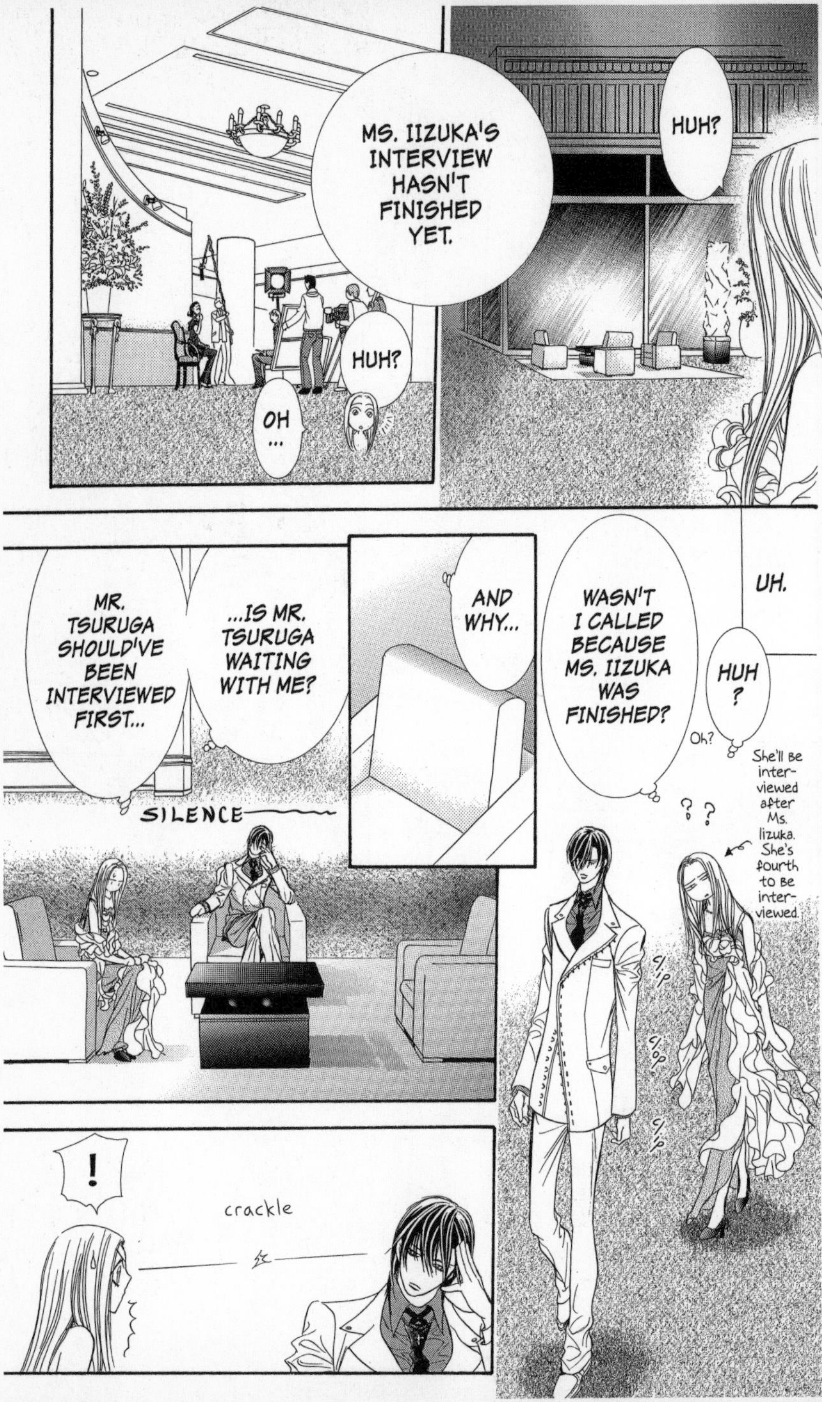
HUH?
MS. IIZUKA'S INTERVIEW HASN'T FINISHED YET.
HUH?
OH ...
UH.
HUH ?
Oh?
She'll be interviewed after Ms. Iizuka. She's fourth to be interviewed.
WASN'T I CALLED BECAUSE MS. IIZUKA WAS FINISHED?
? ?
clip
clop
clip
AND WHY...
...IS MR. TSURUGA WAITING WITH ME?
MR. TSURUGA SHOULD'VE BEEN INTERVIEWED FIRST...
SILENCE
!
crackle

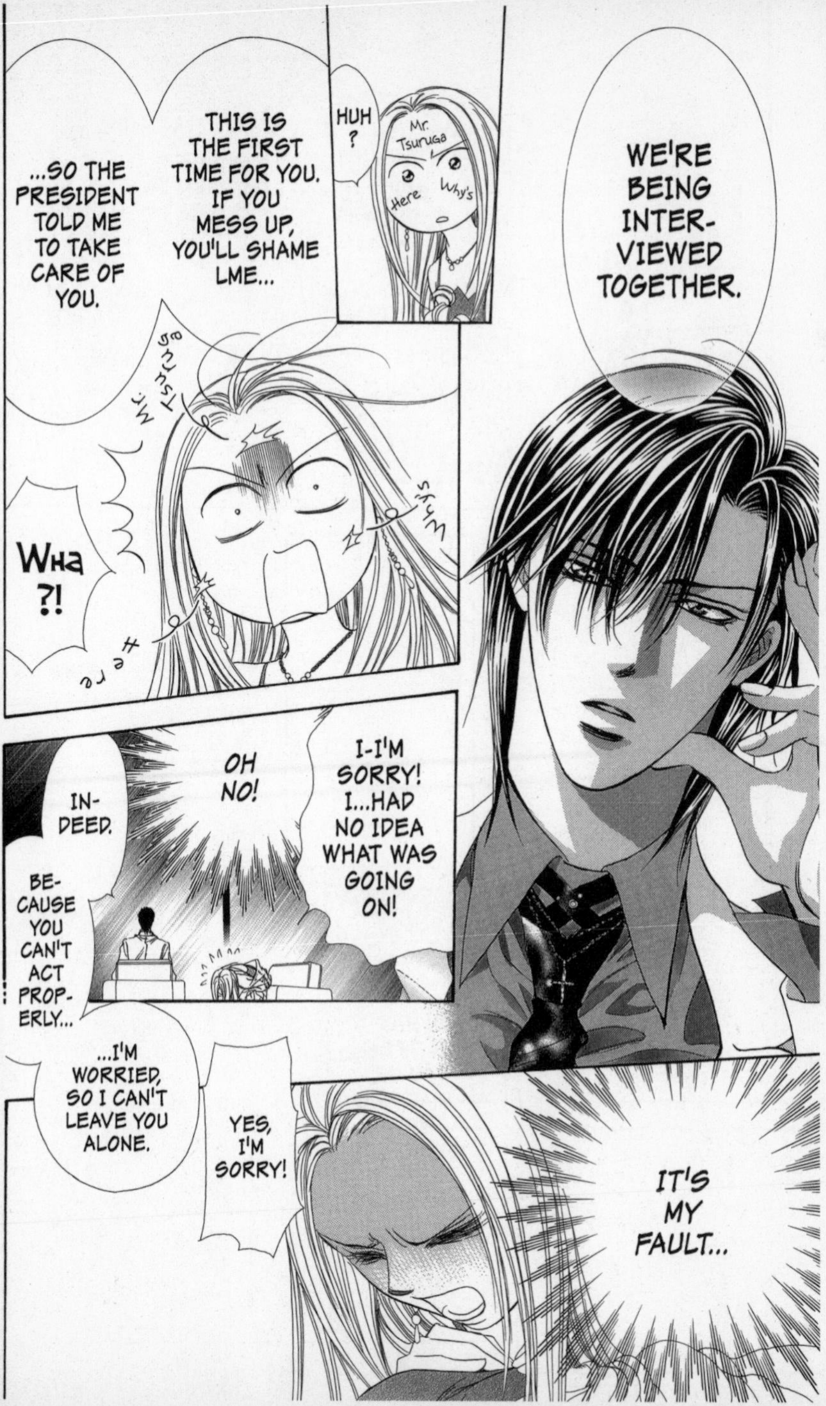
WE'RE BEING INTER-VIEWED TOGETHER.
HUH?
Mr. Tsuruga
Why's Here
THIS IS THE FIRST TIME FOR YOU. IF YOU MESS UP, YOU'LL SHAME LME...
...SO THE PRESIDENT TOLD ME TO TAKE CARE OF YOU.
Mr. Tsuruga
Why's
Here
WHA?!
OH NO!
I-I'M SORRY! I...HAD NO IDEA WHAT WAS GOING ON!
IN-DEED.
BE-CAUSE YOU CAN'T ACT PROP-ERLY...
...I'M WORRIED, SO I CAN'T LEAVE YOU ALONE.
YES, I'M SORRY!
IT'S MY FAULT...

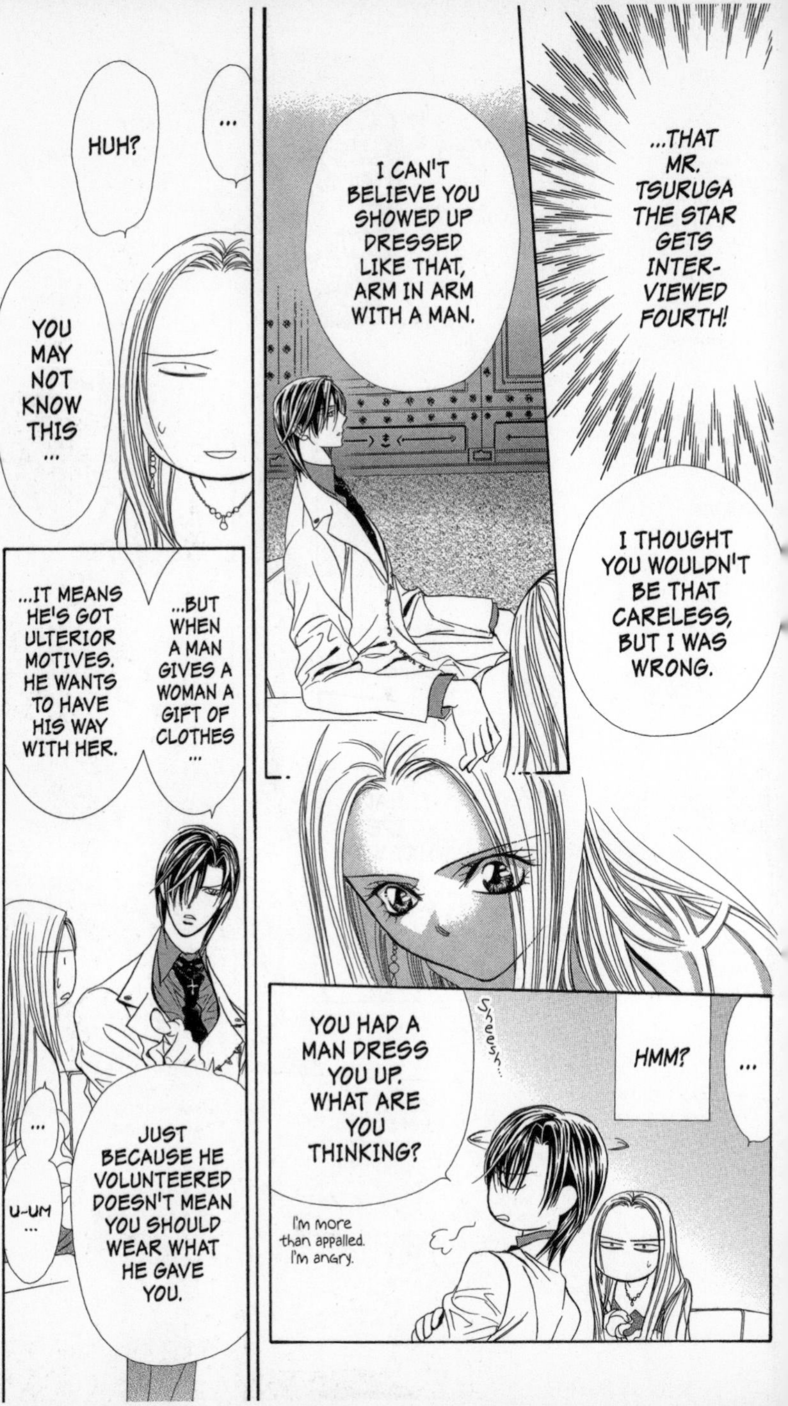
...THAT MR. TSURUGA THE STAR GETS INTER-VIEWED FOURTH!
I CAN'T BELIEVE YOU SHOWED UP DRESSED LIKE THAT, ARM IN ARM WITH A MAN.
I THOUGHT YOU WOULDN'T BE THAT CARELESS, BUT I WAS WRONG.
...
HMM?
YOU HAD A MAN DRESS YOU UP. WHAT ARE YOU THINKING?
Sheesh...
I'm more than appalled. I'm angry.
...
HUH?
YOU MAY NOT KNOW THIS ...
...BUT WHEN A MAN GIVES A WOMAN A GIFT OF CLOTHES ...
...IT MEANS HE'S GOT ULTERIOR MOTIVES. HE WANTS TO HAVE HIS WAY WITH HER.
JUST BECAUSE HE VOLUNTEERED DOESN'T MEAN YOU SHOULD WEAR WHAT HE GAVE YOU.
...
U-UM ...

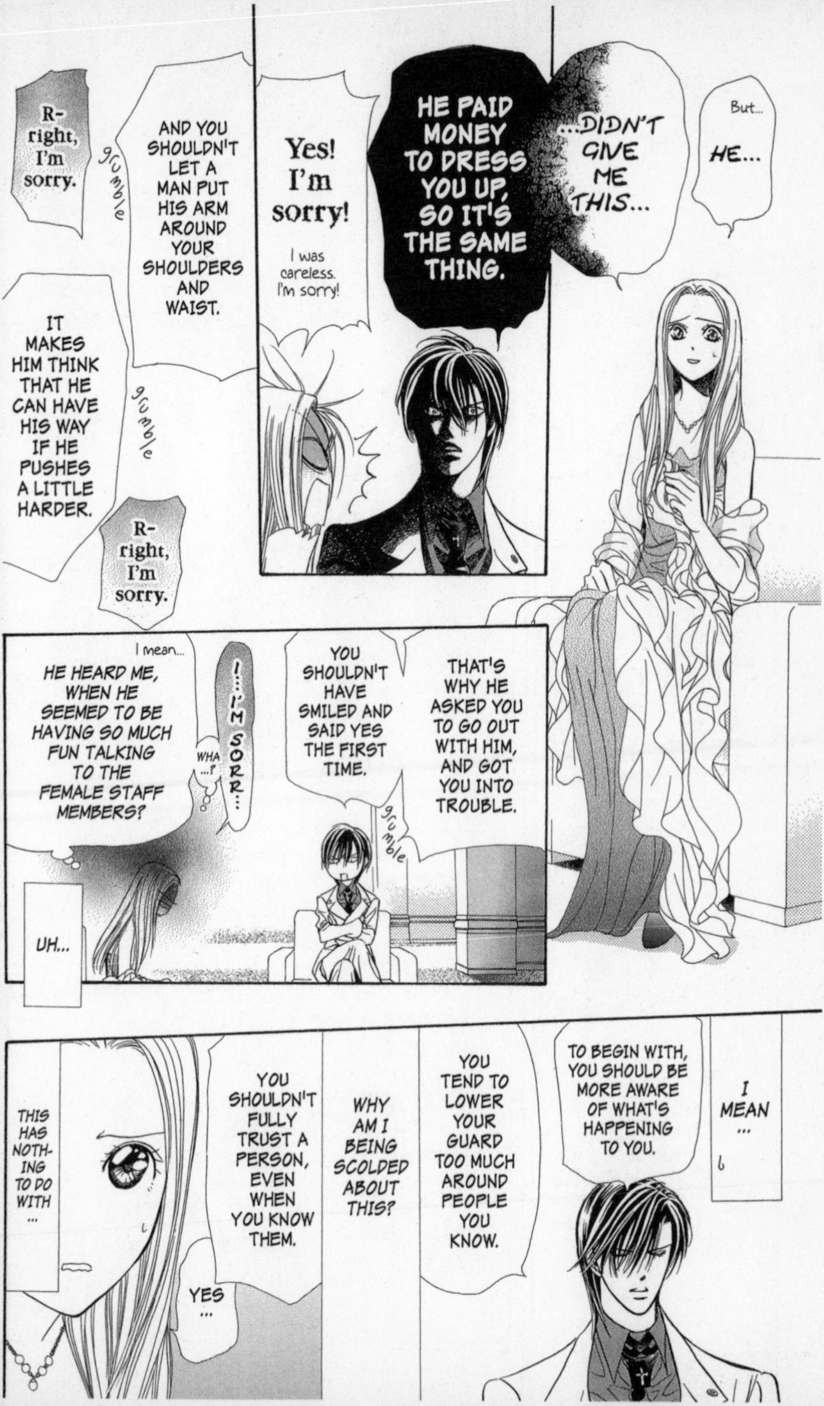
But...
HE...
...DIDN'T GIVE ME THIS...
HE PAID MONEY TO DRESS YOU UP, SO IT'S THE SAME THING.
Yes! I'm sorry!
I was careless. I'm sorry!
AND YOU SHOULDN'T LET A MAN PUT HIS ARM AROUND YOUR SHOULDERS AND WAIST.
grumble
R-right, I'm sorry.
IT MAKES HIM THINK THAT HE CAN HAVE HIS WAY IF HE PUSHES A LITTLE HARDER.
grumble
R-right, I'm sorry.
THAT'S WHY HE ASKED YOU TO GO OUT WITH HIM, AND GOT YOU INTO TROUBLE.
YOU SHOULDN'T HAVE SMILED AND SAID YES THE FIRST TIME.
grumble
I... I'M SORR...
WHA...?
I mean...
HE HEARD ME, WHEN HE SEEMED TO BE HAVING SO MUCH FUN TALKING TO THE FEMALE STAFF MEMBERS?
UH...
I MEAN...
TO BEGIN WITH, YOU SHOULD BE MORE AWARE OF WHAT'S HAPPENING TO YOU.
YOU TEND TO LOWER YOUR GUARD TOO MUCH AROUND PEOPLE YOU KNOW.
WHY AM I BEING SCOLDED ABOUT THIS?
YOU SHOULDN'T FULLY TRUST A PERSON, EVEN WHEN YOU KNOW THEM.
YES...
THIS HAS NOTHING TO DO WITH...

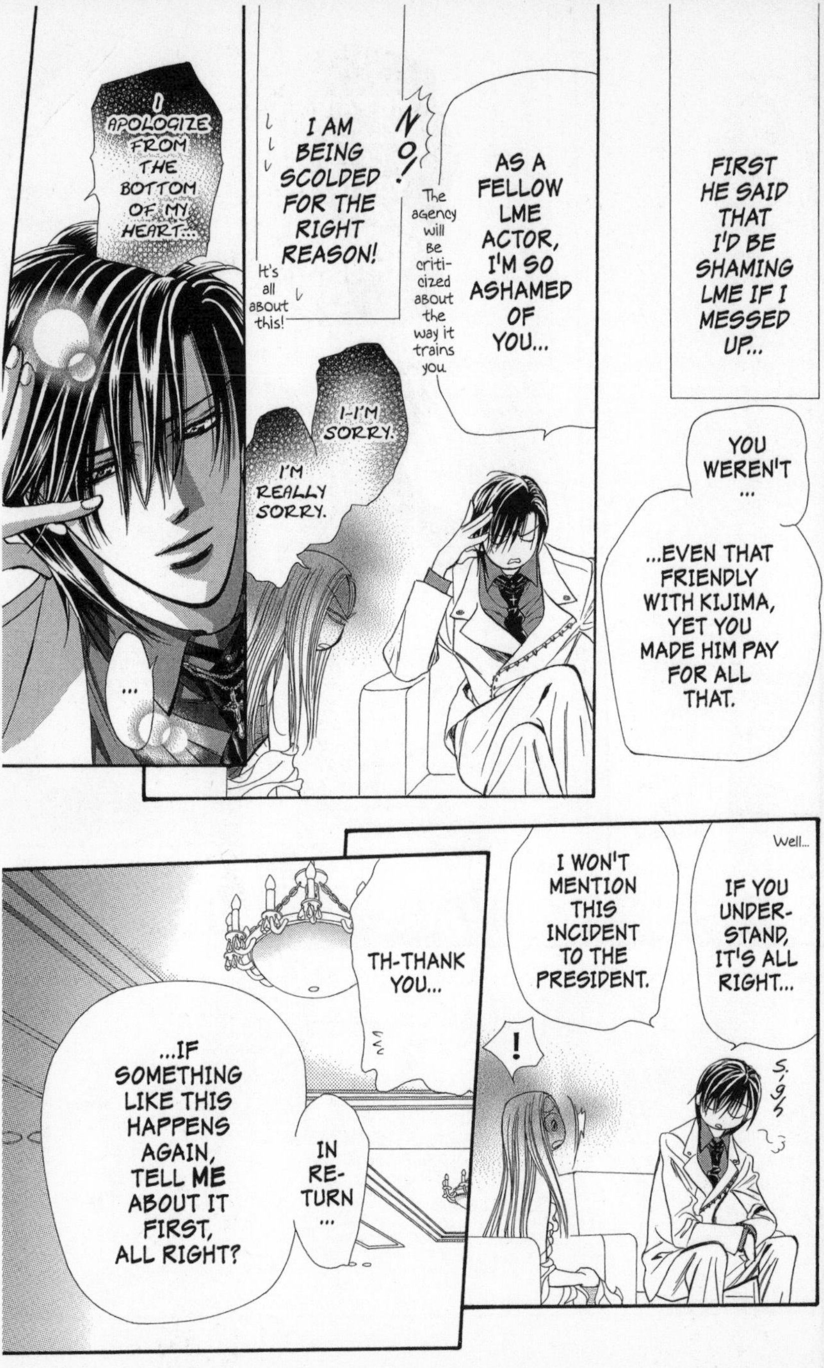
FIRST HE SAID THAT I'D BE SHAMING LME IF I MESSED UP...
YOU WEREN'T ...
...EVEN THAT FRIENDLY WITH KIJIMA, YET YOU MADE HIM PAY FOR ALL THAT.
AS A FELLOW LME ACTOR, I'M SO ASHAMED OF YOU...
The agency will be criti-cized about the way it trains you.
NO!
I AM BEING SCOLDED FOR THE RIGHT REASON!
It's all about this!
I-I'M SORRY.
I'M REALLY SORRY.
I APOLOGIZE FROM THE BOTTOM OF MY HEART...
...
Well...
IF YOU UNDER-STAND, IT'S ALL RIGHT...
I WON'T MENTION THIS INCIDENT TO THE PRESIDENT.
!
TH-THANK YOU...
IN RE-TURN ...
...IF SOMETHING LIKE THIS HAPPENS AGAIN, TELL ME ABOUT IT FIRST, ALL RIGHT?

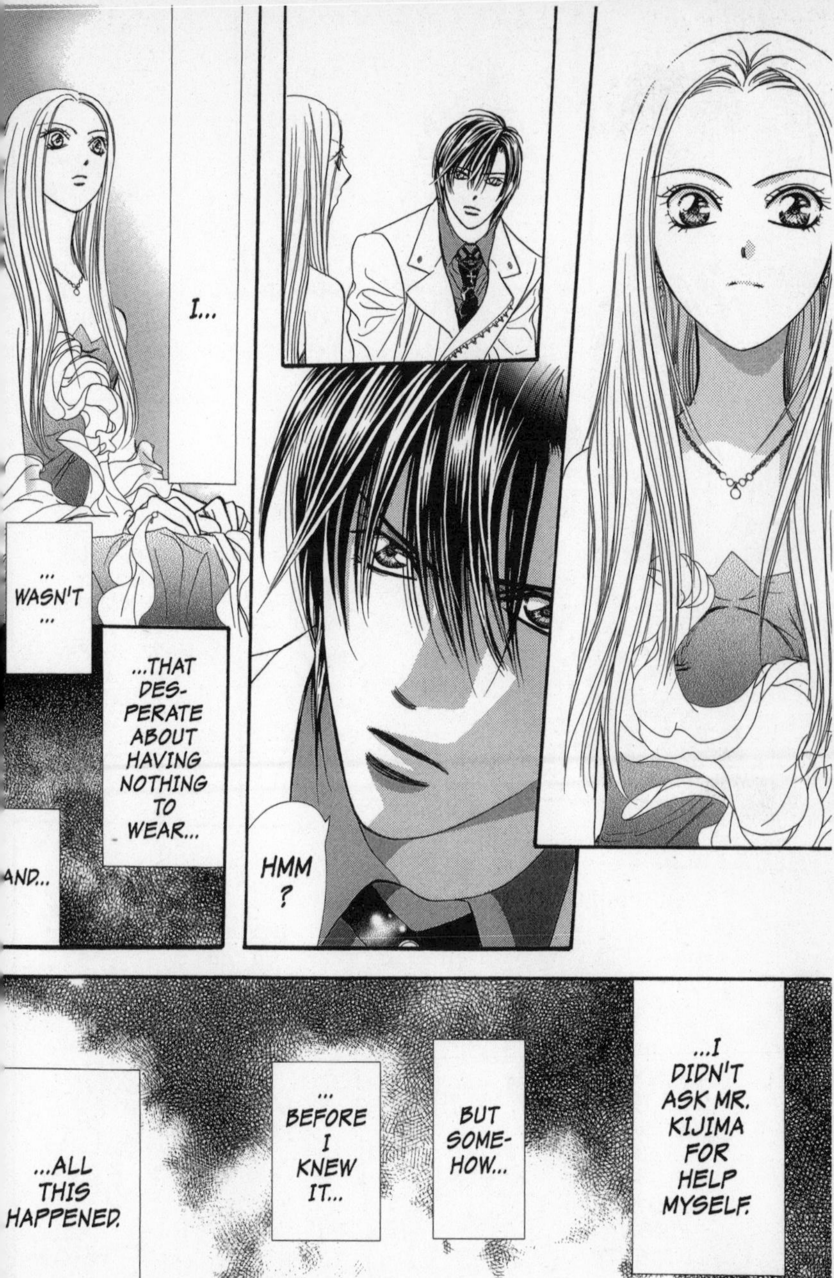
HMM ?
I...
... WASN'T ...
...THAT DES-PERATE ABOUT HAVING NOTHING TO WEAR...
AND...
...I DIDN'T ASK MR. KIJIMA FOR HELP MYSELF.
BUT SOME-HOW...
... BEFORE I KNEW IT...
...ALL THIS HAPPENED.

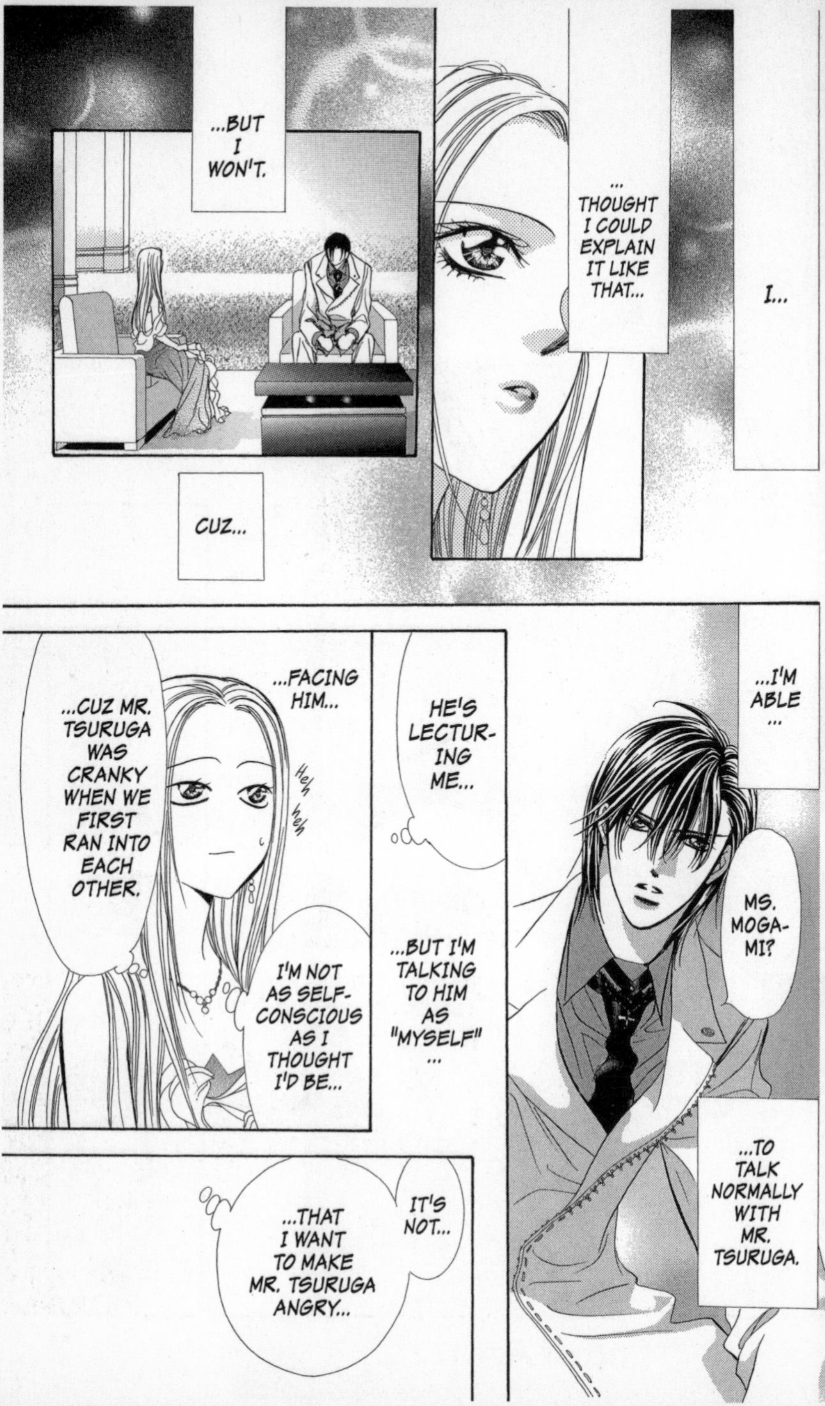
I...
...THOUGHT I COULD EXPLAIN IT LIKE THAT...
...BUT I WON'T.
CUZ...
...I'M ABLE...
MS. MOGAMI?
...TO TALK NORMALLY WITH MR. TSURUGA.
HE'S LECTURING ME...
...BUT I'M TALKING TO HIM AS "MYSELF"...
...FACING HIM...
...CUZ MR. TSURUGA WAS CRANKY WHEN WE FIRST RAN INTO EACH OTHER.
I'M NOT AS SELF-CONSCIOUS AS I THOUGHT I'D BE...
Heh heh
IT'S NOT...
...THAT I WANT TO MAKE MR. TSURUGA ANGRY...

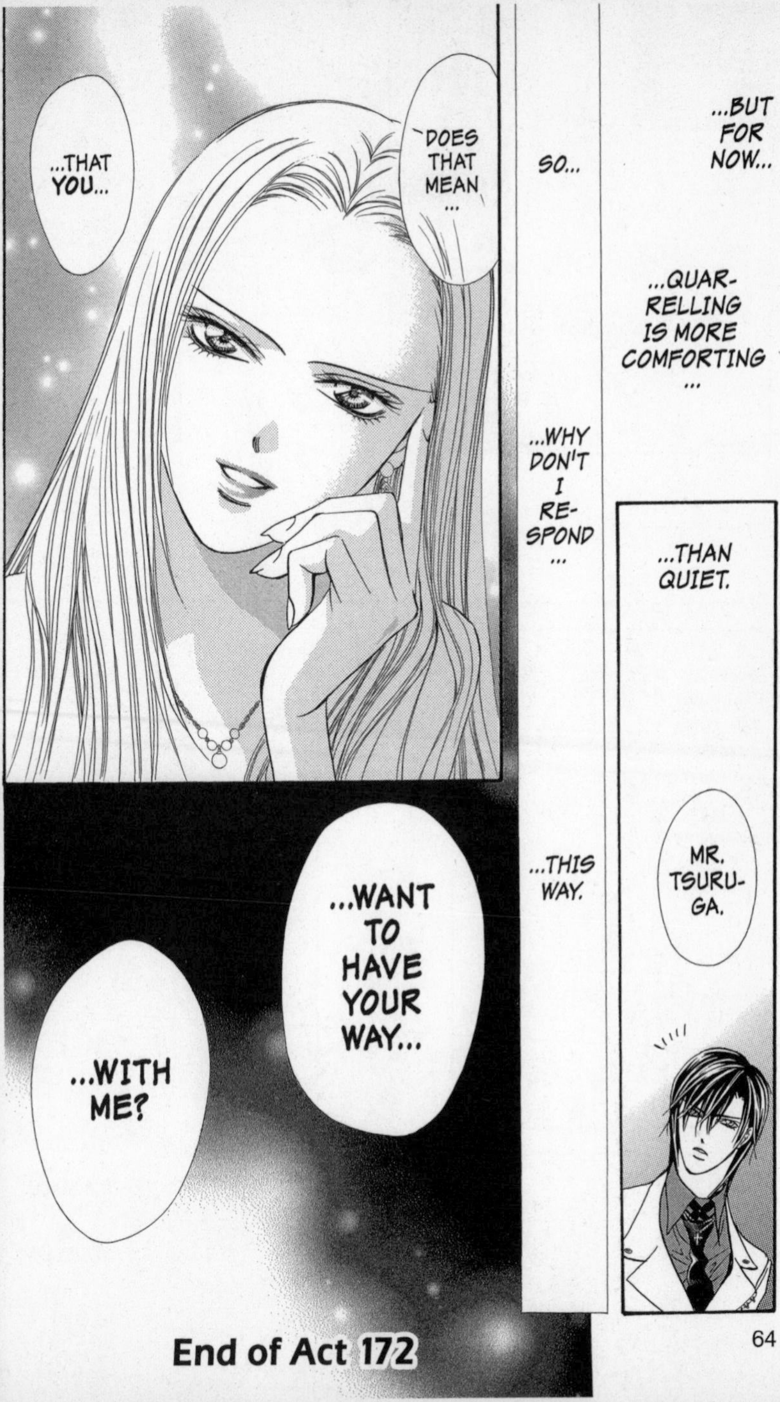
...BUT FOR NOW...
...QUARRELLING IS MORE COMFORTING...
...THAN QUIET.
MR. TSURUGA.
SO...
...WHY DON'T I RESPOND...
...THIS WAY.
DOES THAT MEAN...
...THAT YOU...
...WANT TO HAVE YOUR WAY...
...WITH ME?

End of Act 172

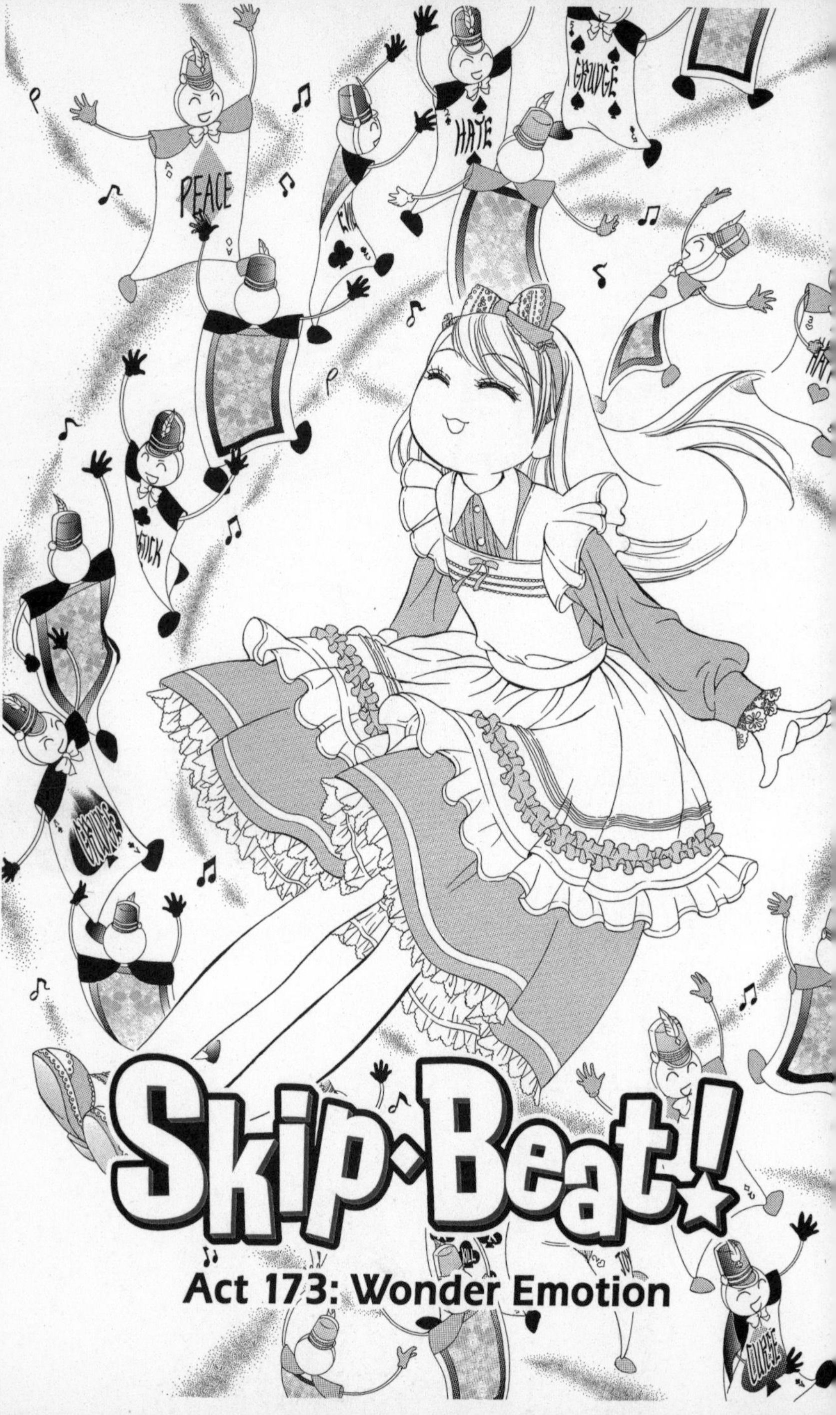
PEACE
HATE
GRUDGE
JOY
Skip·Beat!
Act 173: Wonder Emotion

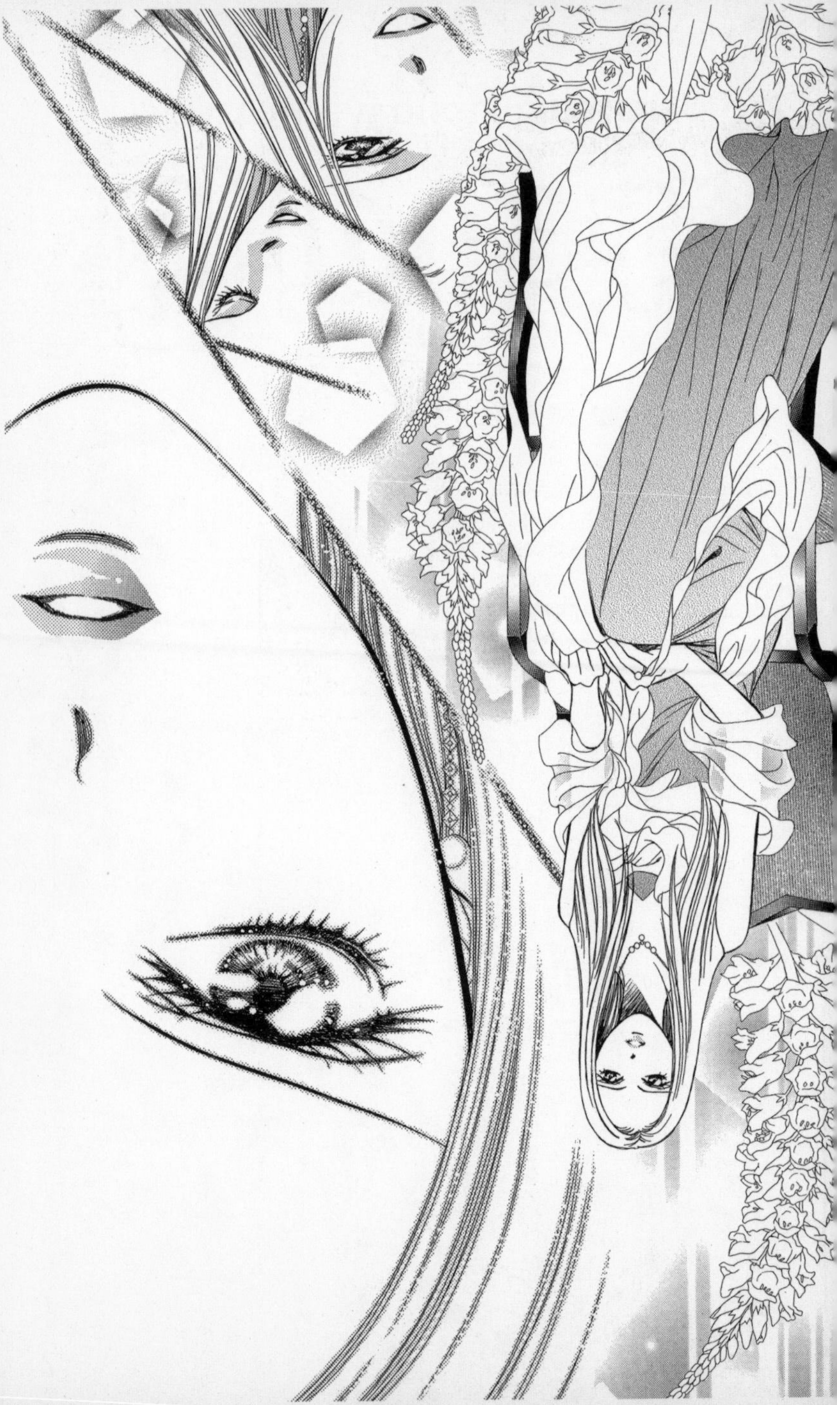

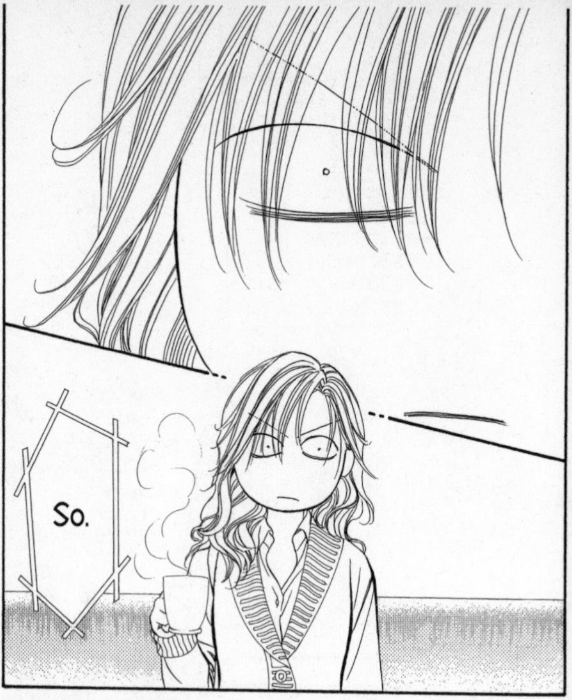
So.

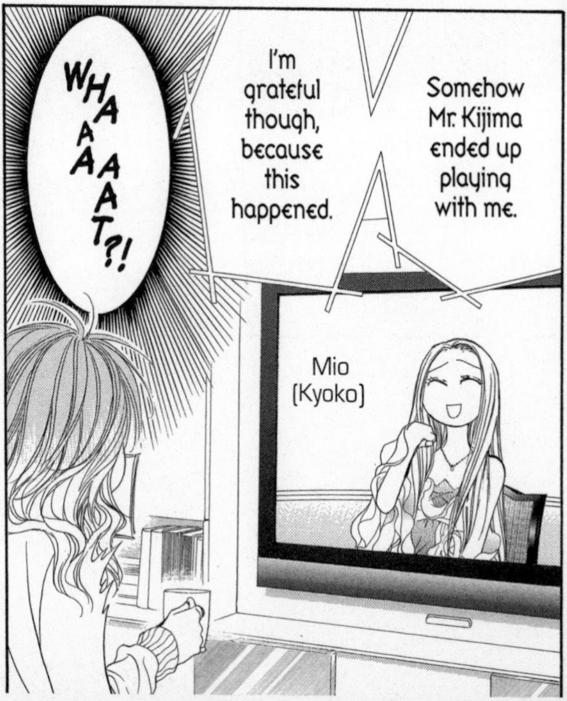
Somehow Mr. Kijima ended up playing with me.
I'm grateful though, because this happened.
WHAAAAAT?!
Mio (Kyoko)

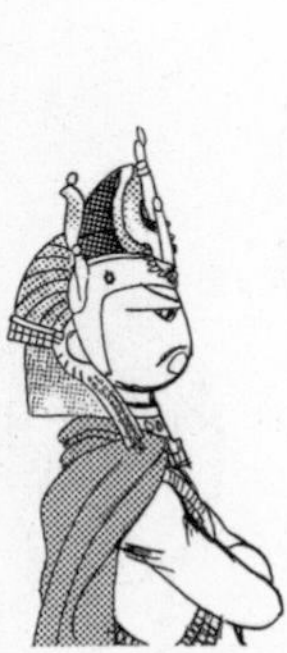

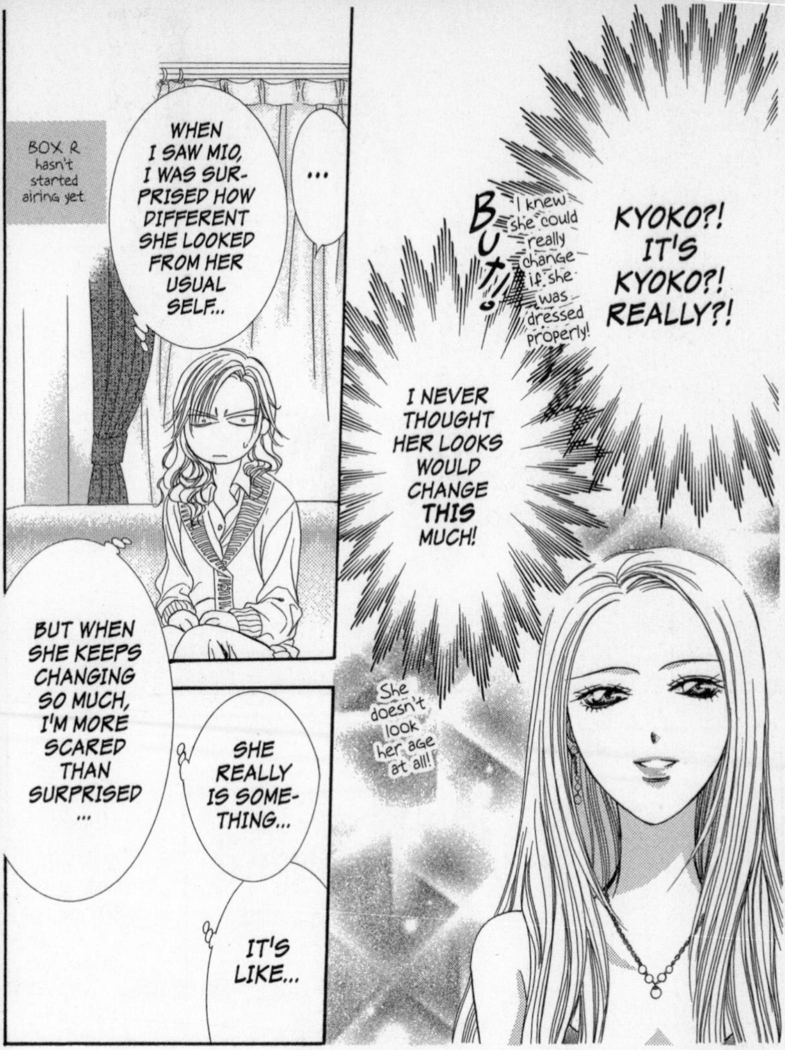
KYOKO?! IT'S KYOKO?! REALLY?!
BUT!
I knew she could really change if she was dressed properly!
I NEVER THOUGHT HER LOOKS WOULD CHANGE THIS MUCH!
She doesn't look her age at all!
BOX R hasn't started airing yet
...
WHEN I SAW MIO, I WAS SUR-PRISED HOW DIFFERENT SHE LOOKED FROM HER USUAL SELF...
BUT WHEN SHE KEEPS CHANGING SO MUCH, I'M MORE SCARED THAN SURPRISED ...
SHE REALLY IS SOME-THING...
IT'S LIKE...
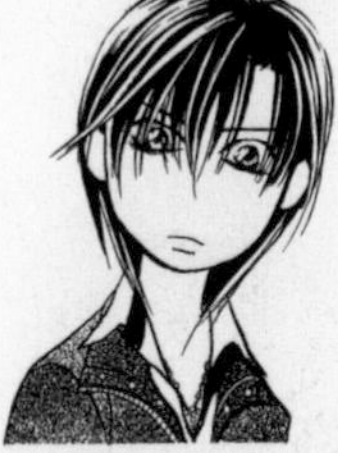

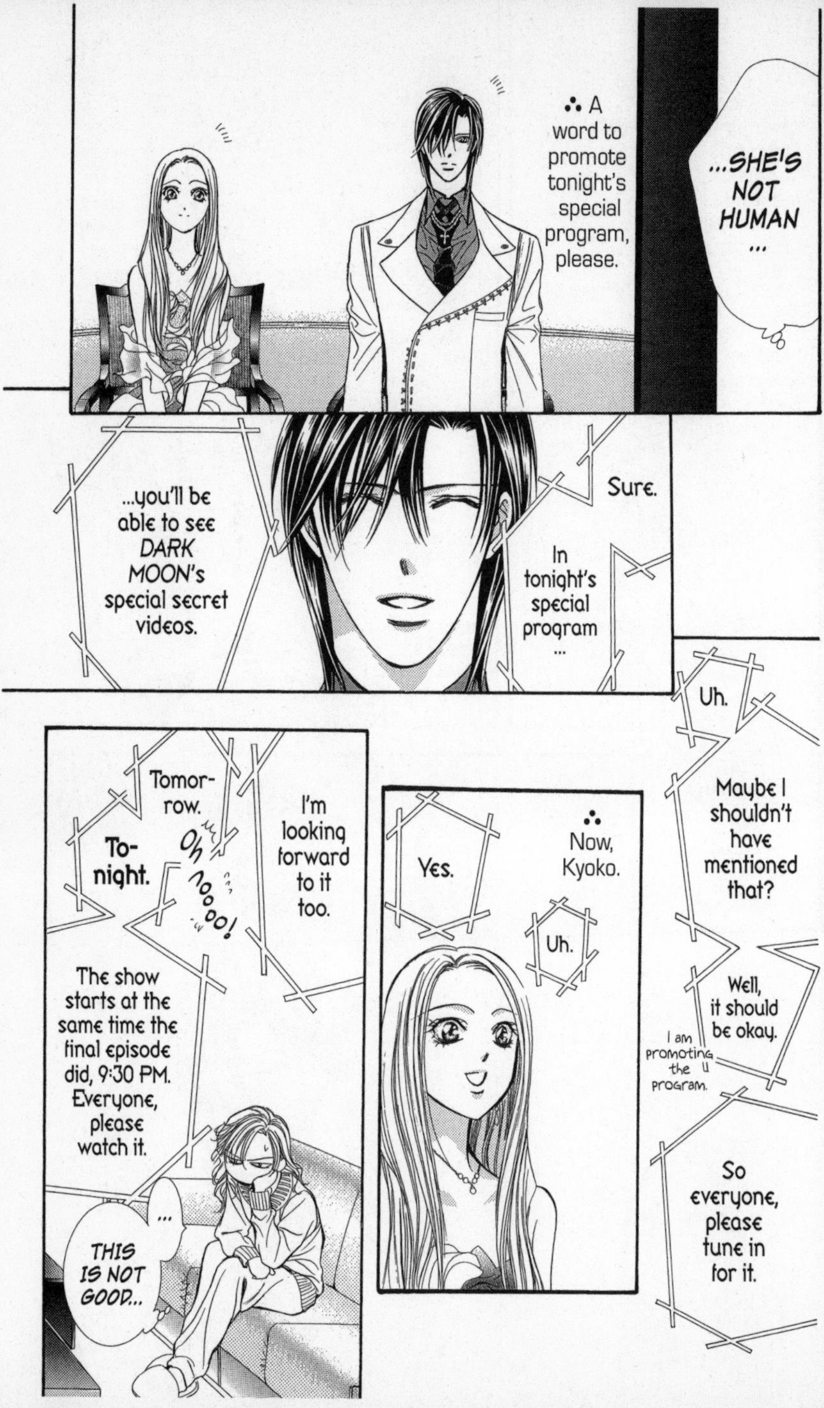
...SHE'S NOT HUMAN ...
∴ A word to promote tonight's special program, please.
Sure.
In tonight's special program ...
...you'll be able to see DARK MOON's special secret videos.
Uh.
Maybe I shouldn't have mentioned that?
Well, it should be okay.
I am promoting the program.
So everyone, please tune in for it.
∴ Now, Kyoko.
Uh.
Yes.
I'm looking forward to it too.
Tomor-row.
To-night.
Oh nooooo!
The show starts at the same time the final episode did, 9:30 PM. Everyone, please watch it.
...
THIS IS NOT GOOD...

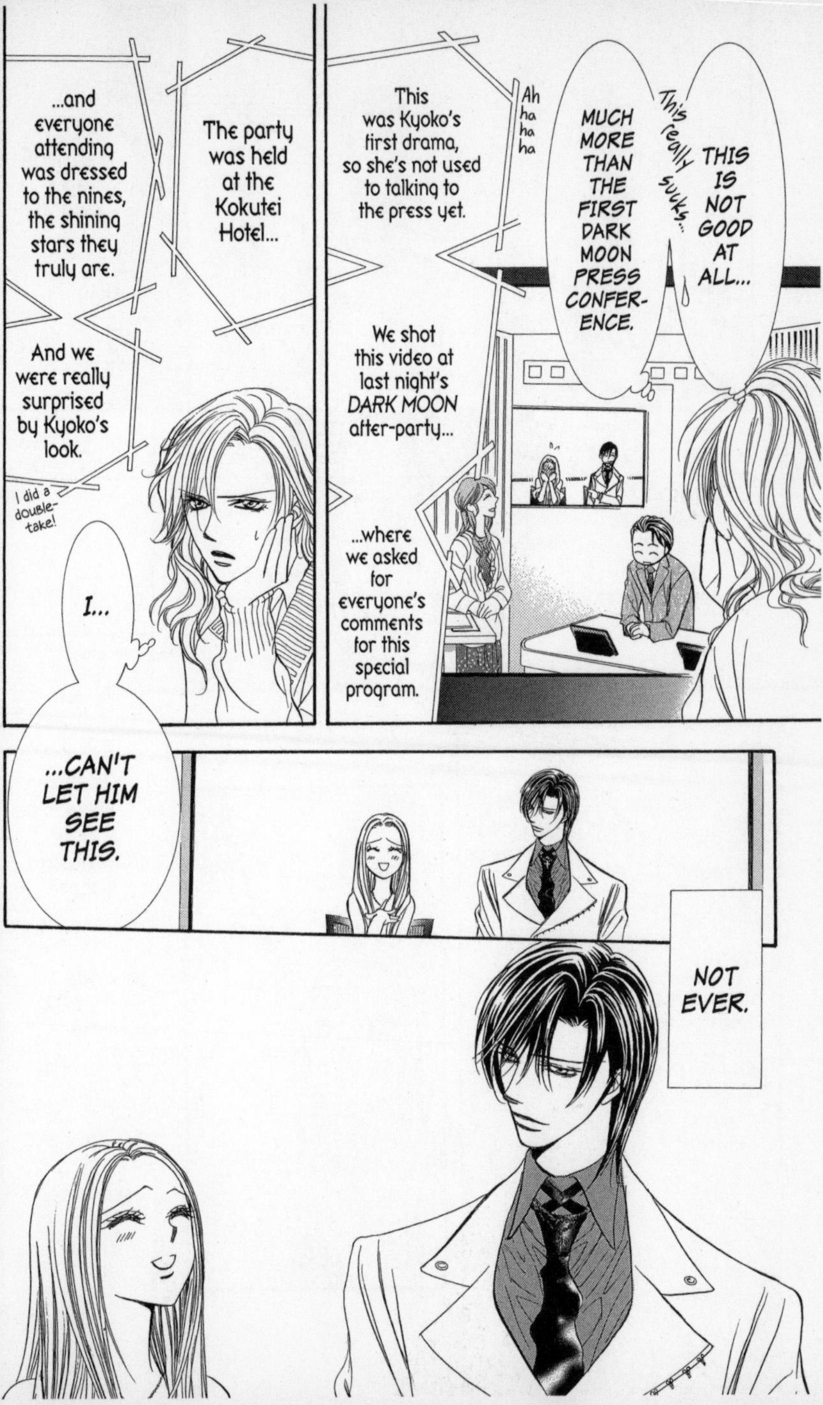
THIS IS NOT GOOD AT ALL...
This really sucks...
MUCH MORE THAN THE FIRST DARK MOON PRESS CONFERENCE.
Ah ha ha ha
This was Kyoko's first drama, so she's not used to talking to the press yet.
We shot this video at last night's DARK MOON after-party...
...where we asked for everyone's comments for this special program.
The party was held at the Kokutei Hotel...
...and everyone attending was dressed to the nines, the shining stars they truly are.
And we were really surprised by Kyoko's look.
I did a double-take!
I...
...CAN'T LET HIM SEE THIS.
NOT EVER.

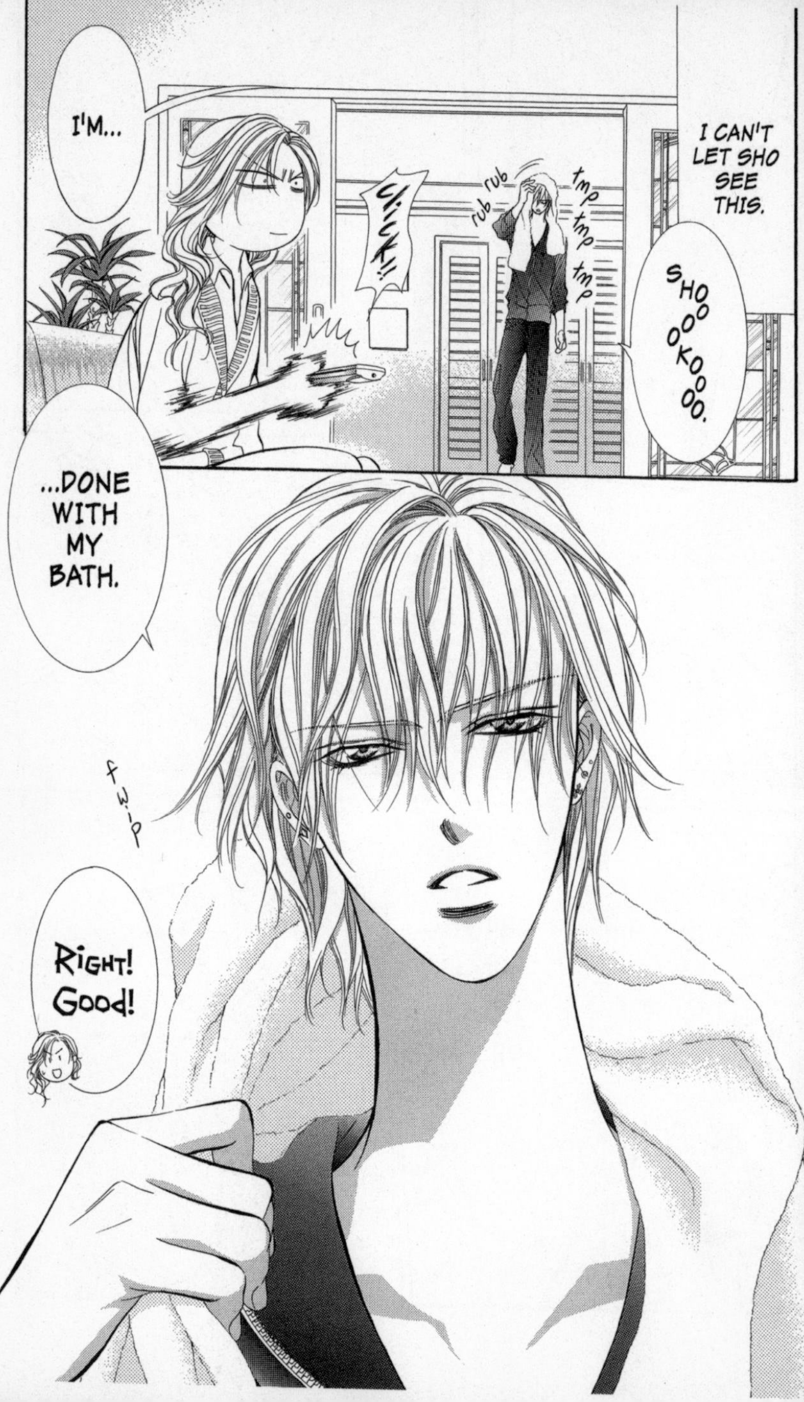
I CAN'T LET SHO SEE THIS.
SHOOOOOKOOOOO.
tmp tmp tmp
rub rub
CLICK!!
I'M...
...DONE WITH MY BATH.
fwip
RIGHT! GOOD!

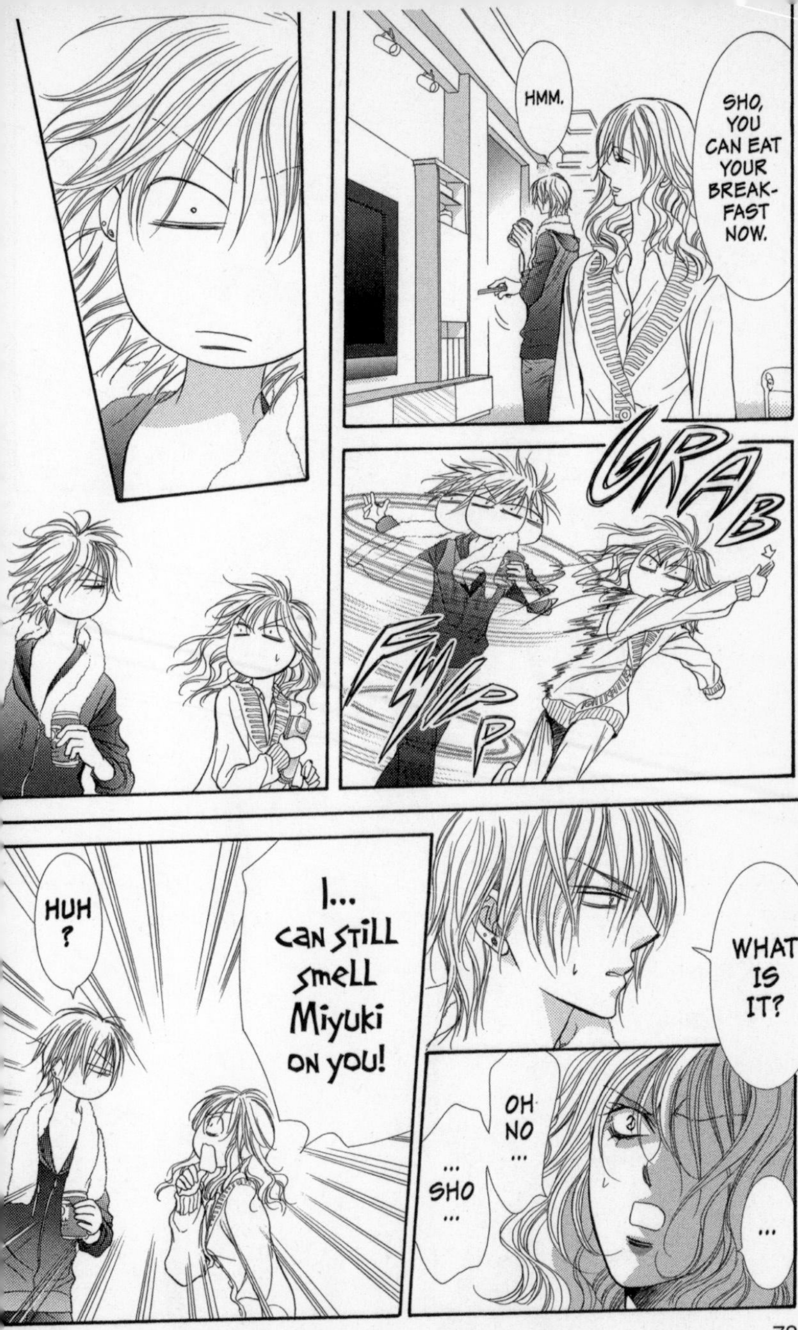
SHO, YOU CAN EAT YOUR BREAK-FAST NOW.
HMM.
GRAB
FWIP
WHAT IS IT?
OH NO ...
... SHO ...
...
I... can still smell Miyuki on you!
HUH ?

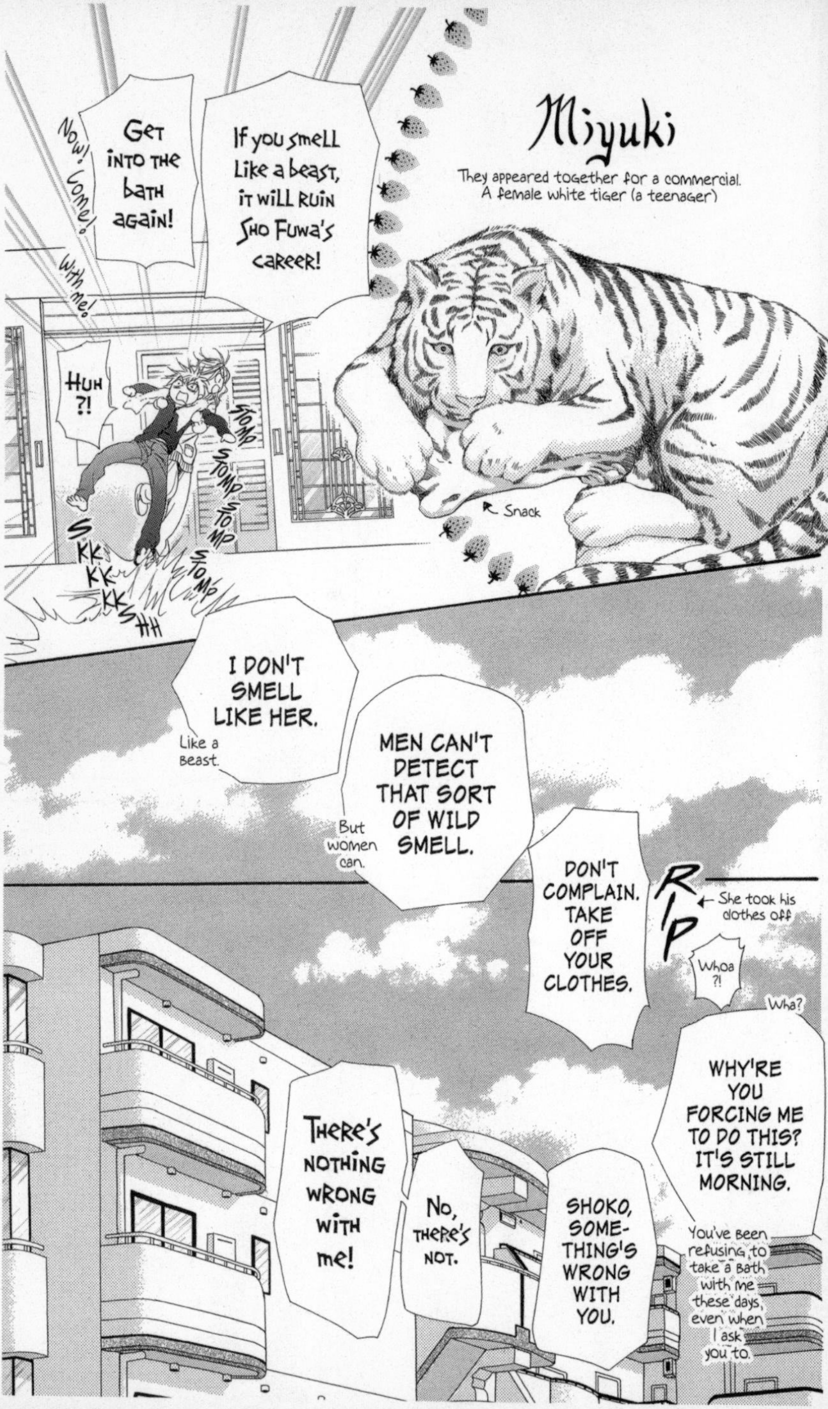
Miyuki
They appeared together for a commercial.
A female white tiger (a teenager)
Snack
If you smell like a beast, it will ruin Sho Fuwa's career!
Get into the bath again!
Now! Come!
With me!
Huh ?!
STOMP STOMP STOMP STOMP
SKKKKKKSHH
I DON'T SMELL LIKE HER.
Like a beast.
MEN CAN'T DETECT THAT SORT OF WILD SMELL.
But women can.
RIP
She took his clothes off
Whoa ?!
DON'T COMPLAIN. TAKE OFF YOUR CLOTHES.
Wha?
WHY'RE YOU FORCING ME TO DO THIS? IT'S STILL MORNING.
You've been refusing to take a bath with me these days, even when I ask you to.
SHOKO, SOME-THING'S WRONG WITH YOU.
No, there's not.
There's nothing wrong with me!

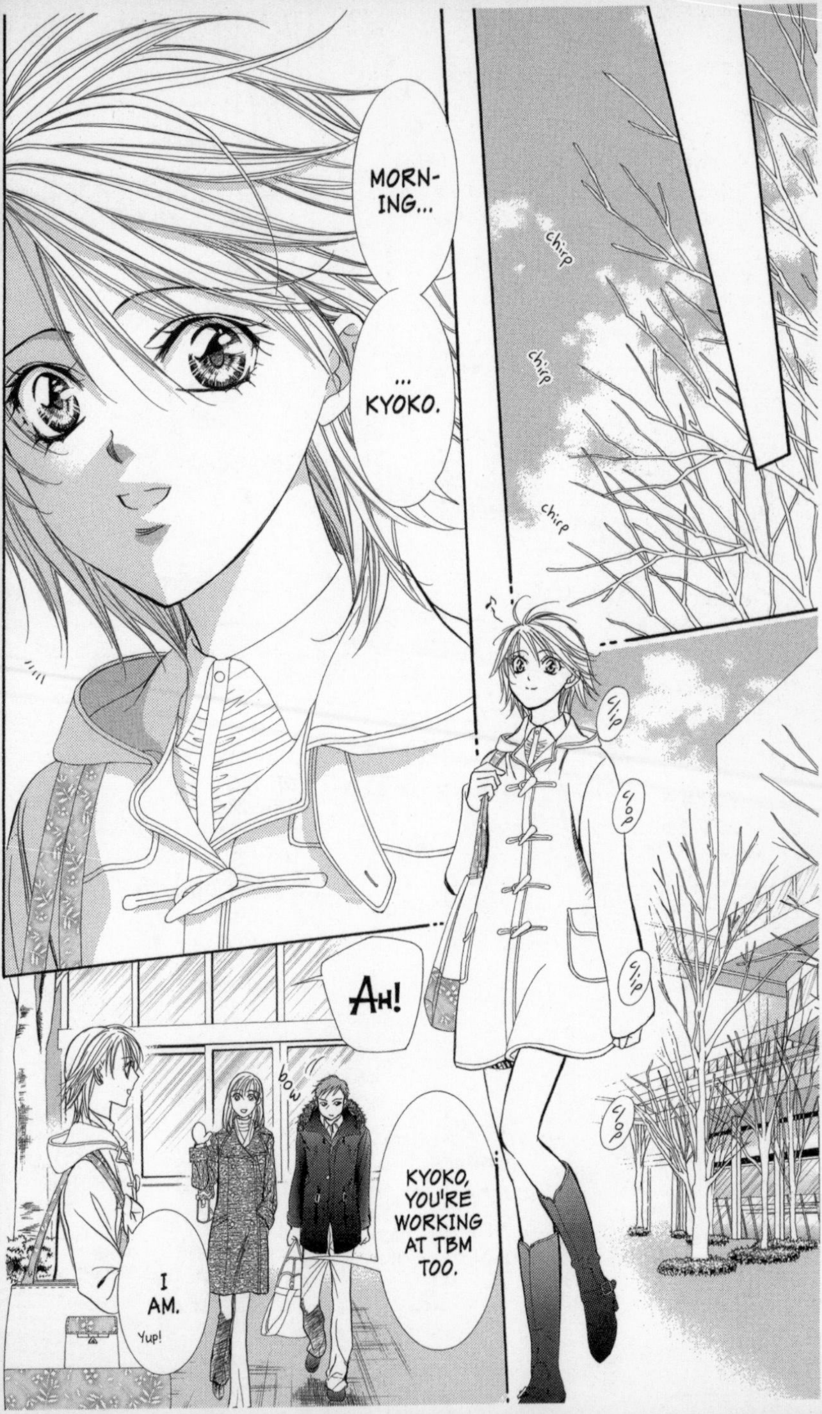
chirp
chirp
chirp
MORNING...
... KYOKO.
clip
clop
clip
clop
AH!
KYOKO, YOU'RE WORKING AT TBM TOO.
bow
I AM.
Yup!

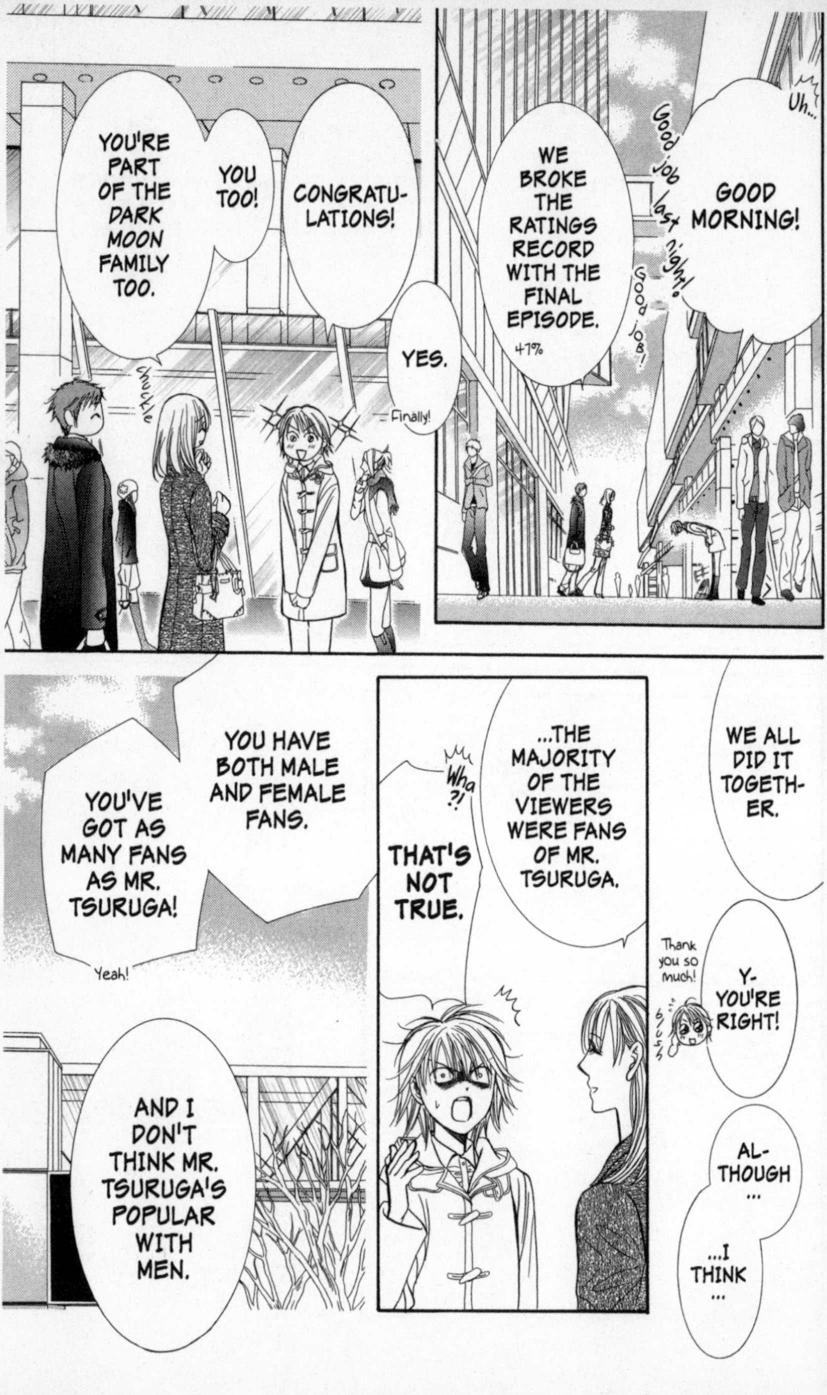
Uh...
GOOD MORNING!
Good job last night!
Good job!
WE BROKE THE RATINGS RECORD WITH THE FINAL EPISODE.
47%
YES.
Finally!
CONGRATULATIONS!
YOU TOO!
YOU'RE PART OF THE DARK MOON FAMILY TOO.
chuckle
WE ALL DID IT TOGETHER.
...THE MAJORITY OF THE VIEWERS WERE FANS OF MR. TSURUGA.
Y-YOU'RE RIGHT!
Thank you so much!
blush
ALTHOUGH...
...I THINK...
Wha?!
THAT'S NOT TRUE.
YOU HAVE BOTH MALE AND FEMALE FANS.
YOU'VE GOT AS MANY FANS AS MR. TSURUGA!
Yeah!
AND I DON'T THINK MR. TSURUGA'S POPULAR WITH MEN.

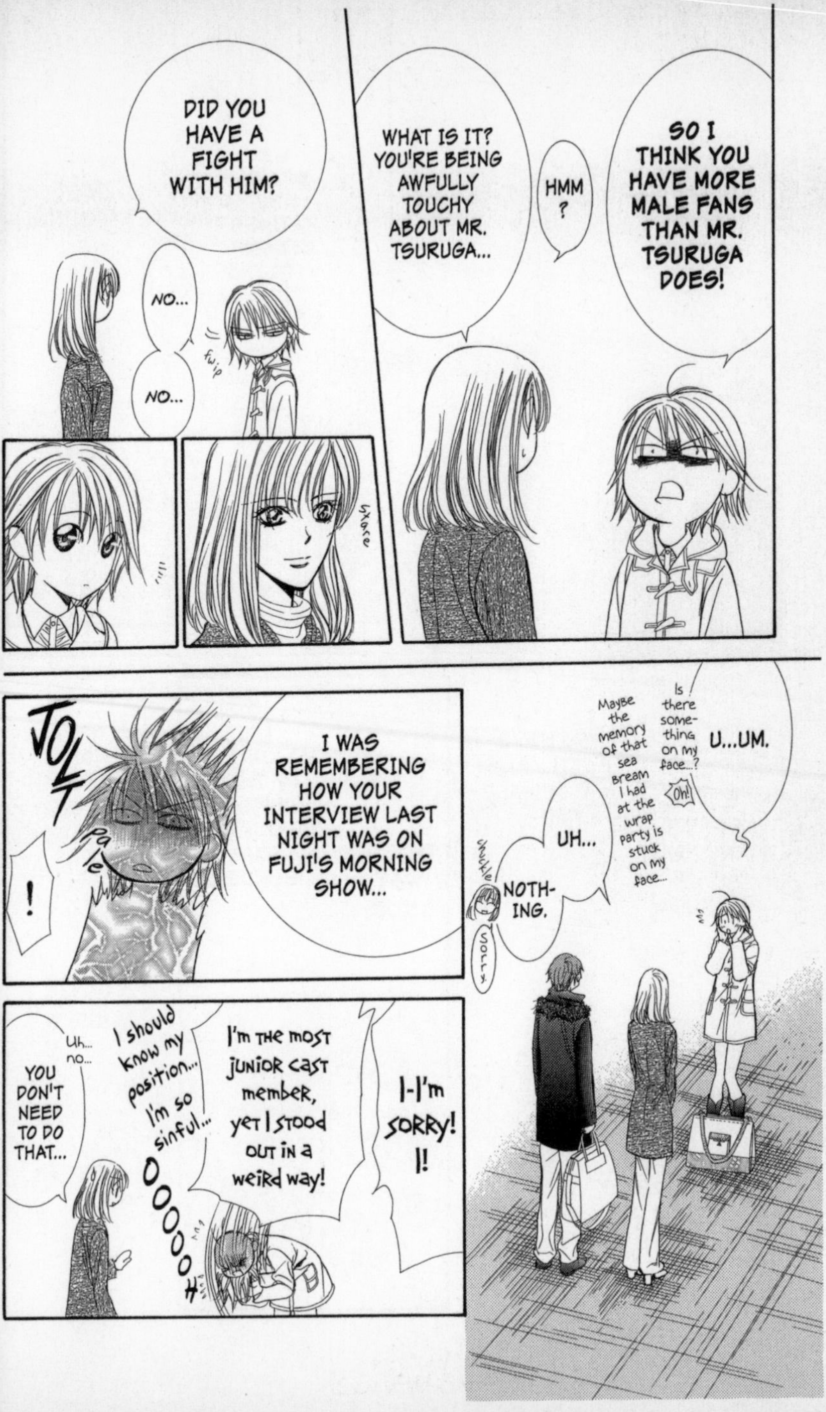
SO I THINK YOU HAVE MORE MALE FANS THAN MR. TSURUGA DOES!
HMM?
WHAT IS IT? YOU'RE BEING AWFULLY TOUCHY ABOUT MR. TSURUGA...
DID YOU HAVE A FIGHT WITH HIM?
NO...
NO...
fwip
stare
U...UM.
Is there something on my face...?
Oh!
Maybe the memory of that sea Bream I had at the wrap party is stuck on my face...
UH...
NOTHING.
shuckle
sorry.
JOLT
pale
I WAS REMEMBERING HOW YOUR INTERVIEW LAST NIGHT WAS ON FUJI'S MORNING SHOW...
!
I-I'm SORRY! !!
I'm THE MOST JUNIOR CAST member, yet I STOOD OUT IN a weird way!
I should know my position... I'm so sinful...
OOOOOH
Uh... no...
YOU DON'T NEED TO DO THAT...

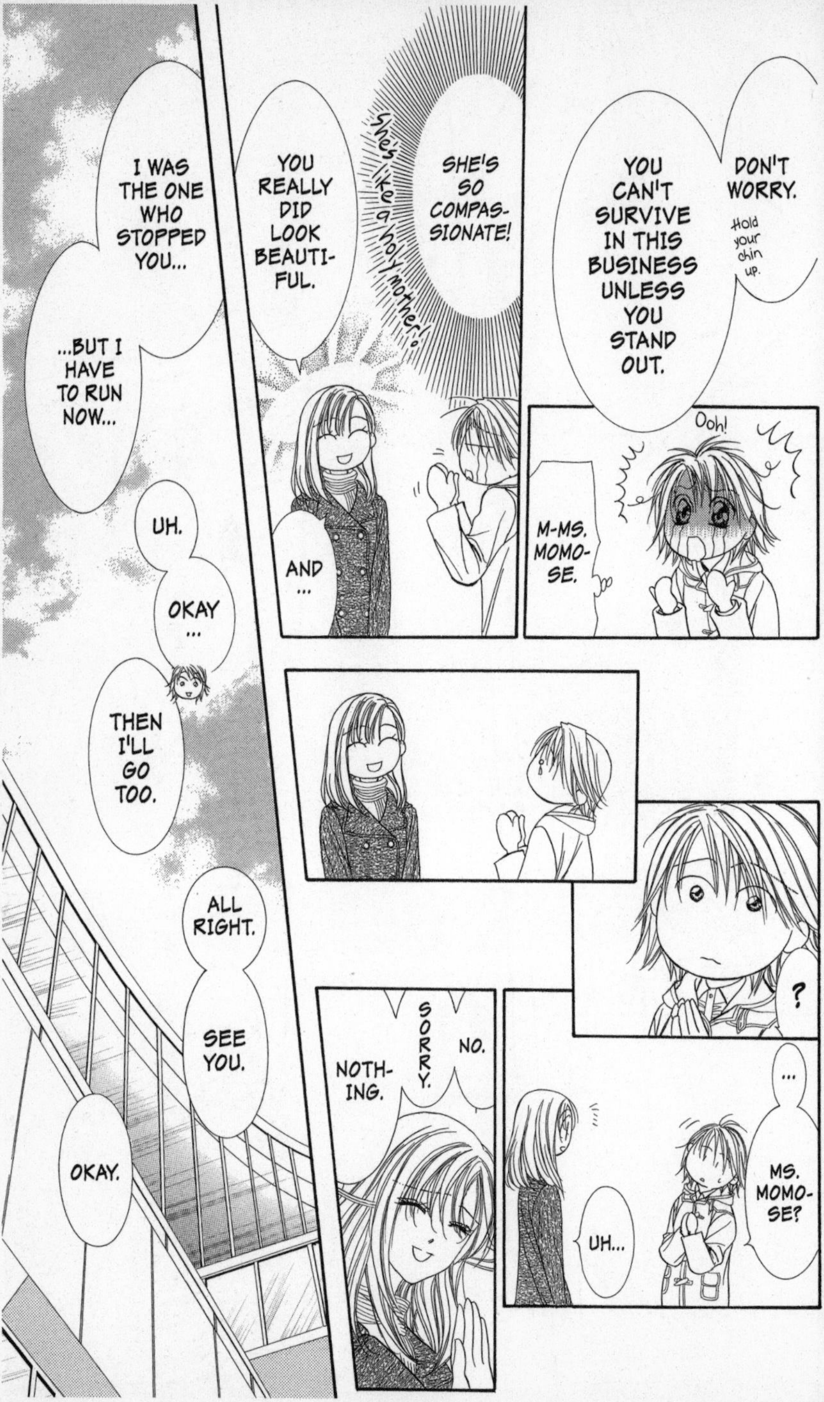
DON'T WORRY.
Hold your chin up.
YOU CAN'T SURVIVE IN THIS BUSINESS UNLESS YOU STAND OUT.
Ooh!
M-MS. MOMOSE.
SHE'S SO COMPASSIONATE!
She's like a holy mother!
YOU REALLY DID LOOK BEAUTIFUL.
AND ...
?
...
MS. MOMOSE?
UH...
NO.
SORRY.
NOTHING.
I WAS THE ONE WHO STOPPED YOU...
...BUT I HAVE TO RUN NOW...
UH.
OKAY ...
THEN I'LL GO TOO.
ALL RIGHT.
SEE YOU.
OKAY.

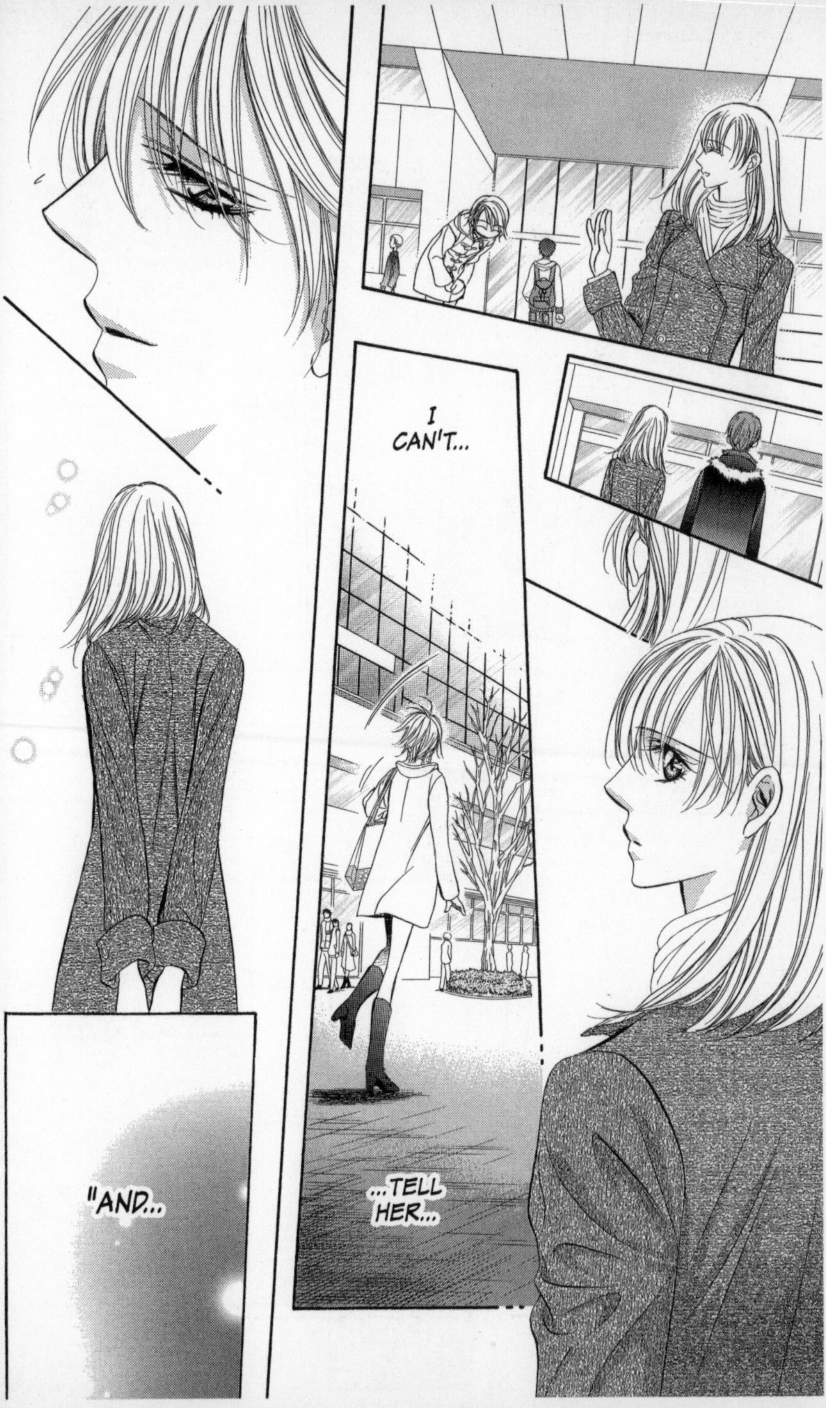
I CAN'T...
...TELL HER...
"AND...

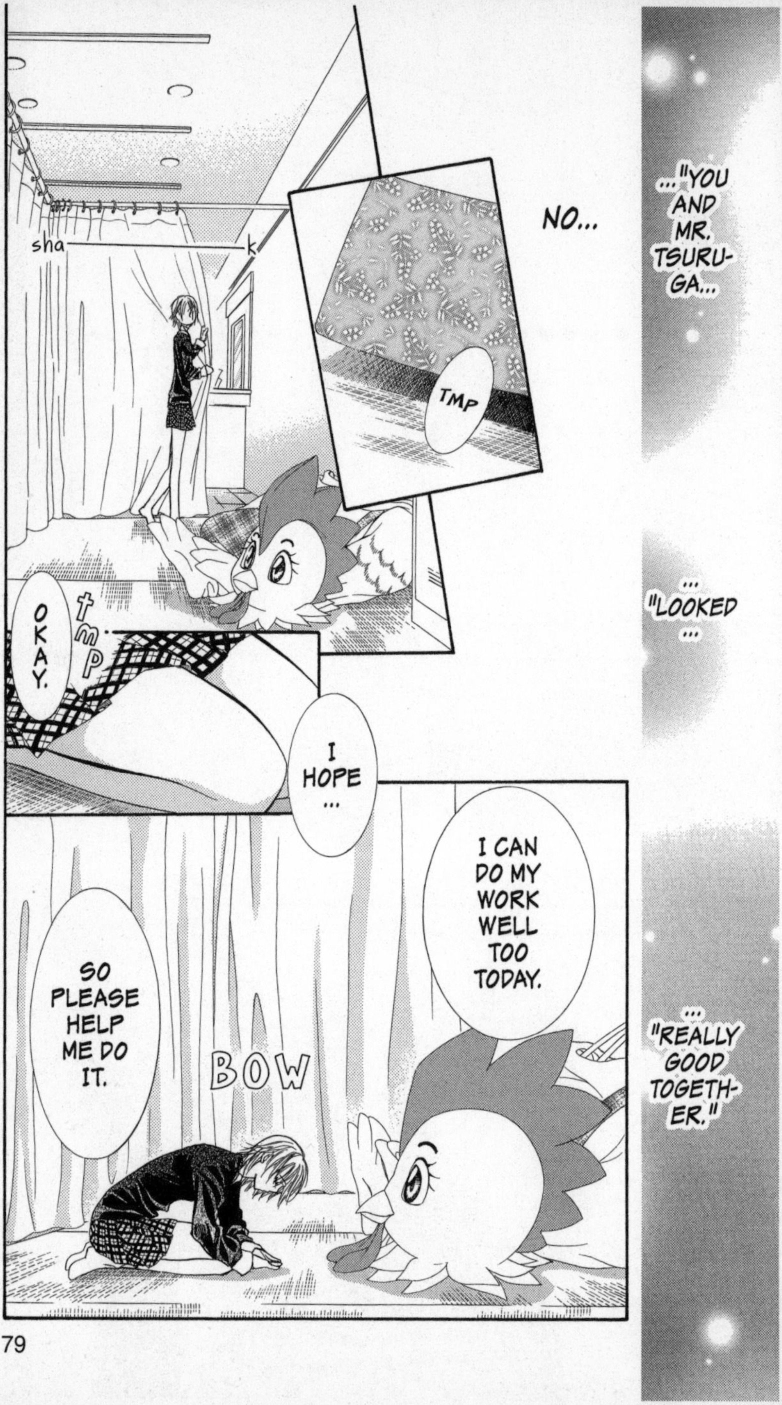
..."YOU AND MR. TSURUGA...
..."LOOKED...
..."REALLY GOOD TOGETHER."
NO...
TMP
sha—k
OKAY.
tmp
I HOPE...
I CAN DO MY WORK WELL TOO TODAY.
SO PLEASE HELP ME DO IT.
BOW

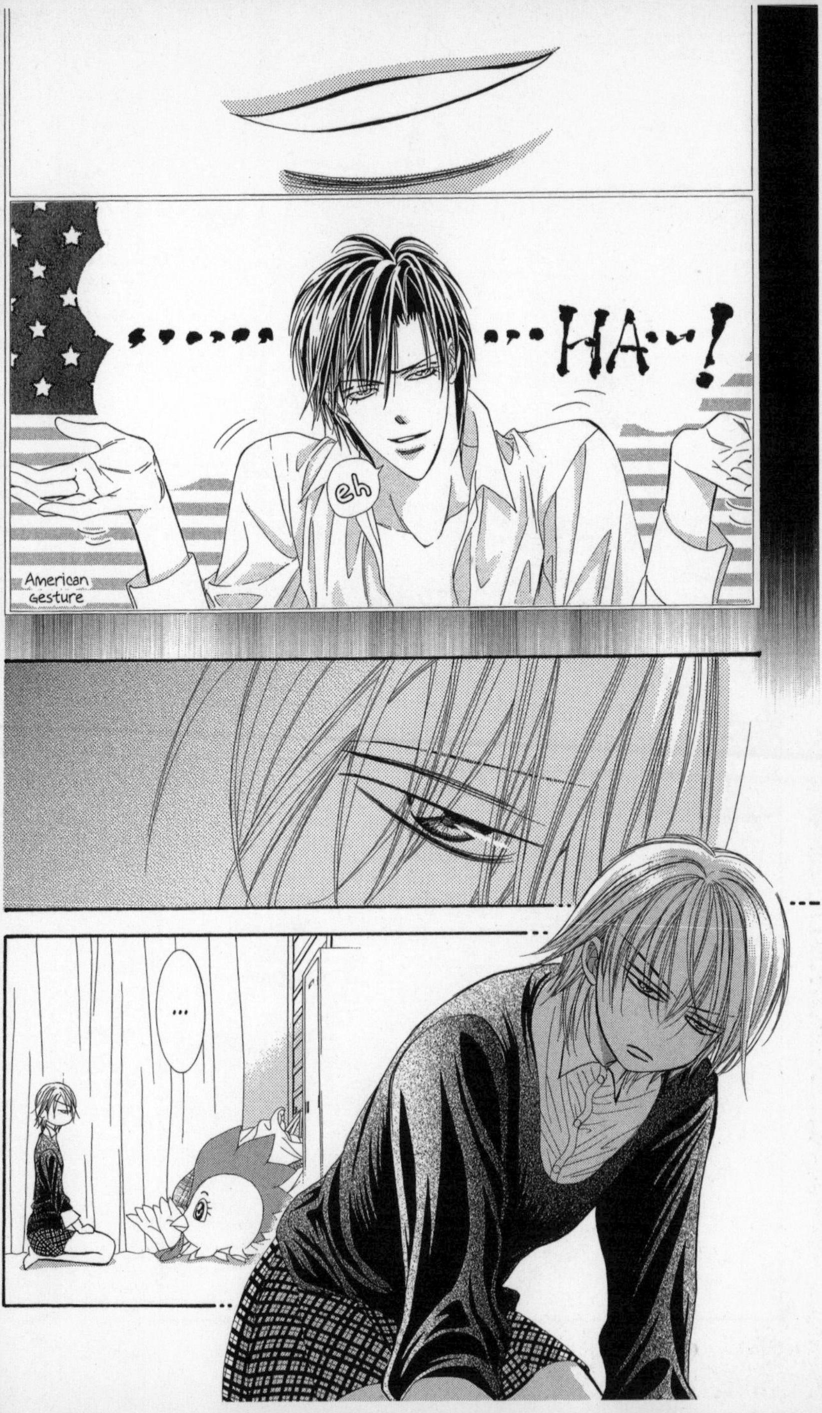

......HA~!
eh
American Gesture
...

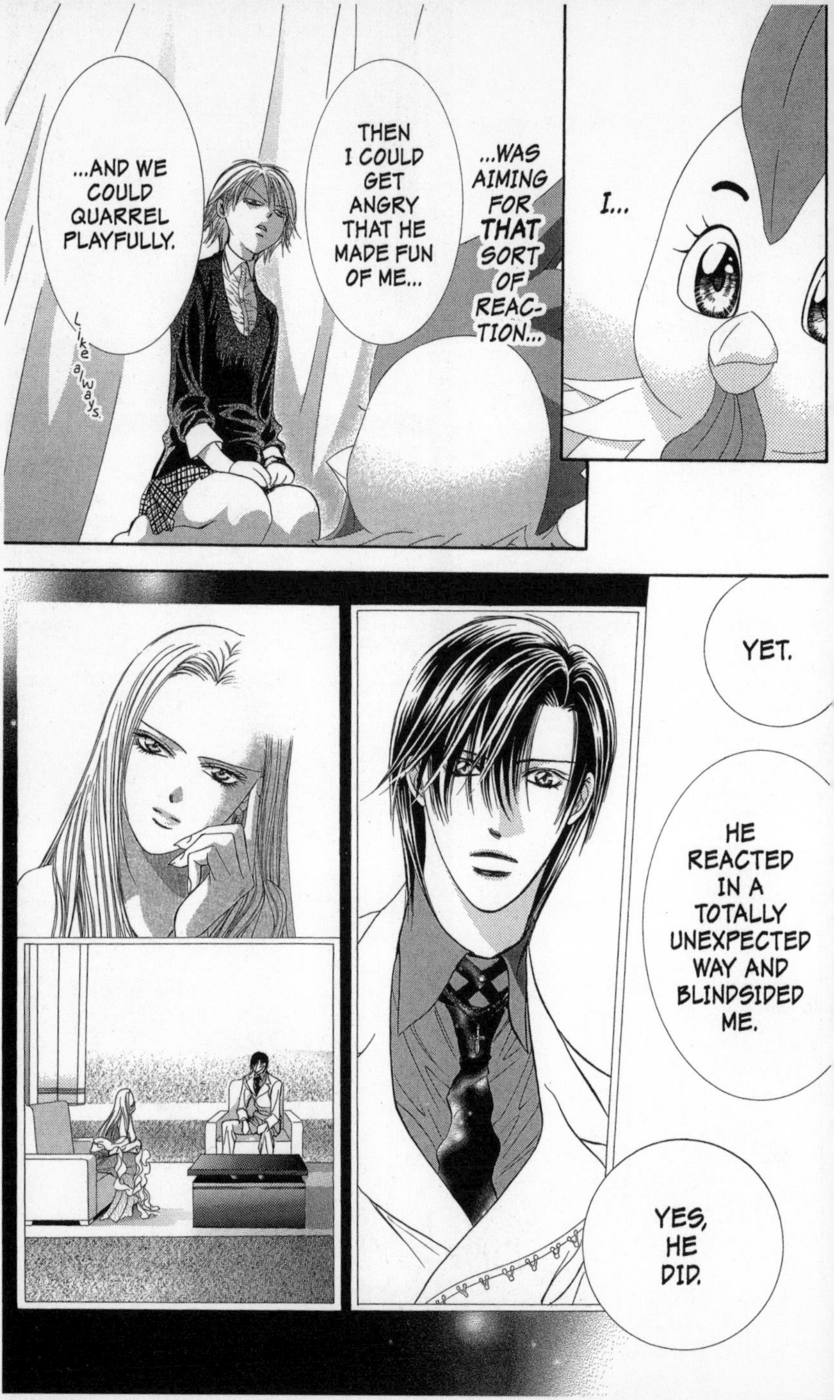
I...
...WAS AIMING FOR THAT SORT OF REAC-TION...
THEN I COULD GET ANGRY THAT HE MADE FUN OF ME...
...AND WE COULD QUARREL PLAYFULLY.
Like always.
YET.
HE REACTED IN A TOTALLY UNEXPECTED WAY AND BLINDSIDED ME.
YES, HE DID.

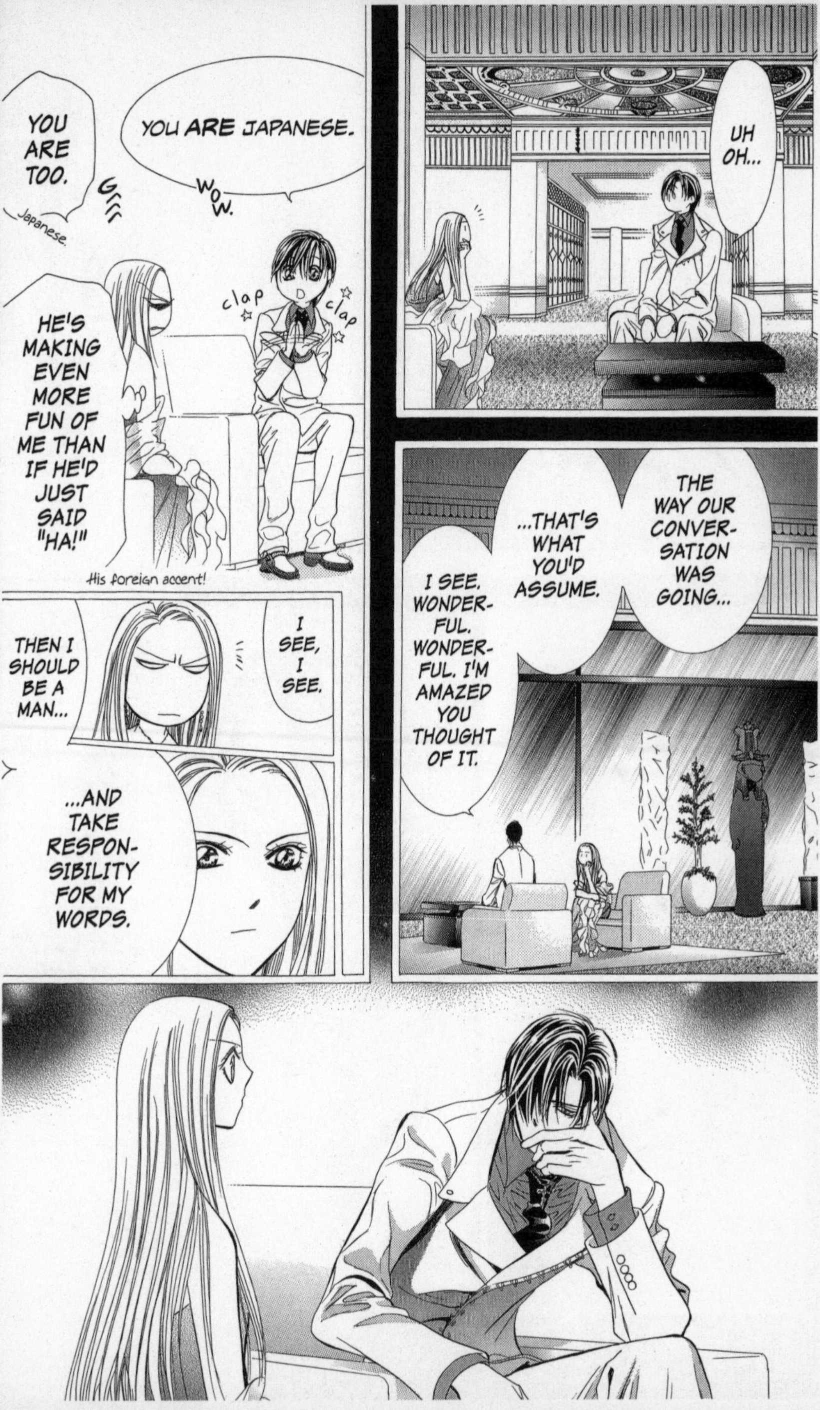
UH OH...
THE WAY OUR CONVERSATION WAS GOING...
...THAT'S WHAT YOU'D ASSUME.
I SEE. WONDERFUL. WONDERFUL. I'M AMAZED YOU THOUGHT OF IT.
YOU ARE JAPANESE.
WOW.
YOU ARE TOO.
Japanese.
clap clap
HE'S MAKING EVEN MORE FUN OF ME THAN IF HE'D JUST SAID "HA!"
His foreign accent!
I SEE, I SEE.
THEN I SHOULD BE A MAN...
...AND TAKE RESPONSIBILITY FOR MY WORDS.

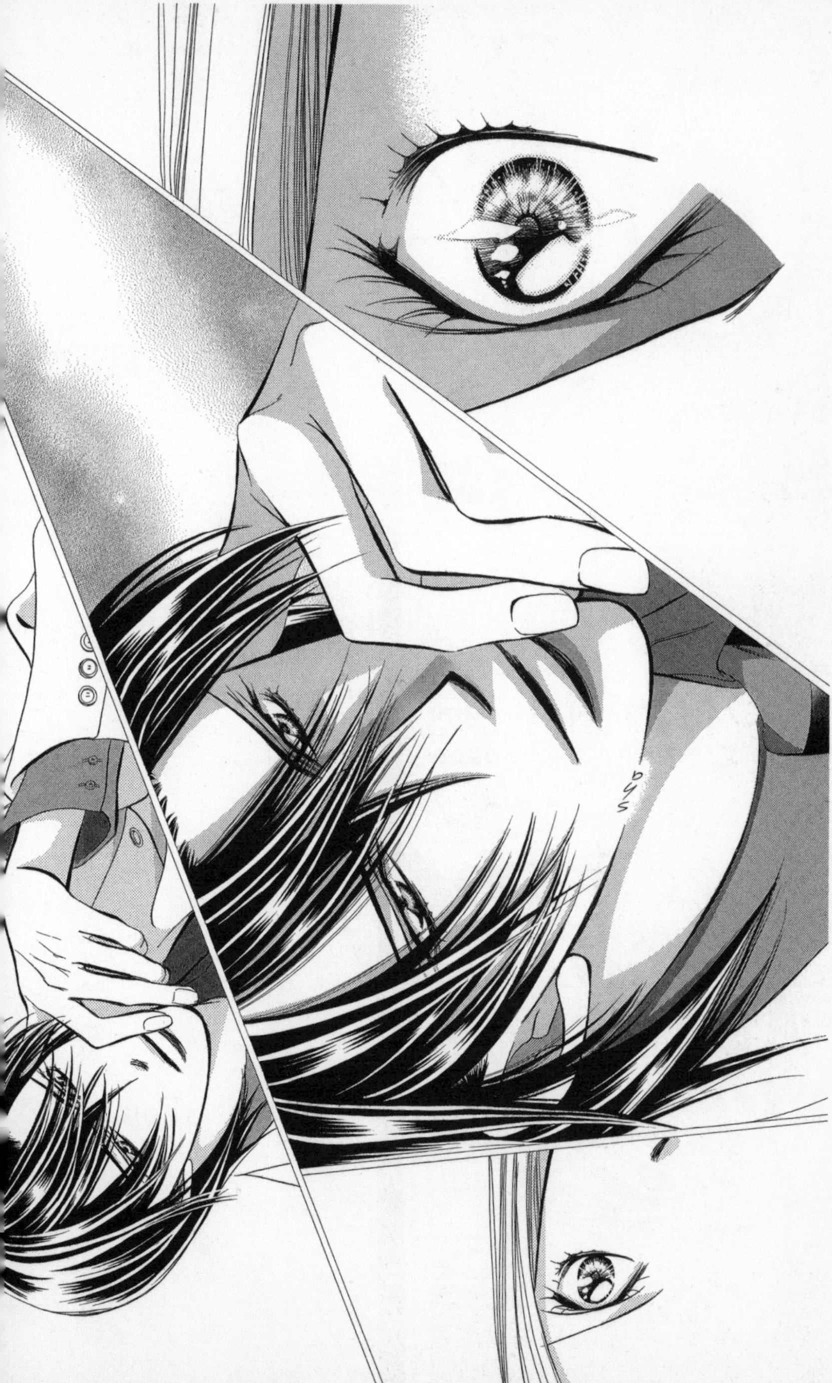
shp

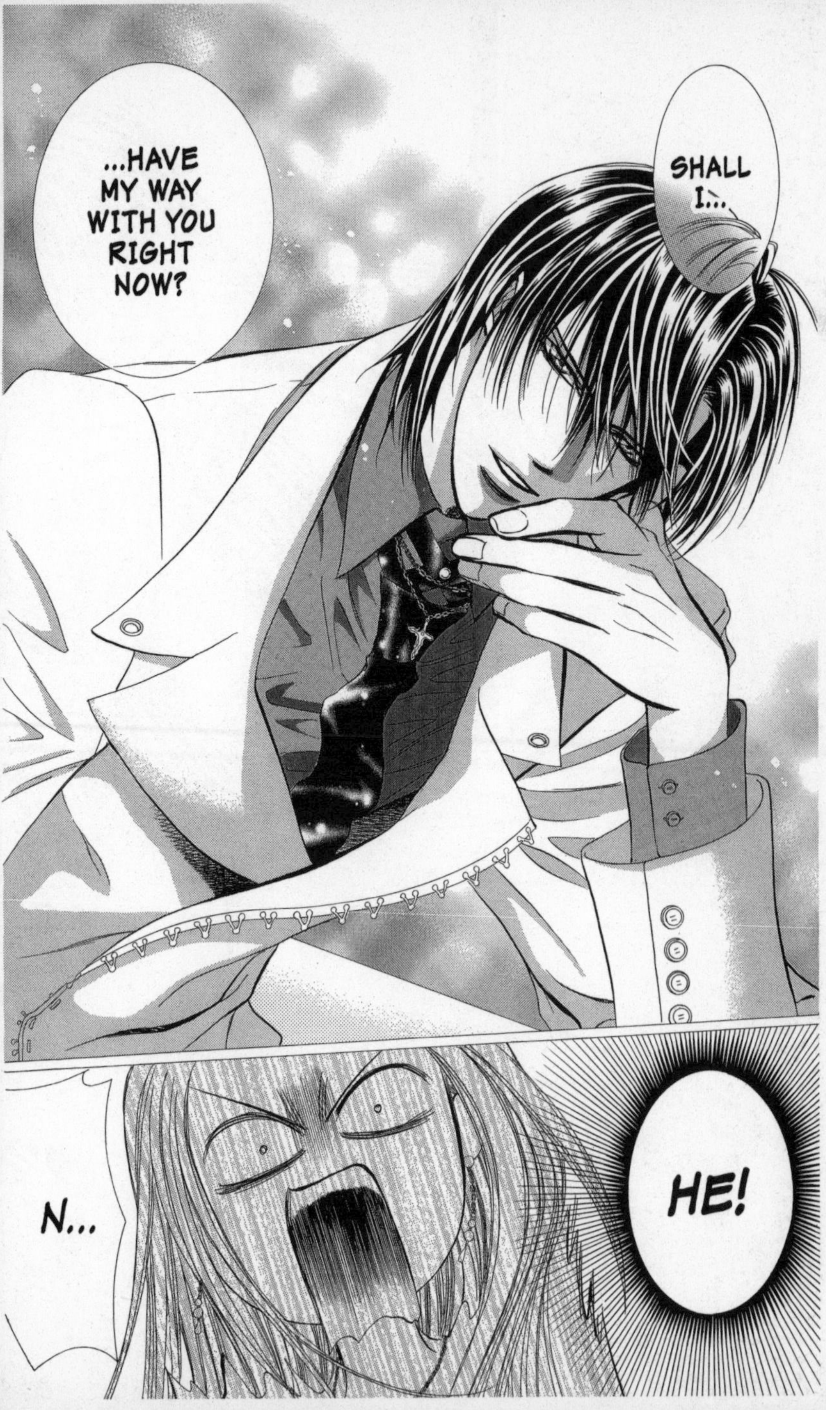
SHALL I...
...HAVE MY WAY WITH YOU RIGHT NOW?
HE!
N...

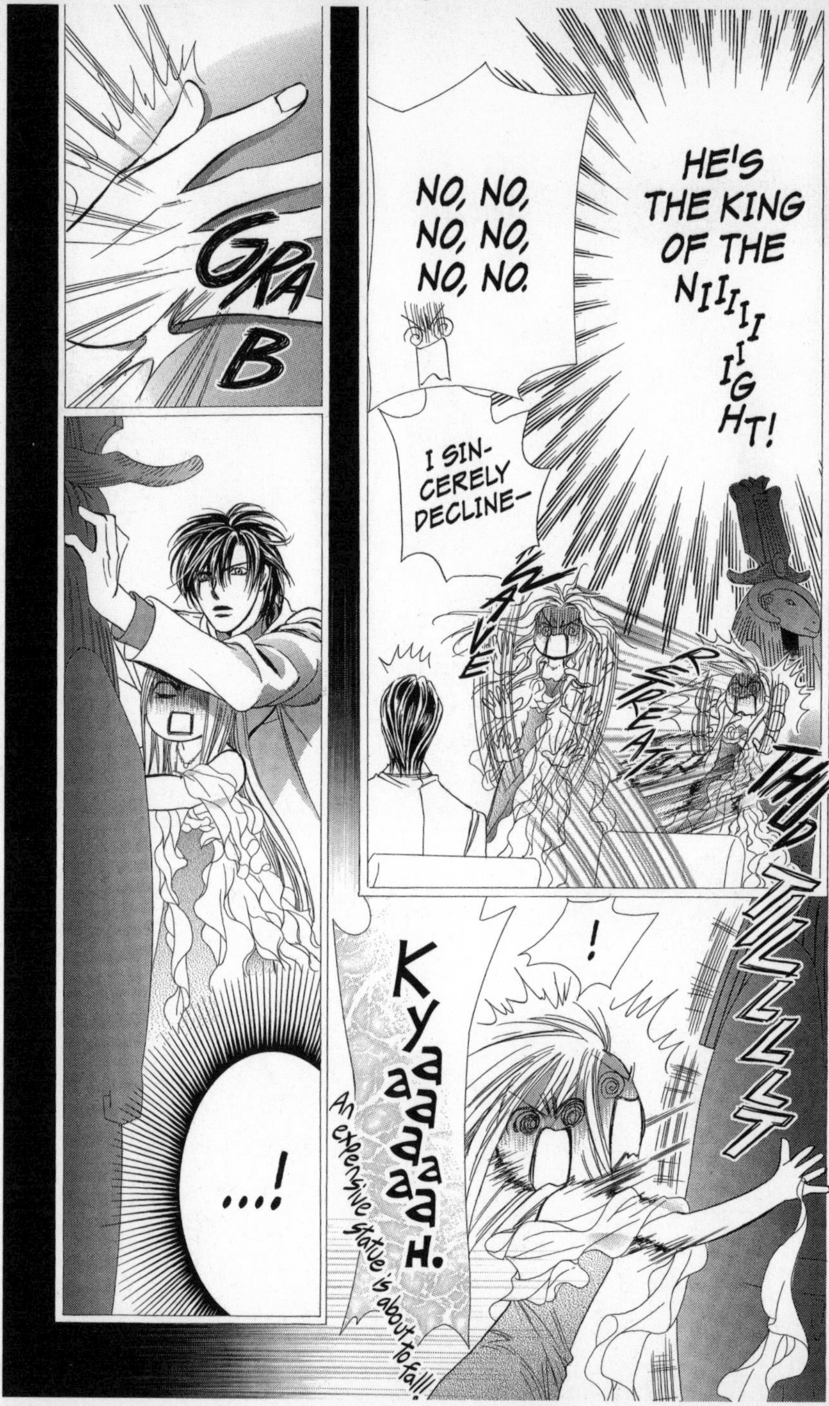
HE'S THE KING OF THE NIIIIIIIGHT!
NO, NO, NO, NO, NO, NO.
I SINCERELY DECLINE—
WAVE
RETREAT
THUD
TILLLLT
!
Kyaaaaaaah.
An expensive statue is about to fall!!
GRAB
...!

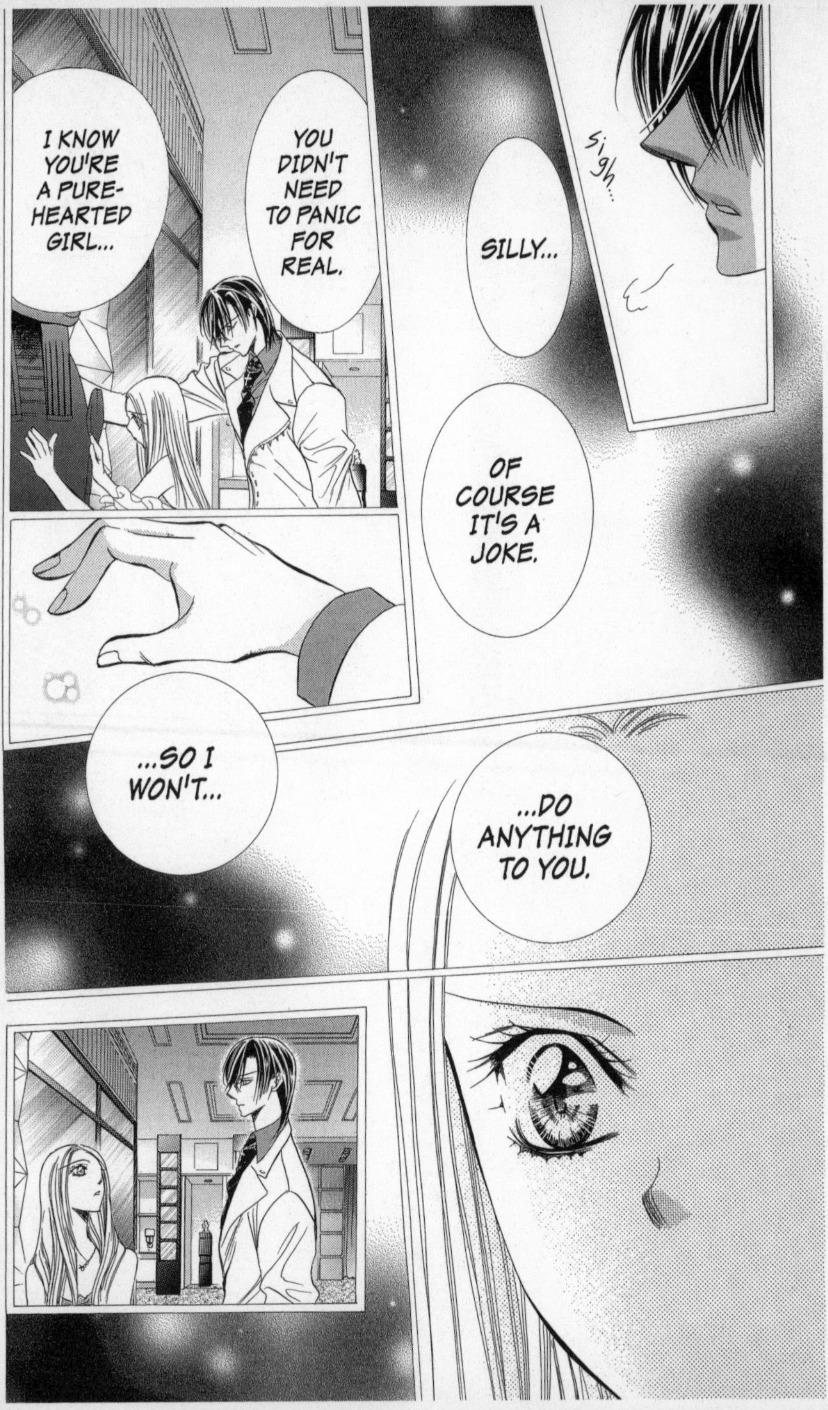
sigh...
SILLY...
I KNOW YOU'RE A PURE-HEARTED GIRL...
YOU DIDN'T NEED TO PANIC FOR REAL.
OF COURSE IT'S A JOKE.
...SO I WON'T...
...DO ANYTHING TO YOU.

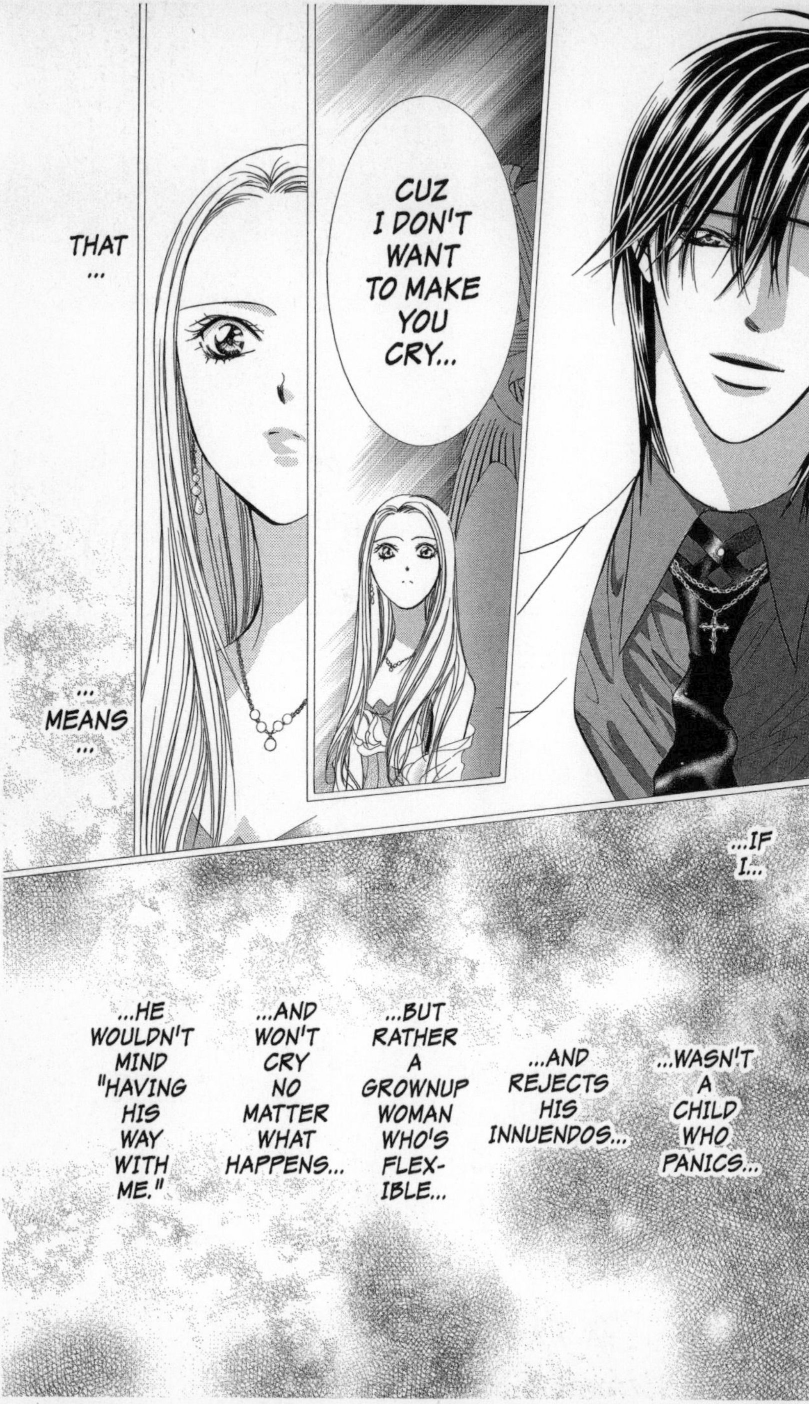
CUZ I DON'T WANT TO MAKE YOU CRY...
THAT ...
... MEANS ...
...IF I...
...WASN'T A CHILD WHO PANICS...
...AND REJECTS HIS INNUENDOS...
...BUT RATHER A GROWNUP WOMAN WHO'S FLEX-IBLE...
...AND WON'T CRY NO MATTER WHAT HAPPENS...
...HE WOULDN'T MIND "HAVING HIS WAY WITH ME."

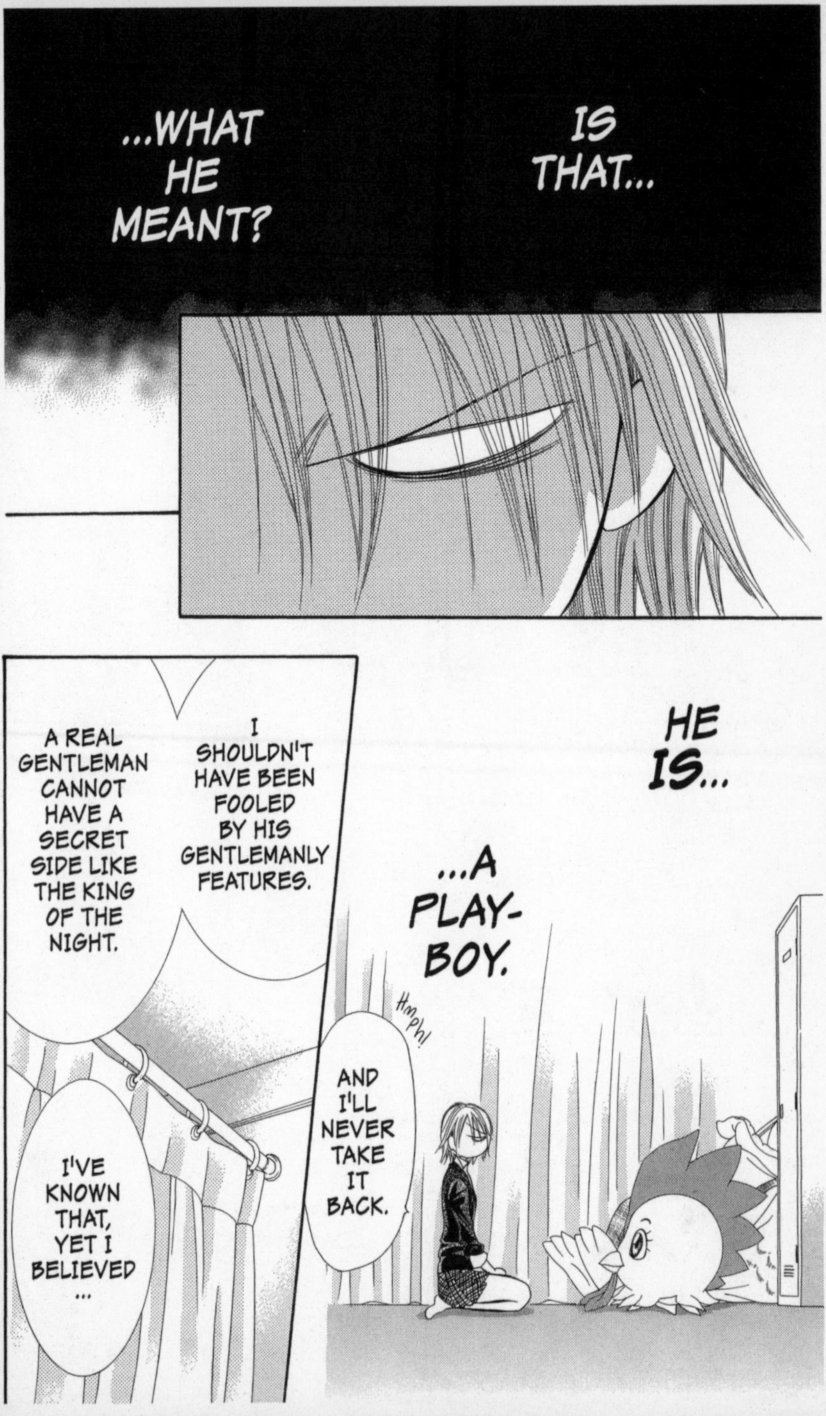
IS THAT...
...WHAT HE MEANT?
HE IS...
...A PLAY-BOY.
A REAL GENTLEMAN CANNOT HAVE A SECRET SIDE LIKE THE KING OF THE NIGHT.
I SHOULDN'T HAVE BEEN FOOLED BY HIS GENTLEMANLY FEATURES.
Hmph!
AND I'LL NEVER TAKE IT BACK.
I'VE KNOWN THAT, YET I BELIEVED ...

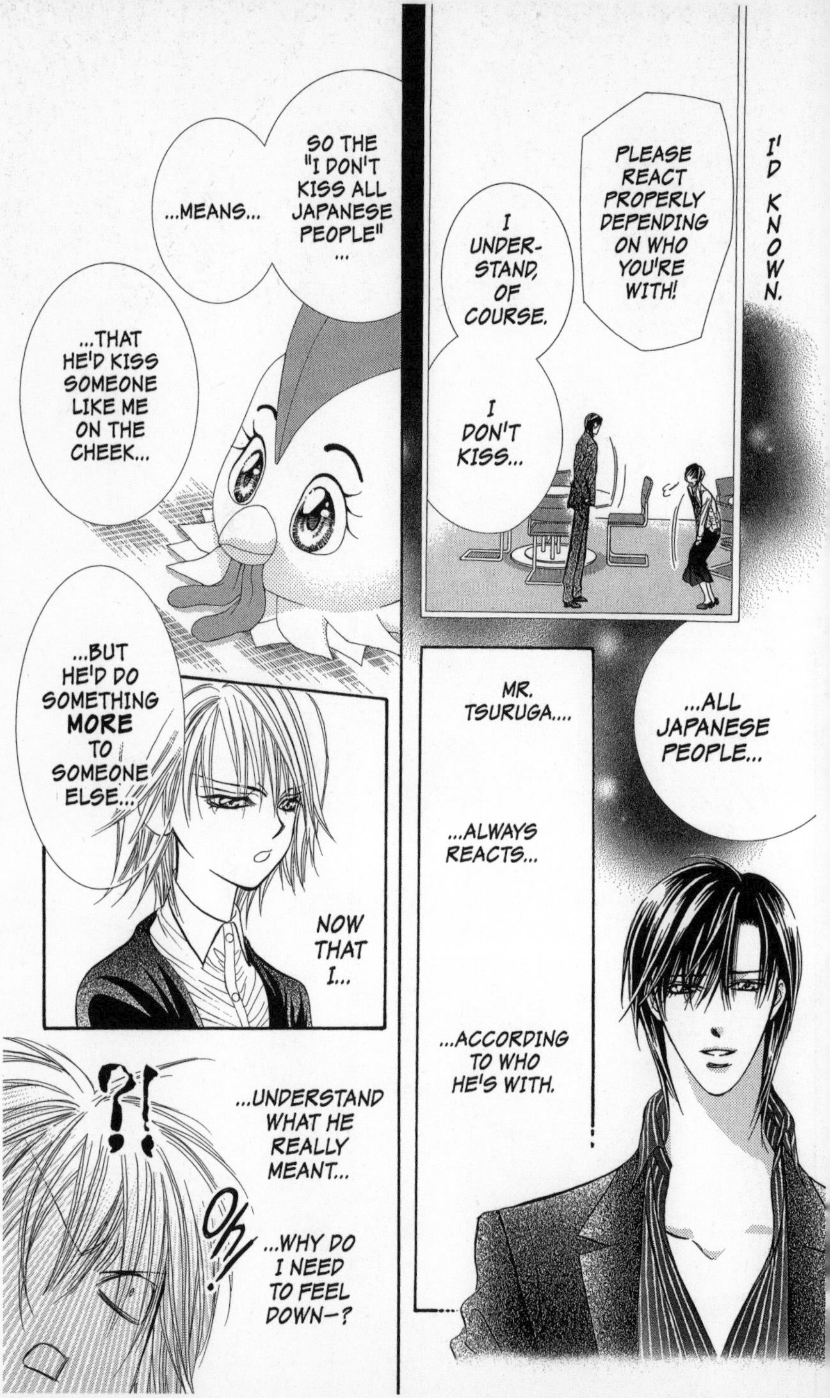
I'D KNOWN.
PLEASE REACT PROPERLY DEPENDING ON WHO YOU'RE WITH!
I UNDER-STAND, OF COURSE.
I DON'T KISS...
...ALL JAPANESE PEOPLE...
MR. TSURUGA....
...ALWAYS REACTS...
...ACCORDING TO WHO HE'S WITH.
SO THE "I DON'T KISS ALL JAPANESE PEOPLE" ...
...MEANS...
...THAT HE'D KISS SOMEONE LIKE ME ON THE CHEEK...
...BUT HE'D DO SOMETHING MORE TO SOMEONE ELSE...
NOW THAT I...
...UNDERSTAND WHAT HE REALLY MEANT...
?!
OH!
...WHY DO I NEED TO FEEL DOWN-?

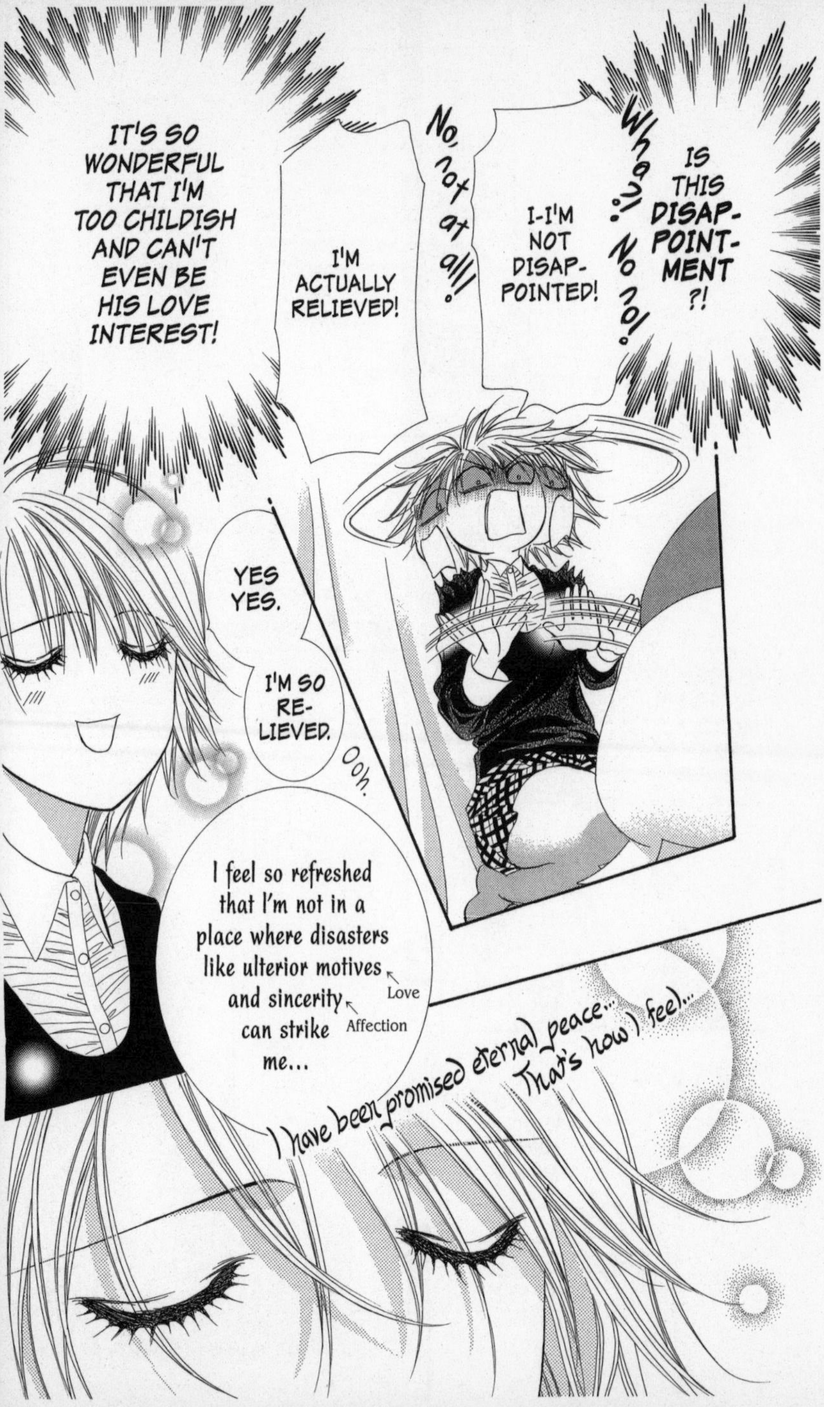
IS THIS DISAPPOINTMENT ?!
Wha?! No no!
I-I'M NOT DISAPPOINTED!
No, not at all!
I'M ACTUALLY RELIEVED!
IT'S SO WONDERFUL THAT I'M TOO CHILDISH AND CAN'T EVEN BE HIS LOVE INTEREST!
Ooh.
YES YES.
I'M SO RELIEVED.
I feel so refreshed that I'm not in a place where disasters like ulterior motives (Love) and sincerity (Affection) can strike me...
I have been promised eternal peace... That's how I feel...

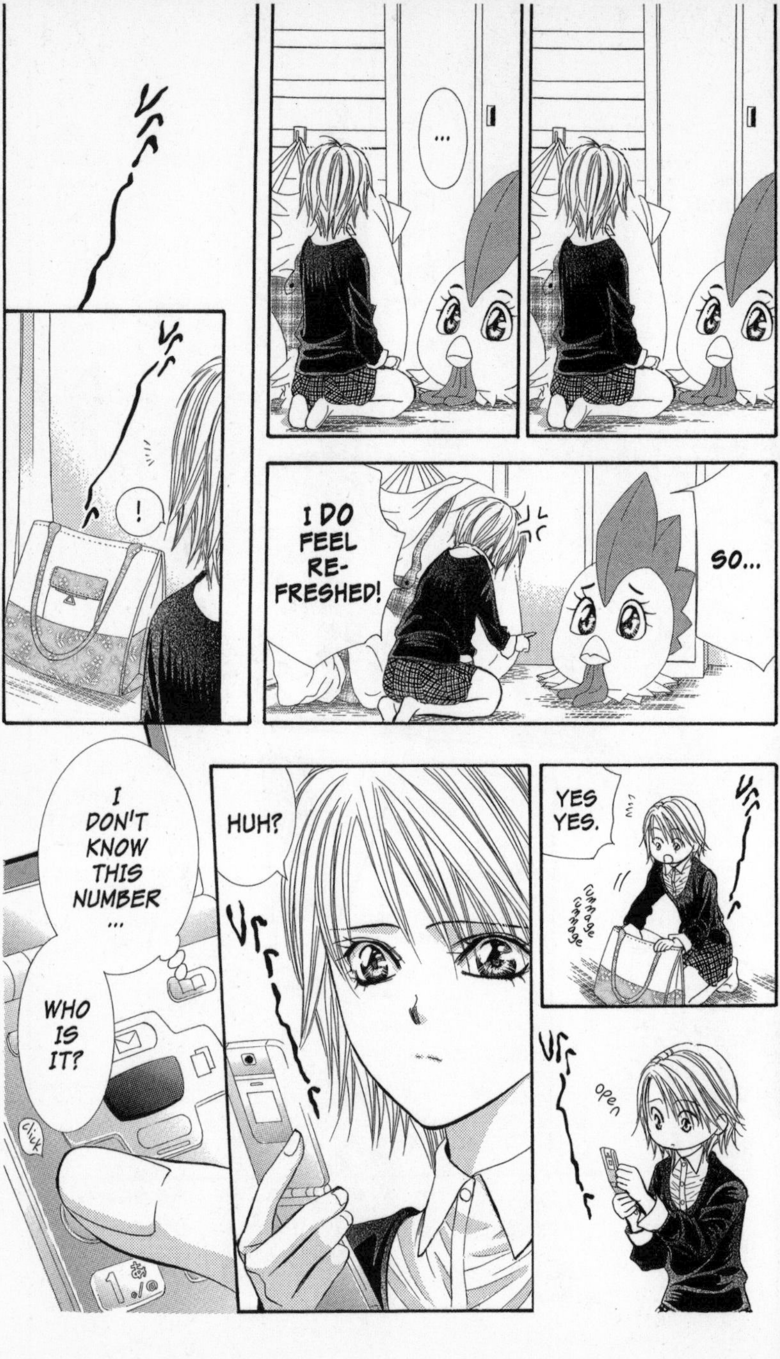
...
SO...
I DO FEEL RE-FRESHED!
!
YES YES.
rummage rummage
HUH?
I DON'T KNOW THIS NUMBER...
WHO IS IT?
click
open

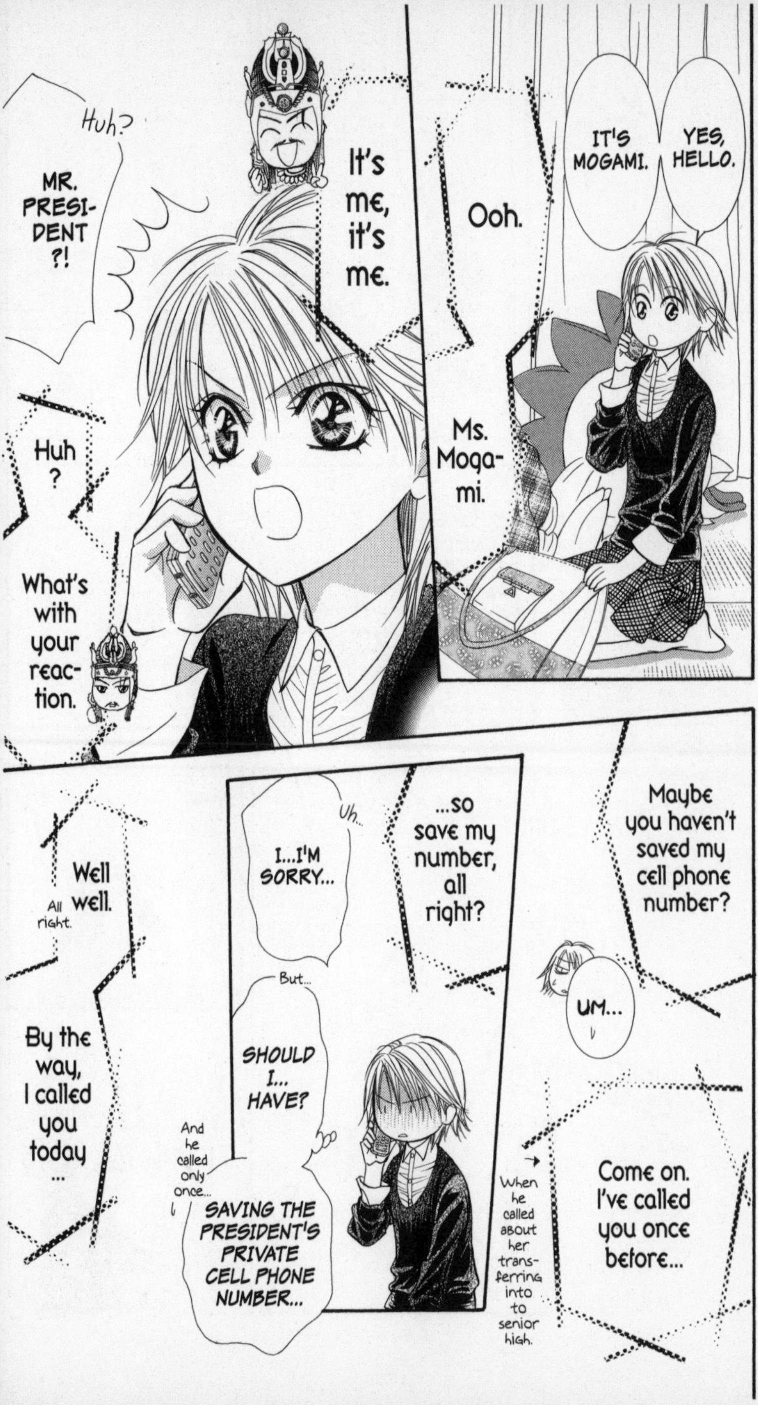
YES, HELLO.
IT'S MOGAMI.
Ooh.
Ms. Moga-mi.
It's me, it's me.
MR. PRESI-DENT ?!
Huh?
Huh ?
What's with your reac-tion.
Maybe you haven't saved my cell phone number?
UM...
Come on. I've called you once before...
When he called about her trans-ferring into to senior high.
...so save my number, all right?
Uh...
I...I'M SORRY...
But...
SHOULD I... HAVE?
SAVING THE PRESIDENT'S PRIVATE CELL PHONE NUMBER...
And he called only once...
Well well.
All right.
By the way, I called you today ...

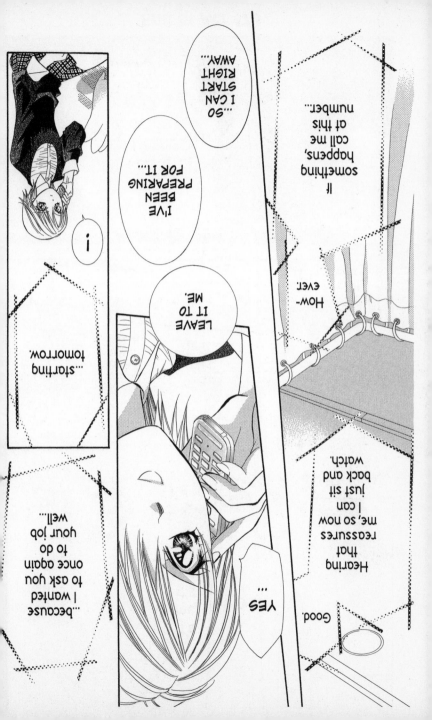

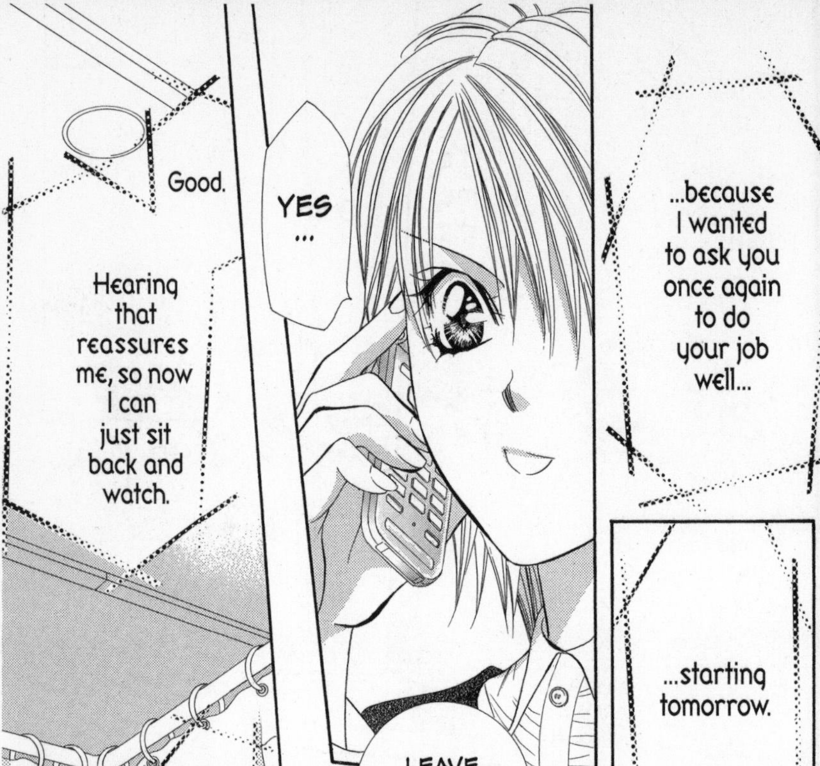
...because I wanted to ask you once again to do your job well...
...starting tomorrow.
!
YES ...
LEAVE IT TO ME.
I'VE BEEN PREPARING FOR IT...
...SO I CAN START RIGHT AWAY...
Good.
Hearing that reassures me, so now I can just sit back and watch.
How-ever.
If something happens, call me at this number...

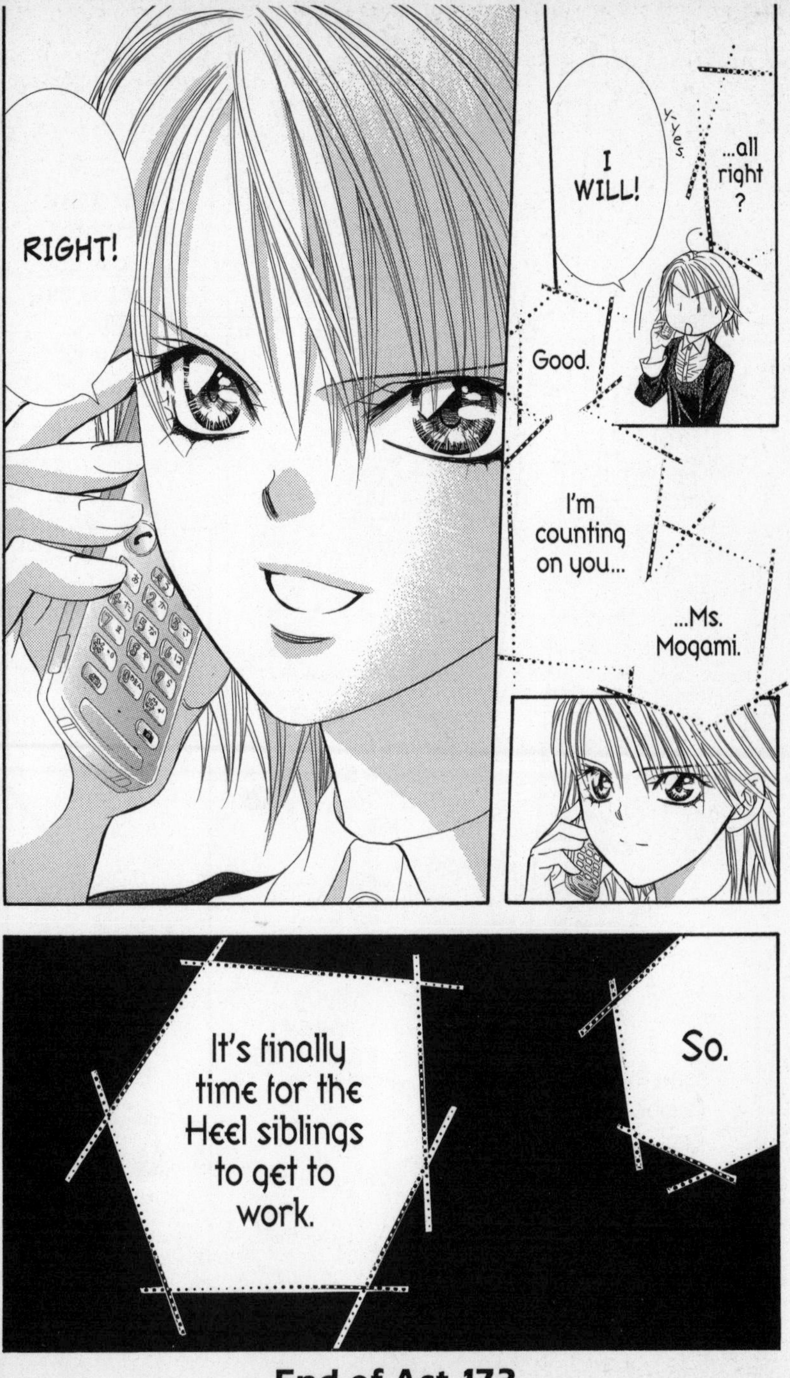
...all right?
Y-yes.
I WILL!
Good.
I'm counting on you...
...Ms. Mogami.
RIGHT!
So.
It's finally time for the Heel siblings to get to work.

End of Act 173

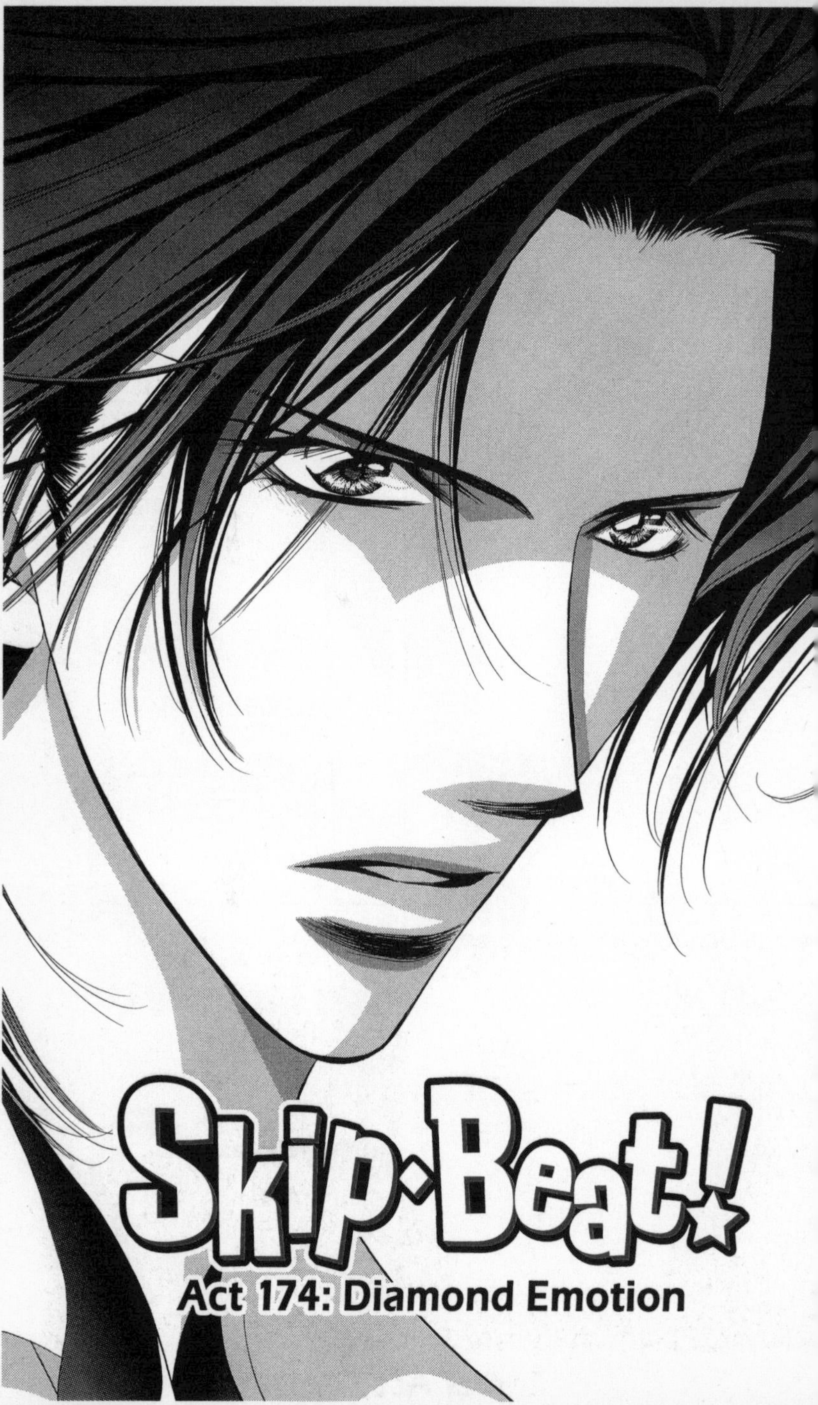
Skip·Beat!
Act 174: Diamond Emotion

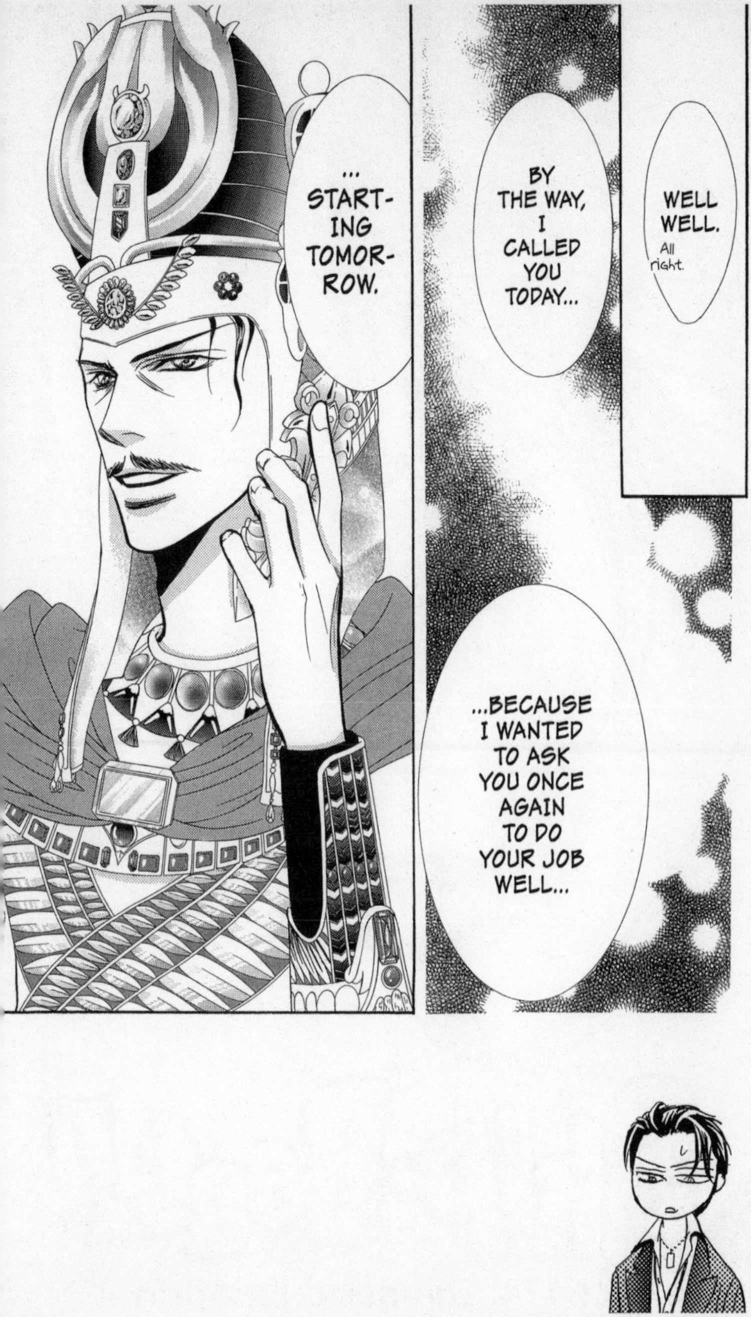
WELL WELL.
All right.
BY THE WAY, I CALLED YOU TODAY...
...BECAUSE I WANTED TO ASK YOU ONCE AGAIN TO DO YOUR JOB WELL...
... STARTING TOMORROW.

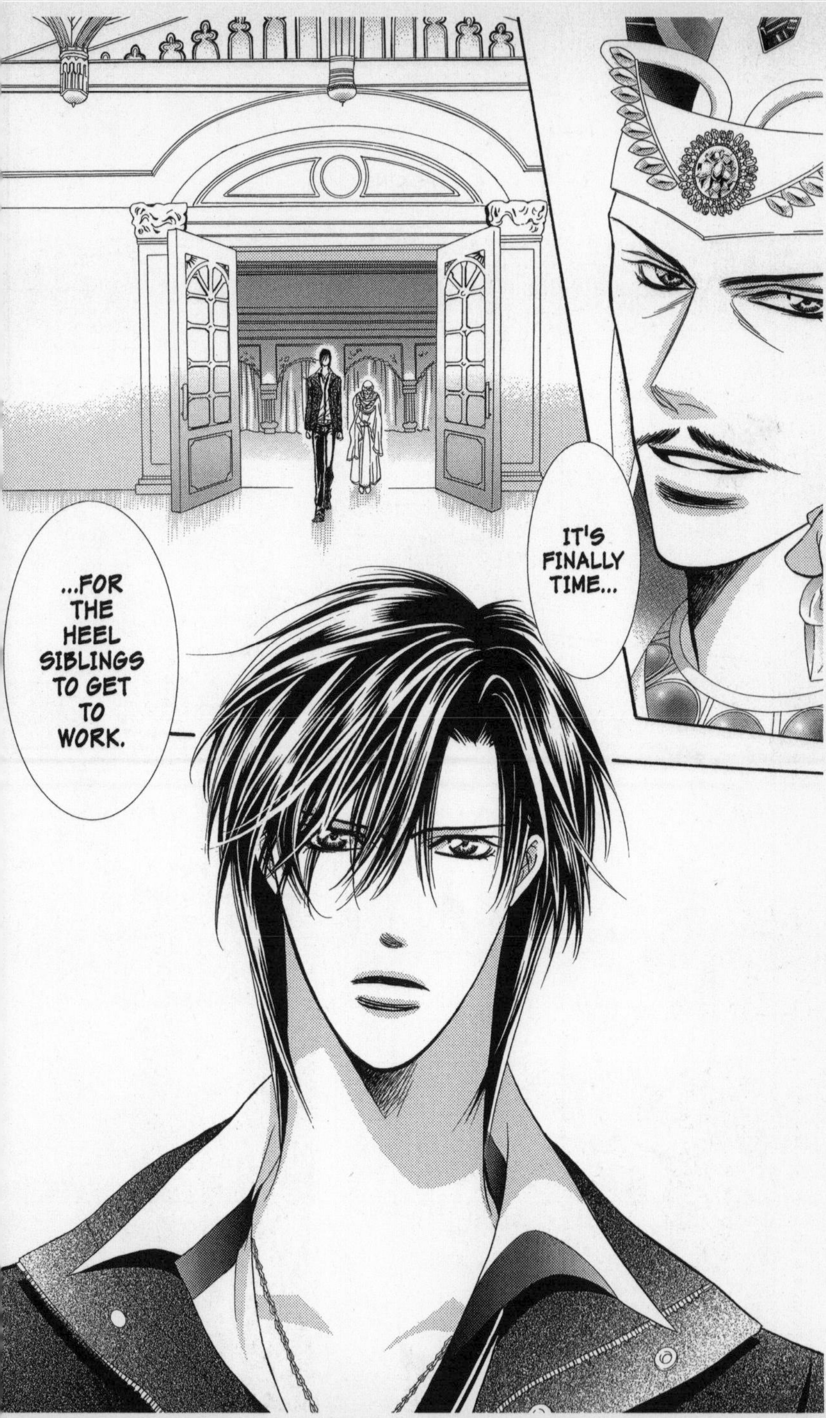
IT'S FINALLY TIME...
...FOR THE HEEL SIBLINGS TO GET TO WORK.

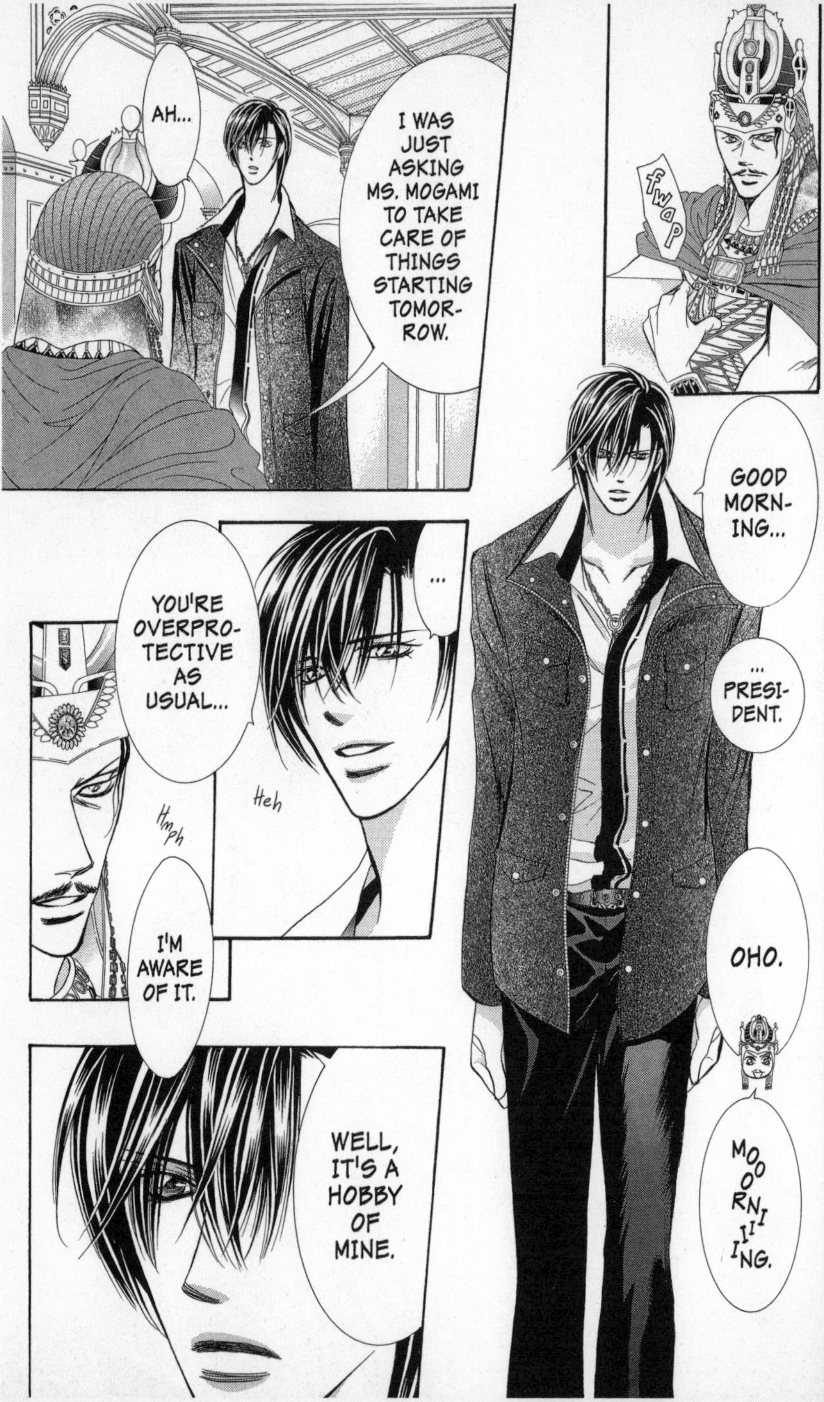
fwap
AH...
I WAS JUST ASKING MS. MOGAMI TO TAKE CARE OF THINGS STARTING TOMOR-ROW.
GOOD MORN-ING...
... PRESI-DENT.
OHO.
MOOOORNIIIING.
YOU'RE OVERPRO-TECTIVE AS USUAL...
...
Heh
Hmph
I'M AWARE OF IT.
WELL, IT'S A HOBBY OF MINE.

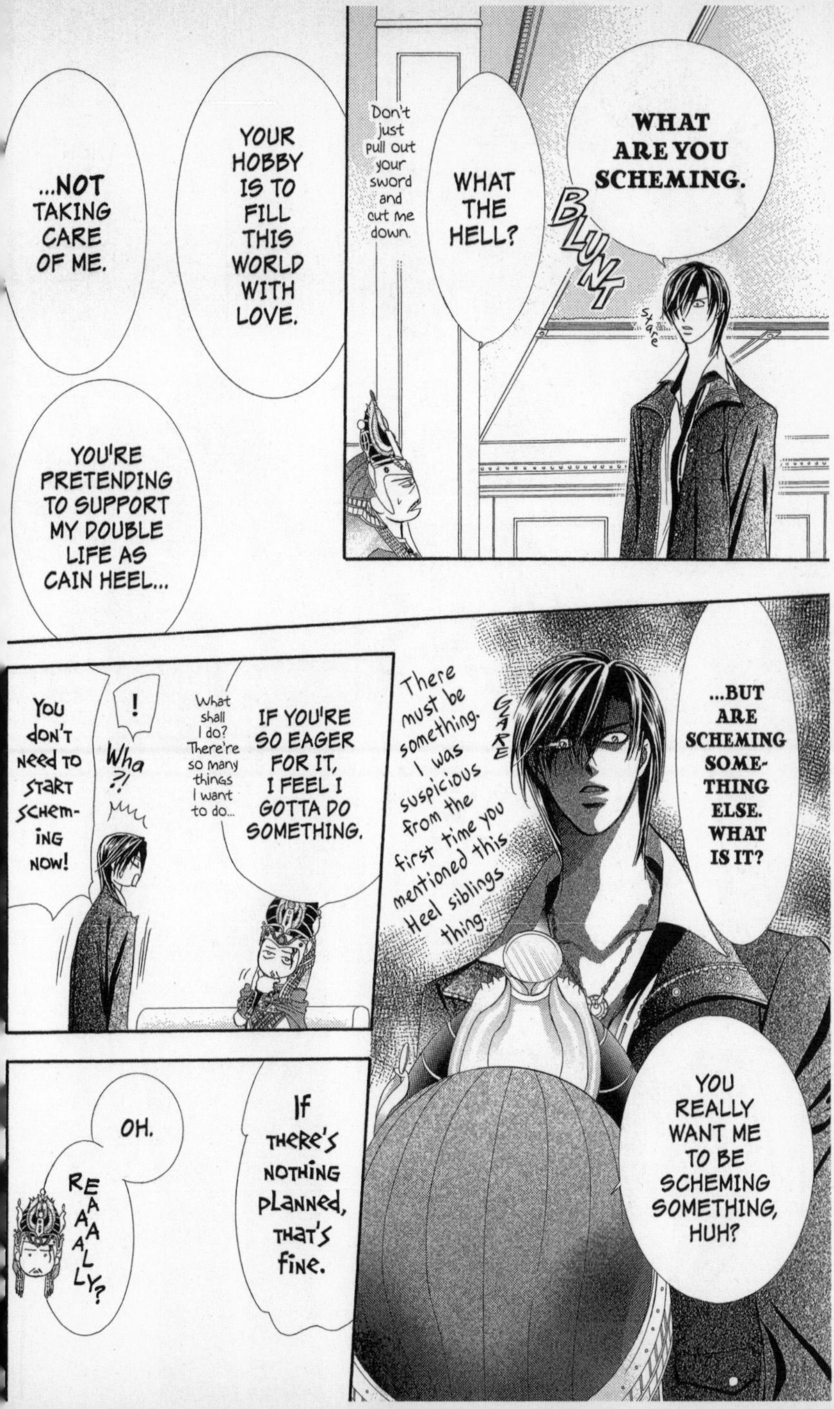
WHAT ARE YOU SCHEMING.
BLUNT
stare
WHAT THE HELL?
Don't just pull out your sword and cut me down.
YOUR HOBBY IS TO FILL THIS WORLD WITH LOVE.
...NOT TAKING CARE OF ME.
YOU'RE PRETENDING TO SUPPORT MY DOUBLE LIFE AS CAIN HEEL...
...BUT ARE SCHEMING SOMETHING ELSE. WHAT IS IT?
GLARE
There must be something. I was suspicious from the first time you mentioned this Heel siblings thing.
IF YOU'RE SO EAGER FOR IT, I FEEL I GOTTA DO SOMETHING.
What shall I do? There're so many things I want to do...
!
Wha ?!
You don't need to start scheming now!
YOU REALLY WANT ME TO BE SCHEMING SOMETHING, HUH?
If there's nothing planned, that's fine.
OH.
REAAAALLY?

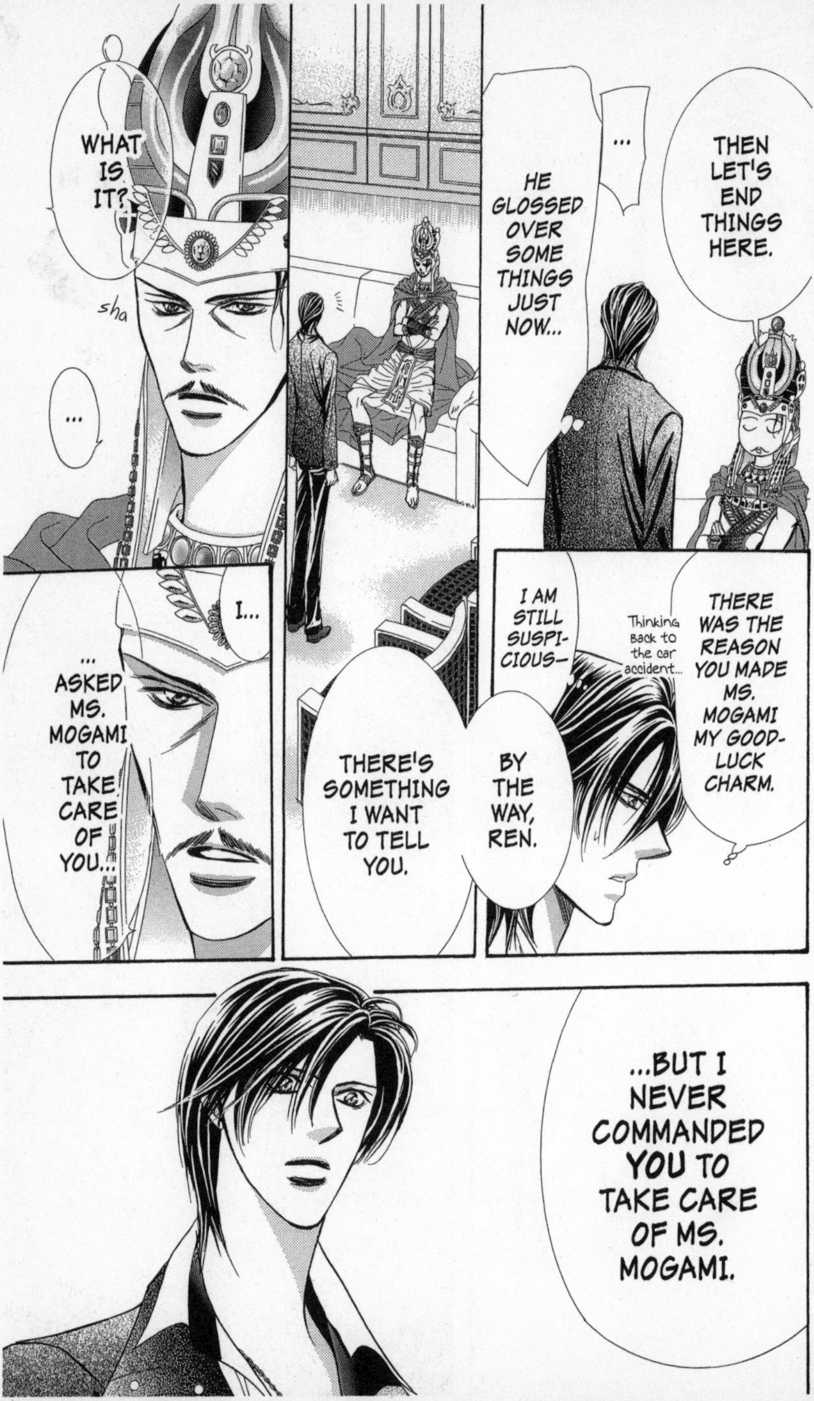
THEN LET'S END THINGS HERE.
...
HE GLOSSED OVER SOME THINGS JUST NOW...
WHAT IS IT?
sha
...
THERE WAS THE REASON YOU MADE MS. MOGAMI MY GOOD-LUCK CHARM.
Thinking back to the car accident...
I AM STILL SUSPICIOUS—
BY THE WAY, REN.
THERE'S SOMETHING I WANT TO TELL YOU.
I...
...ASKED MS. MOGAMI TO TAKE CARE OF YOU...
...BUT I NEVER COMMANDED YOU TO TAKE CARE OF MS. MOGAMI.

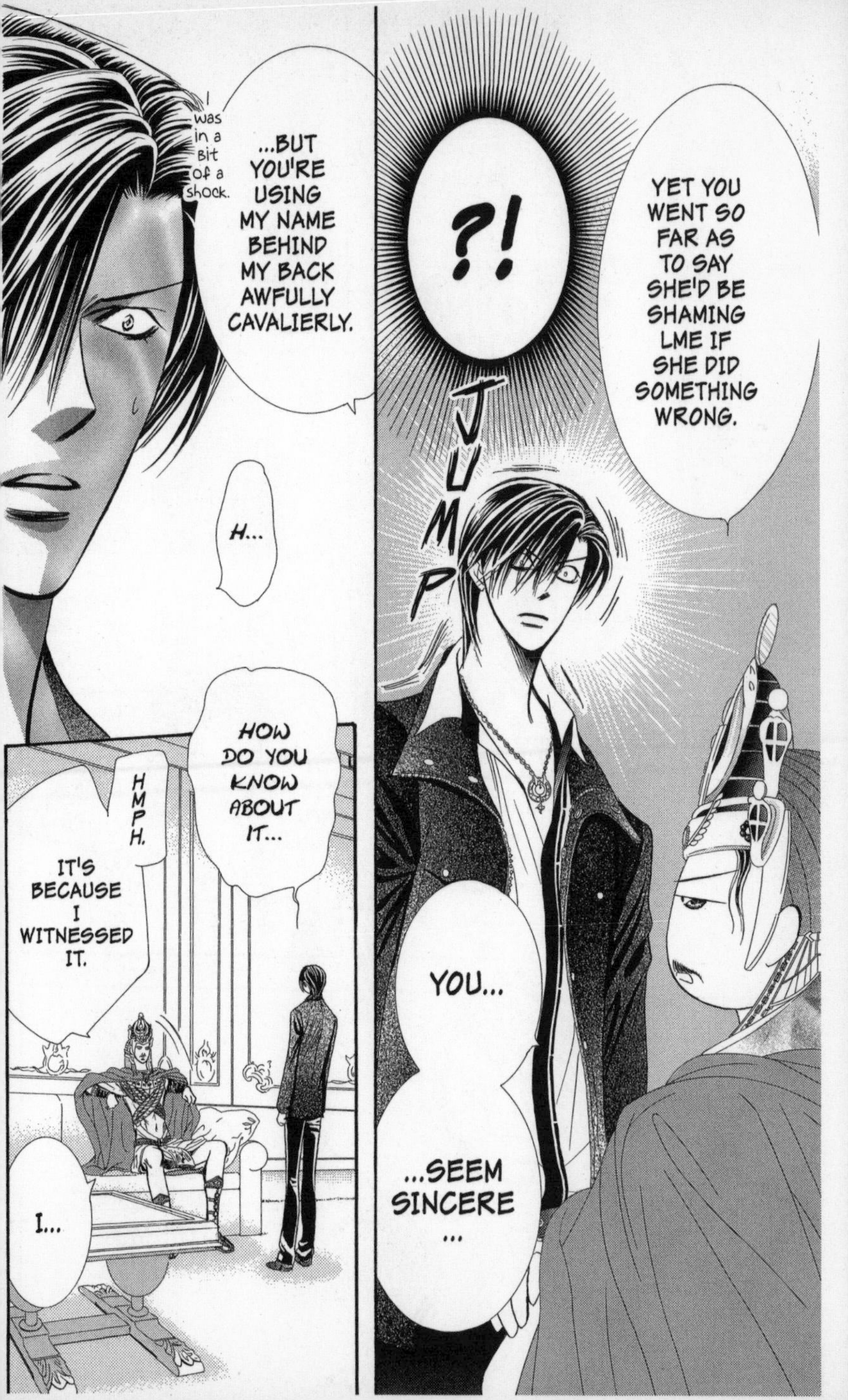
YET YOU WENT SO FAR AS TO SAY SHE'D BE SHAMING LME IF SHE DID SOMETHING WRONG.
?!
JUMP
YOU...
...SEEM SINCERE ...
...BUT YOU'RE USING MY NAME BEHIND MY BACK AWFULLY CAVALIERLY.
I was in a bit of a shock.
H...
HOW DO YOU KNOW ABOUT IT...
HMPH.
IT'S BECAUSE I WITNESSED IT.
I...

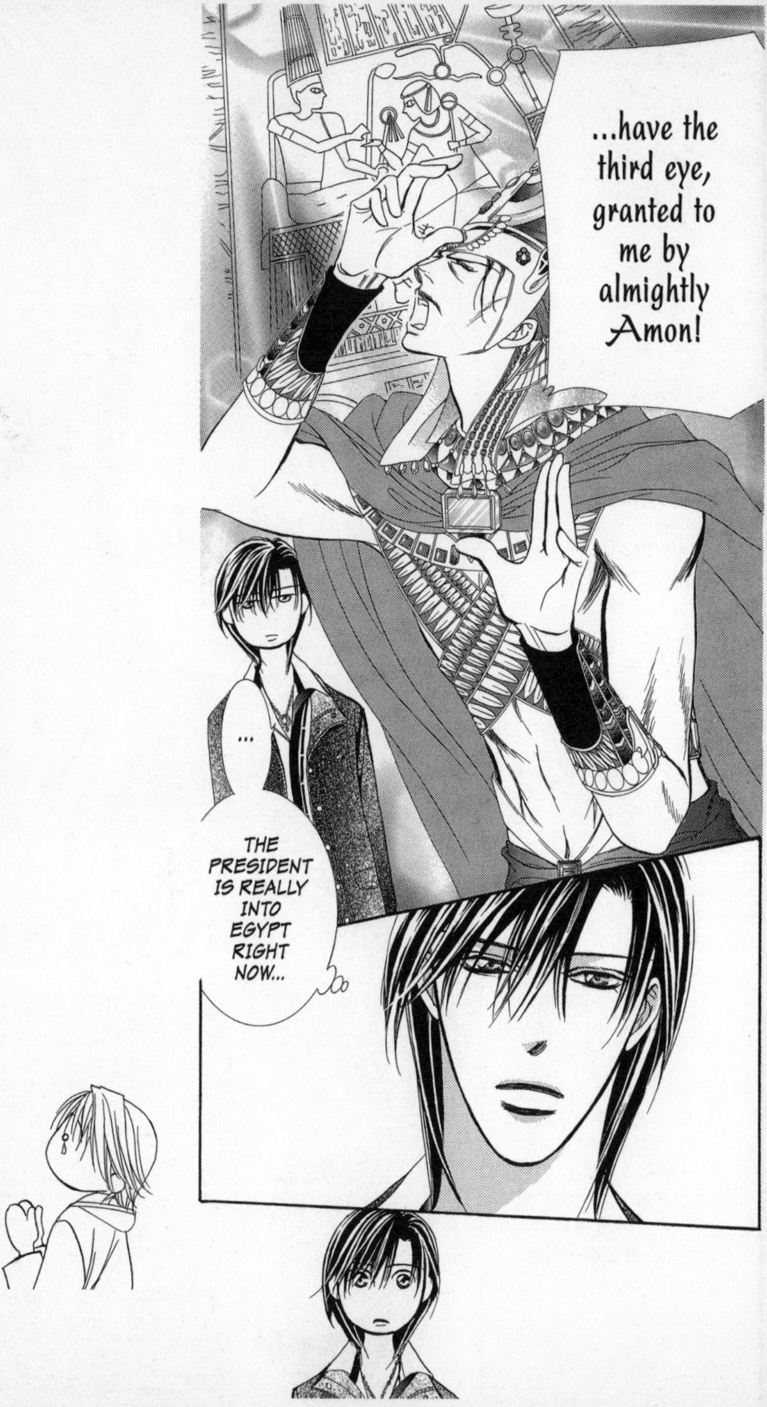
...have the third eye, granted to me by almightly Amon!
...
THE PRESIDENT IS REALLY INTO EGYPT RIGHT NOW...

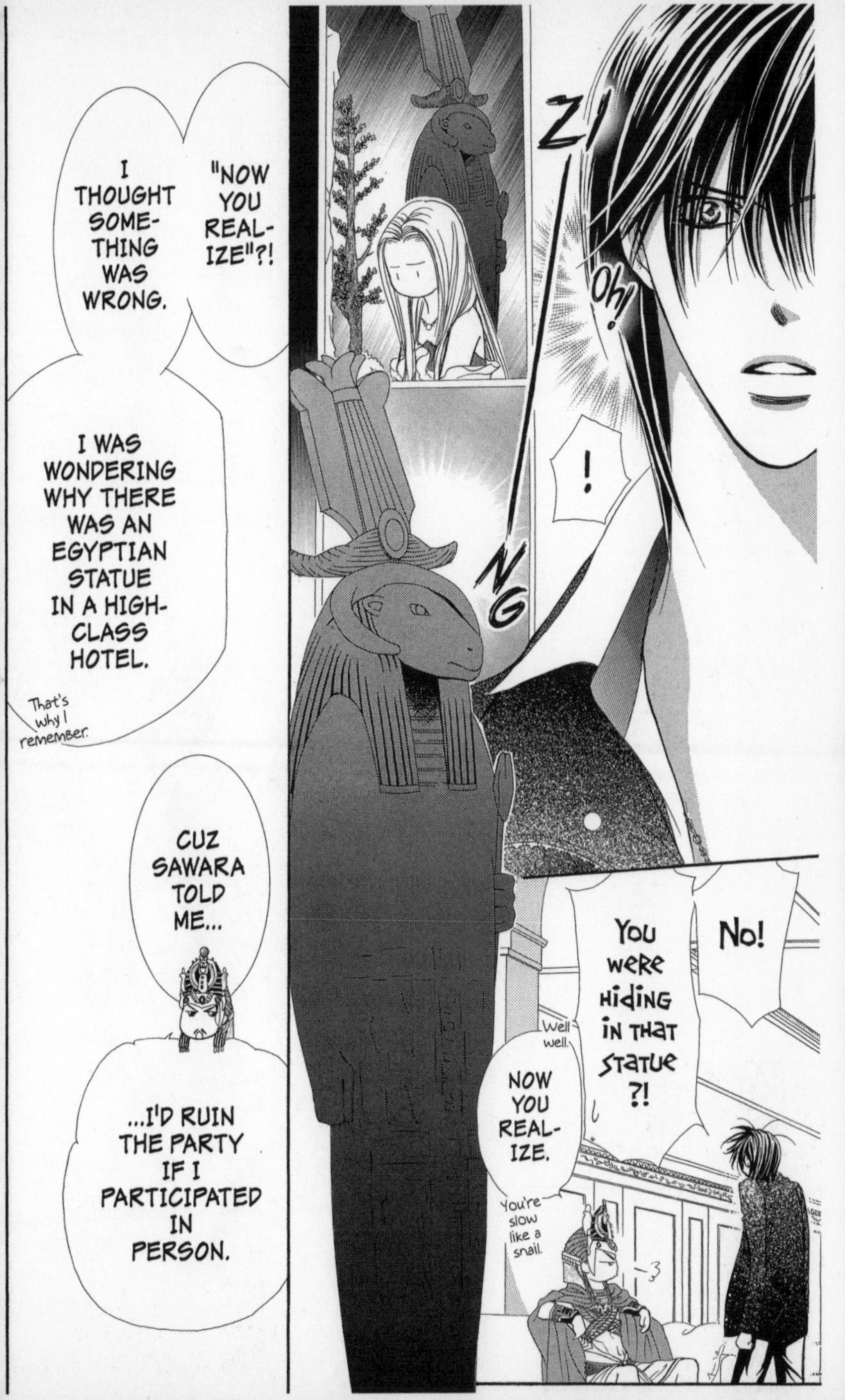
ZING
Oh!
!
No!
You were hiding in that statue?!
Well well.
NOW YOU REAL-IZE.
You're slow like a snail.
"NOW YOU REAL-IZE"?!
I THOUGHT SOME-THING WAS WRONG.
I WAS WONDERING WHY THERE WAS AN EGYPTIAN STATUE IN A HIGH-CLASS HOTEL.
That's why I remember.
CUZ SAWARA TOLD ME...
...I'D RUIN THE PARTY IF I PARTICIPATED IN PERSON.

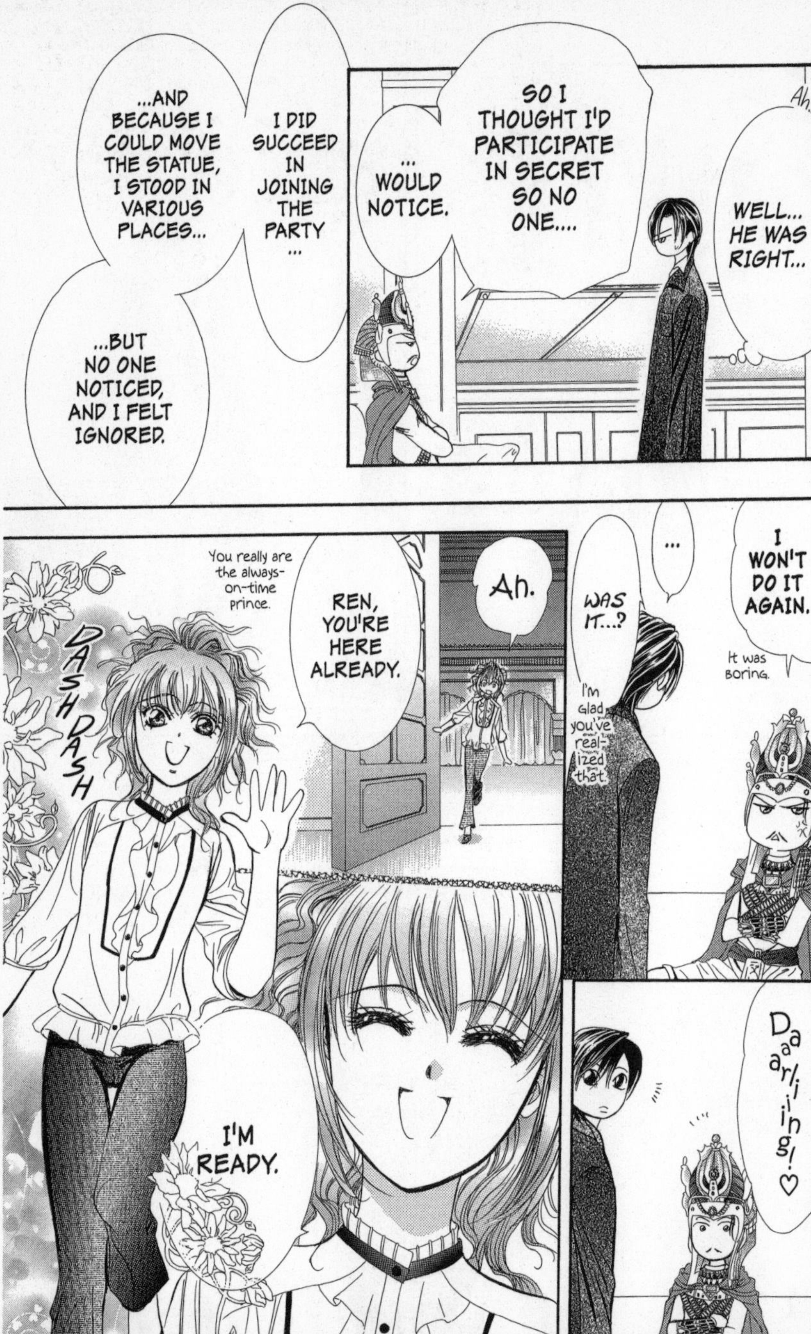
Ah...
WELL... HE WAS RIGHT...
SO I THOUGHT I'D PARTICIPATE IN SECRET SO NO ONE....
... WOULD NOTICE.
I DID SUCCEED IN JOINING THE PARTY ...
...AND BECAUSE I COULD MOVE THE STATUE, I STOOD IN VARIOUS PLACES...
...BUT NO ONE NOTICED, AND I FELT IGNORED.
I WON'T DO IT AGAIN.
It was boring.
...
WAS IT...?
I'm glad you've real-ized that.
Daarliiing! ♡
Ah.
REN, YOU'RE HERE ALREADY.
You really are the always-on-time prince.
DASH DASH
I'M READY.

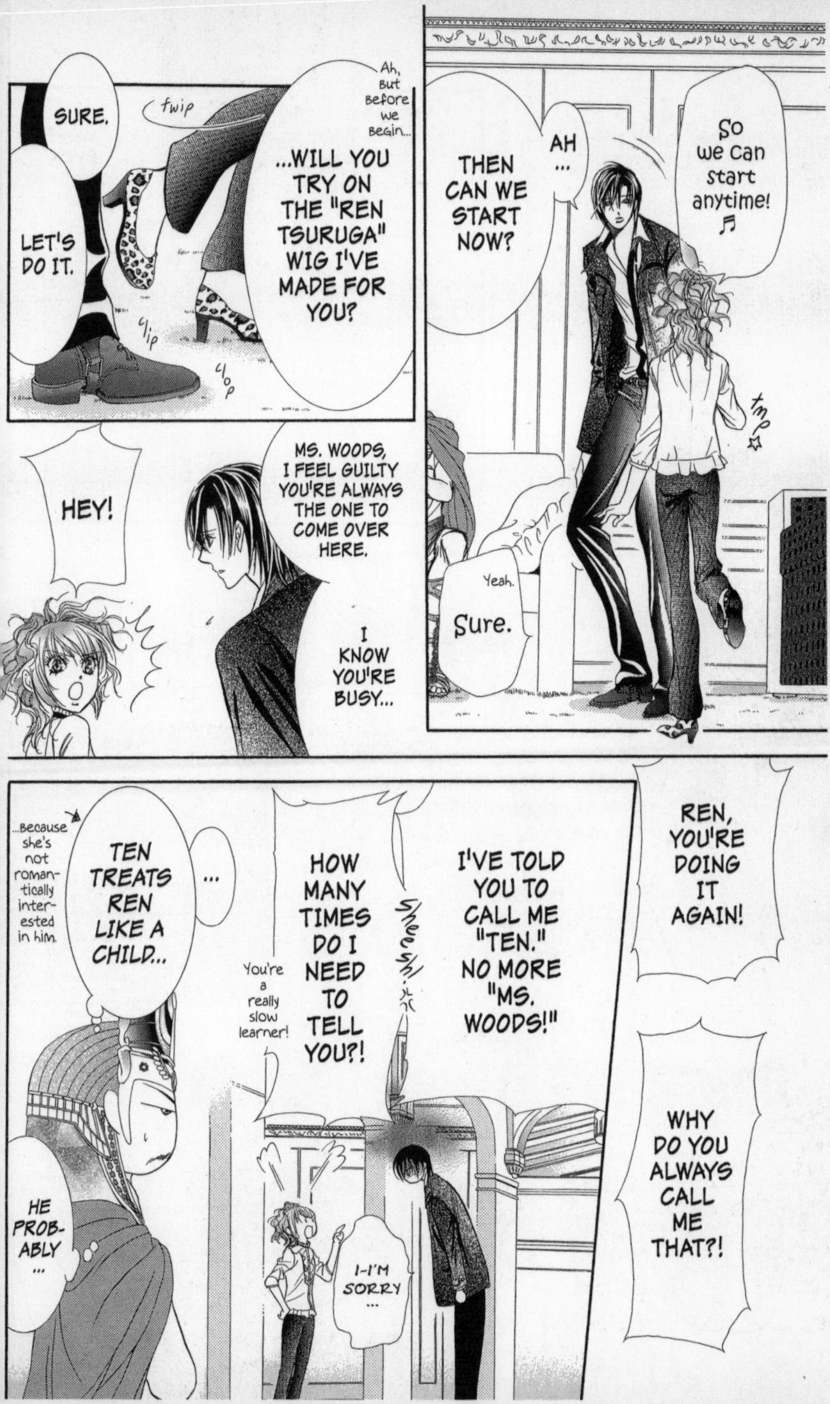
So we can start anytime! ♬
AH ...
THEN CAN WE START NOW?
Yeah.
Sure.
tmp
Ah, But Before we Begin...
...WILL YOU TRY ON THE "REN TSURUGA" WIG I'VE MADE FOR YOU?
fwip
clip
clop
SURE.
LET'S DO IT.
MS. WOODS, I FEEL GUILTY YOU'RE ALWAYS THE ONE TO COME OVER HERE.
I KNOW YOU'RE BUSY...
HEY!
REN, YOU'RE DOING IT AGAIN!
WHY DO YOU ALWAYS CALL ME THAT?!
I'VE TOLD YOU TO CALL ME "TEN." NO MORE "MS. WOODS!"
HOW MANY TIMES DO I NEED TO TELL YOU?!
Sheesh!
You're a really slow learner!
I-I'M SORRY ...
...
TEN TREATS REN LIKE A CHILD...
...Because she's not romantically interested in him.
HE PROBABLY ...

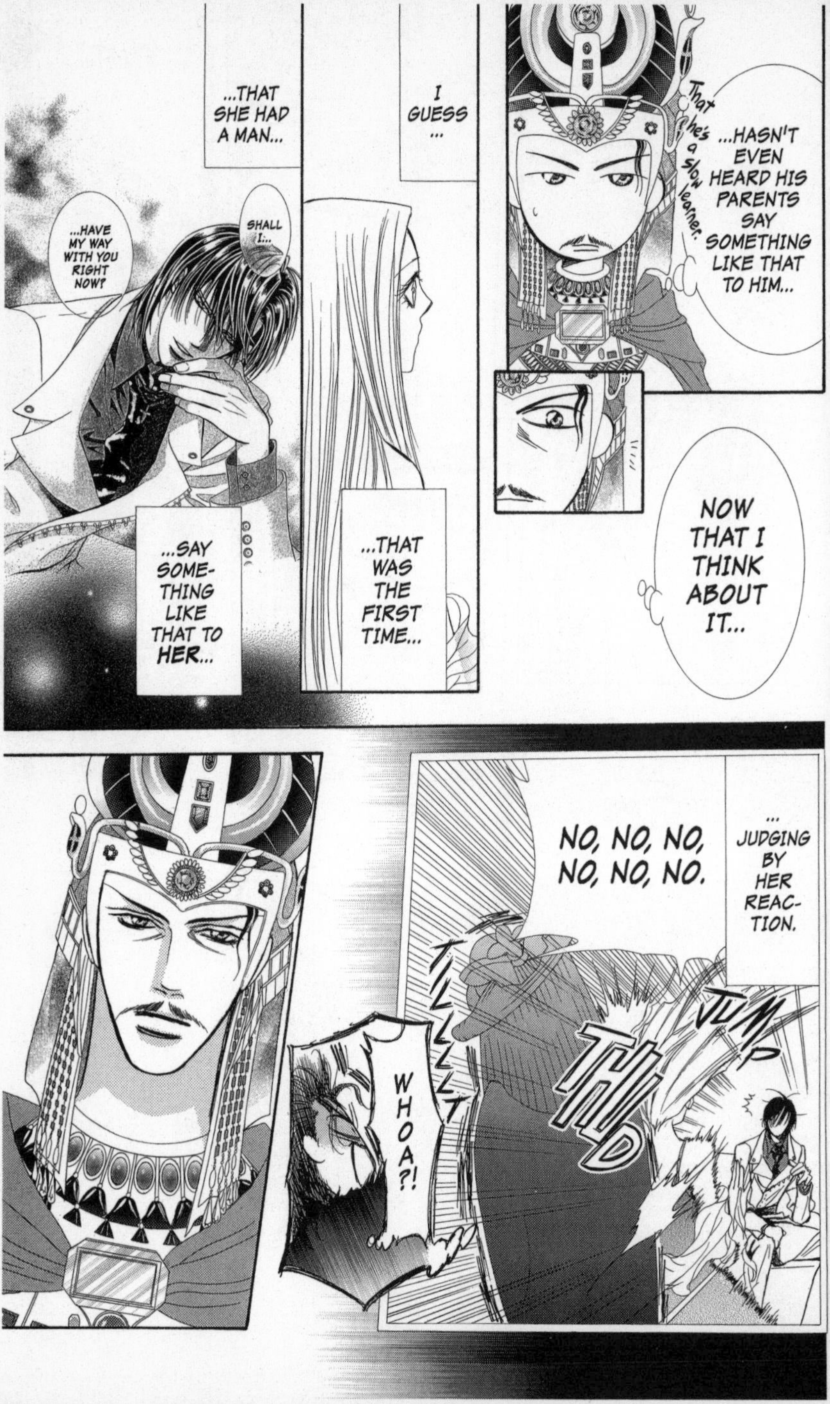
...HASN'T EVEN HEARD HIS PARENTS SAY SOMETHING LIKE THAT TO HIM...
That he's a slow learner.
NOW THAT I THINK ABOUT IT...
I GUESS ...
...THAT WAS THE FIRST TIME...
...THAT SHE HAD A MAN...
SHALL I...
...HAVE MY WAY WITH YOU RIGHT NOW?
...SAY SOME-THING LIKE THAT TO HER...
... JUDGING BY HER REAC-TION.
NO, NO, NO, NO, NO, NO.
JUMP
THUD
TILLLT
WHOA?!

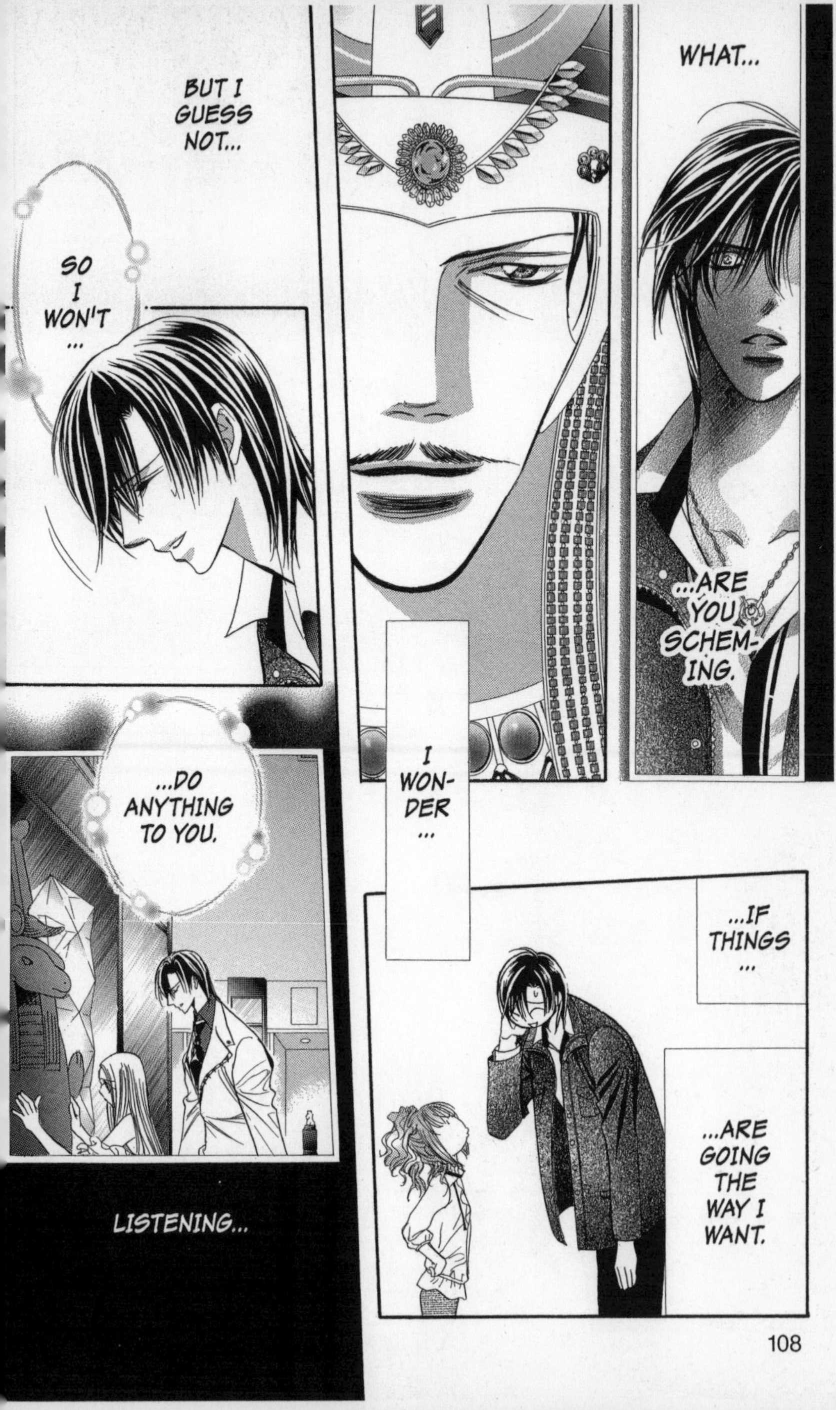
WHAT...
...ARE YOU SCHEMING.
I WONDER...
...IF THINGS...
...ARE GOING THE WAY I WANT.
BUT I GUESS NOT...
SO I WON'T...
...DO ANYTHING TO YOU.
LISTENING...

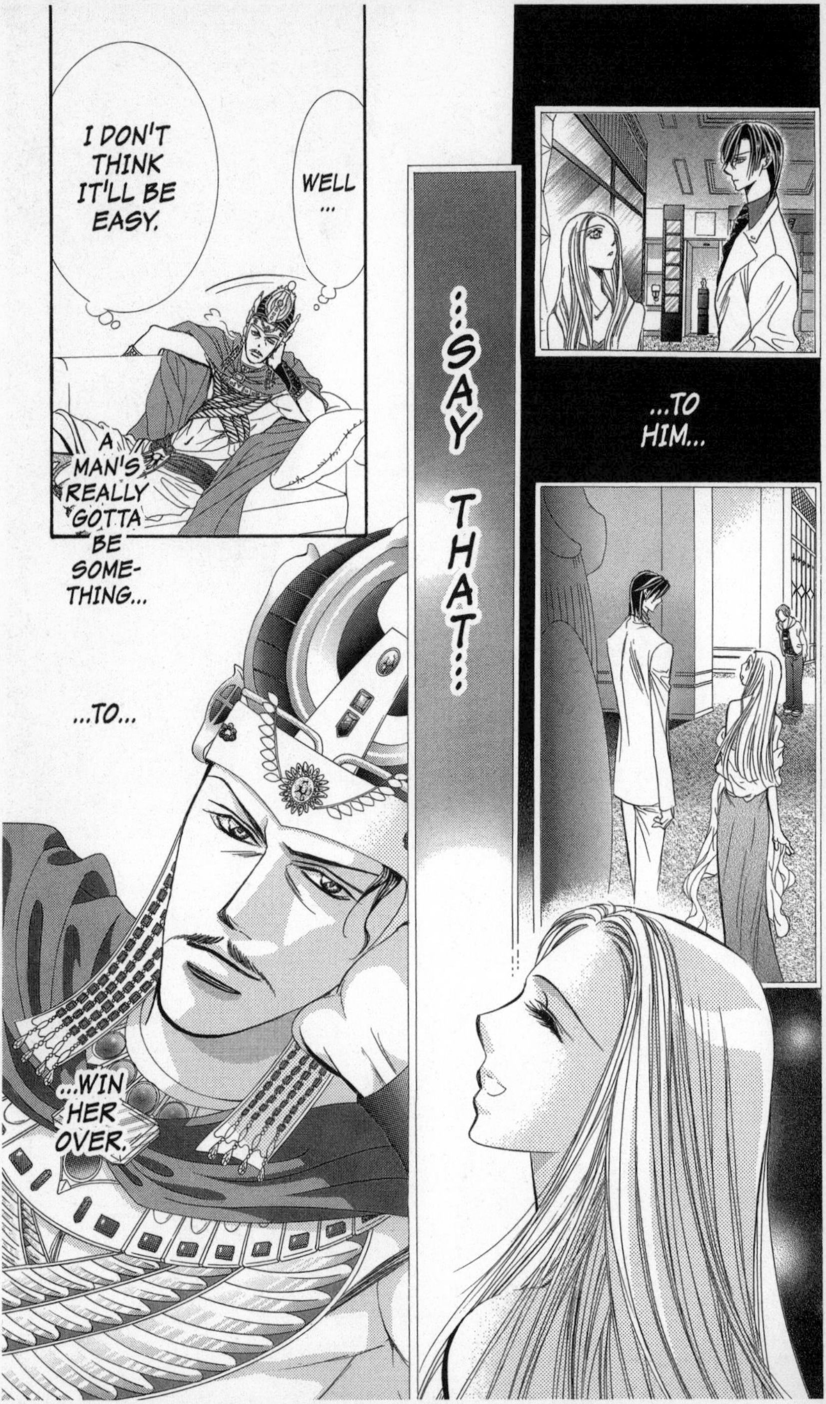
...TO HIM...
...SAY THAT...
WELL ...
I DON'T THINK IT'LL BE EASY.
A MAN'S REALLY GOTTA BE SOME-THING...
...TO...
...WIN HER OVER.

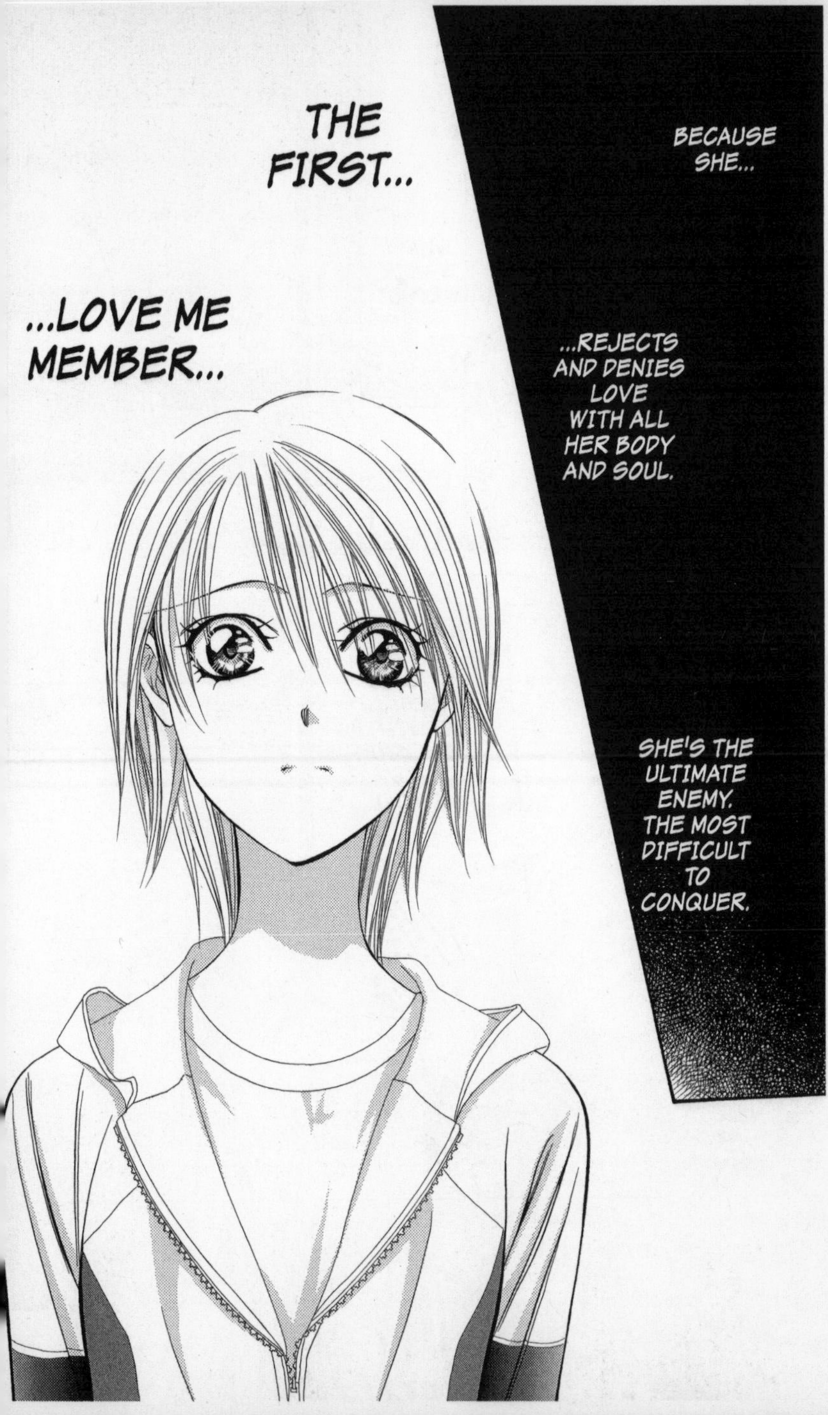
BECAUSE SHE...
THE FIRST...
...REJECTS AND DENIES LOVE WITH ALL HER BODY AND SOUL.
...LOVE ME MEMBER...
SHE'S THE ULTIMATE ENEMY. THE MOST DIFFICULT TO CONQUER.

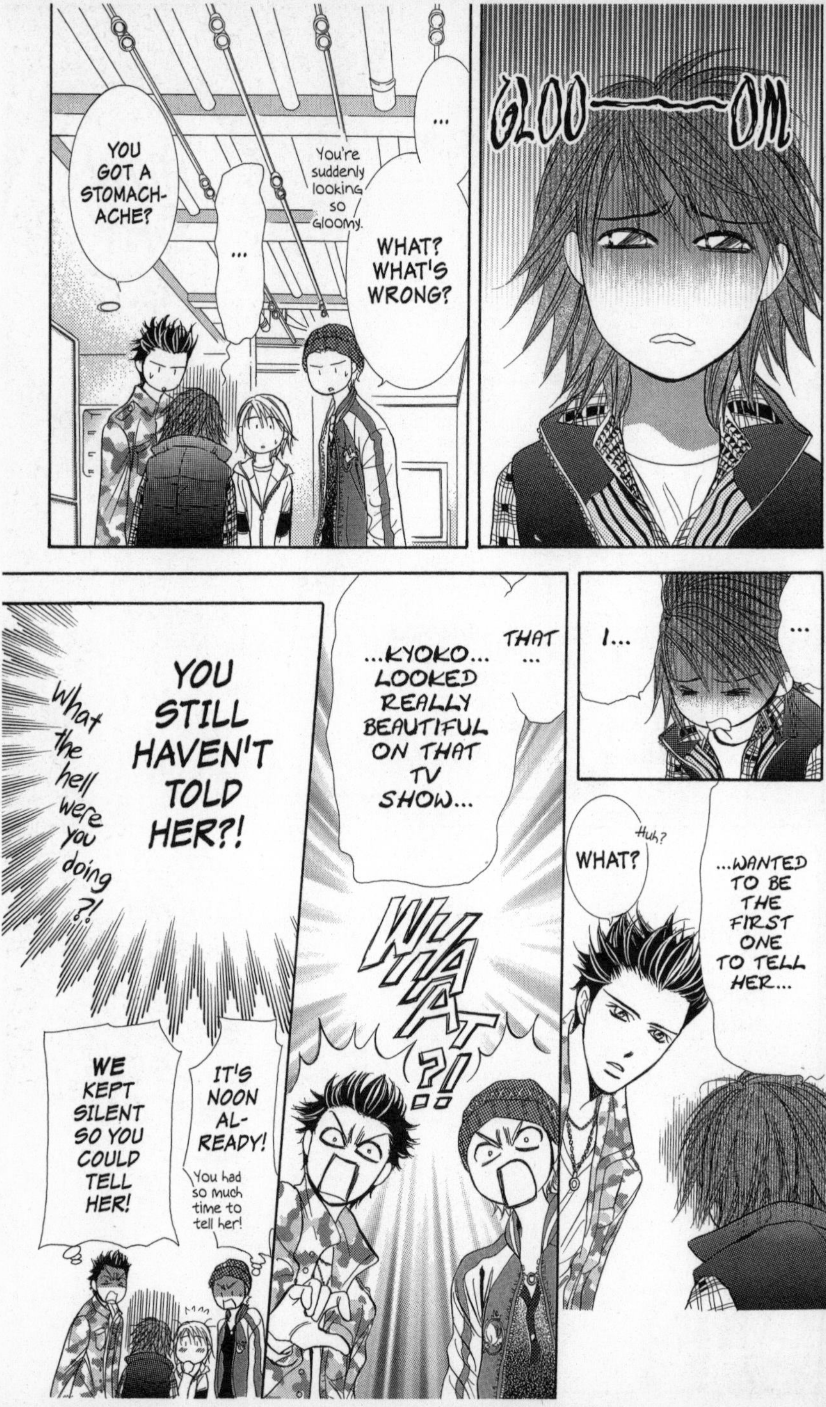
GLOO———OM
...
You're suddenly looking so gloomy.
WHAT? WHAT'S WRONG?
...
YOU GOT A STOMACH-ACHE?
...
I...
THAT ...
...KYOKO... LOOKED REALLY BEAUTIFUL ON THAT TV SHOW...
...WANTED TO BE THE FIRST ONE TO TELL HER...
WHAT?
Huh?
WHAT?!
YOU STILL HAVEN'T TOLD HER?!
What the hell were you doing?!
IT'S NOON AL-READY!
You had so much time to tell her!
WE KEPT SILENT SO YOU COULD TELL HER!
MMM

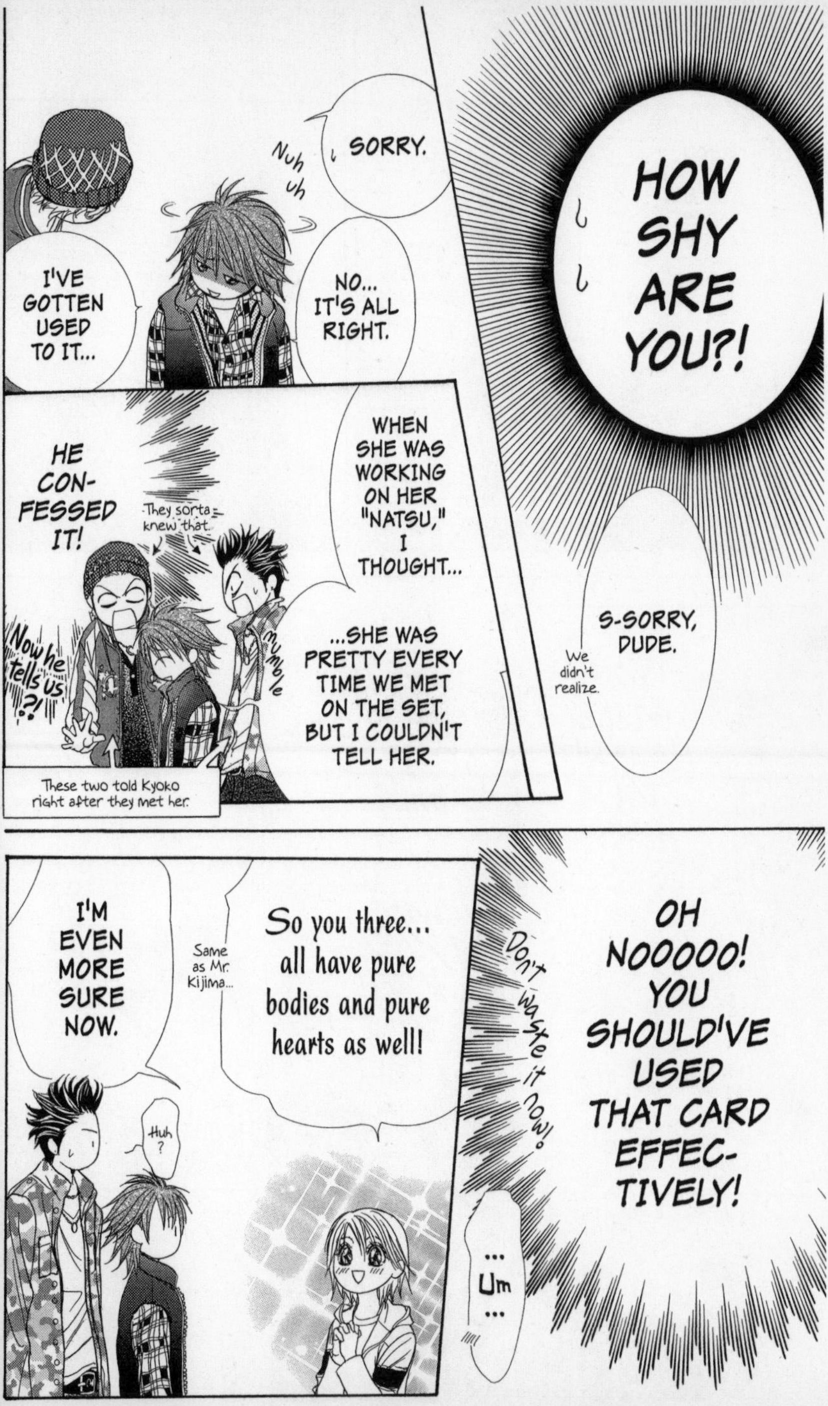
HOW SHY ARE YOU?!
S-SORRY, DUDE.
We didn't realize.
SORRY.
Nuh uh
NO... IT'S ALL RIGHT.
I'VE GOTTEN USED TO IT...
WHEN SHE WAS WORKING ON HER "NATSU," I THOUGHT...
...SHE WAS PRETTY EVERY TIME WE MET ON THE SET, BUT I COULDN'T TELL HER.
mumble
HE CON-FESSED IT!
They sorta knew that.
Now he tells us?!
These two told Kyoko right after they met her.
OH NOOOOO! YOU SHOULD'VE USED THAT CARD EFFEC-TIVELY!
Don't waste it now!
...Um...
So you three... all have pure bodies and pure hearts as well!
Same as Mr. Kijima...
I'M EVEN MORE SURE NOW.
Huh?

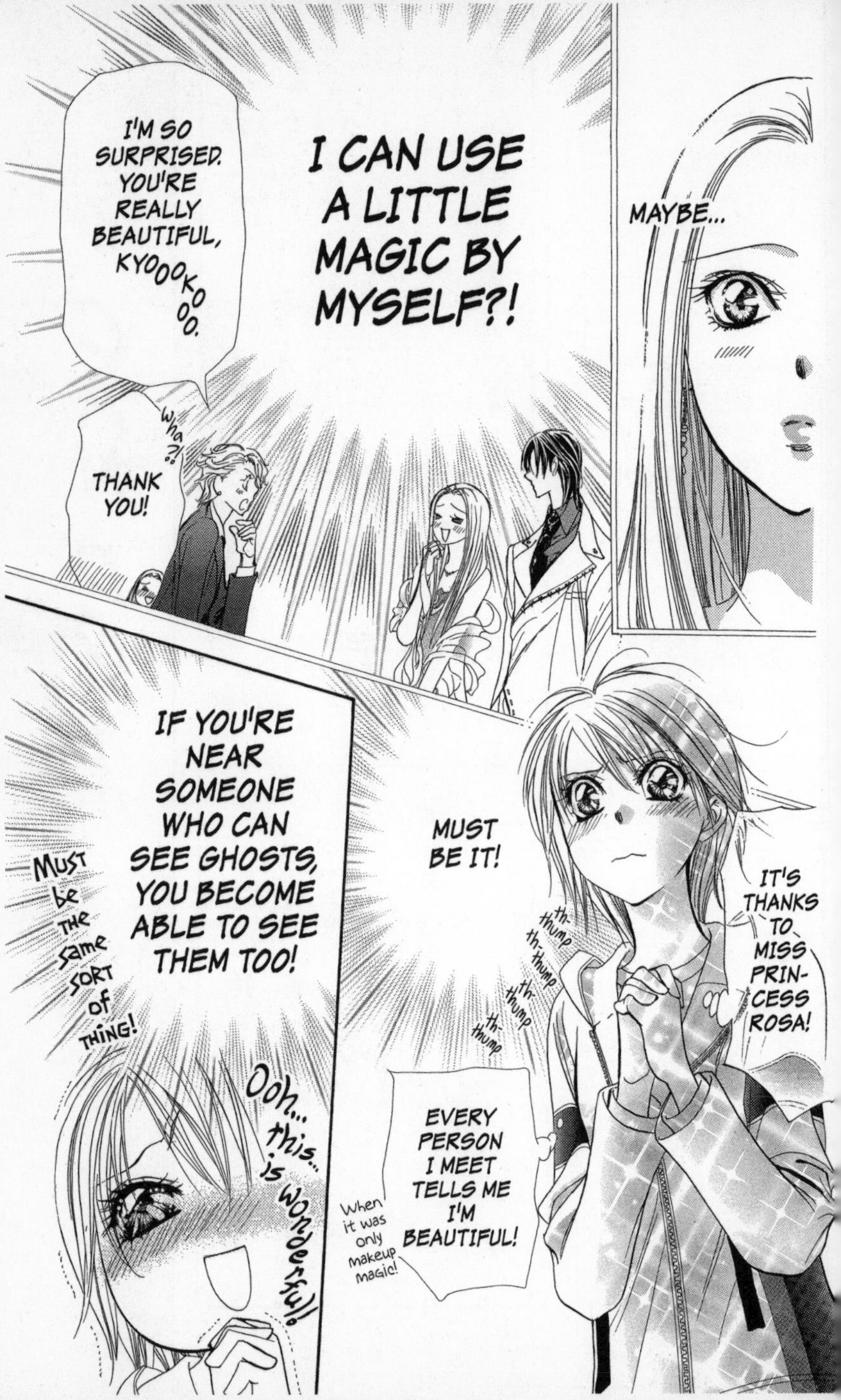
MAYBE...
I CAN USE A LITTLE MAGIC BY MYSELF?!
I'M SO SURPRISED. YOU'RE REALLY BEAUTIFUL, KYOOOKOOO.
wha?!
THANK YOU!
IT'S THANKS TO MISS PRINCESS ROSA!
MUST BE IT!
th-thump th-thump th-thump th-thump
EVERY PERSON I MEET TELLS ME I'M BEAUTIFUL!
When it was only makeup magic!
IF YOU'RE NEAR SOMEONE WHO CAN SEE GHOSTS, YOU BECOME ABLE TO SEE THEM TOO!
Must be the same sort of thing!
Ooh... this... is wonderful!

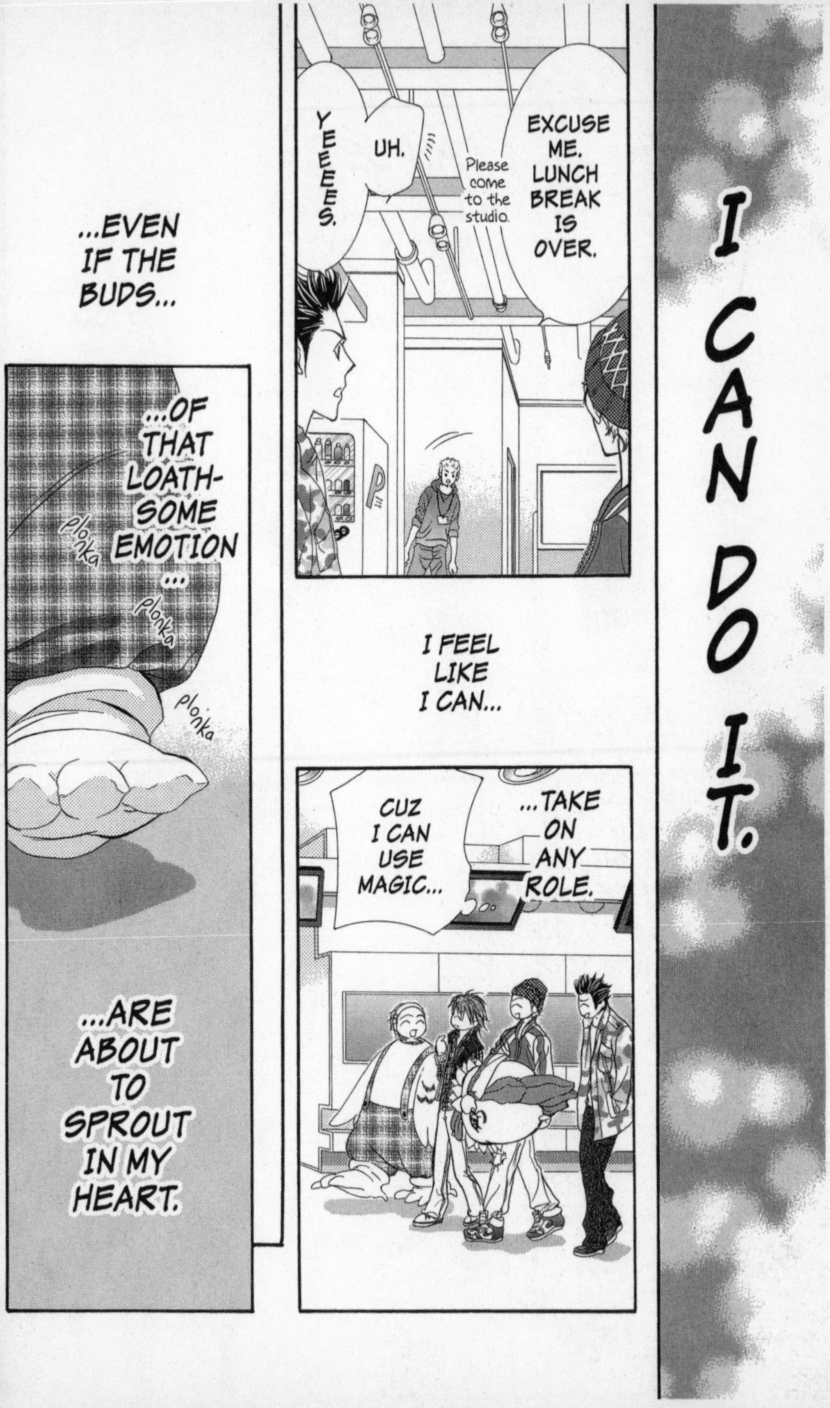
I CAN DO IT.
EXCUSE ME. LUNCH BREAK IS OVER.
Please come to the studio.
UH.
YEEEES.
I FEEL LIKE I CAN...
...TAKE ON ANY ROLE.
CUZ I CAN USE MAGIC...
...EVEN IF THE BUDS...
...OF THAT LOATH-SOME EMOTION...
plonka
plonka
plonka
...ARE ABOUT TO SPROUT IN MY HEART.

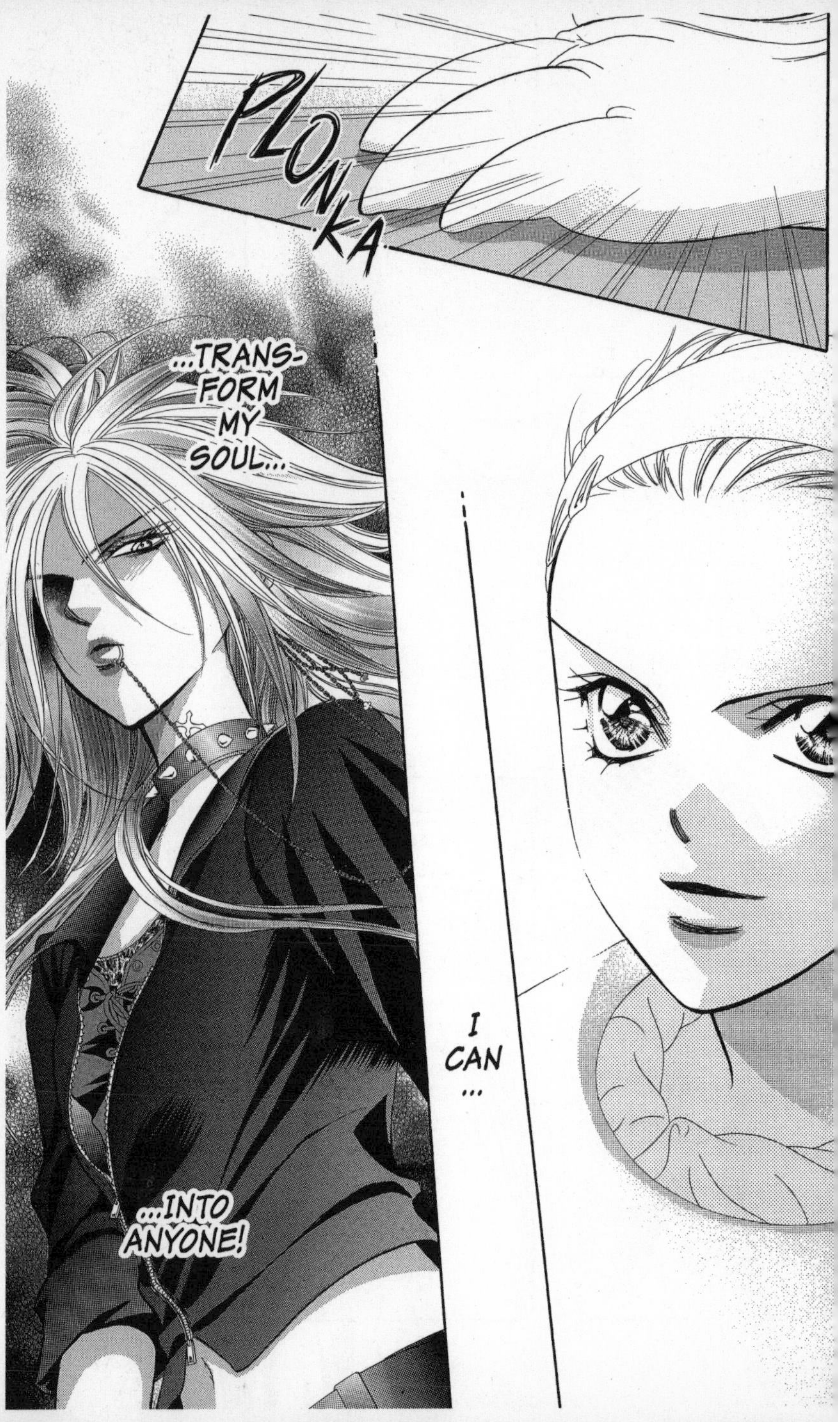
PLONKA
I CAN...
...TRANS-FORM MY SOUL...
...INTO ANYONE!

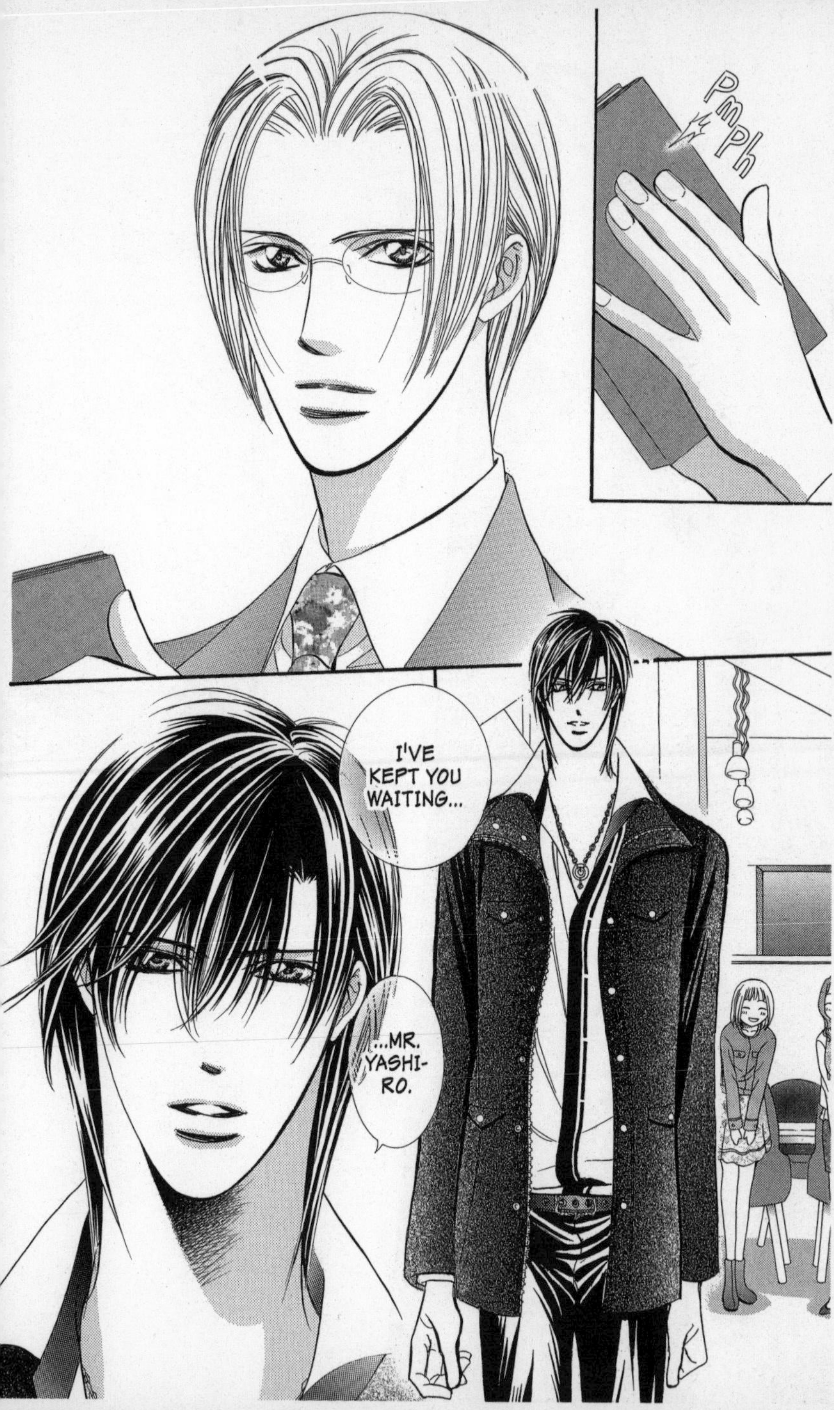
PmPh
I'VE KEPT YOU WAITING...
...MR. YASHIRO.

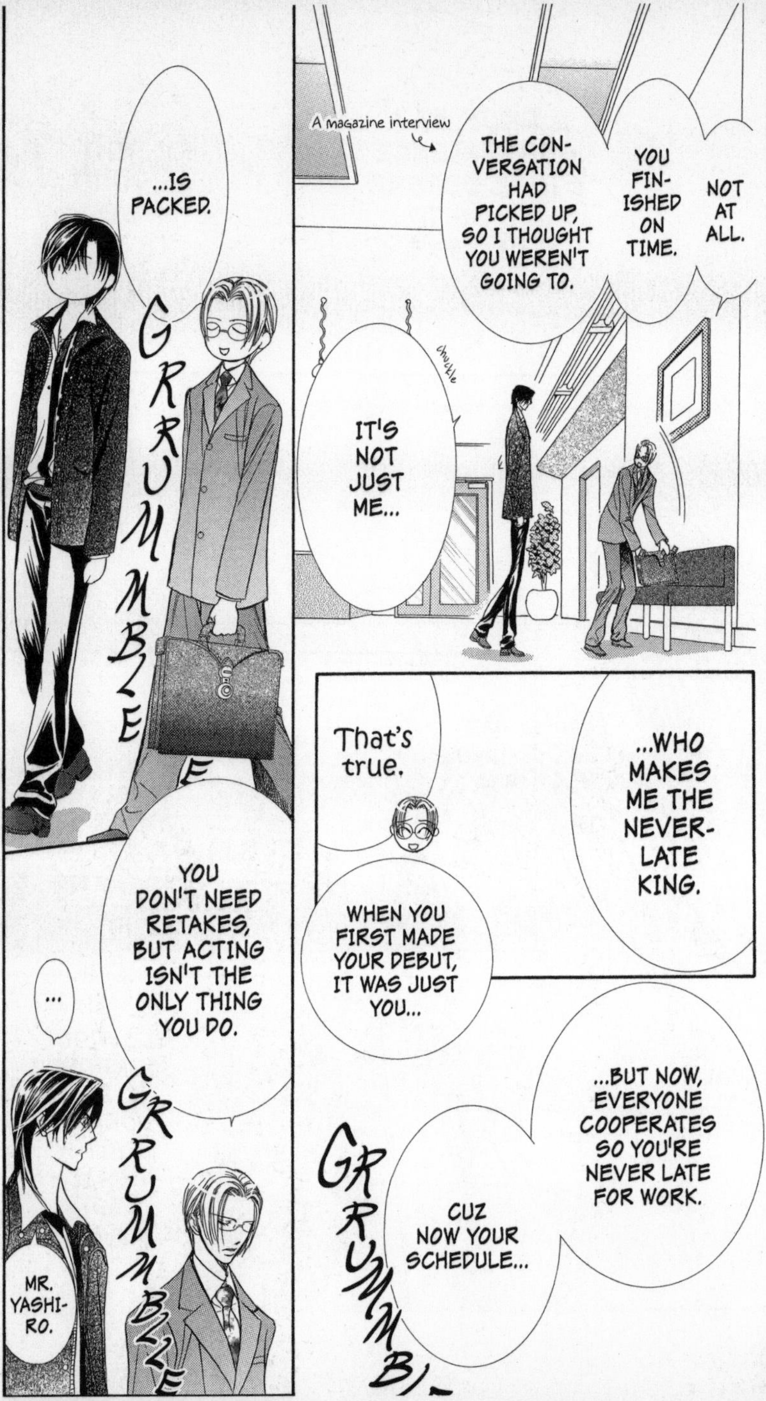
YOU FIN-ISHED ON TIME.
NOT AT ALL.
A magazine interview
THE CON-VERSATION HAD PICKED UP, SO I THOUGHT YOU WEREN'T GOING TO.
chuckle
IT'S NOT JUST ME...
...WHO MAKES ME THE NEVER-LATE KING.
That's true.
WHEN YOU FIRST MADE YOUR DEBUT, IT WAS JUST YOU...
...BUT NOW, EVERYONE COOPERATES SO YOU'RE NEVER LATE FOR WORK.
CUZ NOW YOUR SCHEDULE...
GRUMMBL
...IS PACKED.
GRUMMBLE
YOU DON'T NEED RETAKES, BUT ACTING ISN'T THE ONLY THING YOU DO.
...
GRUMMBLE
MR. YASHI-RO.

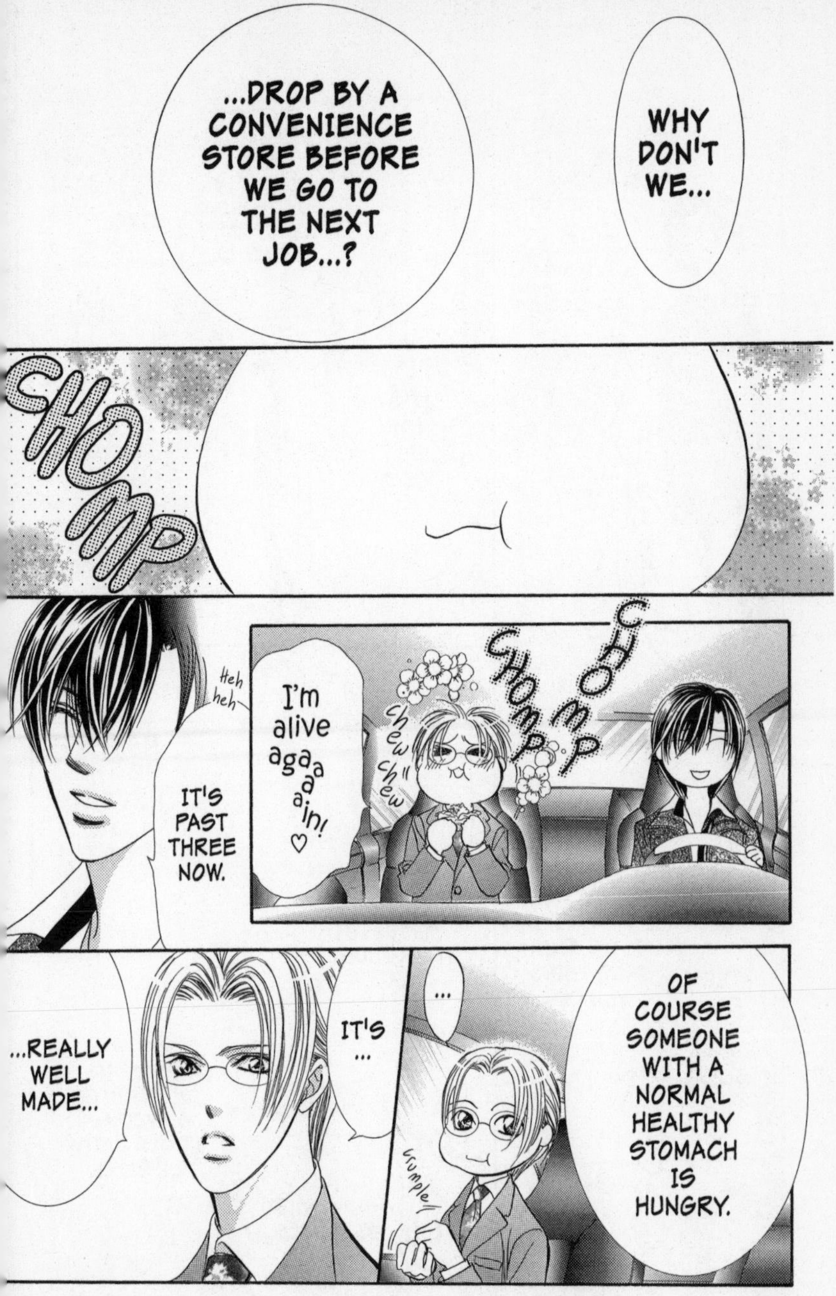
WHY DON'T WE...
...DROP BY A CONVENIENCE STORE BEFORE WE GO TO THE NEXT JOB...?
CHOMP
CHOMP CHOMP
chew chew
I'm alive agaaaain! ♡
Heh heh
IT'S PAST THREE NOW.
OF COURSE SOMEONE WITH A NORMAL HEALTHY STOMACH IS HUNGRY.
...
crumple
IT'S ...
...REALLY WELL MADE...

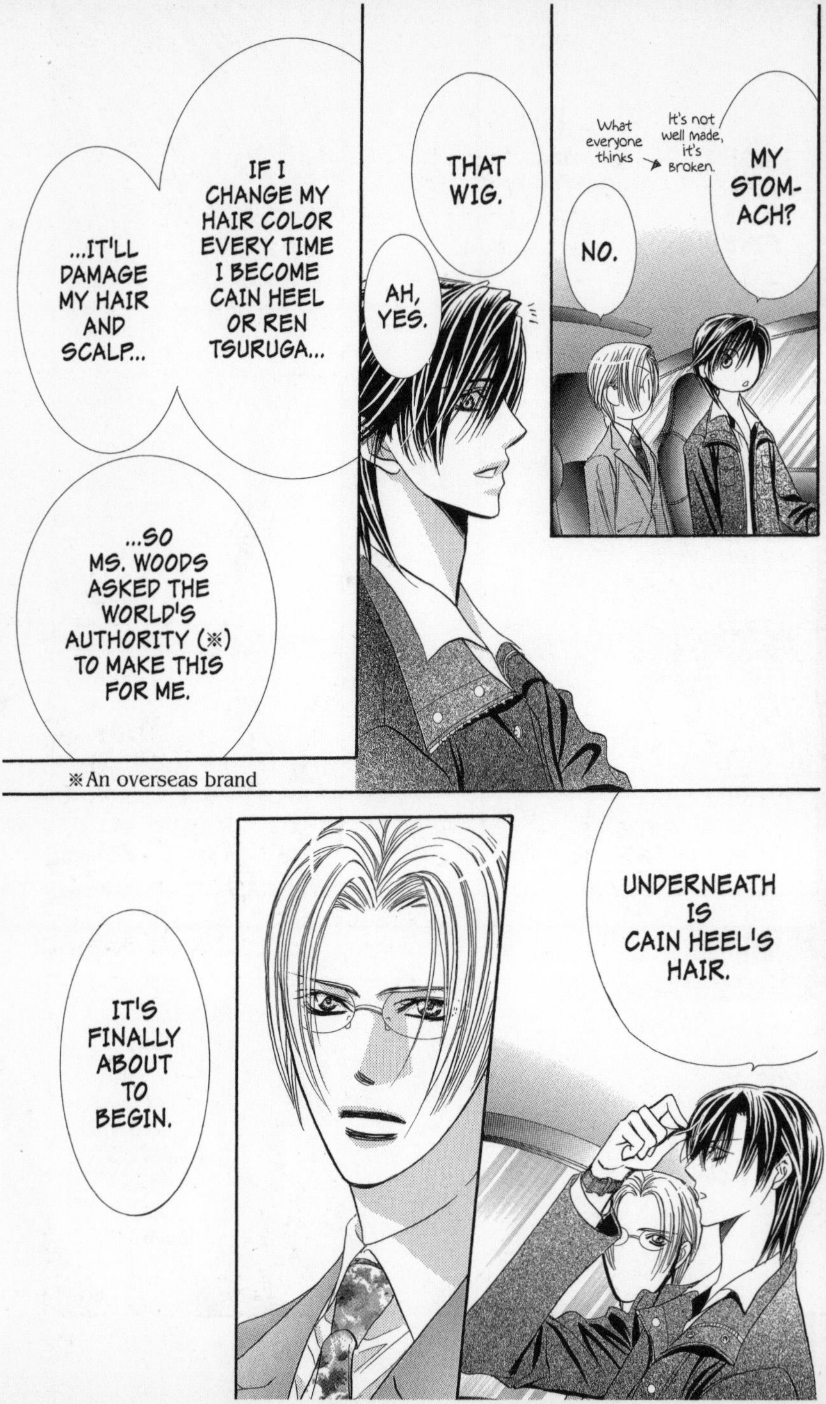
MY STOM-ACH?
It's not well made, it's broken.
What everyone thinks
NO.
THAT WIG.
AH, YES.
IF I CHANGE MY HAIR COLOR EVERY TIME I BECOME CAIN HEEL OR REN TSURUGA...
...IT'LL DAMAGE MY HAIR AND SCALP...
...SO MS. WOODS ASKED THE WORLD'S AUTHORITY (※) TO MAKE THIS FOR ME.
※An overseas brand
UNDERNEATH IS CAIN HEEL'S HAIR.
IT'S FINALLY ABOUT TO BEGIN.

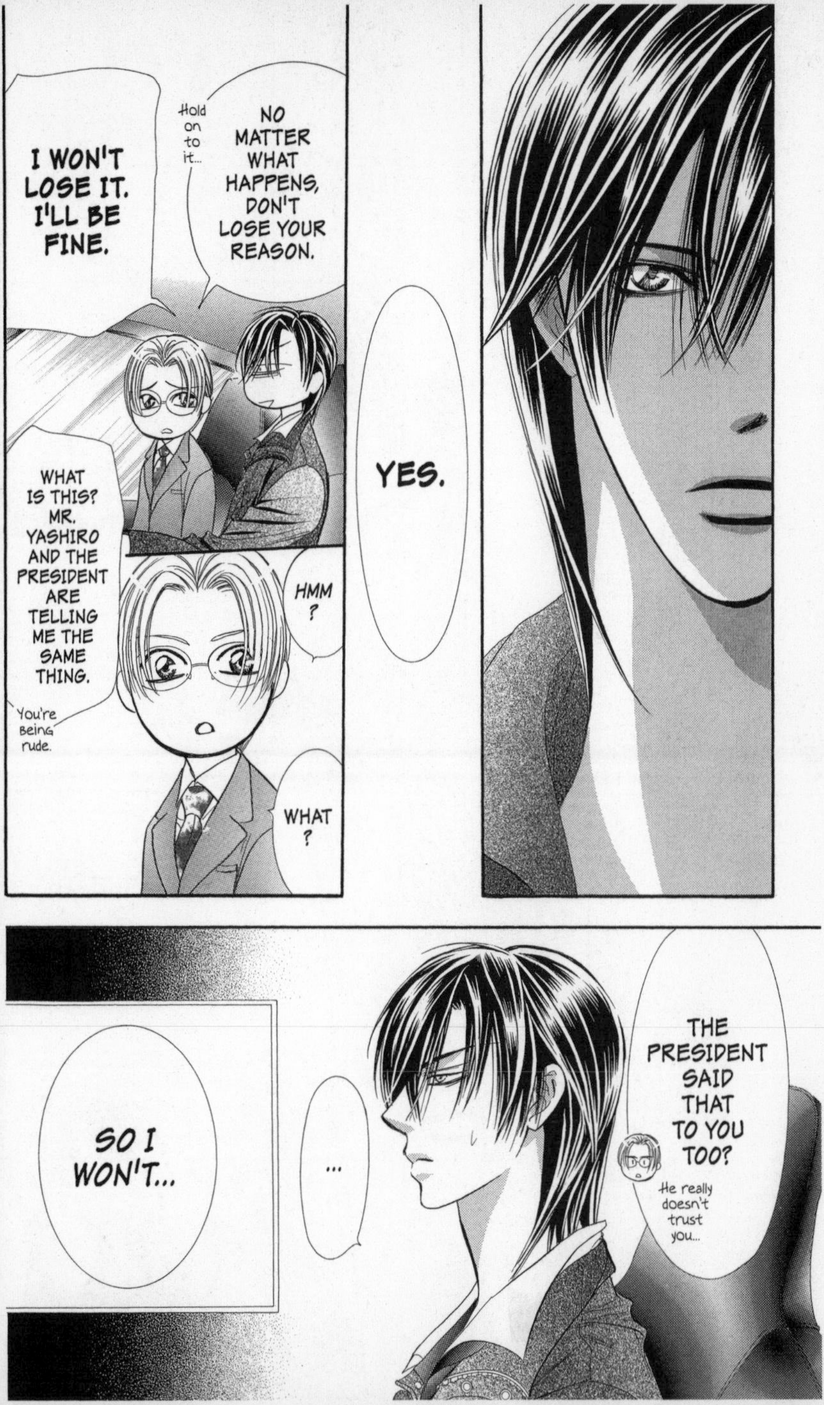
YES.
NO MATTER WHAT HAPPENS, DON'T LOSE YOUR REASON.
Hold on to it...
I WON'T LOSE IT. I'LL BE FINE.
HMM?
WHAT IS THIS? MR. YASHIRO AND THE PRESIDENT ARE TELLING ME THE SAME THING.
You're being rude.
WHAT?
THE PRESIDENT SAID THAT TO YOU TOO?
He really doesn't trust you...
...
SO I WON'T...

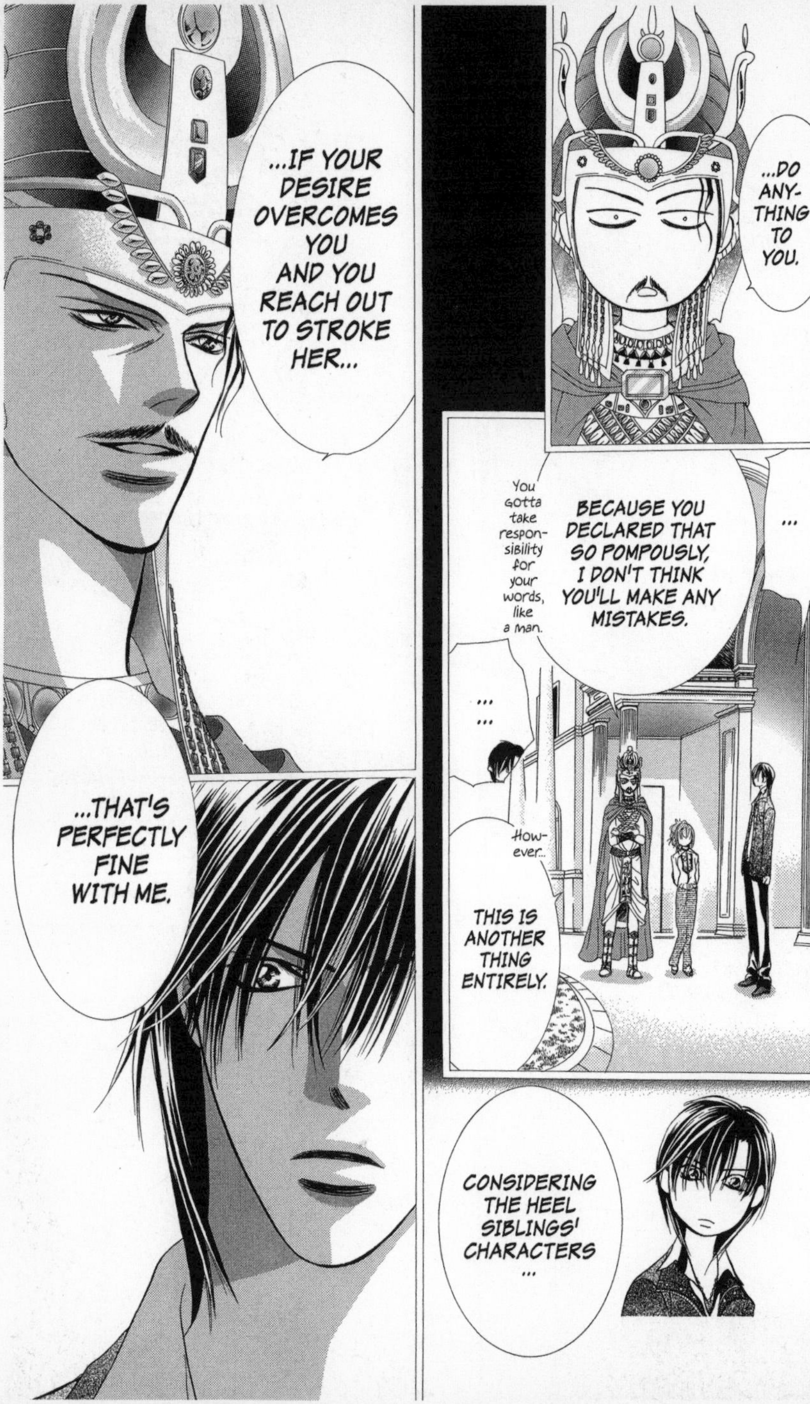
...DO ANY-THING TO YOU.
...
BECAUSE YOU DECLARED THAT SO POMPOUSLY, I DON'T THINK YOU'LL MAKE ANY MISTAKES.
You gotta take respon-sibility for your words, like a man.
...
...
How-ever...
THIS IS ANOTHER THING ENTIRELY.
CONSIDERING THE HEEL SIBLINGS' CHARACTERS ...
...IF YOUR DESIRE OVERCOMES YOU AND YOU REACH OUT TO STROKE HER...
...THAT'S PERFECTLY FINE WITH ME.

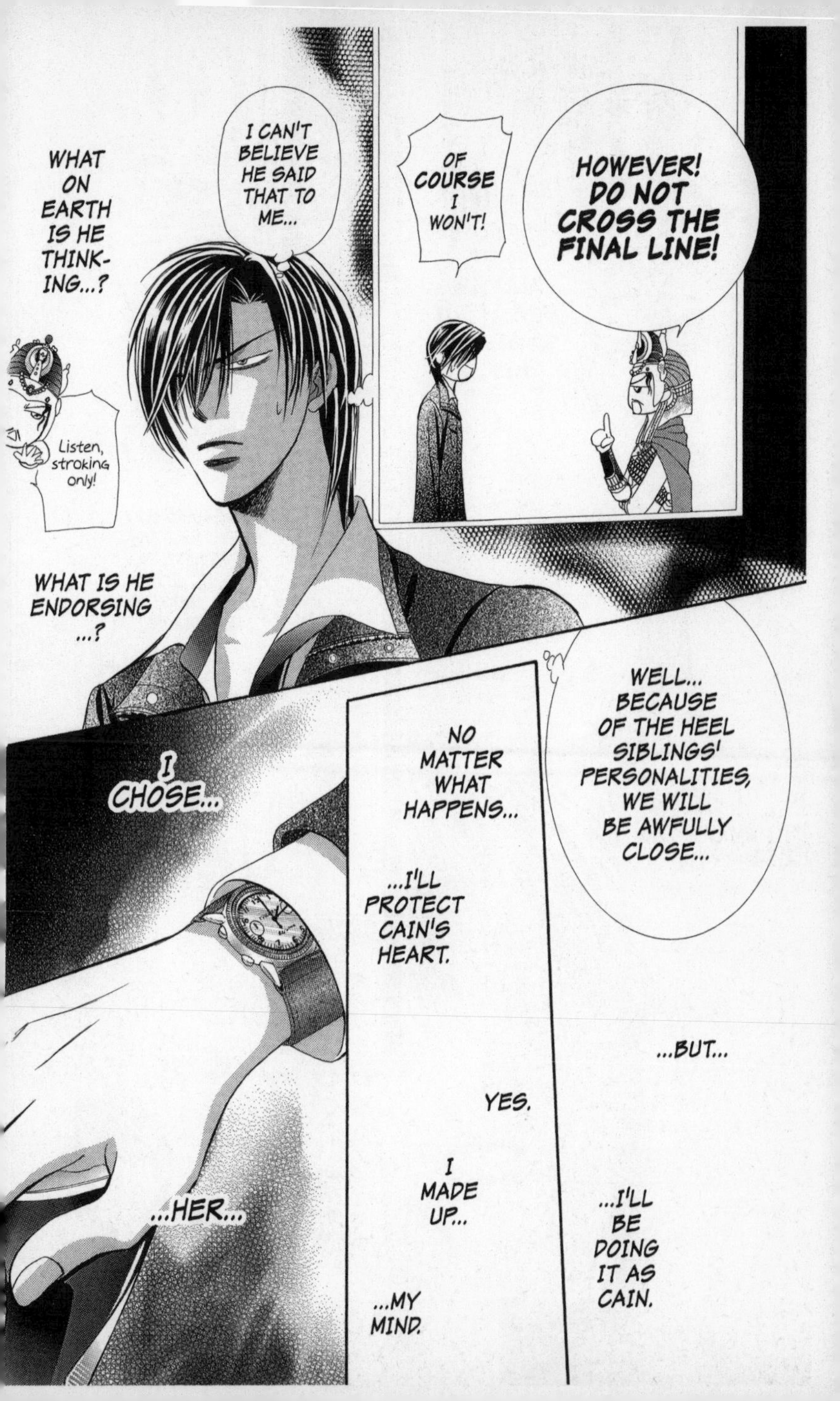
HOWEVER! DO NOT CROSS THE FINAL LINE!
OF COURSE I WON'T!
I CAN'T BELIEVE HE SAID THAT TO ME...
WHAT ON EARTH IS HE THINKING...?
Listen, stroking only!
WHAT IS HE ENDORSING ...?
WELL... BECAUSE OF THE HEEL SIBLINGS' PERSONALITIES, WE WILL BE AWFULLY CLOSE...
NO MATTER WHAT HAPPENS...
...I'LL PROTECT CAIN'S HEART.
I CHOSE...
...BUT...
YES.
...I'LL BE DOING IT AS CAIN.
I MADE UP...
...MY MIND.
...HER...

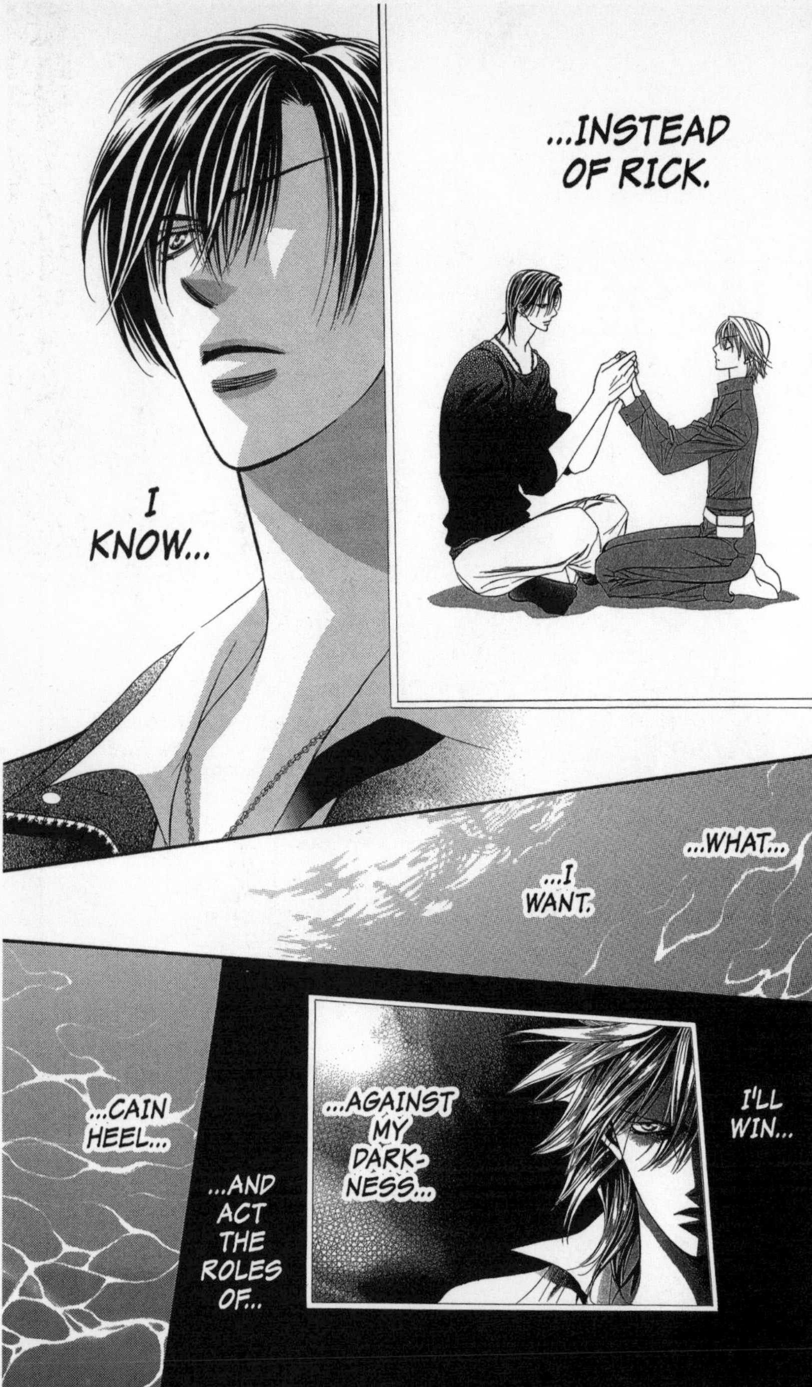
...INSTEAD OF RICK.
I KNOW...
...WHAT...
...I WANT.
I'LL WIN...
...AGAINST MY DARK-NESS...
...AND ACT THE ROLES OF...
...CAIN HEEL...

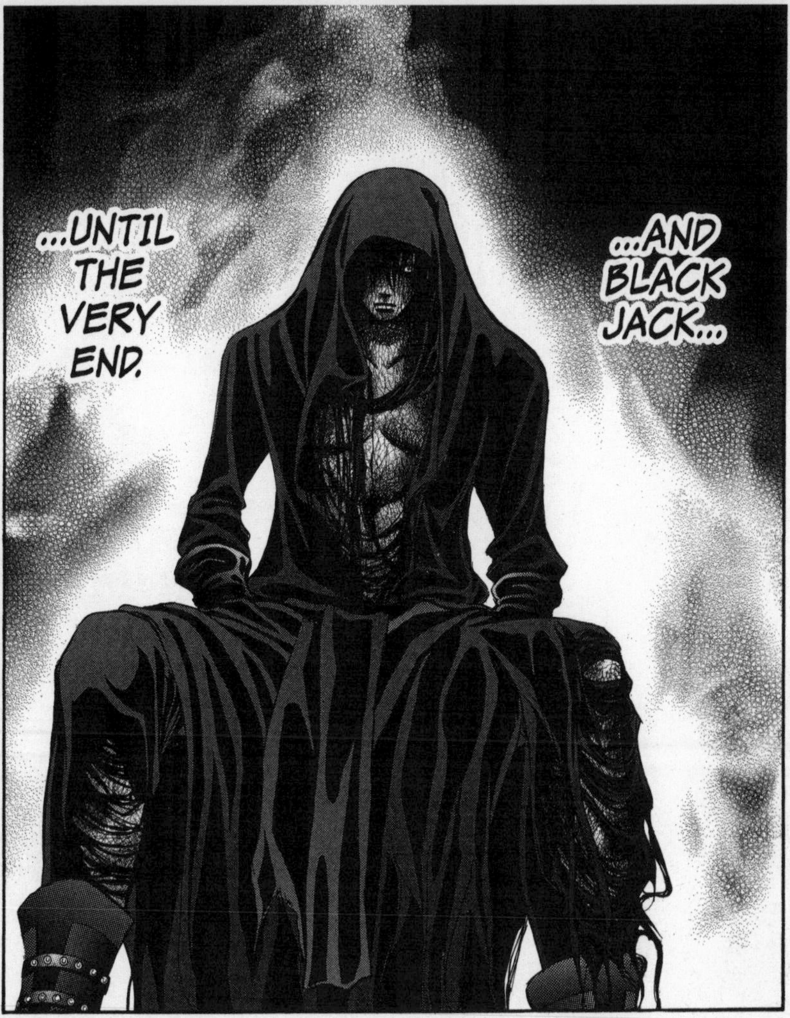
...AND BLACK JACK...
...UNTIL THE VERY END.

AND I'LL DO IT PERFECTLY.

End of Act 174

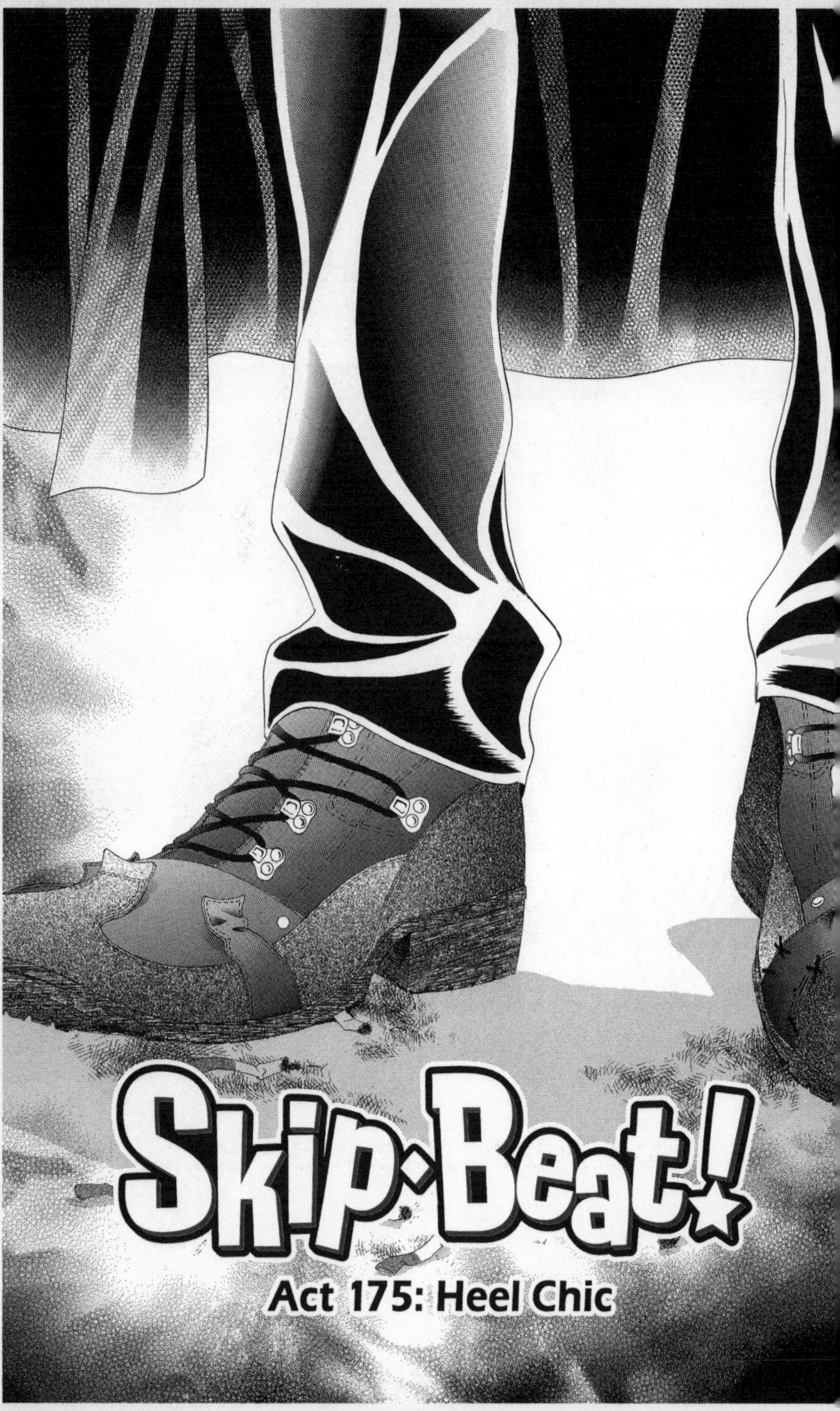
Skip·Beat!
Act 175: Heel Chic

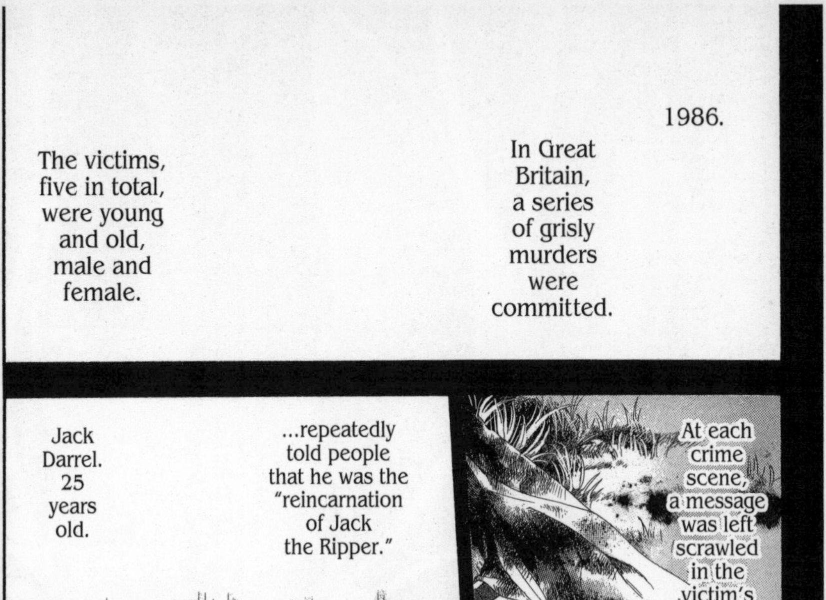
1986.
In Great Britain, a series of grisly murders were committed.
The victims, five in total, were young and old, male and female.
At each crime scene, a message was left scrawled in the victim's blood...
...and their hearts were missing. The perpetrator of these bizarre and lust-fueled murders...
...repeatedly told people that he was the "reincarnation of Jack the Ripper."
Jack Darrel. 25 years old.
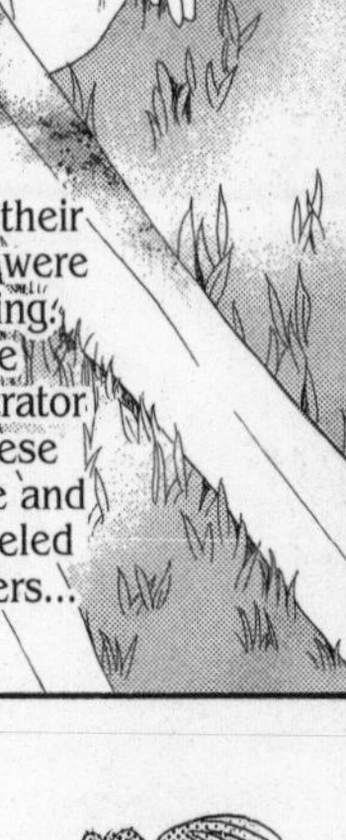

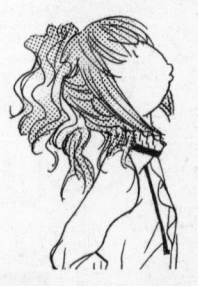

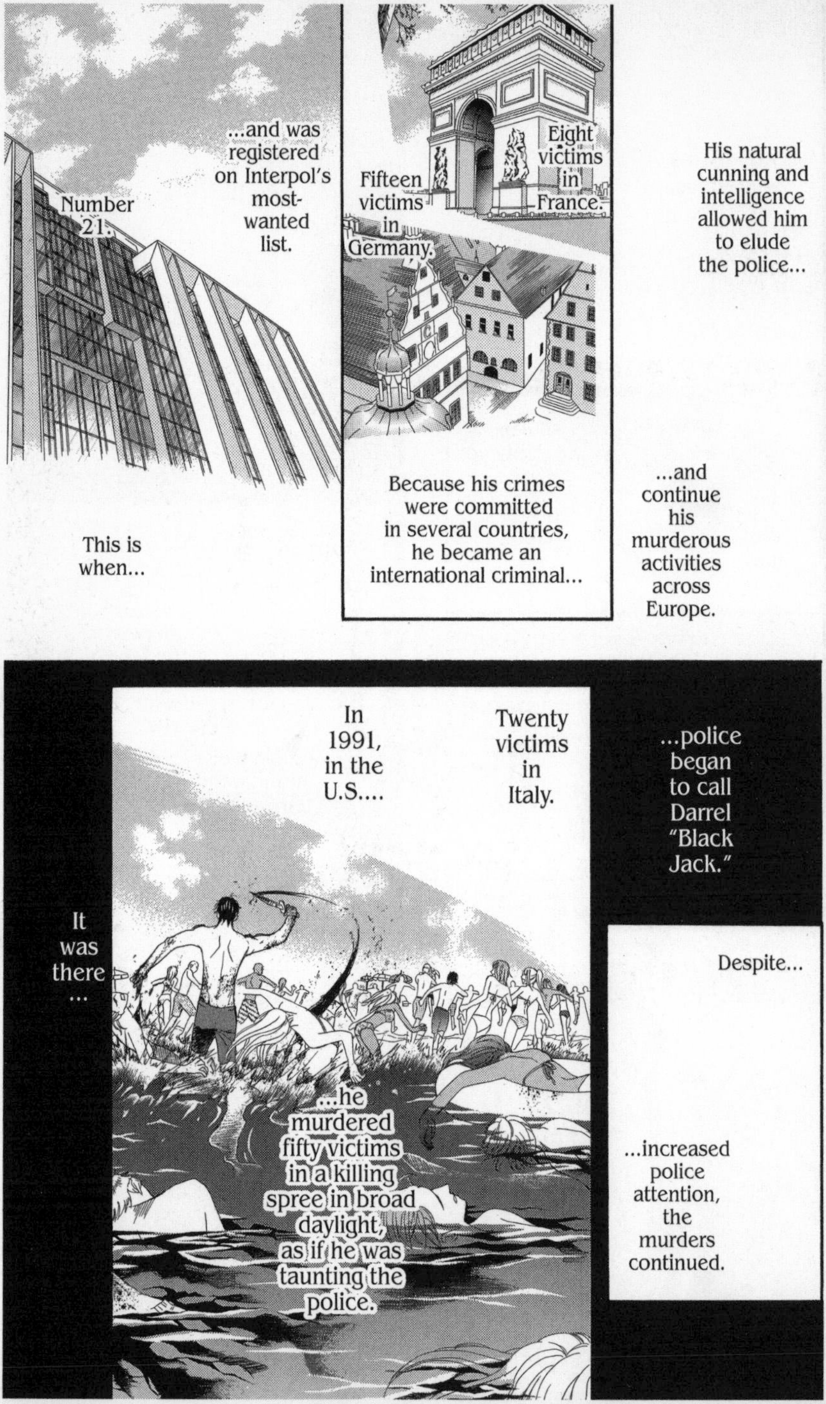
His natural cunning and intelligence allowed him to elude the police...
...and continue his murderous activities across Europe.
Eight victims in France.
Fifteen victims in Germany.
Because his crimes were committed in several countries, he became an international criminal...
...and was registered on Interpol's most-wanted list.
Number 21.
This is when...
...police began to call Darrel "Black Jack."
Despite...
...increased police attention, the murders continued.
Twenty victims in Italy.
In 1991, in the U.S....
...he murdered fifty victims in a killing spree in broad daylight, as if he was taunting the police.
It was there...

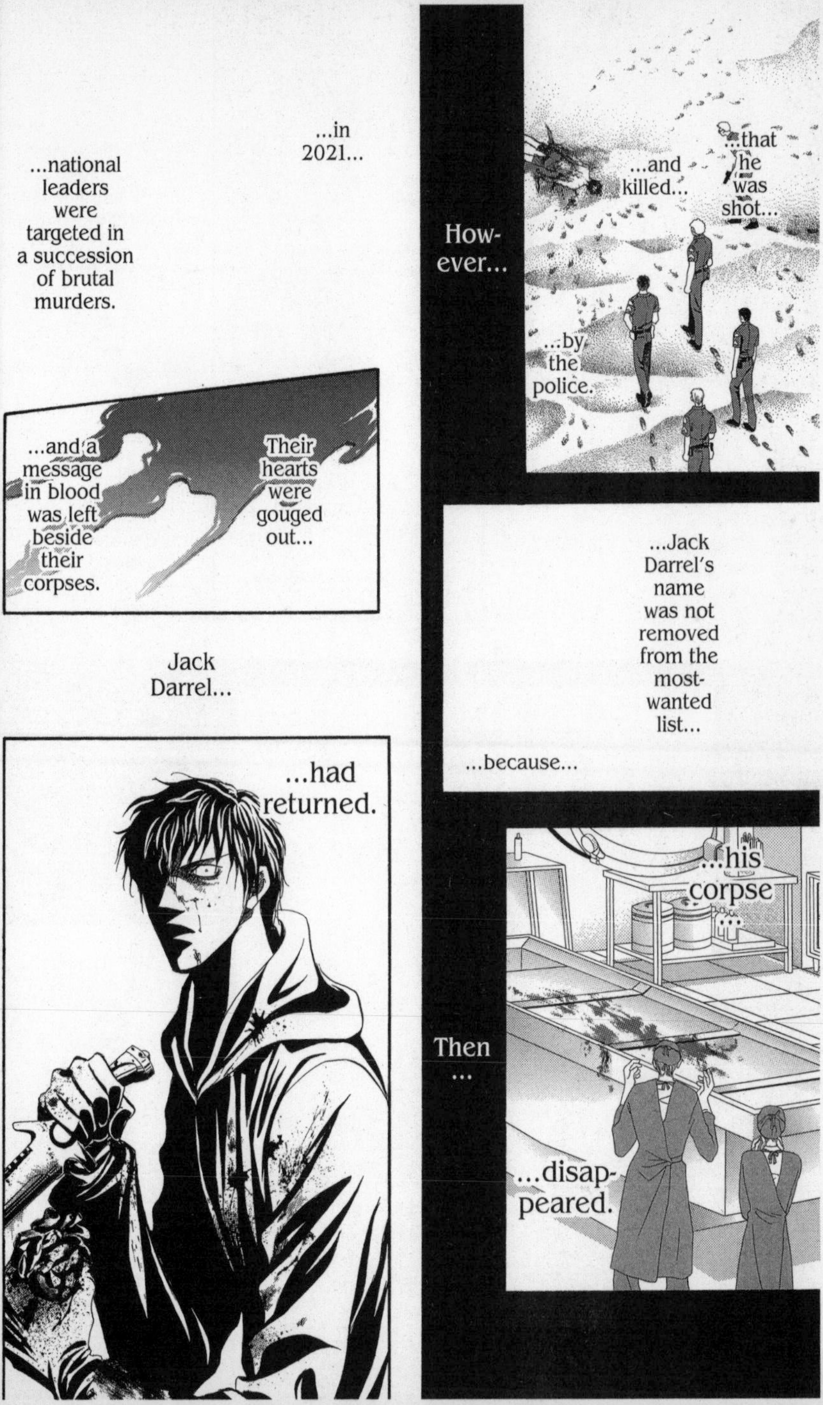

How-ever...
...that he was shot...
...and killed...
...by the police.
...Jack Darrel's name was not removed from the most-wanted list...
...because...
Then ...
...his corpse ...
...disap-peared.
...in 2021...
...national leaders were targeted in a succession of brutal murders.
Their hearts were gouged out...
...and a message in blood was left beside their corpses.
Jack Darrel...
...had returned.

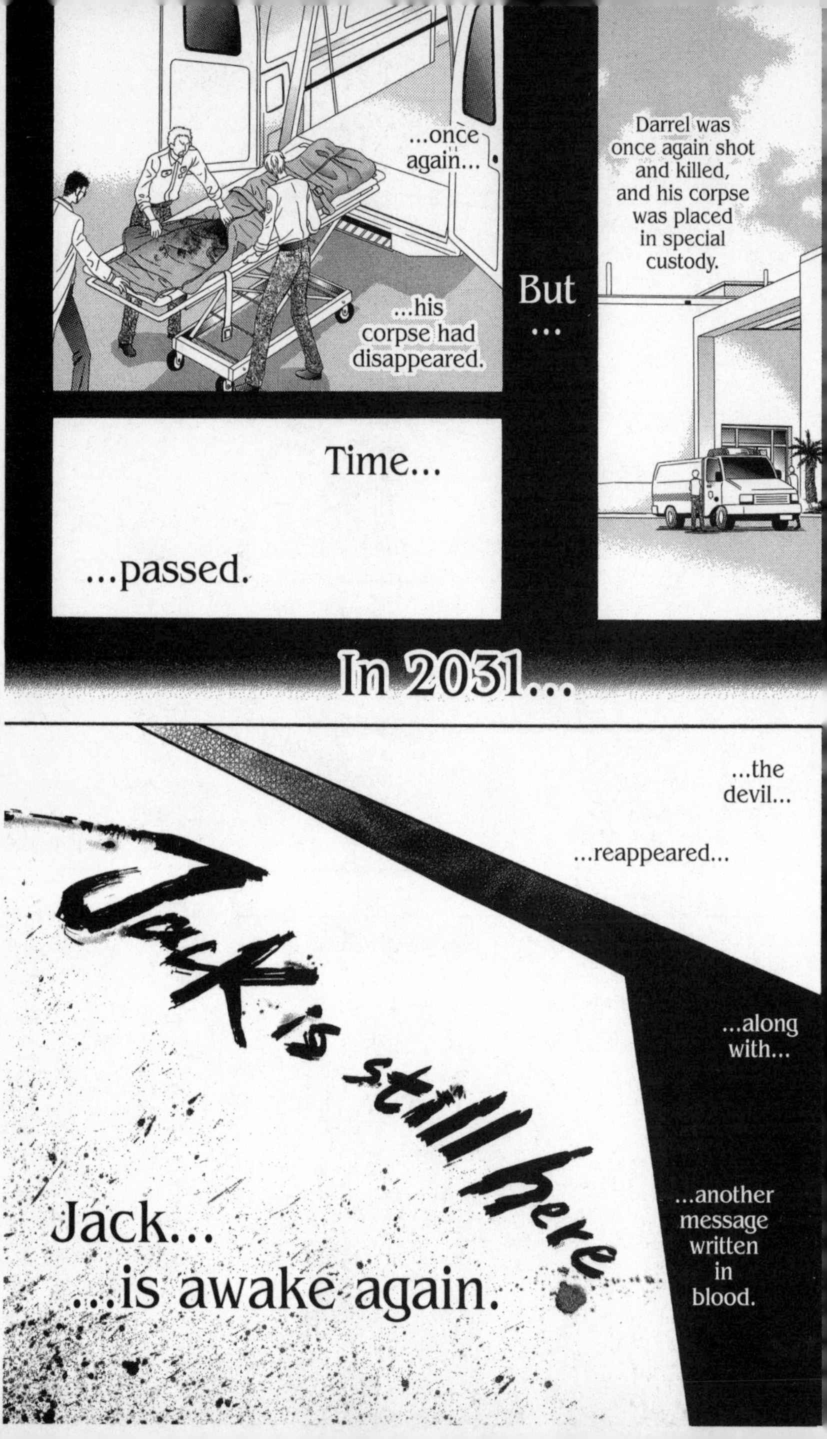
Darrel was once again shot and killed, and his corpse was placed in special custody.
But ...
...once again...
...his corpse had disappeared.
Time...
...passed.
In 2031...
...the devil...
...reappeared...
...along with...
...another message written in blood.
Jack is still here
Jack...
...is awake again.

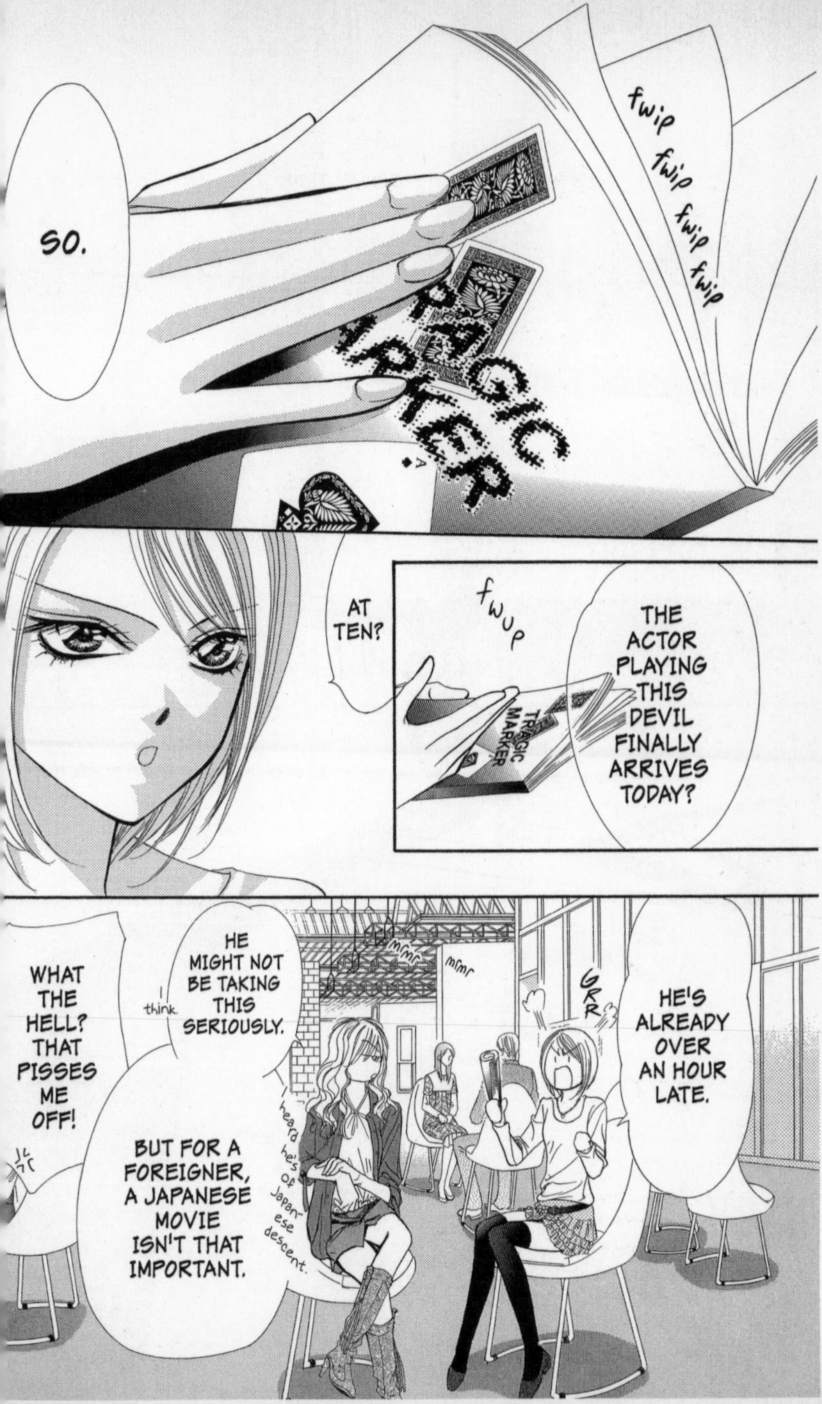
fwip fwip fwip fwip
TRAGIC MARKER
SO.
THE ACTOR PLAYING THIS DEVIL FINALLY ARRIVES TODAY?
fwup
TRAGIC MARKER
AT TEN?
HE'S ALREADY OVER AN HOUR LATE.
GRR
mrmr
mrmr
HE MIGHT NOT BE TAKING THIS SERIOUSLY.
I think.
I heard he's of Japanese descent.
BUT FOR A FOREIGNER, A JAPANESE MOVIE ISN'T THAT IMPORTANT.
WHAT THE HELL? THAT PISSES ME OFF!

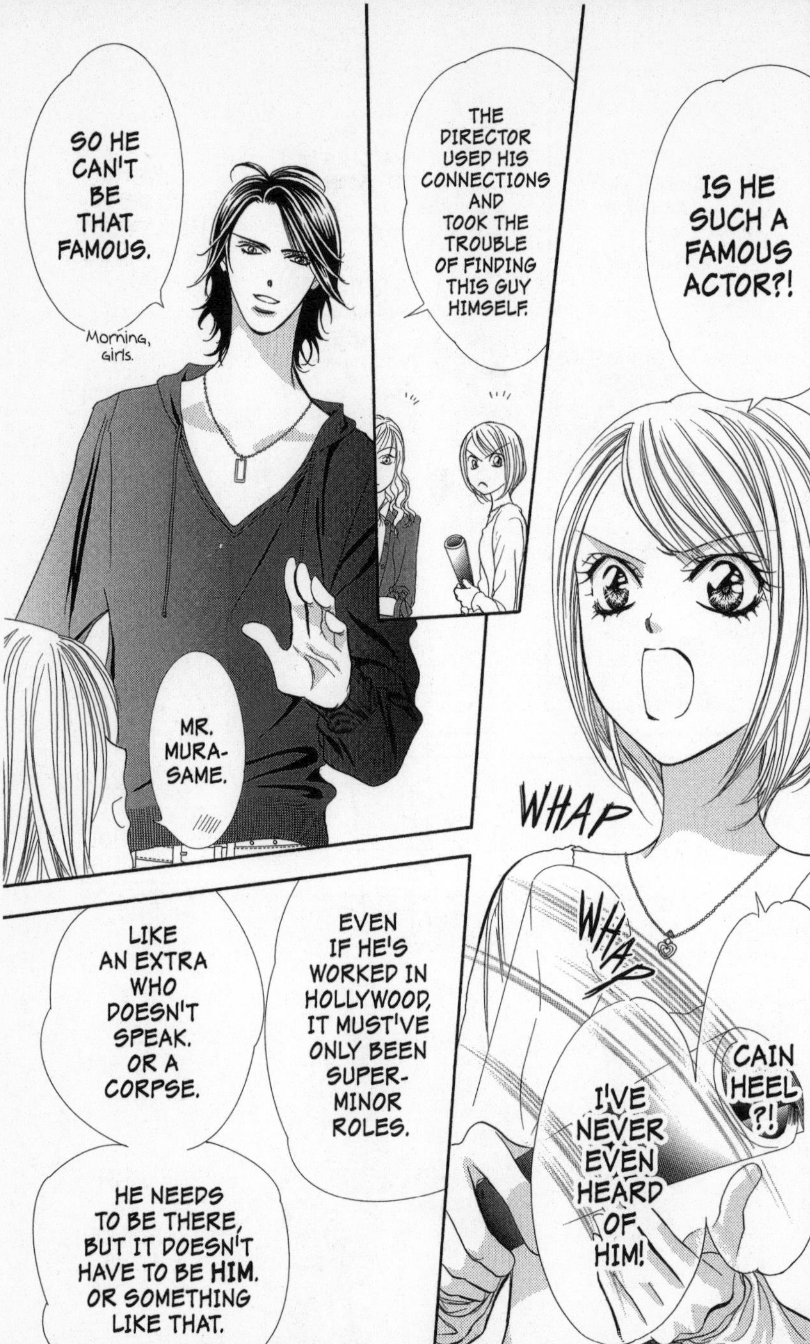
IS HE SUCH A FAMOUS ACTOR?!
WHAP
WHAP
CAIN HEEL?!
I'VE NEVER EVEN HEARD OF HIM!
THE DIRECTOR USED HIS CONNECTIONS AND TOOK THE TROUBLE OF FINDING THIS GUY HIMSELF.
SO HE CAN'T BE THAT FAMOUS.
Morning, girls.
MR. MURA-SAME.
EVEN IF HE'S WORKED IN HOLLYWOOD, IT MUST'VE ONLY BEEN SUPER-MINOR ROLES.
LIKE AN EXTRA WHO DOESN'T SPEAK. OR A CORPSE.
HE NEEDS TO BE THERE, BUT IT DOESN'T HAVE TO BE HIM. OR SOMETHING LIKE THAT.

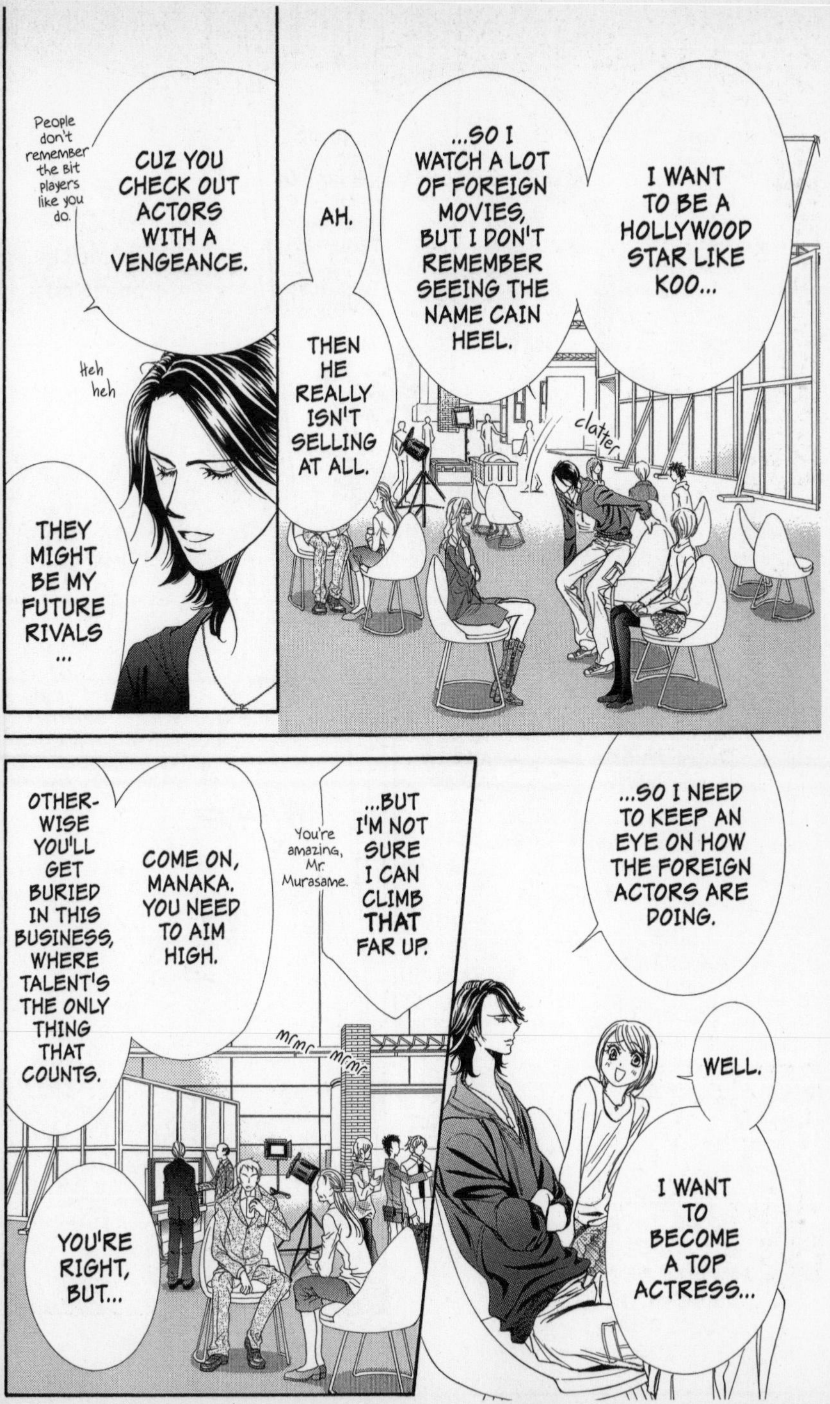
I WANT TO BE A HOLLYWOOD STAR LIKE KOO...
...SO I WATCH A LOT OF FOREIGN MOVIES, BUT I DON'T REMEMBER SEEING THE NAME CAIN HEEL.
AH.
THEN HE REALLY ISN'T SELLING AT ALL.
clatter
CUZ YOU CHECK OUT ACTORS WITH A VENGEANCE.
People don't remember the bit players like you do.
Heh heh
THEY MIGHT BE MY FUTURE RIVALS ...
WELL.
I WANT TO BECOME A TOP ACTRESS...
...SO I NEED TO KEEP AN EYE ON HOW THE FOREIGN ACTORS ARE DOING.
COME ON, MANAKA. YOU NEED TO AIM HIGH.
OTHER-WISE YOU'LL GET BURIED IN THIS BUSINESS, WHERE TALENT'S THE ONLY THING THAT COUNTS.
YOU'RE RIGHT, BUT...
...BUT I'M NOT SURE I CAN CLIMB THAT FAR UP.
You're amazing, Mr. Murasame.
mrmr mrmr

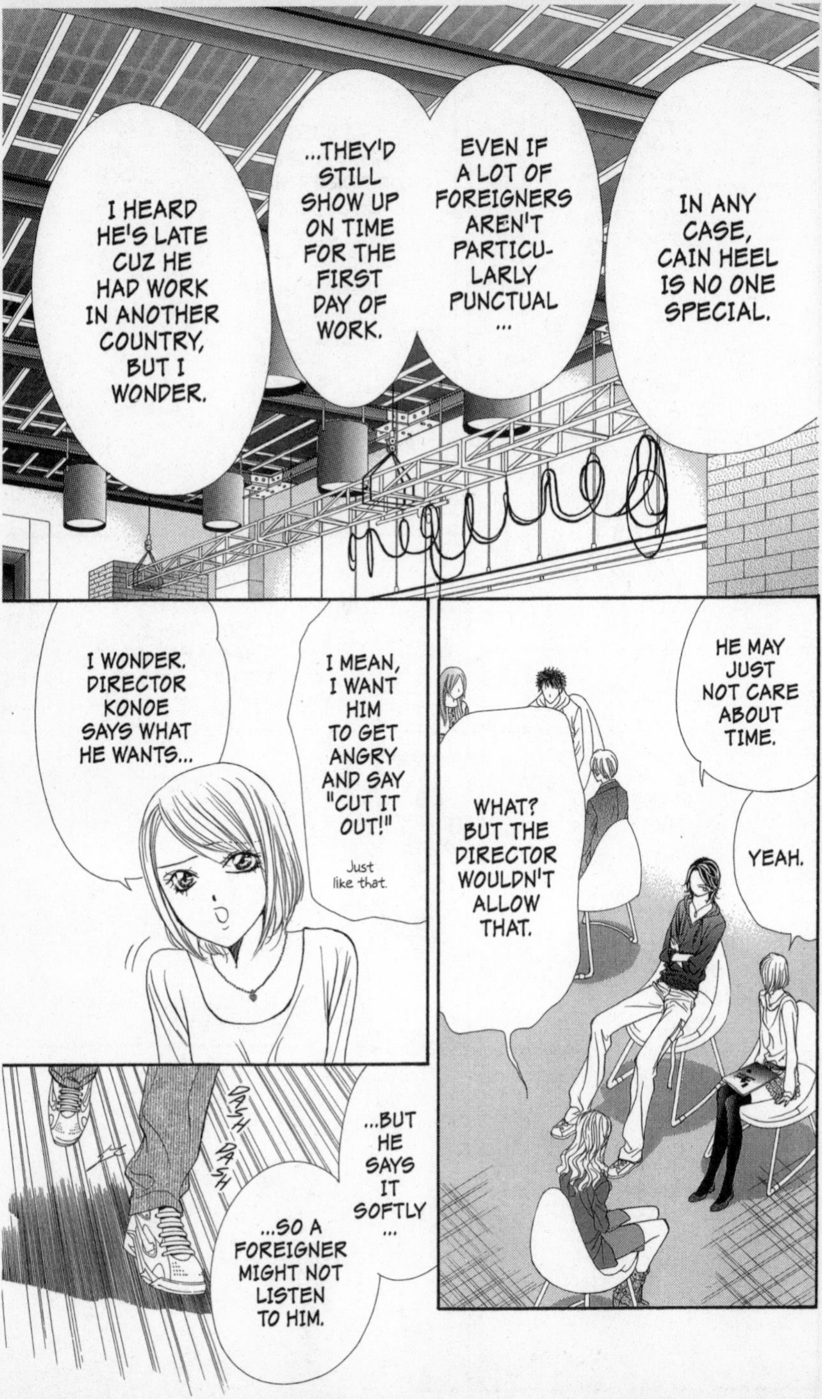
IN ANY CASE, CAIN HEEL IS NO ONE SPECIAL.
EVEN IF A LOT OF FOREIGNERS AREN'T PARTICU-LARLY PUNCTUAL ...
...THEY'D STILL SHOW UP ON TIME FOR THE FIRST DAY OF WORK.
I HEARD HE'S LATE CUZ HE HAD WORK IN ANOTHER COUNTRY, BUT I WONDER.
HE MAY JUST NOT CARE ABOUT TIME.
YEAH.
WHAT? BUT THE DIRECTOR WOULDN'T ALLOW THAT.
I MEAN, I WANT HIM TO GET ANGRY AND SAY "CUT IT OUT!"
Just like that.
I WONDER. DIRECTOR KONOE SAYS WHAT HE WANTS...
...BUT HE SAYS IT SOFTLY ...
DASH DASH
...SO A FOREIGNER MIGHT NOT LISTEN TO HIM.

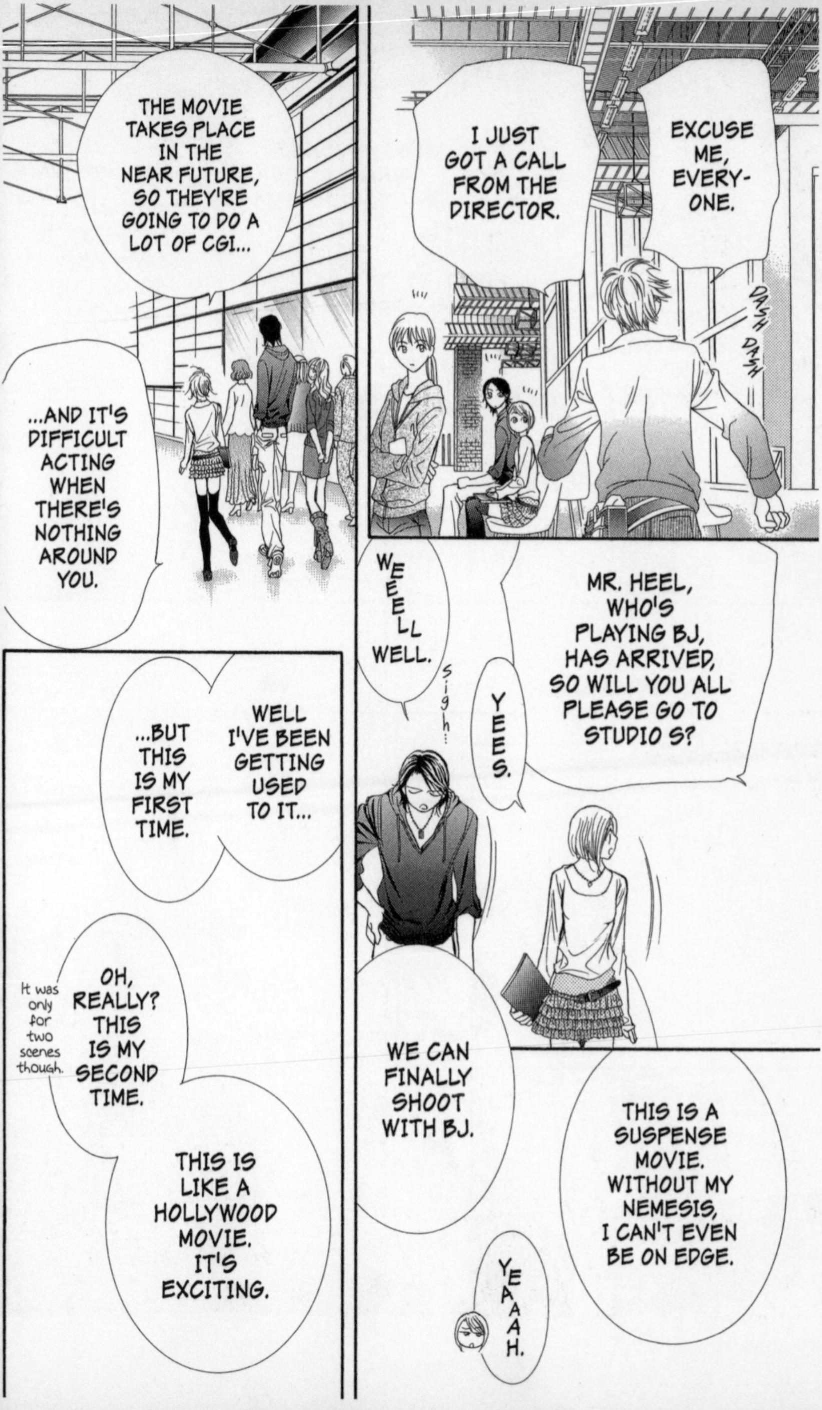
EXCUSE ME, EVERY-ONE.
I JUST GOT A CALL FROM THE DIRECTOR.
DASH DASH
MR. HEEL, WHO'S PLAYING BJ, HAS ARRIVED, SO WILL YOU ALL PLEASE GO TO STUDIO S?
YEES.
Sigh...
WEEELL WELL.
THIS IS A SUSPENSE MOVIE. WITHOUT MY NEMESIS, I CAN'T EVEN BE ON EDGE.
WE CAN FINALLY SHOOT WITH BJ.
YEAAAH.
THE MOVIE TAKES PLACE IN THE NEAR FUTURE, SO THEY'RE GOING TO DO A LOT OF CGI...
...AND IT'S DIFFICULT ACTING WHEN THERE'S NOTHING AROUND YOU.
WELL I'VE BEEN GETTING USED TO IT...
...BUT THIS IS MY FIRST TIME.
OH, REALLY? THIS IS MY SECOND TIME.
It was only for two scenes though.
THIS IS LIKE A HOLLYWOOD MOVIE. IT'S EXCITING.

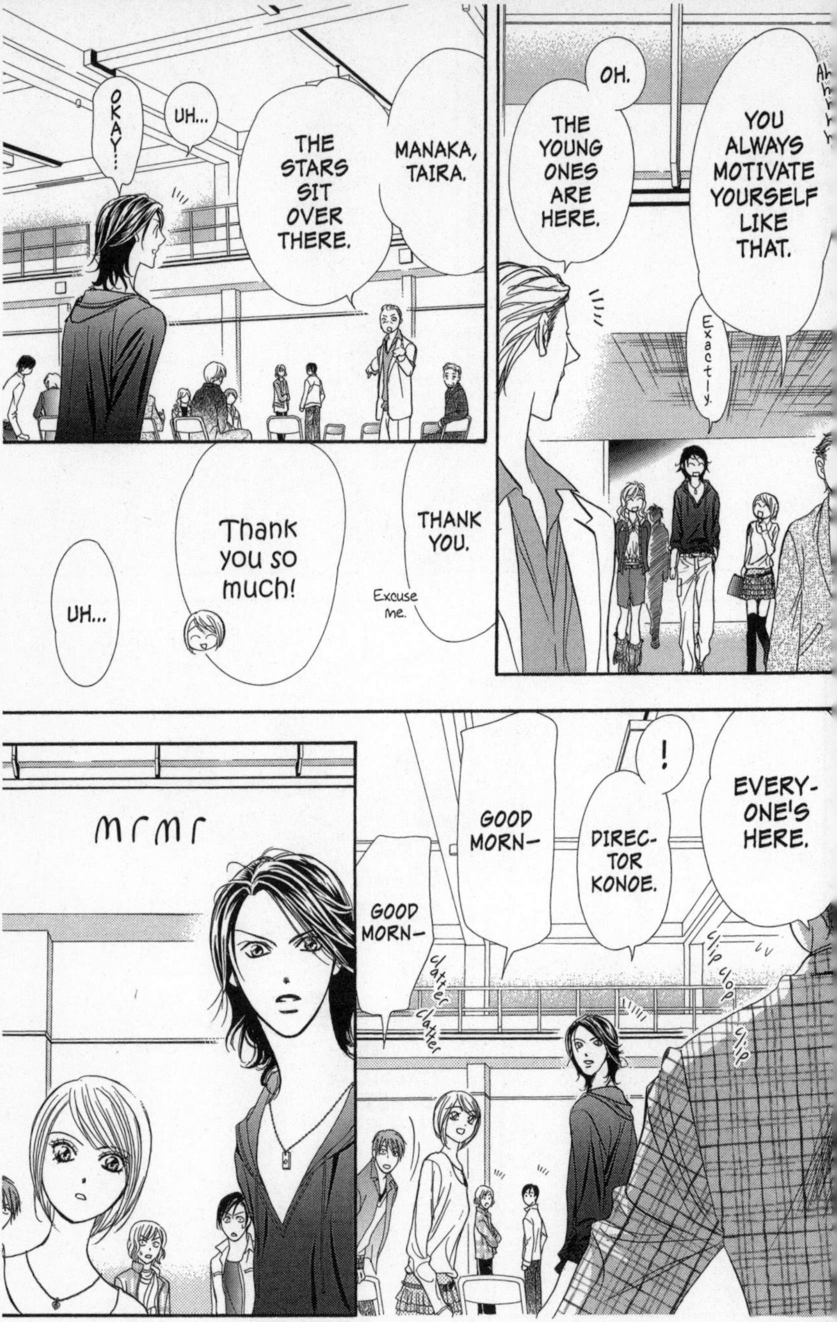
Ahhhh
YOU ALWAYS MOTIVATE YOURSELF LIKE THAT.
Exactly.
OH.
THE YOUNG ONES ARE HERE.
MANAKA, TAIRA.
THE STARS SIT OVER THERE.
UH...
OKAY...
THANK YOU.
Excuse me.
Thank you so much!
UH...
EVERY-ONE'S HERE.
!
DIREC-TOR KONOE.
GOOD MORN-
clip clop
clip
GOOD MORN-
clatter clatter
mrmr

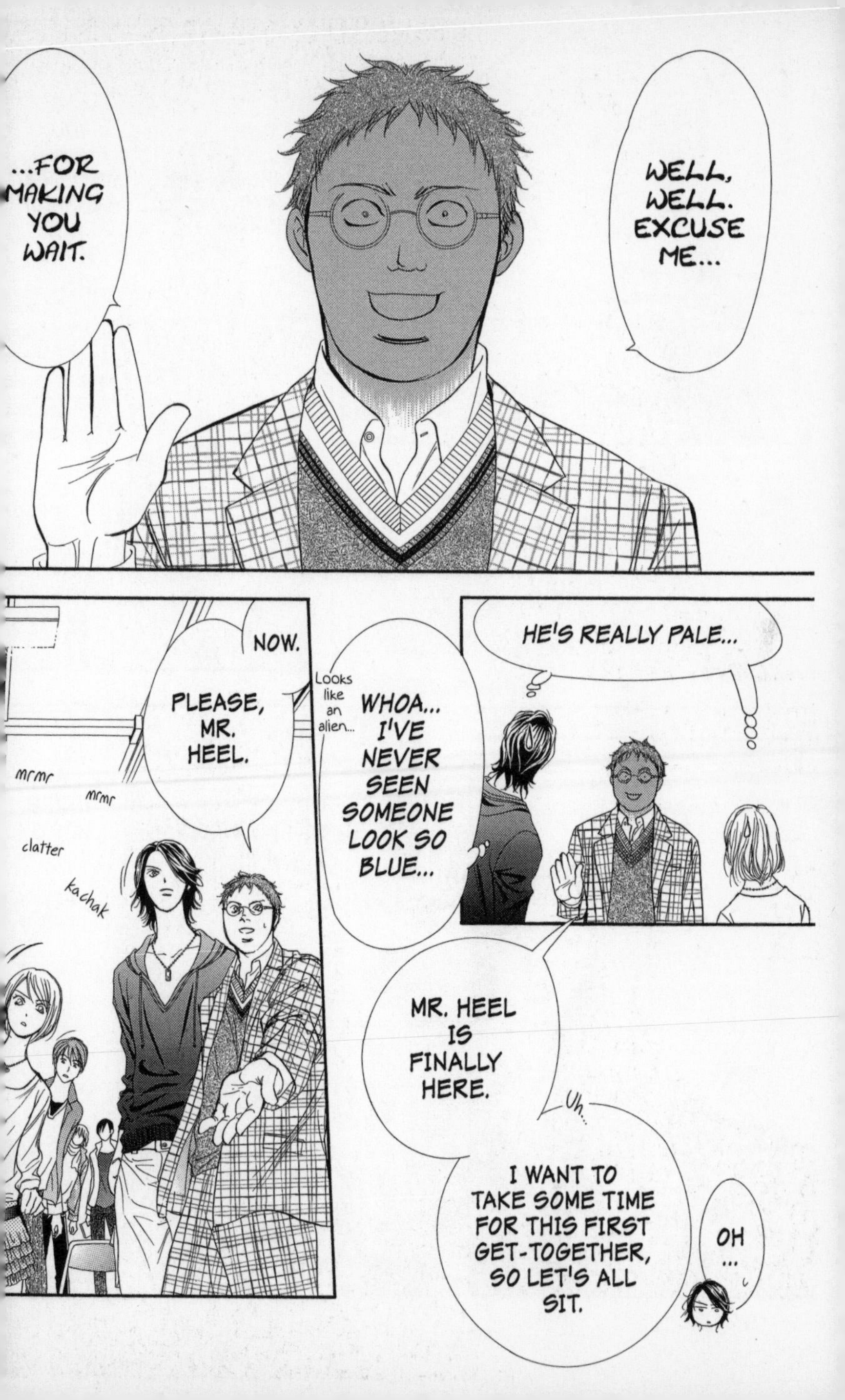
WELL, WELL. EXCUSE ME...
...FOR MAKING YOU WAIT.
HE'S REALLY PALE...
MR. HEEL IS FINALLY HERE.
Uh...
I WANT TO TAKE SOME TIME FOR THIS FIRST GET-TOGETHER, SO LET'S ALL SIT.
OH ...
WHOA... I'VE NEVER SEEN SOMEONE LOOK SO BLUE...
Looks like an alien...
NOW.
PLEASE, MR. HEEL.
mrmr
mrmr
clatter
kachak

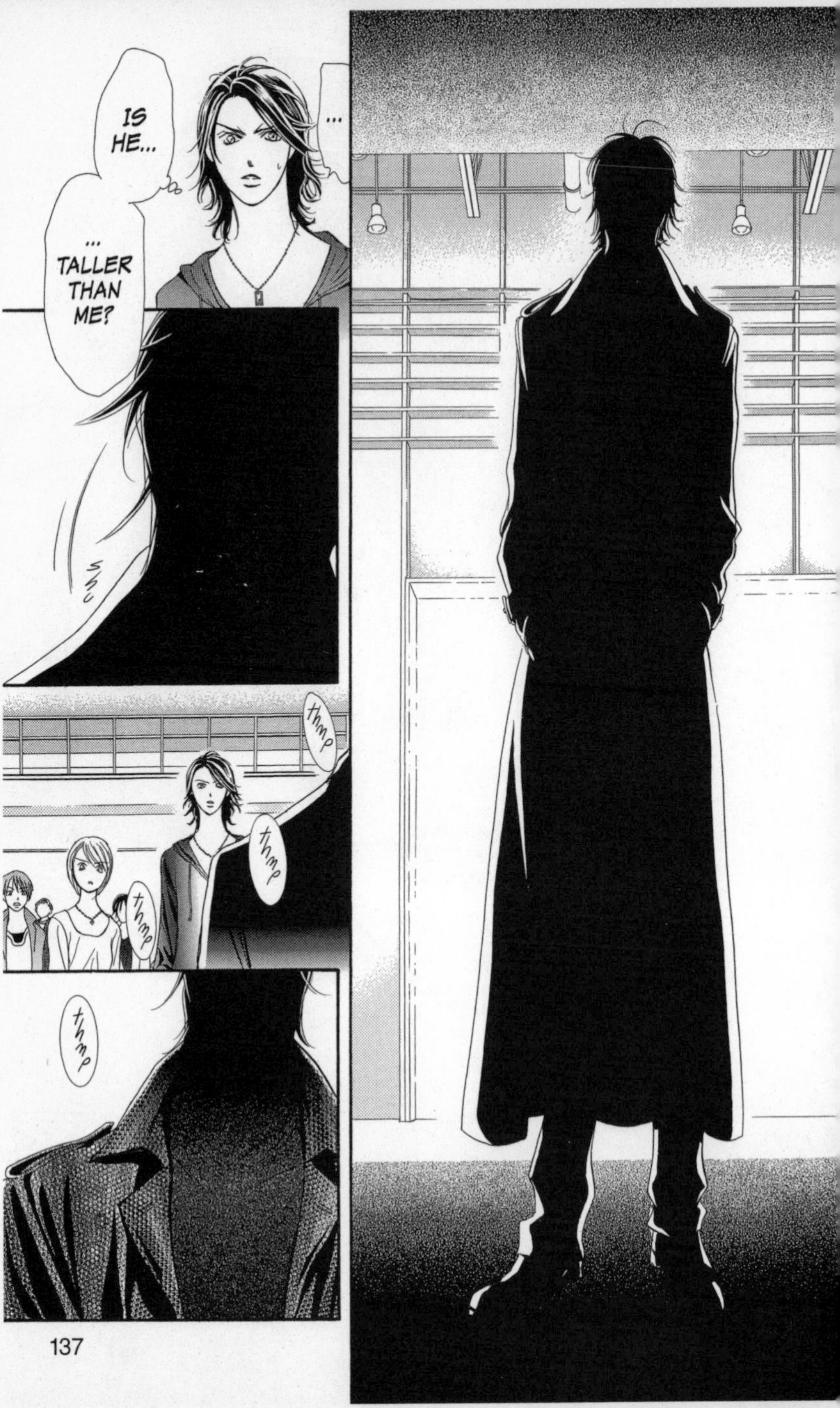
...
IS HE...
...TALLER THAN ME?
shu
thmp
thmp
thmp
thmp

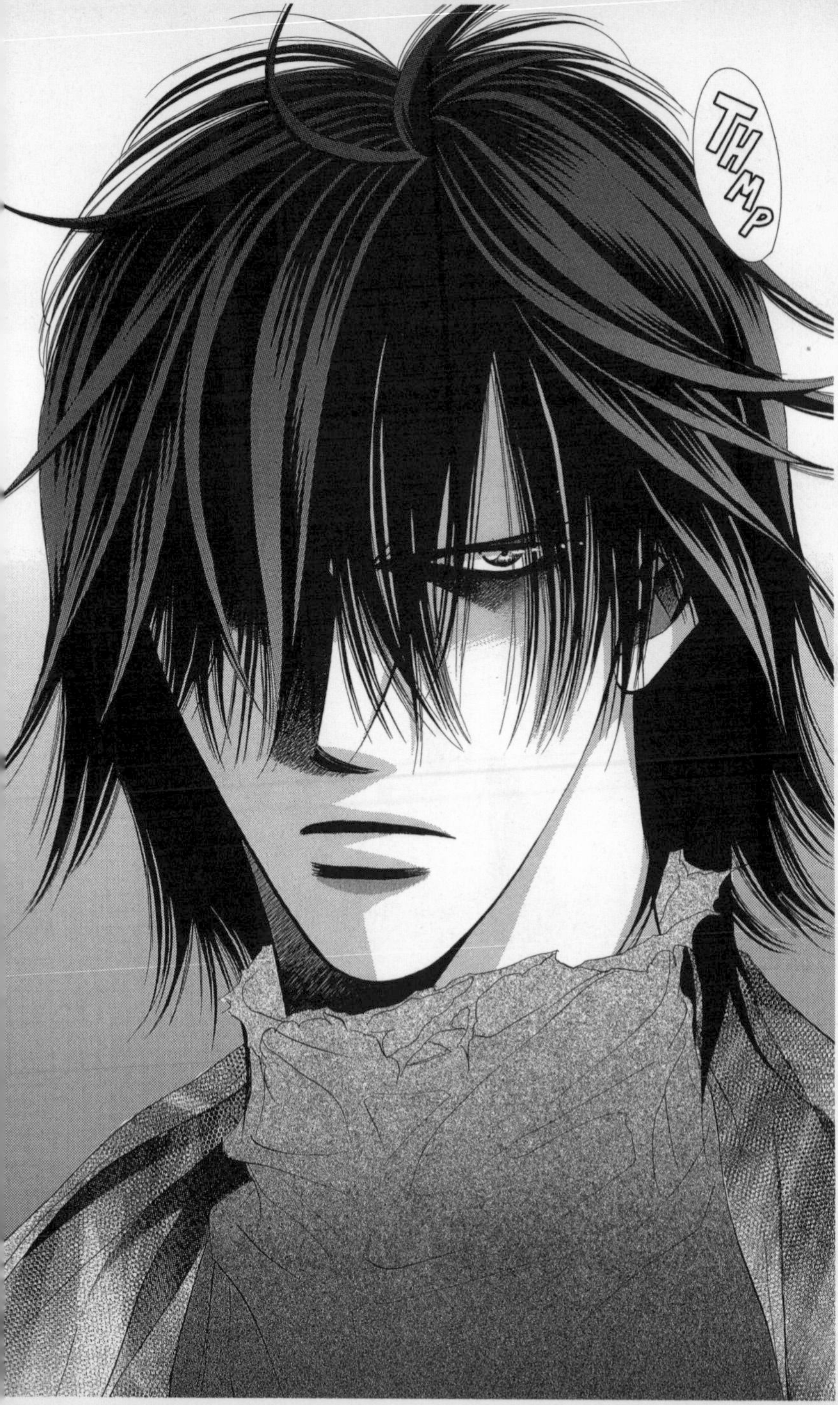
THMP

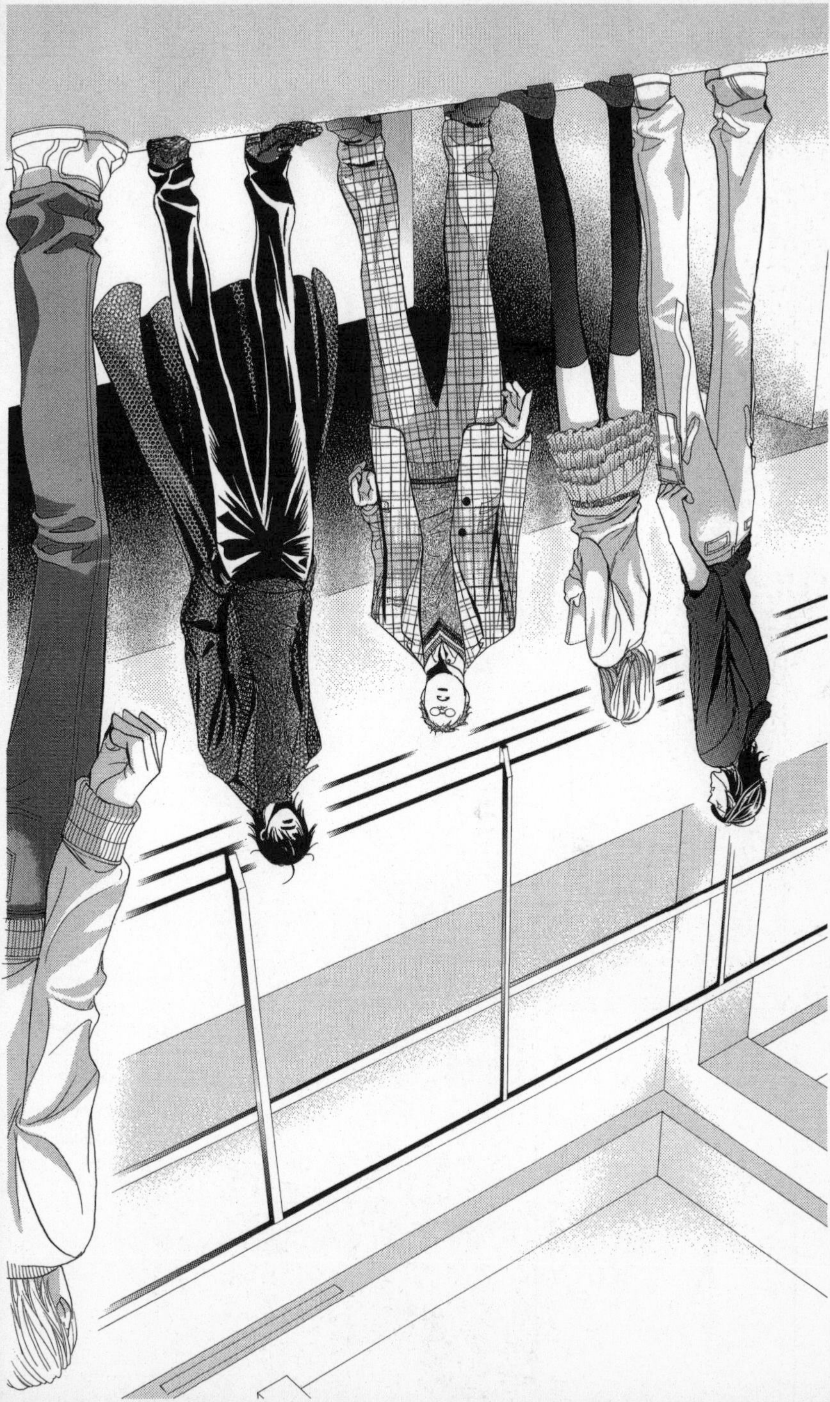

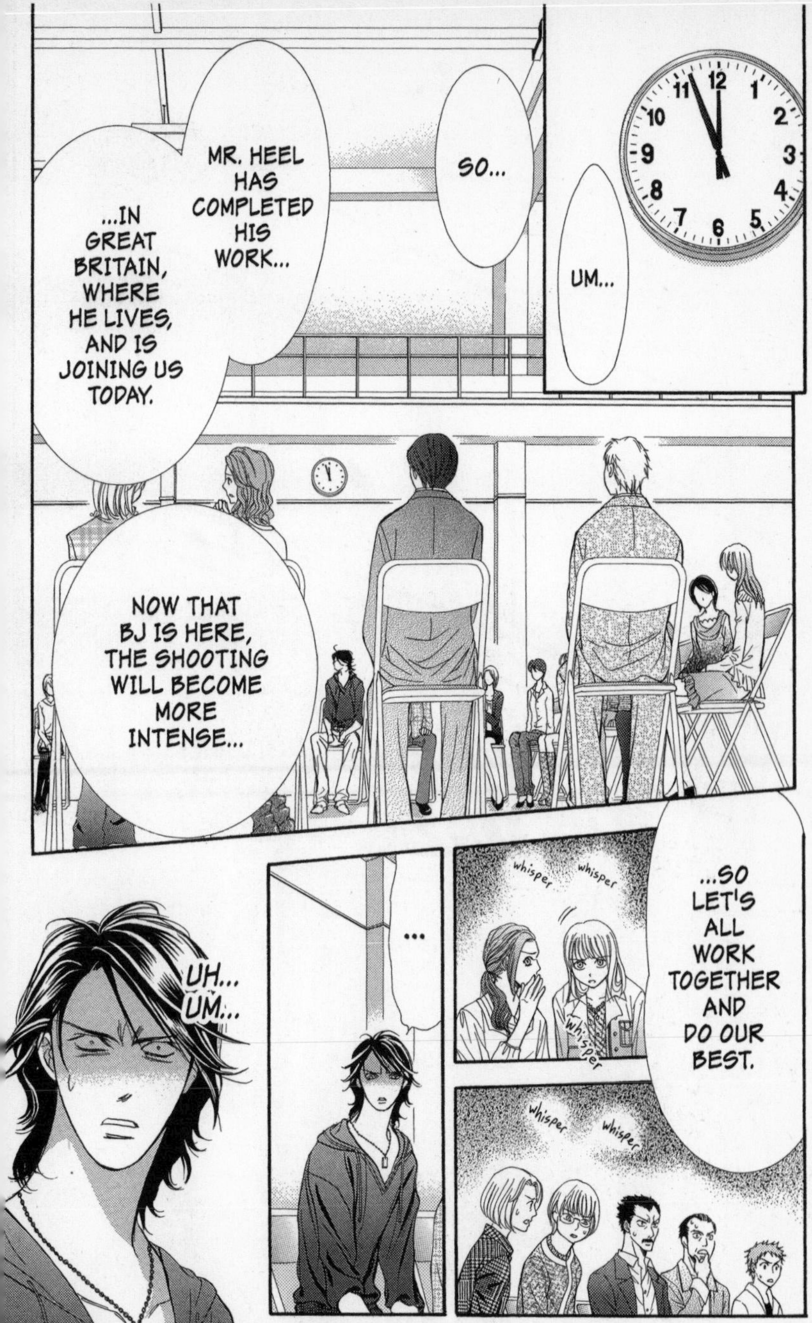
UM...
SO...
MR. HEEL HAS COMPLETED HIS WORK...
...IN GREAT BRITAIN, WHERE HE LIVES, AND IS JOINING US TODAY.
NOW THAT BJ IS HERE, THE SHOOTING WILL BECOME MORE INTENSE...
...SO LET'S ALL WORK TOGETHER AND DO OUR BEST.
whisper
whisper
whisper
whisper
whisper
...
UH... UM...

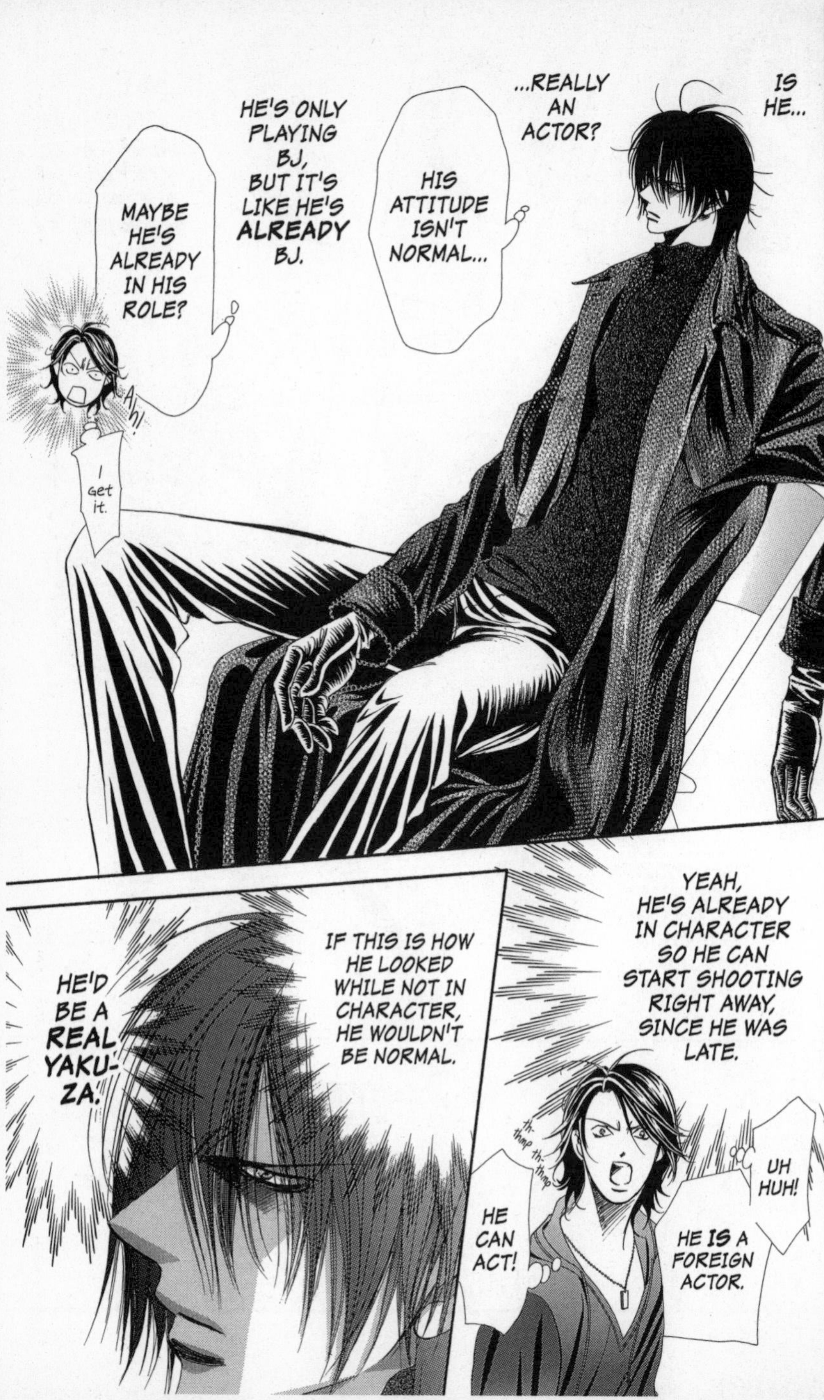
IS HE...
...REALLY AN ACTOR?
HIS ATTITUDE ISN'T NORMAL...
HE'S ONLY PLAYING BJ, BUT IT'S LIKE HE'S ALREADY BJ.
MAYBE HE'S ALREADY IN HIS ROLE?
Ah!
I Get it.
YEAH, HE'S ALREADY IN CHARACTER SO HE CAN START SHOOTING RIGHT AWAY, SINCE HE WAS LATE.
UH HUH!
HE IS A FOREIGN ACTOR.
th-thmp th-thmp
HE CAN ACT!
IF THIS IS HOW HE LOOKED WHILE NOT IN CHARACTER, HE WOULDN'T BE NORMAL.
HE'D BE A REAL YAKU-ZA!

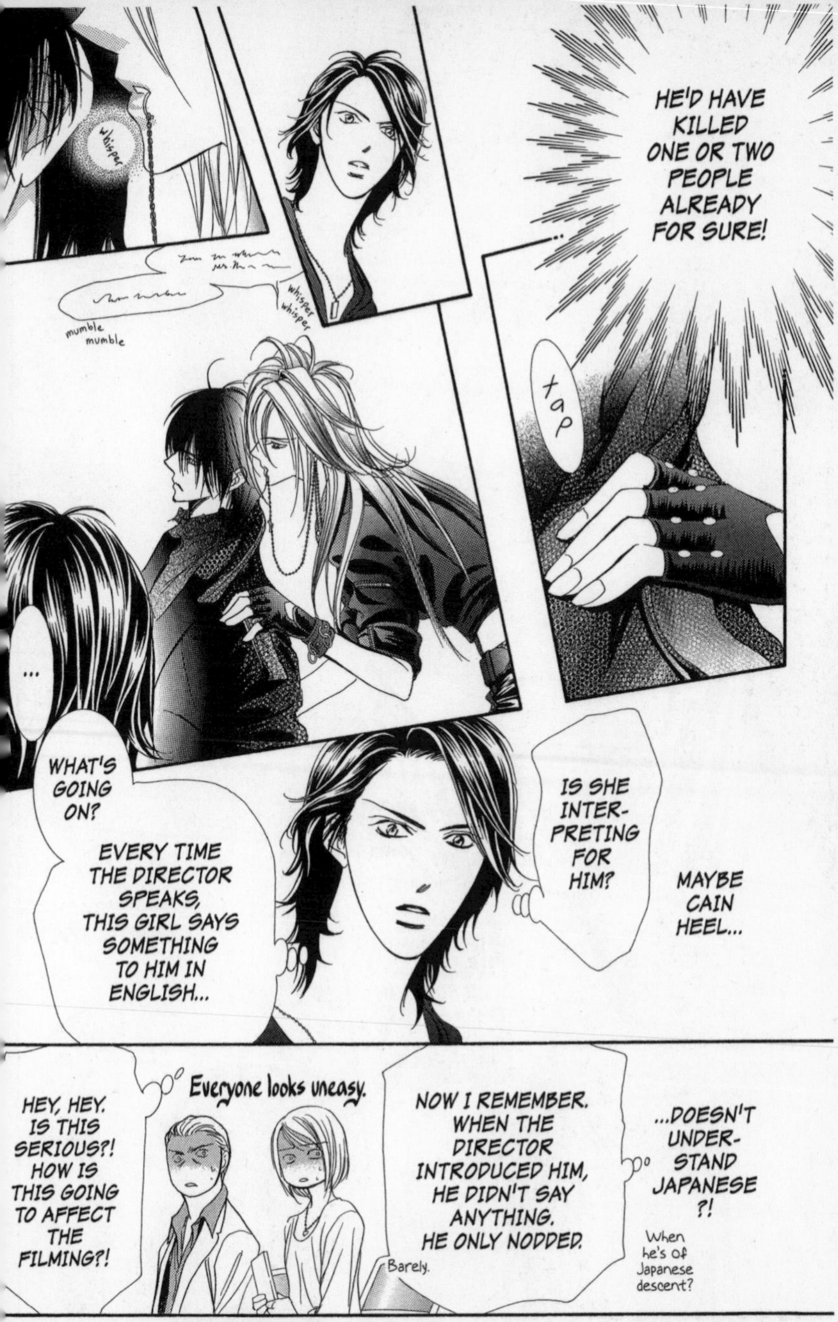
HE'D HAVE KILLED ONE OR TWO PEOPLE ALREADY FOR SURE!
whisper
whisper whisper
mumble mumble
tap
...
WHAT'S GOING ON?
EVERY TIME THE DIRECTOR SPEAKS, THIS GIRL SAYS SOMETHING TO HIM IN ENGLISH...
IS SHE INTER-PRETING FOR HIM?
MAYBE CAIN HEEL...
HEY, HEY. IS THIS SERIOUS?! HOW IS THIS GOING TO AFFECT THE FILMING?!
Everyone looks uneasy.
NOW I REMEMBER. WHEN THE DIRECTOR INTRODUCED HIM, HE DIDN'T SAY ANYTHING. HE ONLY NODDED.
Barely.
...DOESN'T UNDER-STAND JAPANESE ?!
When he's of Japanese descent?

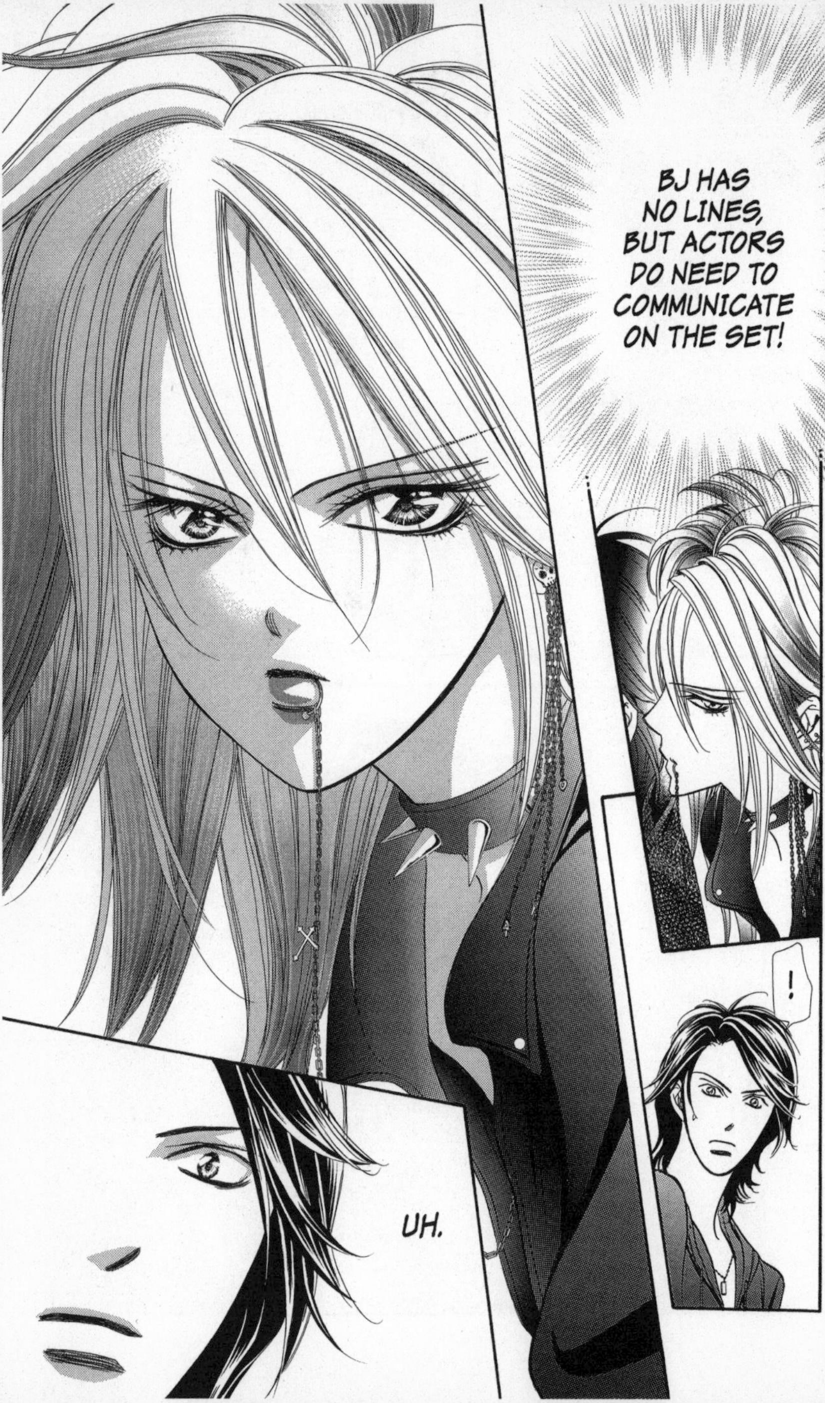
BJ HAS NO LINES, BUT ACTORS DO NEED TO COMMUNICATE ON THE SET!
!
UH.

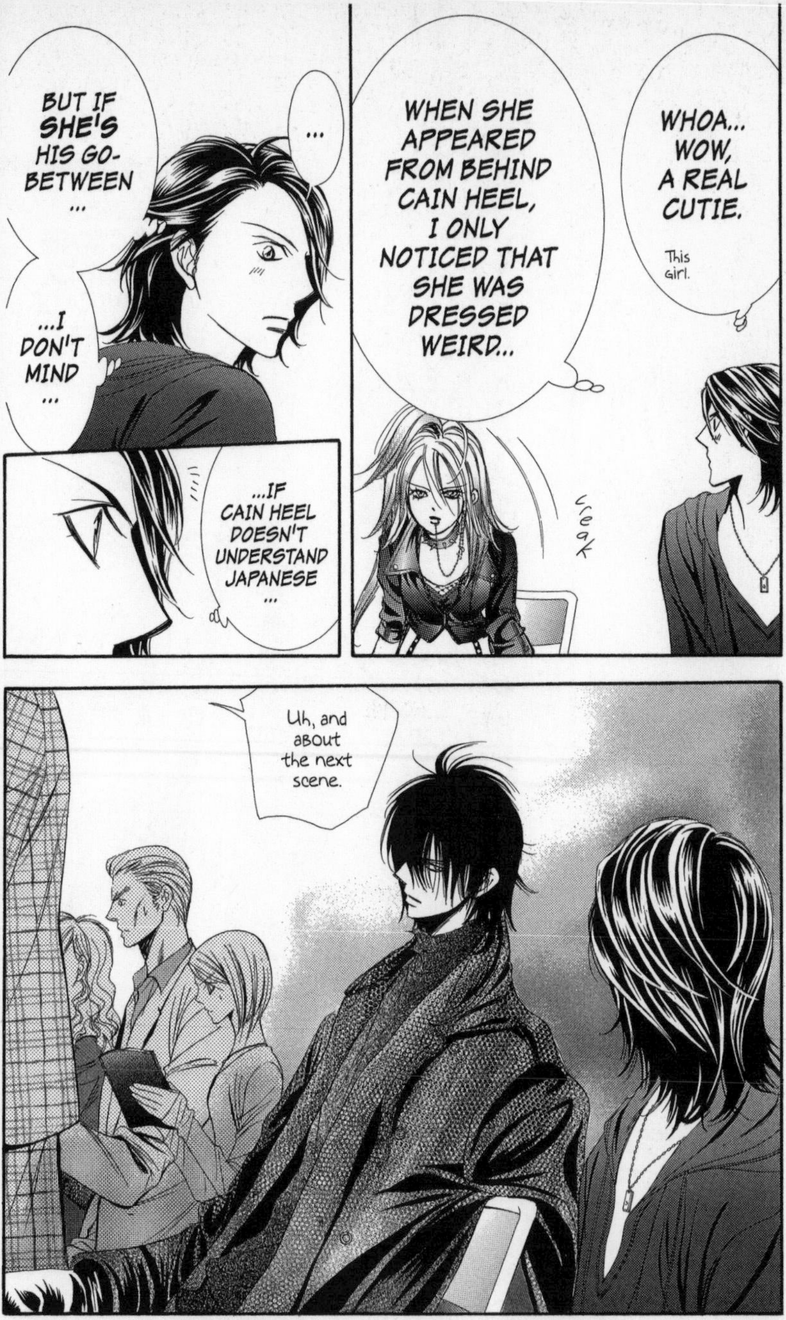
WHOA... WOW, A REAL CUTIE.
This girl.
creak
WHEN SHE APPEARED FROM BEHIND CAIN HEEL, I ONLY NOTICED THAT SHE WAS DRESSED WEIRD...
...
BUT IF SHE'S HIS GO-BETWEEN ...
...I DON'T MIND ...
...IF CAIN HEEL DOESN'T UNDERSTAND JAPANESE ...
Uh, and about the next scene.

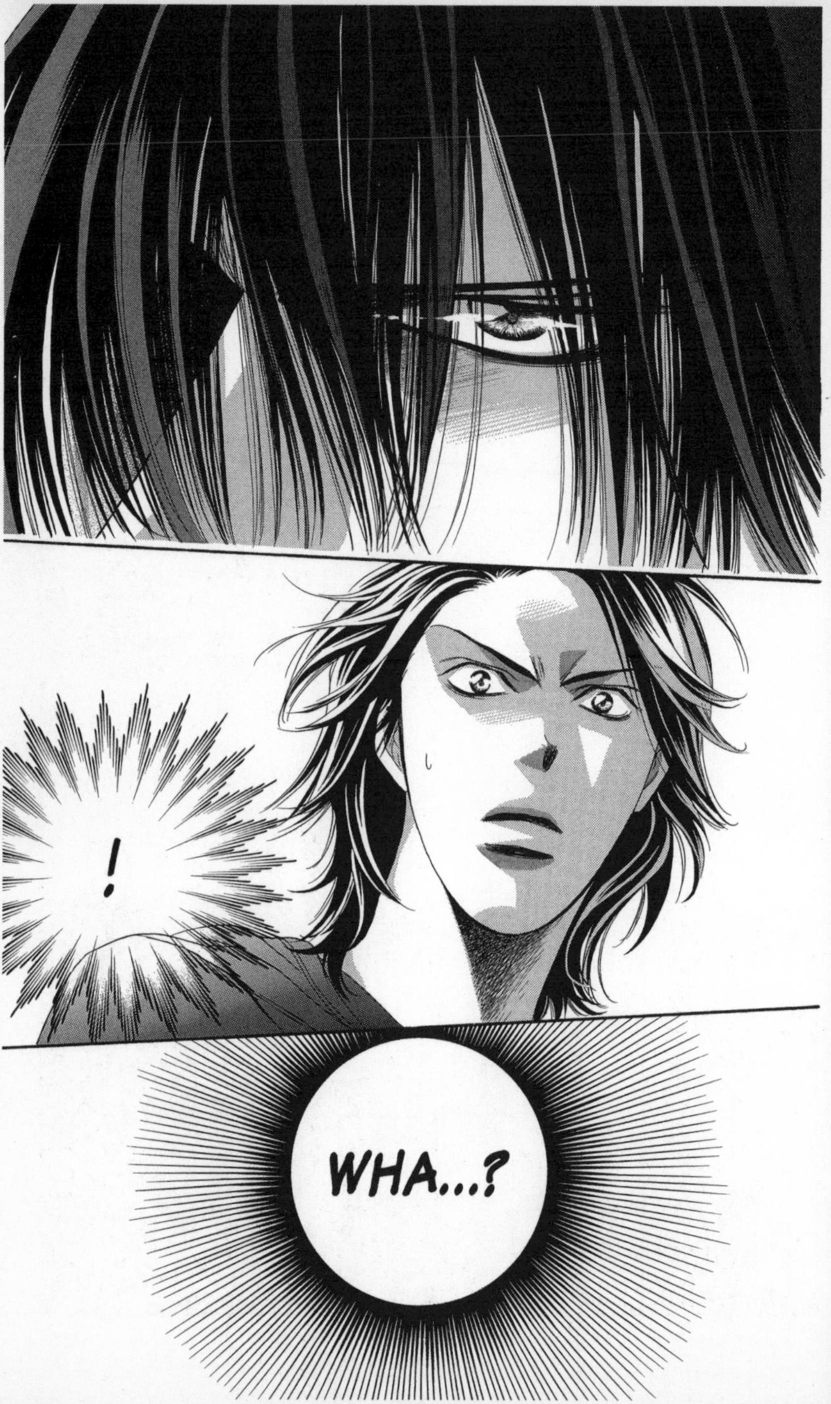
!
WHA...?

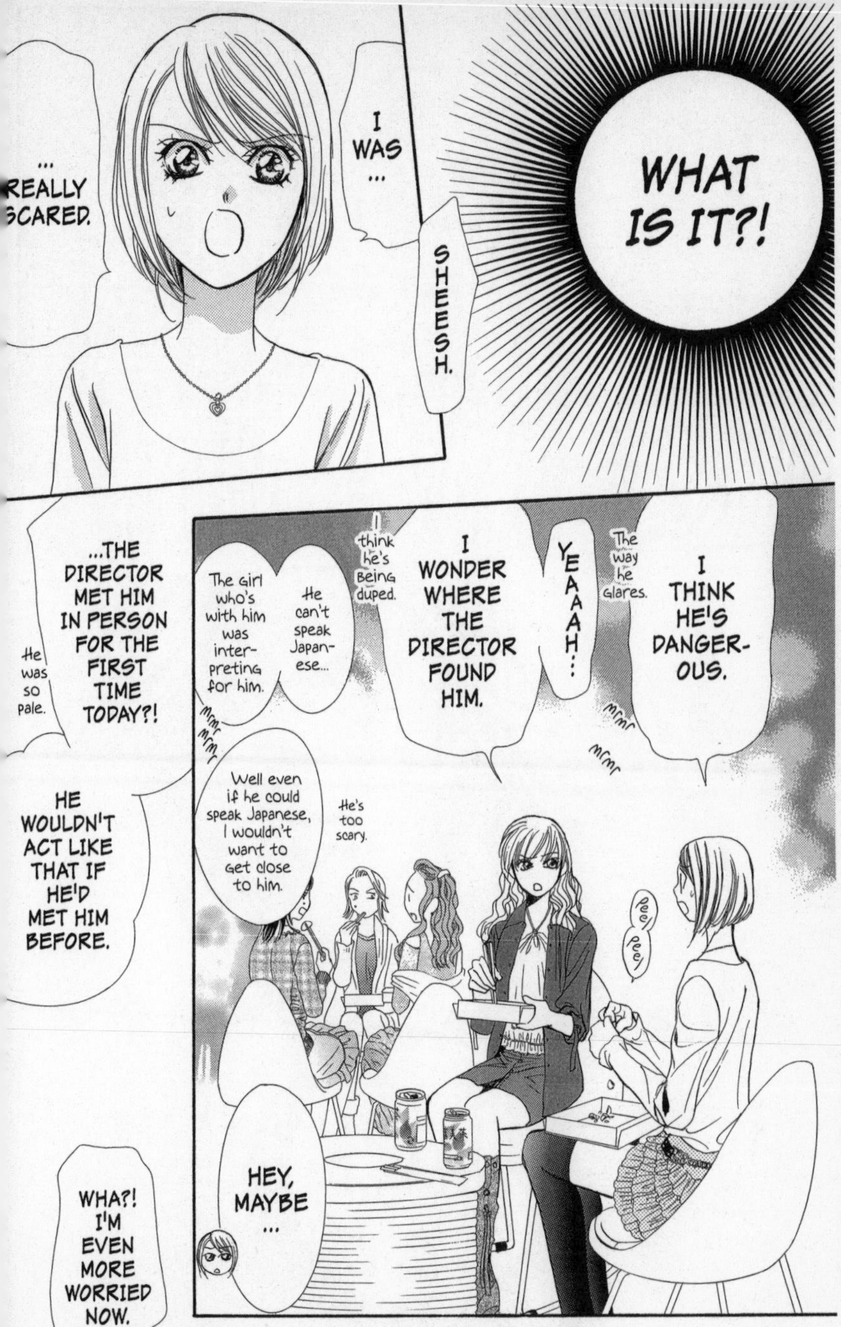
WHAT IS IT?!
I WAS...
SHEESH.
...REALLY SCARED.
The way he glares.
I THINK HE'S DANGER-OUS.
mrmr
mrmr
YEAAAAH...
I WONDER WHERE THE DIRECTOR FOUND HIM.
I think he's being duped.
He can't speak Japan-ese...
The girl who's with him was inter-preting for him.
mrmr mrmr
...THE DIRECTOR MET HIM IN PERSON FOR THE FIRST TIME TODAY?!
He was so pale.
He's too scary.
Well even if he could speak Japanese, I wouldn't want to get close to him.
HE WOULDN'T ACT LIKE THAT IF HE'D MET HIM BEFORE.
Peel Peel
HEY, MAYBE...
WHA?! I'M EVEN MORE WORRIED NOW.

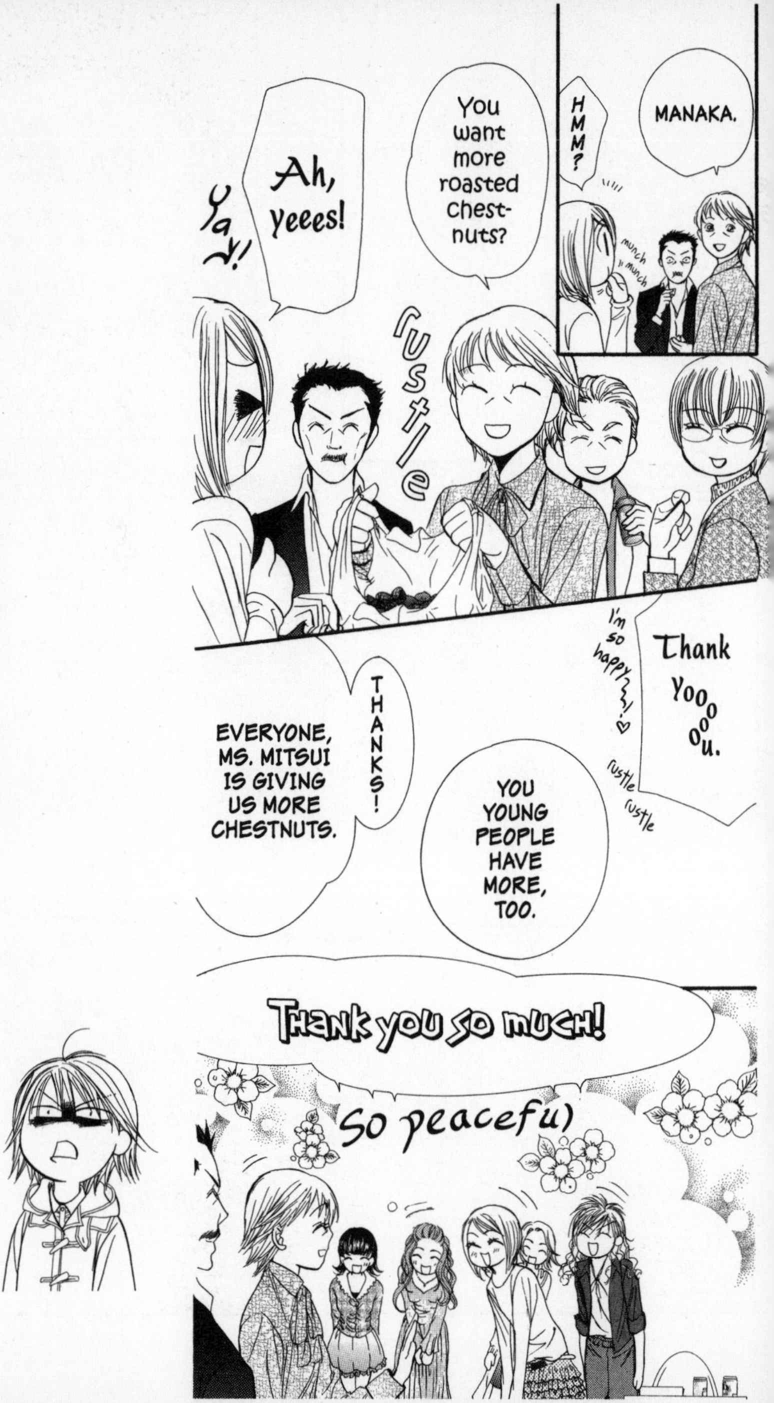
MANAKA.
HMM?
munch munch
You want more roasted chest-nuts?
Ah, yeees!
Yay!
rustle
Thank yooooou.
I'm so happy~!♡
rustle rustle
THANKS!
EVERYONE, MS. MITSUI IS GIVING US MORE CHESTNUTS.
YOU YOUNG PEOPLE HAVE MORE, TOO.
THANK YOU SO MUCH!
So peacefu)

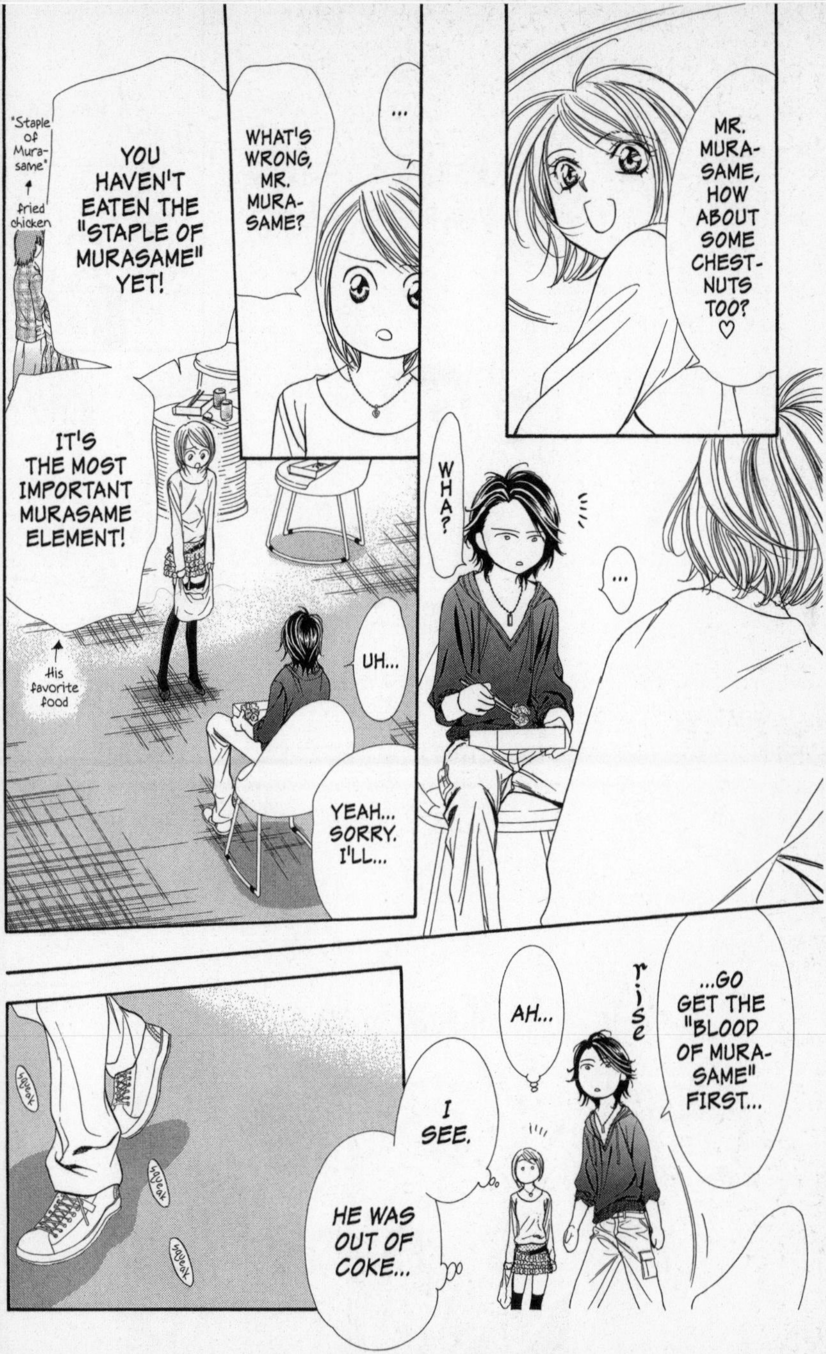
MR. MURA-SAME, HOW ABOUT SOME CHEST-NUTS TOO? ♡
...
WHAT'S WRONG, MR. MURA-SAME?
YOU HAVEN'T EATEN THE "STAPLE OF MURASAME" YET!
"Staple of Mura-same" ↑ fried chicken
IT'S THE MOST IMPORTANT MURASAME ELEMENT!
↑ His favorite food
...
WHA?
UH...
YEAH... SORRY. I'LL...
...GO GET THE "BLOOD OF MURA-SAME" FIRST...
rise
AH...
I SEE.
HE WAS OUT OF COKE...
squeak
squeak
squeak

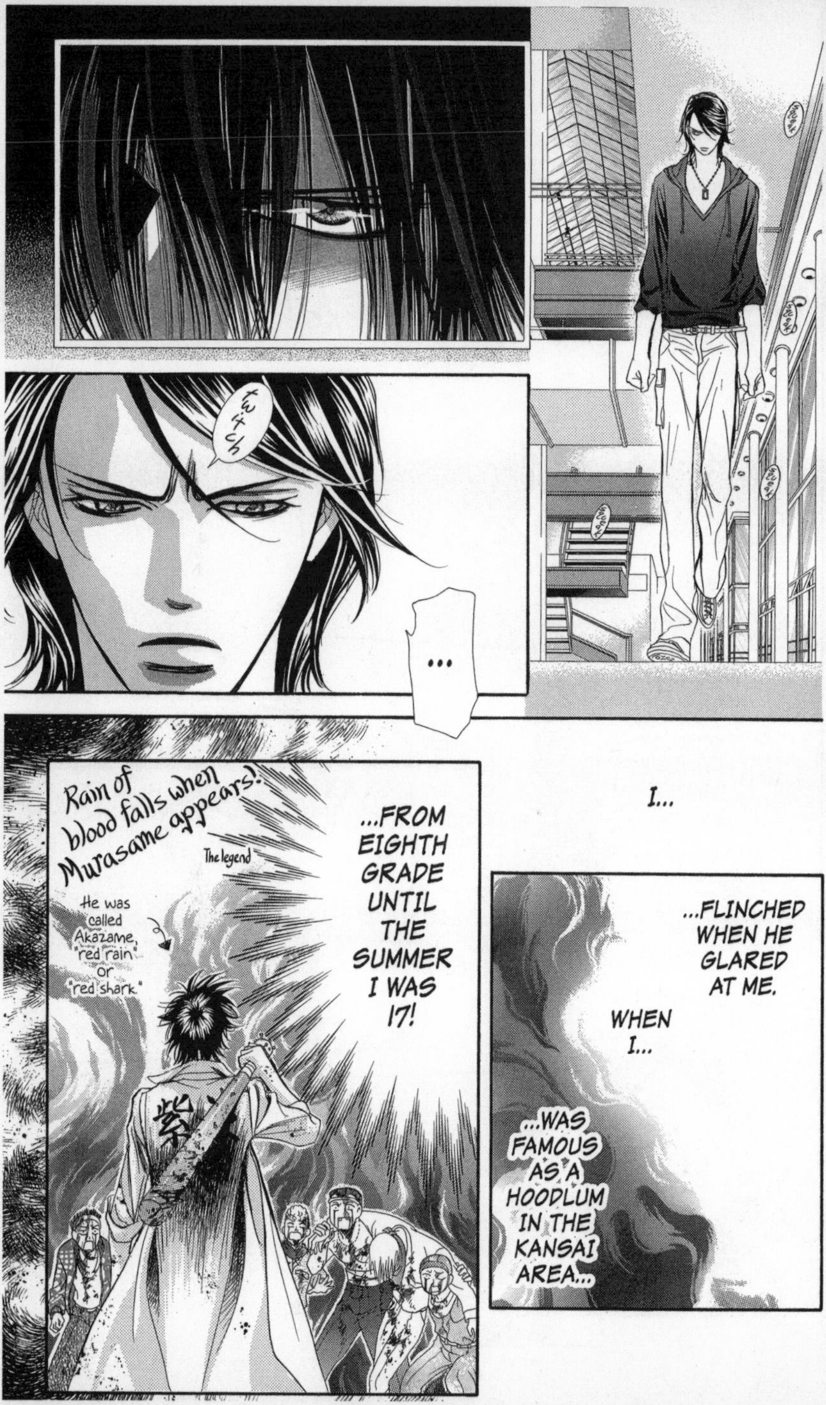
squeak
squeak
squeak
squeak
twitch
...
I...
...FLINCHED WHEN HE GLARED AT ME.
WHEN I...
...WAS FAMOUS AS A HOODLUM IN THE KANSAI AREA...
...FROM EIGHTH GRADE UNTIL THE SUMMER I WAS 17!
Rain of blood falls when Murasame appears!
The legend
He was called Akazame, "red rain" or "red shark."

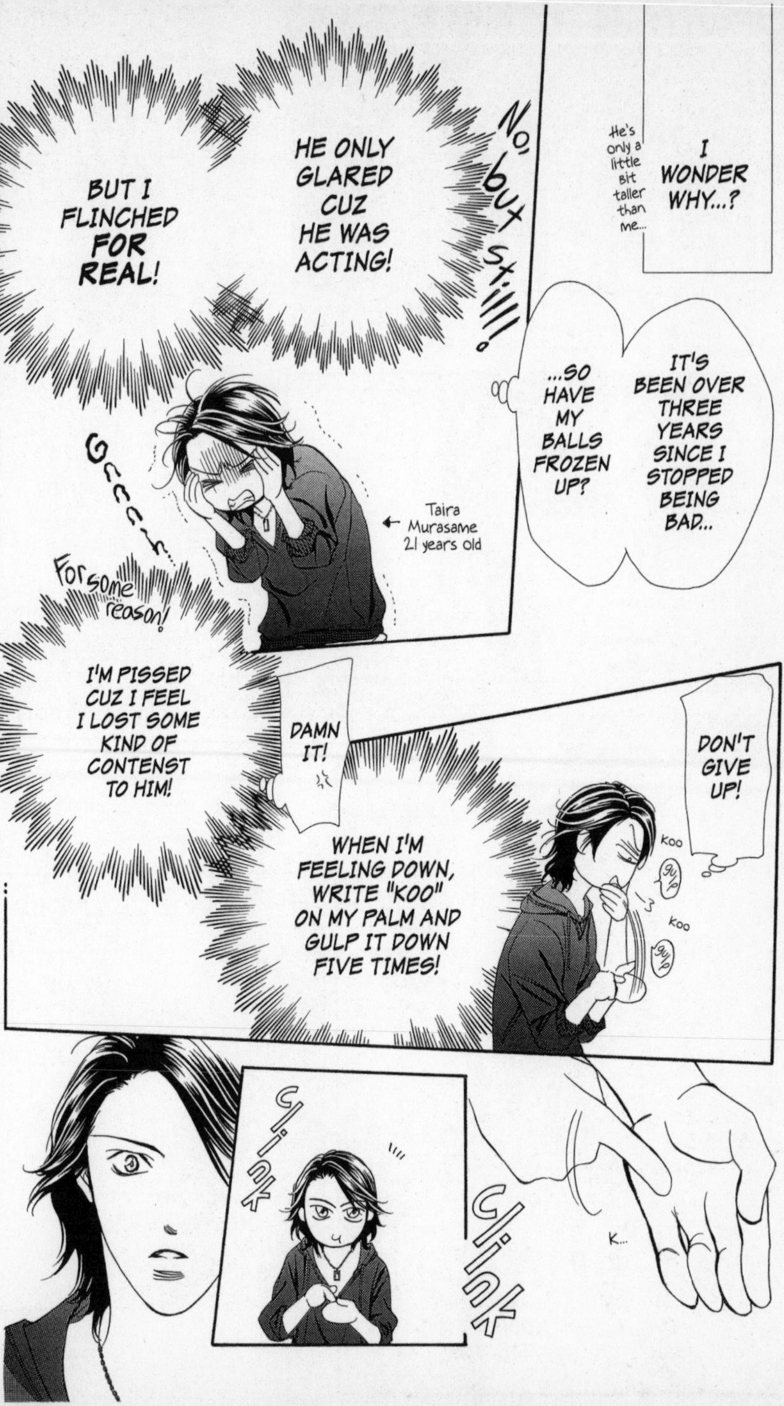
I WONDER WHY...?
He's only a little bit taller than me...
IT'S BEEN OVER THREE YEARS SINCE I STOPPED BEING BAD...
...SO HAVE MY BALLS FROZEN UP?
No, but still!!!
HE ONLY GLARED CUZ HE WAS ACTING!
BUT I FLINCHED FOR REAL!
Taira Murasame 21 years old
Gccccr...
For some reason!
I'M PISSED CUZ I FEEL I LOST SOME KIND OF CONTENST TO HIM!
DAMN IT!
DON'T GIVE UP!
koo
gulp
koo
gulp
WHEN I'M FEELING DOWN, WRITE "KOO" ON MY PALM AND GULP IT DOWN FIVE TIMES!
K...
clink
clink

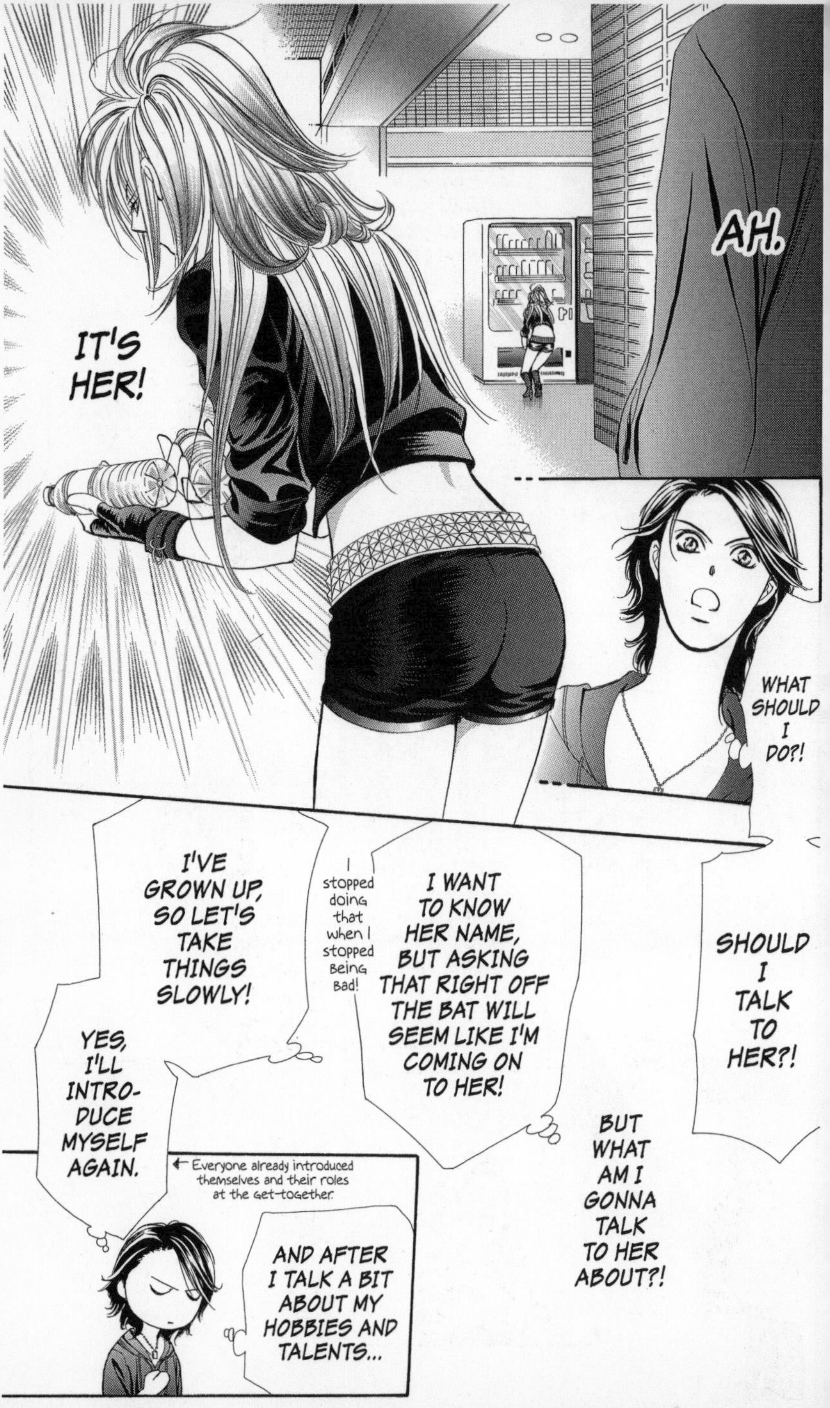
AH.
IT'S HER!
WHAT SHOULD I DO?!
SHOULD I TALK TO HER?!
BUT WHAT AM I GONNA TALK TO HER ABOUT?!
I WANT TO KNOW HER NAME, BUT ASKING THAT RIGHT OFF THE BAT WILL SEEM LIKE I'M COMING ON TO HER!
I stopped doing that when I stopped Being Bad!
I'VE GROWN UP, SO LET'S TAKE THINGS SLOWLY!
YES, I'LL INTRO-DUCE MYSELF AGAIN.
← Everyone already introduced themselves and their roles at the Get-together.
AND AFTER I TALK A BIT ABOUT MY HOBBIES AND TALENTS...

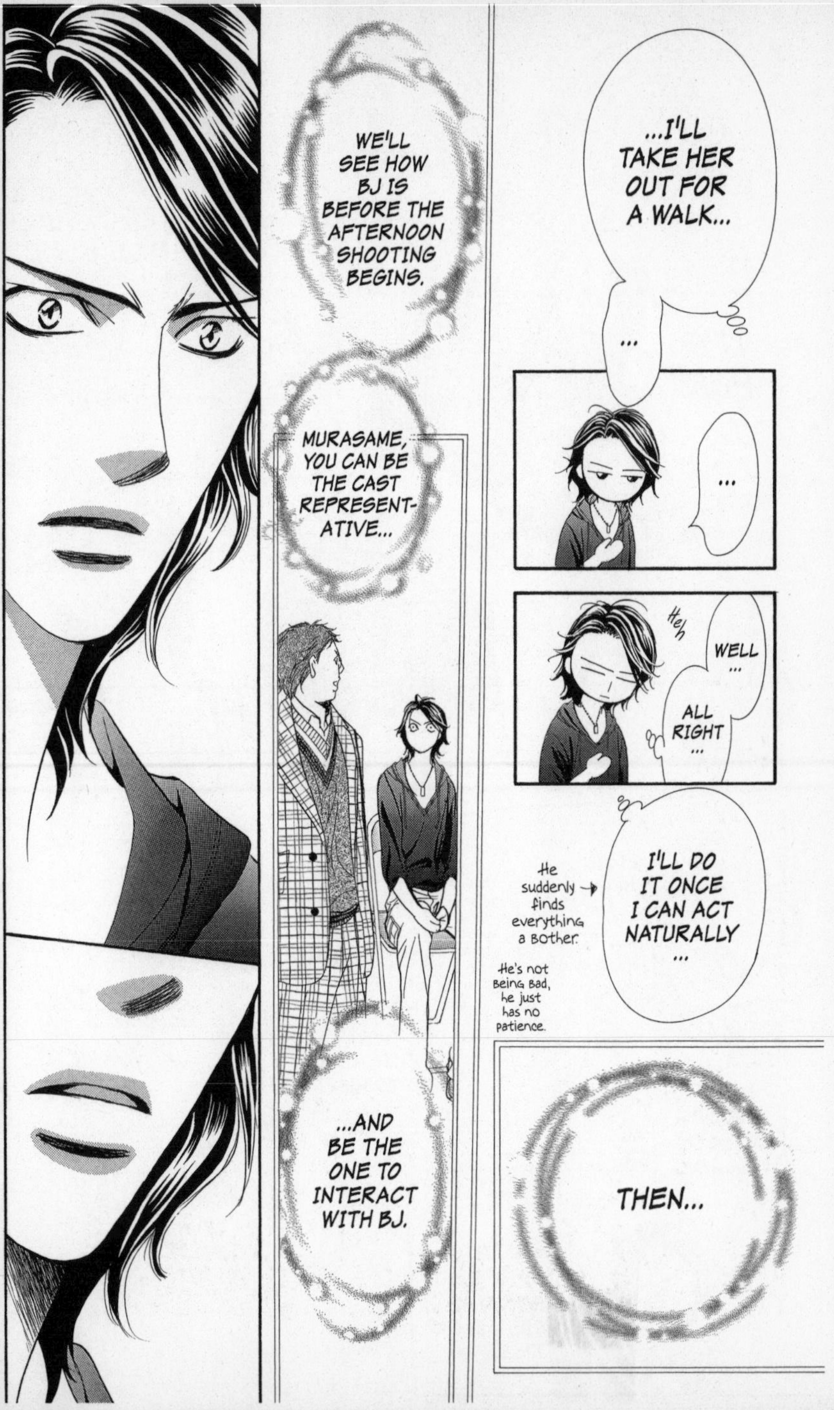
...I'LL TAKE HER OUT FOR A WALK...
...
...
WELL...
Heh
ALL RIGHT...
I'LL DO IT ONCE I CAN ACT NATURALLY...
He suddenly finds everything a Bother.
He's not Being Bad, he just has no patience.
THEN...
WE'LL SEE HOW BJ IS BEFORE THE AFTERNOON SHOOTING BEGINS.
MURASAME, YOU CAN BE THE CAST REPRESENT-ATIVE...
...AND BE THE ONE TO INTERACT WITH BJ.

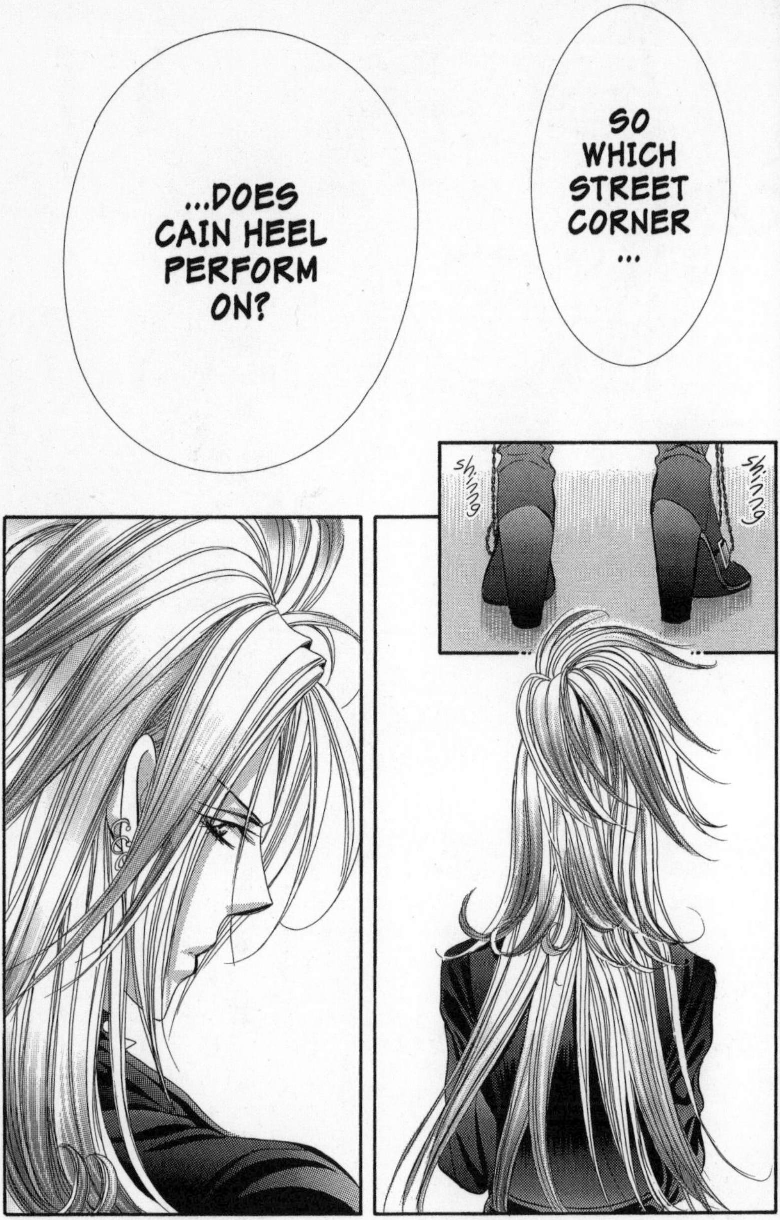
SO WHICH STREET CORNER ...
...DOES CAIN HEEL PERFORM ON?
shiiing
shiiing

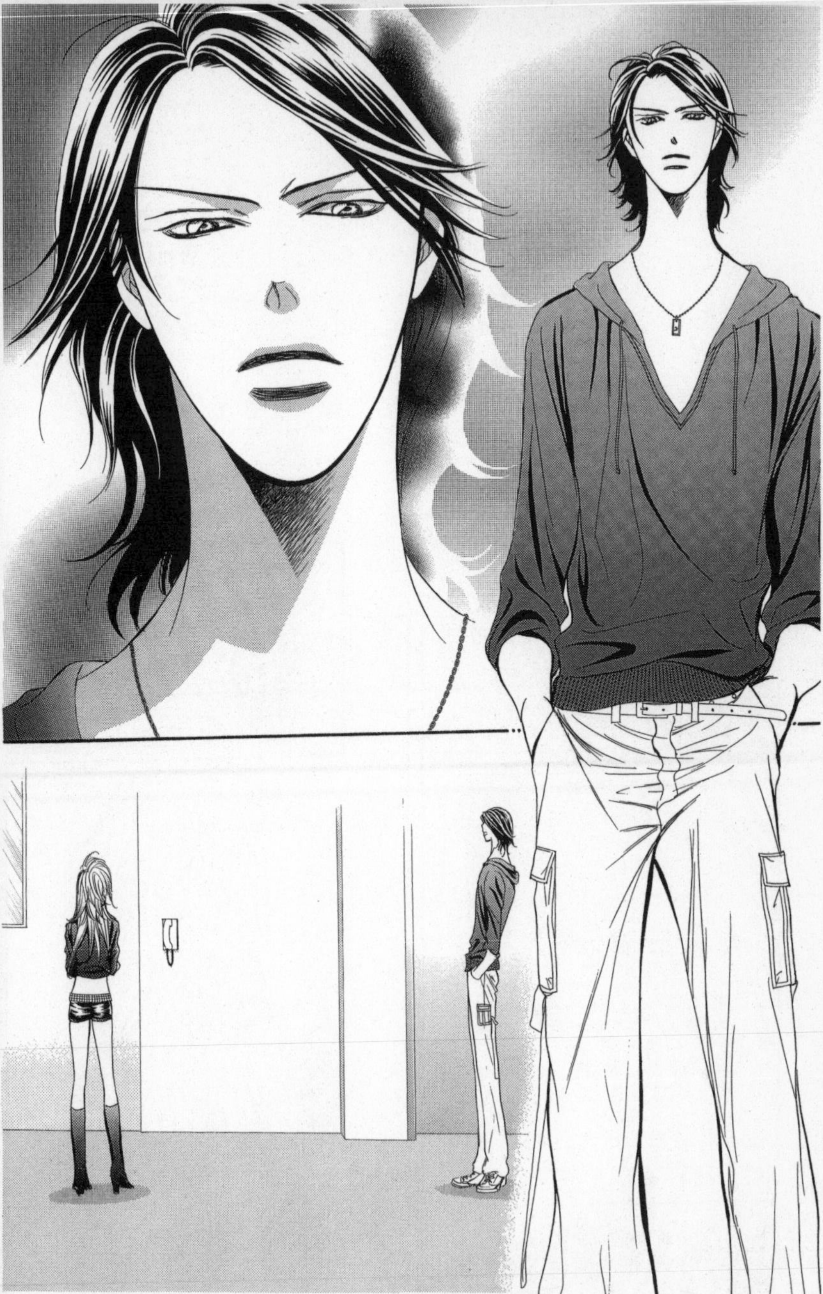

End of Act 175

Skip·Beat!

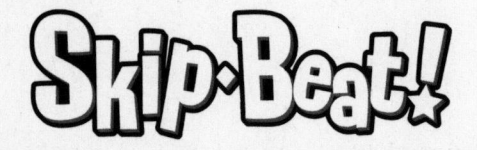

Act 176: Hero's High

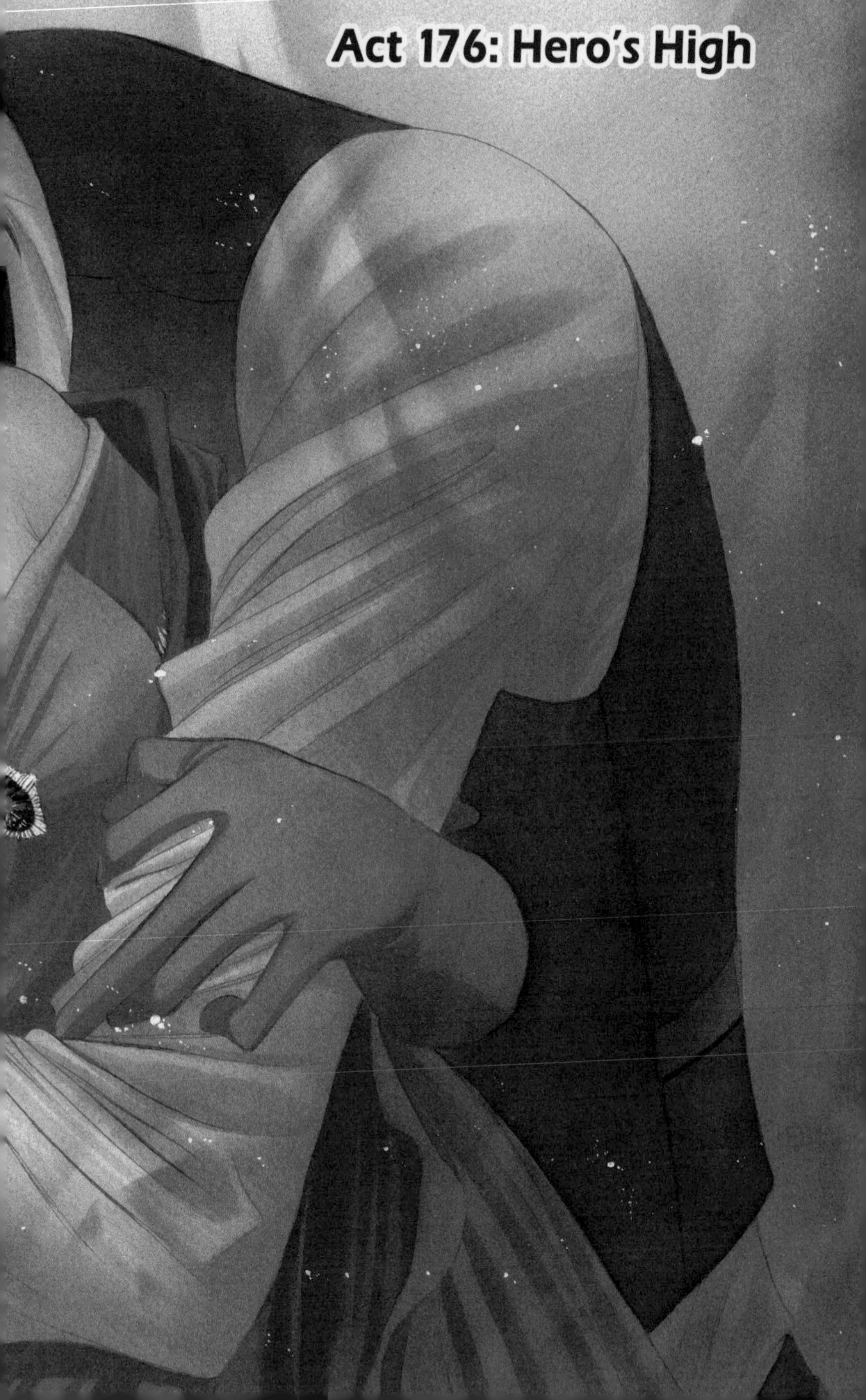

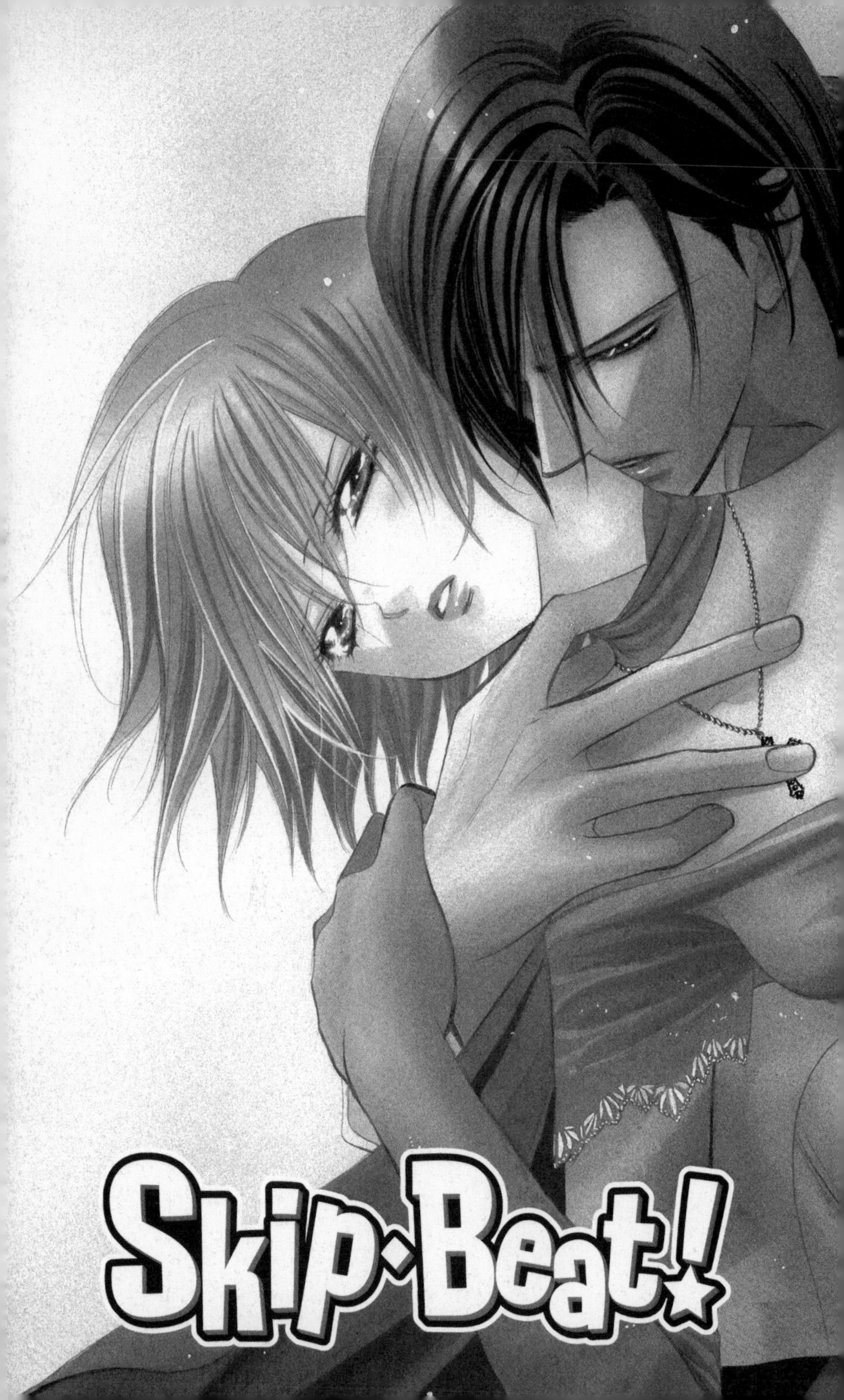
Skip·Beat!

Skip·Beat!

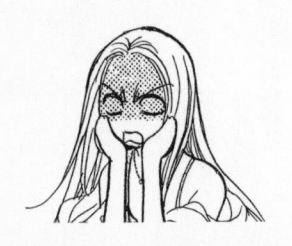

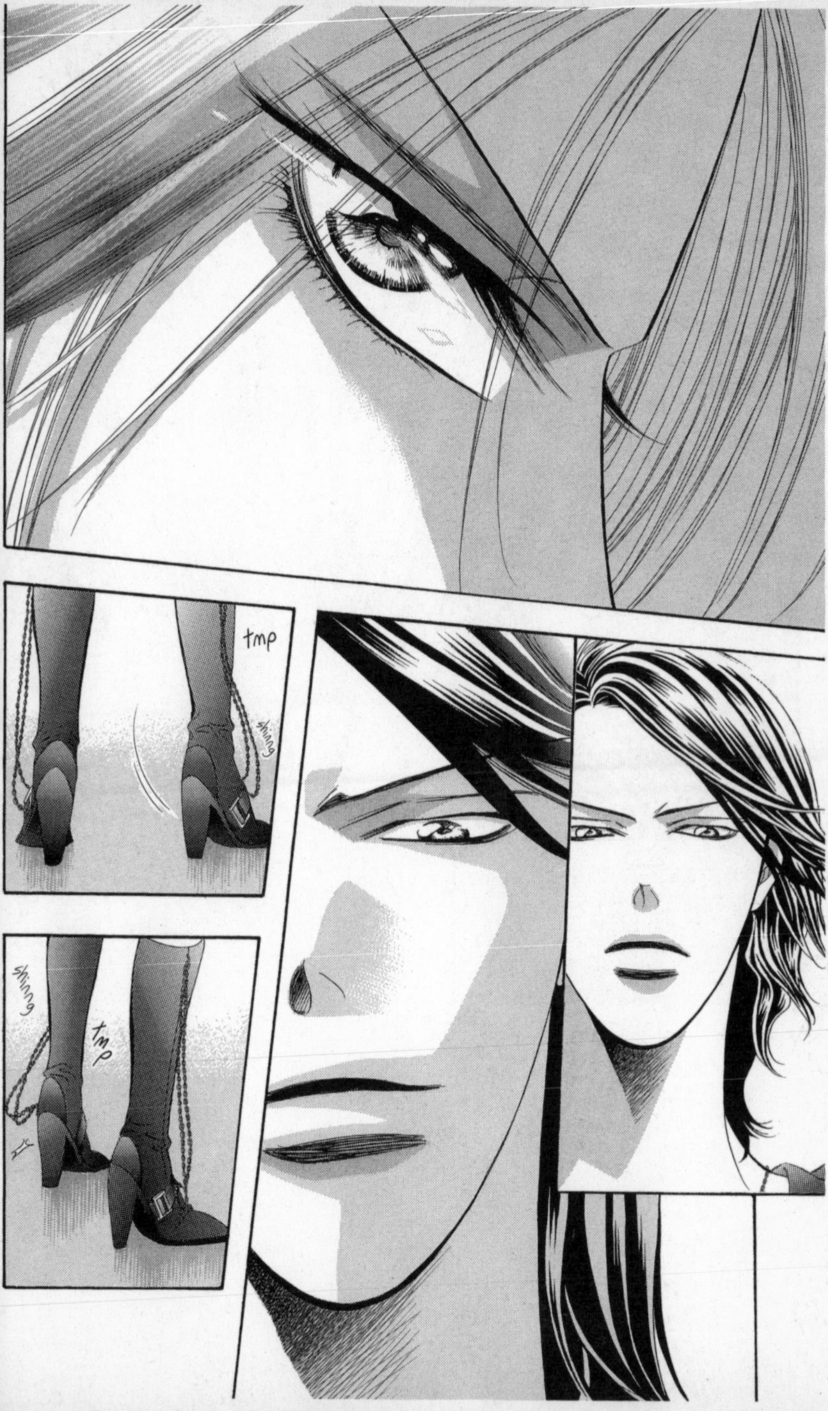
tmp
shiing
shiing
tmp

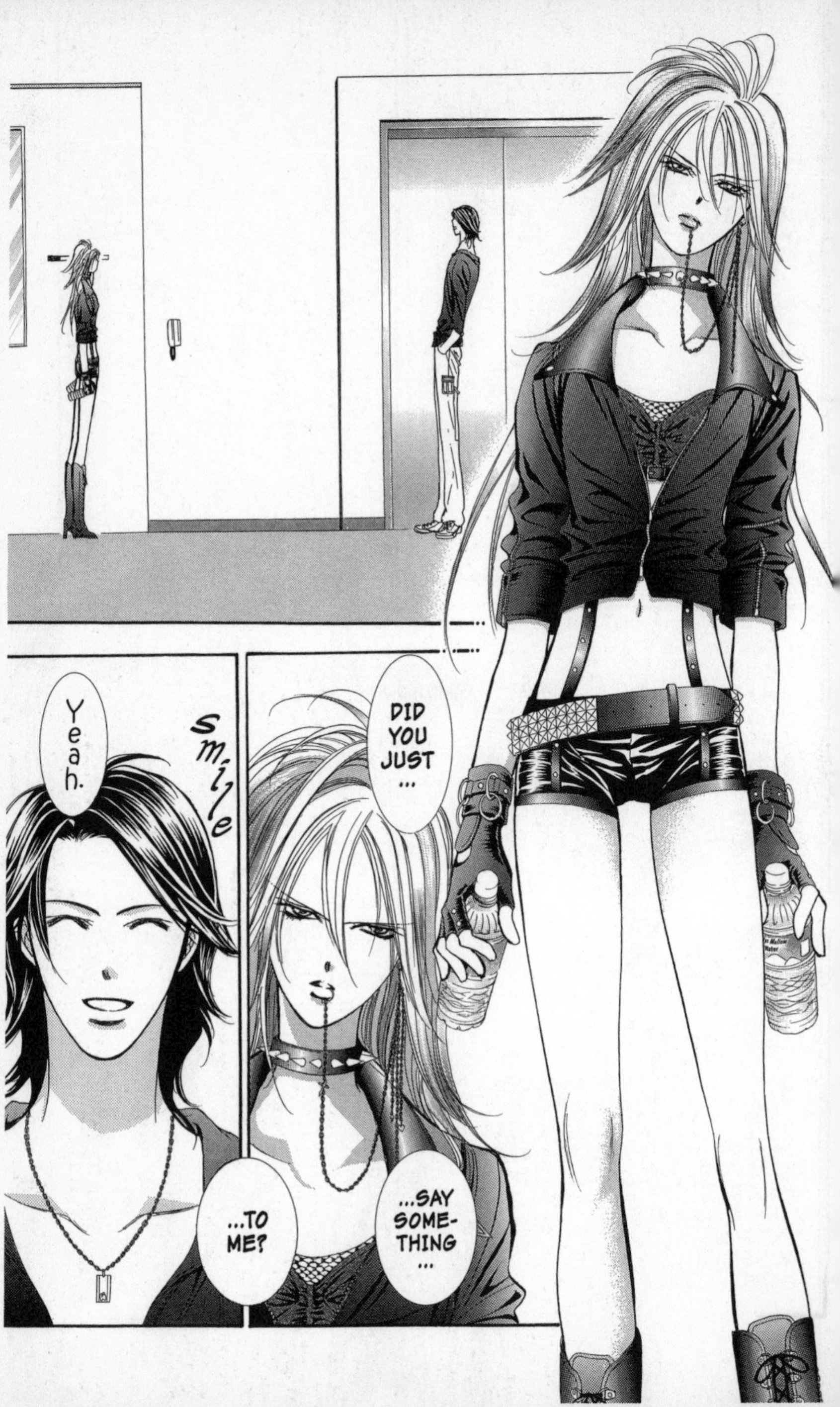
DID YOU JUST ...
...SAY SOME-THING ...
...TO ME?
smile
Yeah.

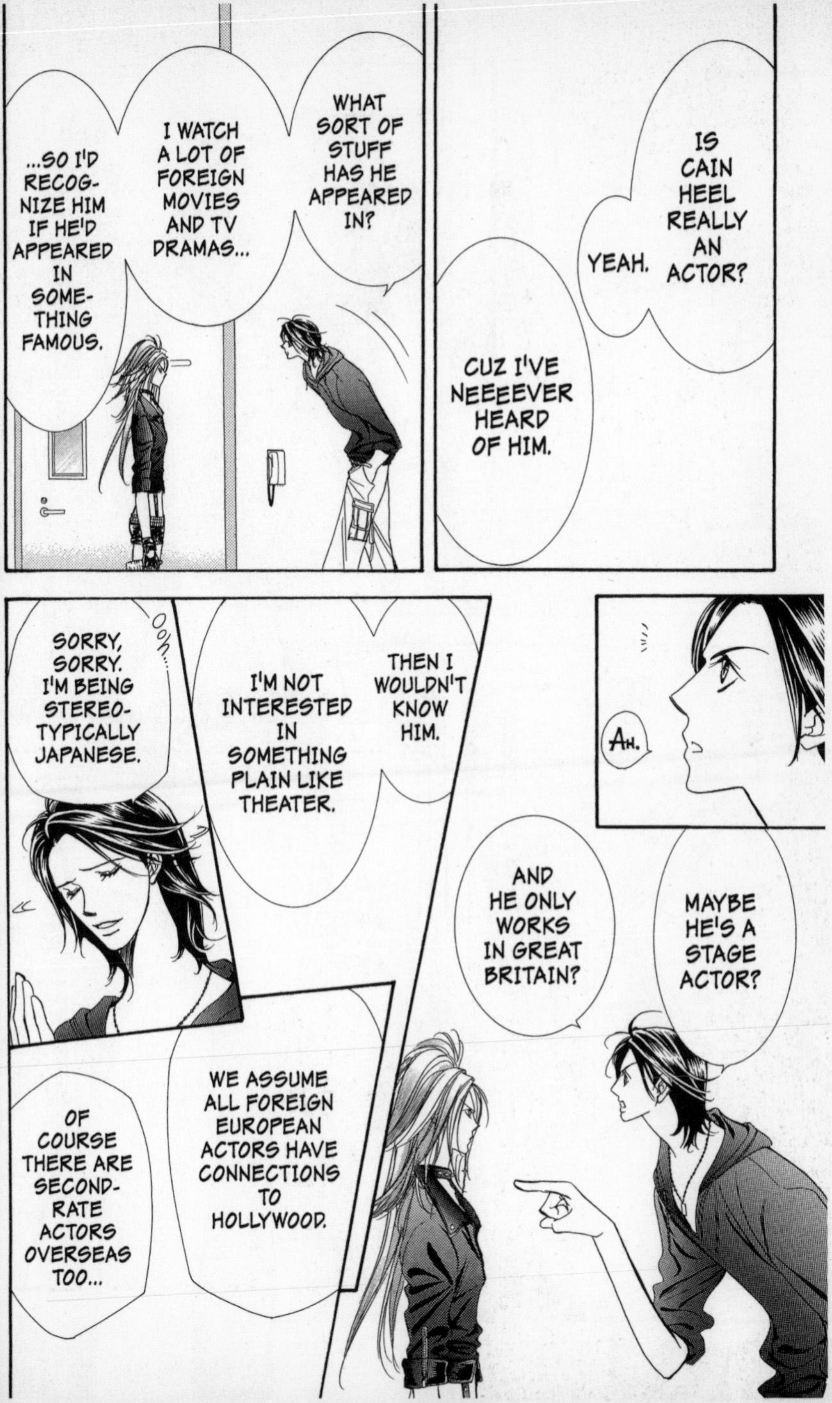
IS CAIN HEEL REALLY AN ACTOR?
YEAH.
CUZ I'VE NEEEEVER HEARD OF HIM.
WHAT SORT OF STUFF HAS HE APPEARED IN?
I WATCH A LOT OF FOREIGN MOVIES AND TV DRAMAS...
...SO I'D RECOG-NIZE HIM IF HE'D APPEARED IN SOME-THING FAMOUS.
AH.
MAYBE HE'S A STAGE ACTOR?
AND HE ONLY WORKS IN GREAT BRITAIN?
THEN I WOULDN'T KNOW HIM.
I'M NOT INTERESTED IN SOMETHING PLAIN LIKE THEATER.
OOH...
SORRY, SORRY. I'M BEING STEREO-TYPICALLY JAPANESE.
WE ASSUME ALL FOREIGN EUROPEAN ACTORS HAVE CONNECTIONS TO HOLLYWOOD.
OF COURSE THERE ARE SECOND-RATE ACTORS OVERSEAS TOO...

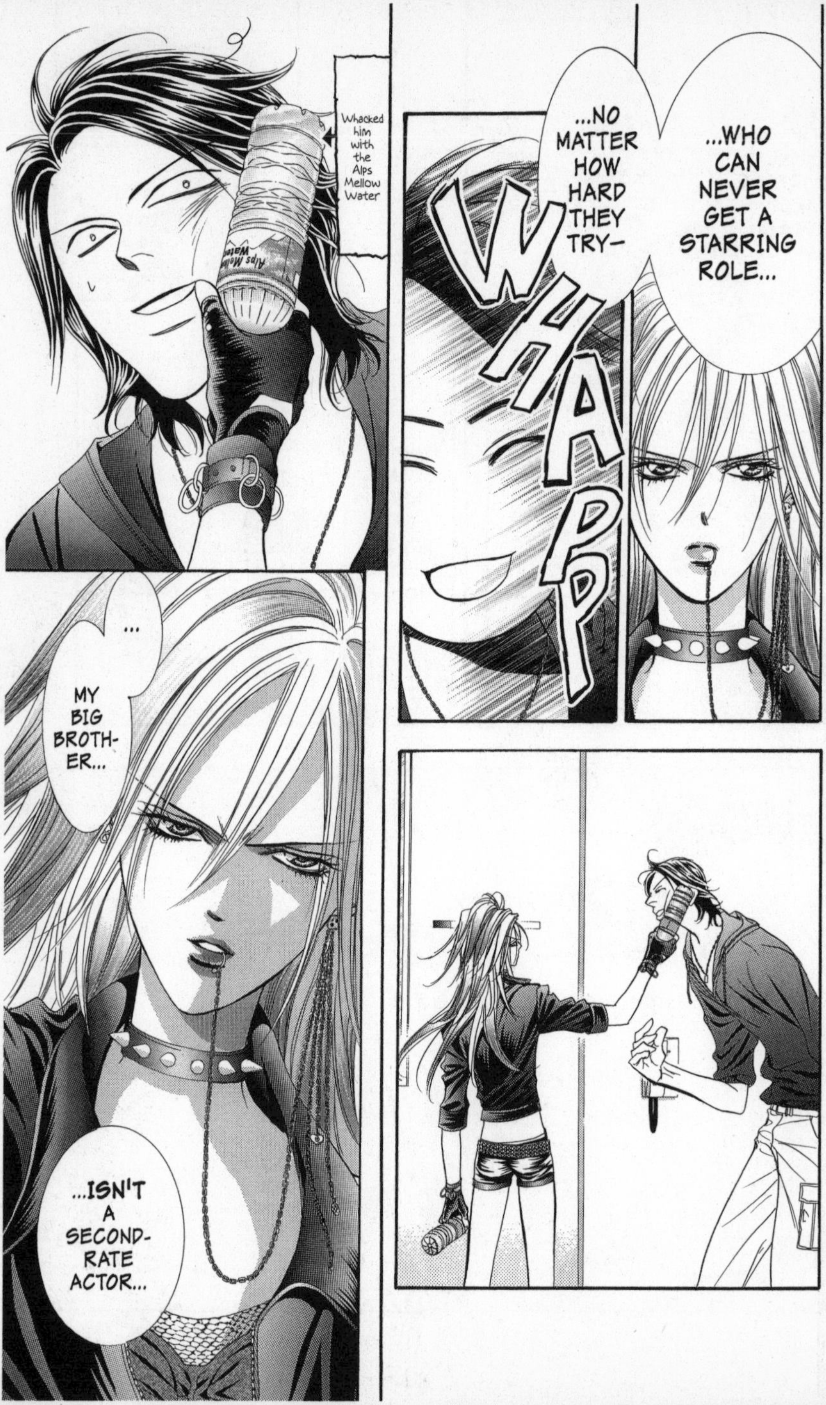
...NO MATTER HOW HARD THEY TRY-
...WHO CAN NEVER GET A STARRING ROLE...
WHAPP
Whacked him with the Alps Mellow Water
Alps Mellow Water
...
MY BIG BROTHER-ER...
...ISN'T A SECOND-RATE ACTOR...

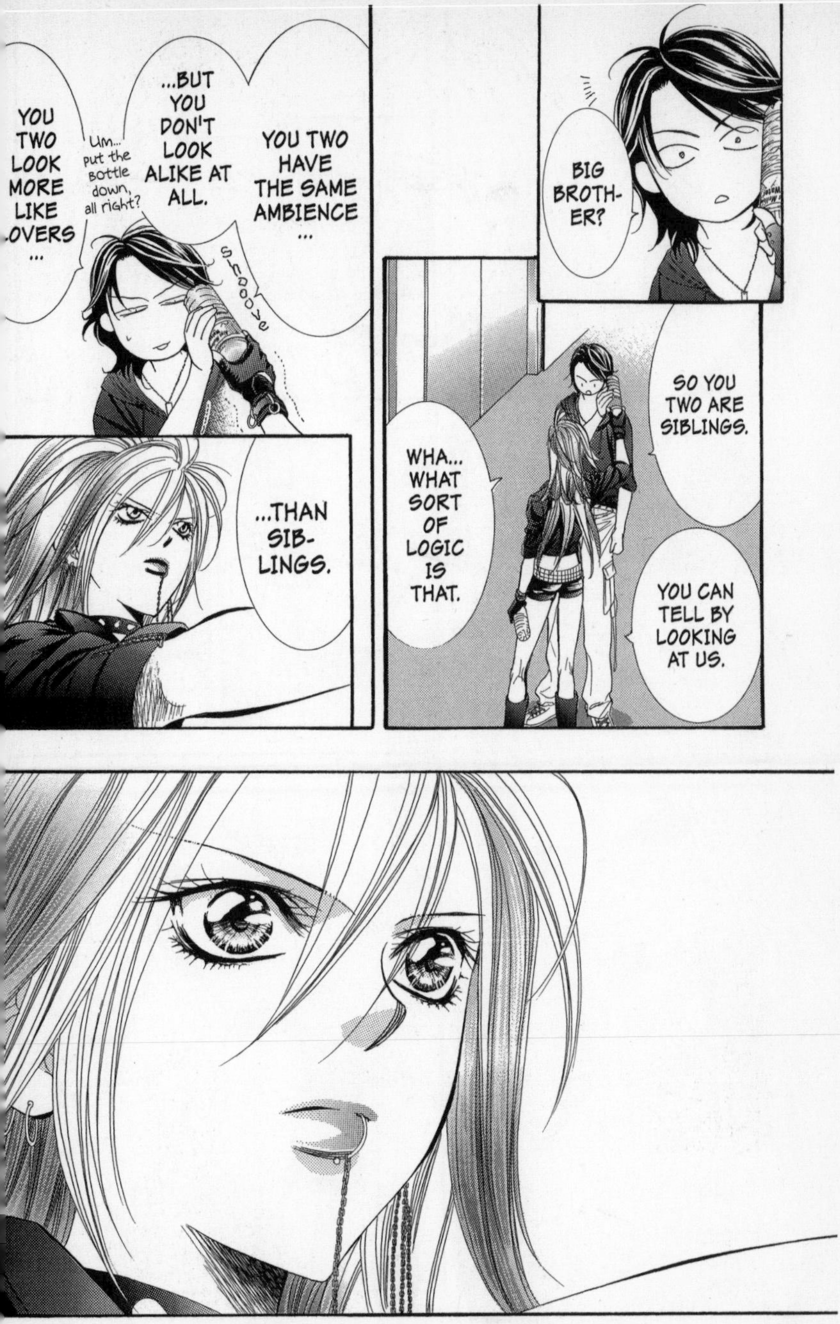
BIG BROTH-ER?
SO YOU TWO ARE SIBLINGS.
YOU CAN TELL BY LOOKING AT US.
WHA... WHAT SORT OF LOGIC IS THAT.
YOU TWO HAVE THE SAME AMBIENCE ...
...BUT YOU DON'T LOOK ALIKE AT ALL.
Um... put the bottle down, all right?
shooove
YOU TWO LOOK MORE LIKE LOVERS ...
...THAN SIB-LINGS.

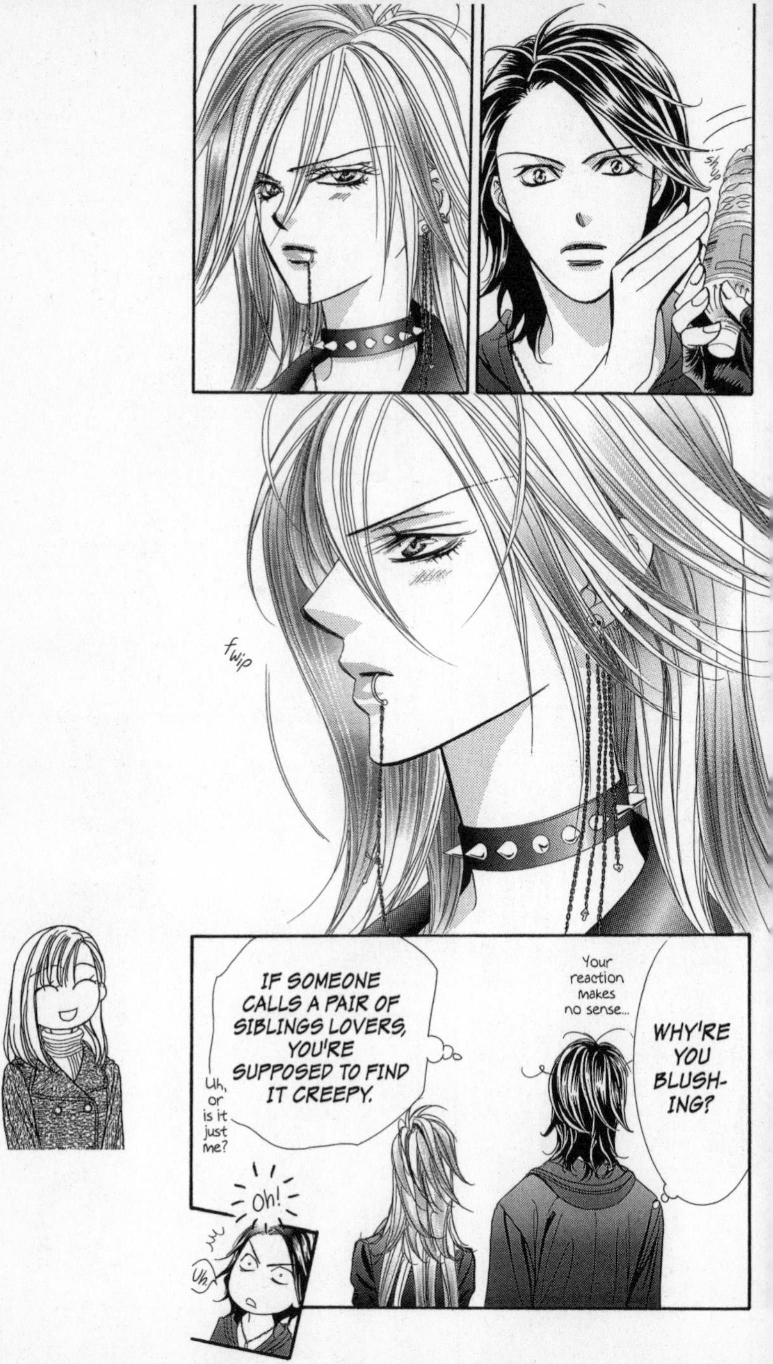
shup
fwip
WHY'RE YOU BLUSHING?
Your reaction makes no sense...
IF SOMEONE CALLS A PAIR OF SIBLINGS LOVERS, YOU'RE SUPPOSED TO FIND IT CREEPY.
Uh, or is it just me?
Oh!
Uh.

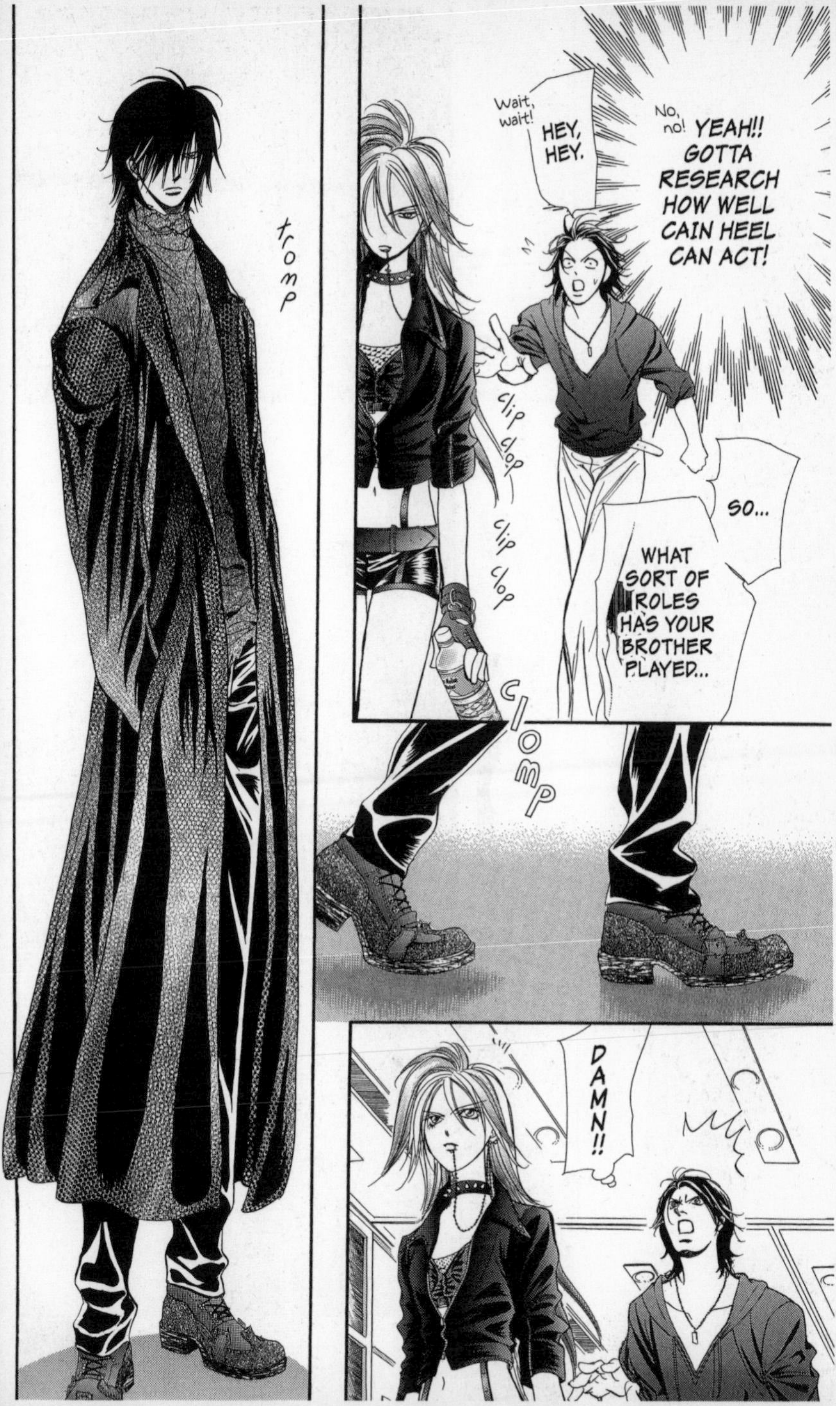
No, no! YEAH!! GOTTA RESEARCH HOW WELL CAIN HEEL CAN ACT!
Wait, wait!
HEY, HEY.
clip clop
clip clop
SO...
WHAT SORT OF ROLES HAS YOUR BROTHER PLAYED...
CLOMP
DAMN!!
tromp

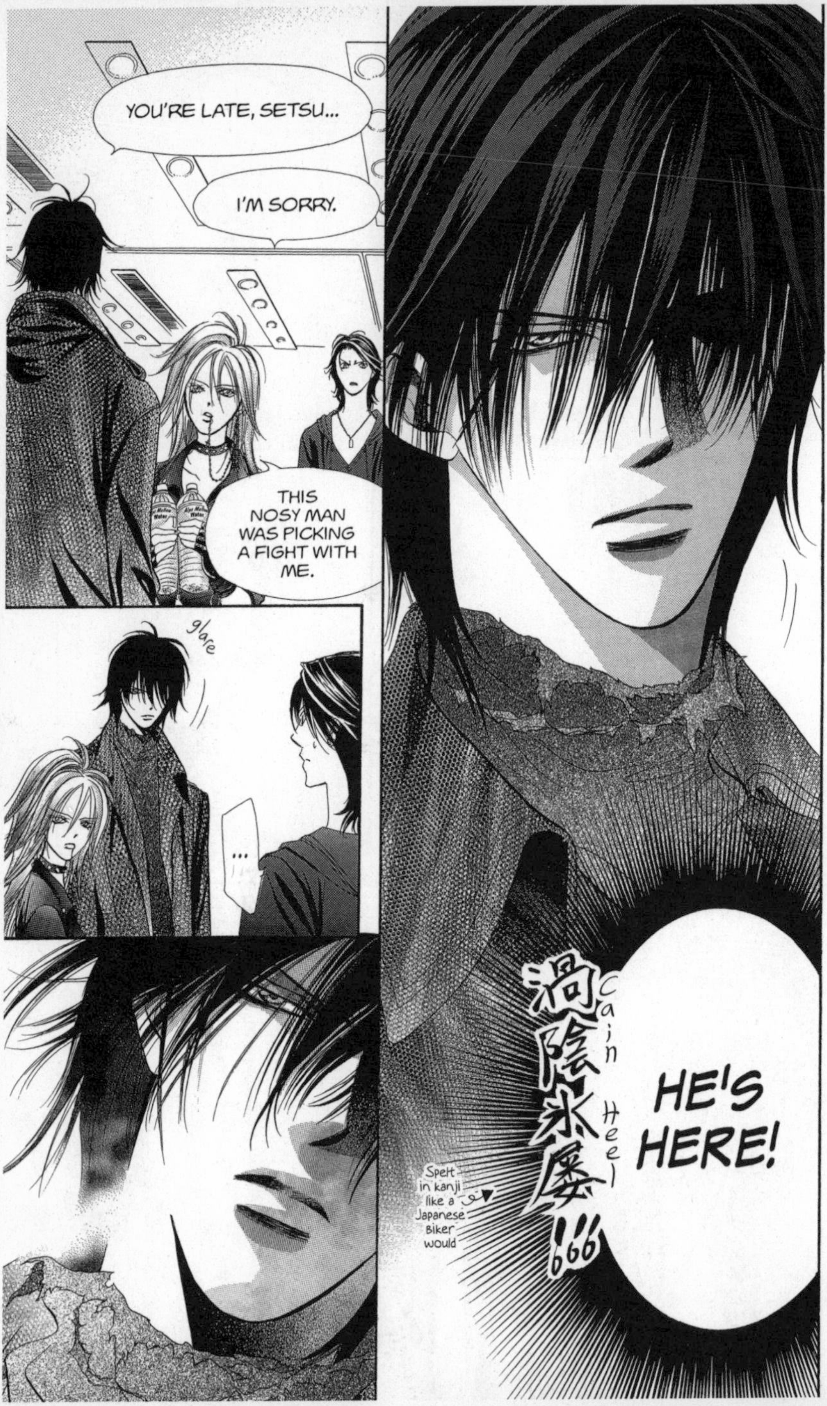
Cain Heel
666
HE'S HERE!
Spelt in kanji like a Japanese Biker would
YOU'RE LATE, SETSU...
I'M SORRY.
THIS NOSY MAN WAS PICKING A FIGHT WITH ME.
glare
...

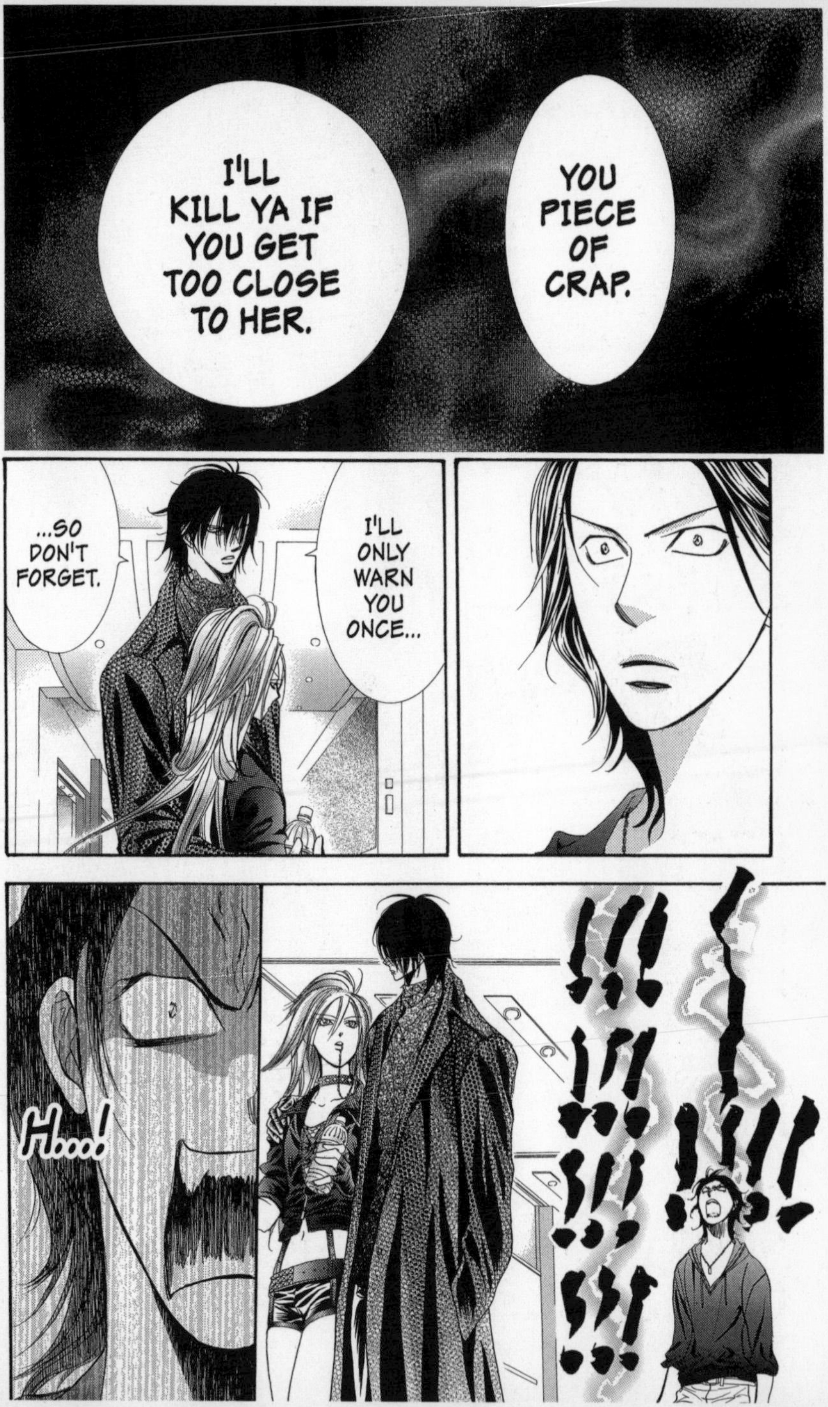
I'LL KILL YA IF YOU GET TOO CLOSE TO HER.
YOU PIECE OF CRAP.
I'LL ONLY WARN YOU ONCE...
...SO DON'T FORGET.
Hoo!

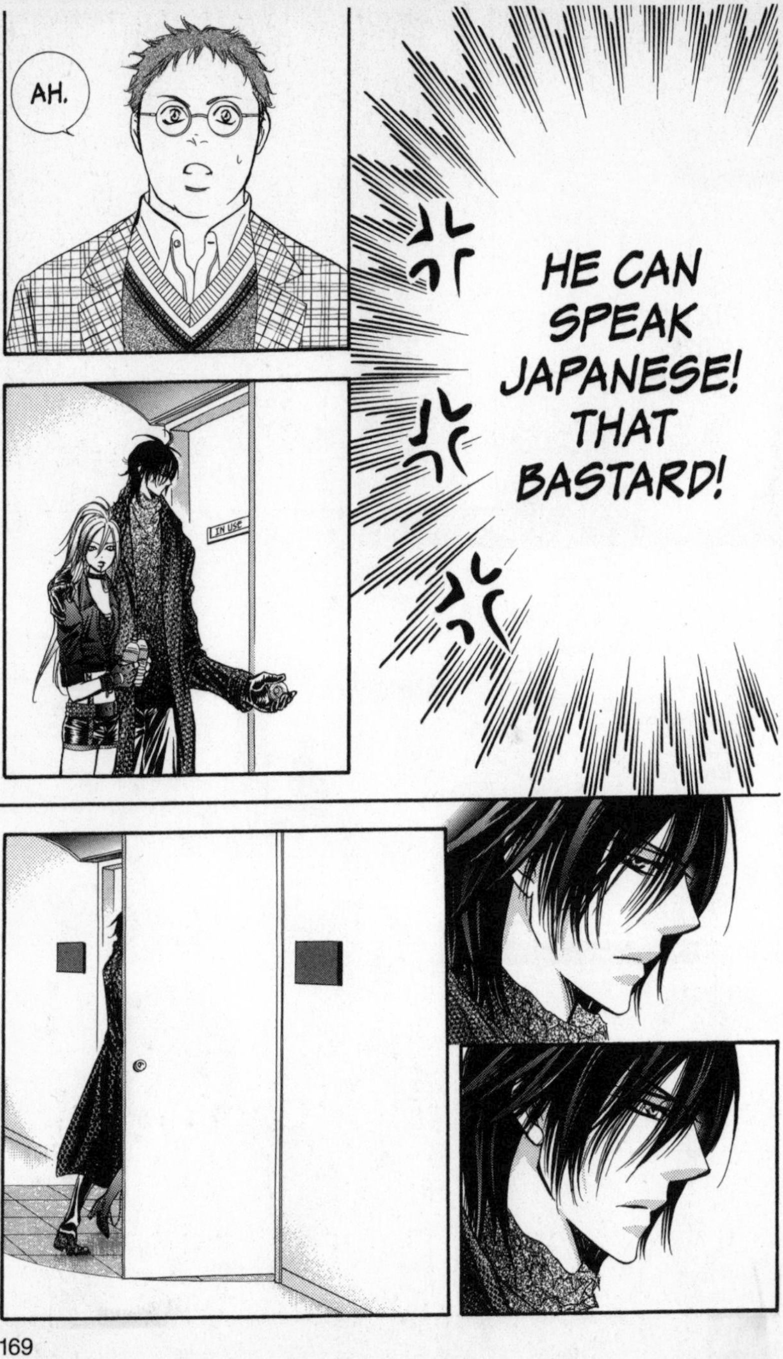
HE CAN SPEAK JAPANESE! THAT BASTARD!
AH.
IN USE

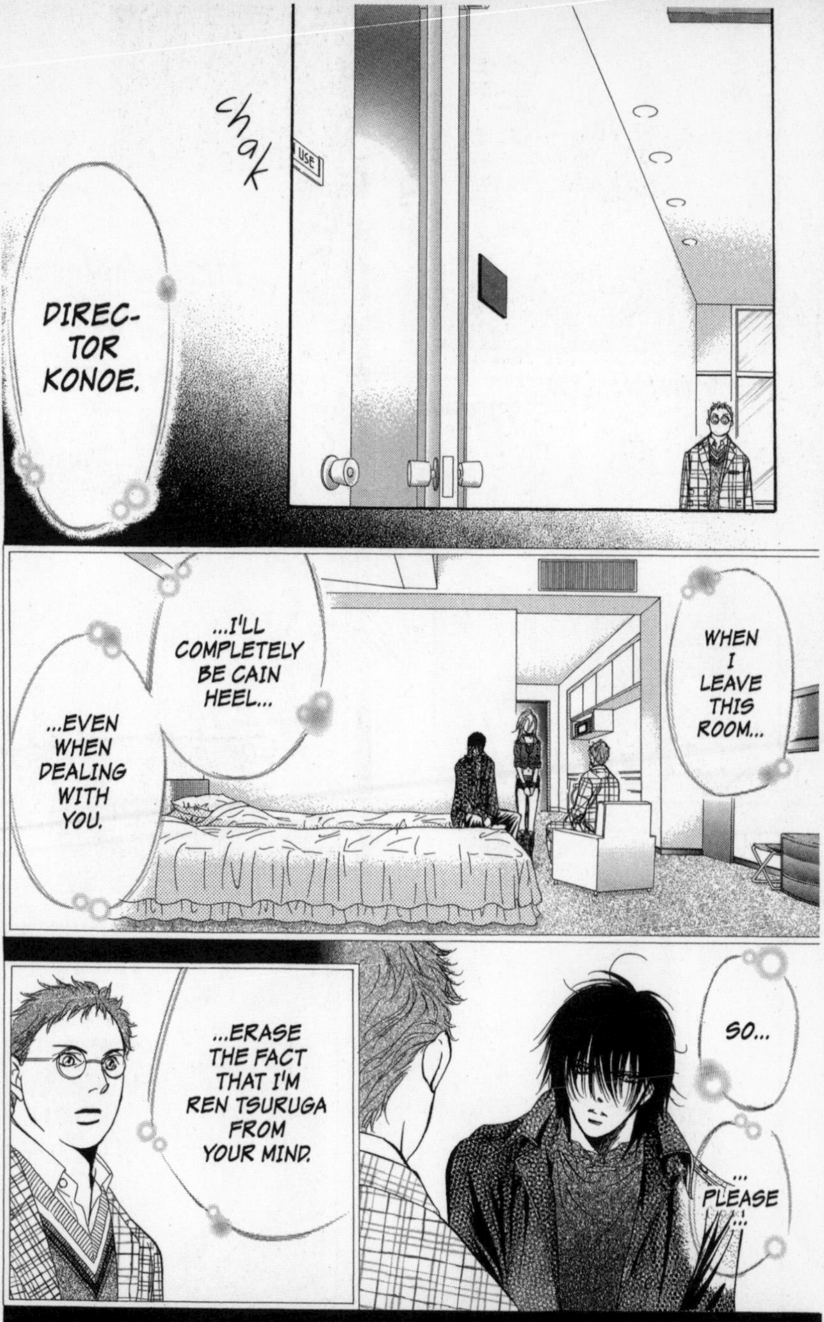

USE
chak
DIREC-TOR KONOE.
WHEN I LEAVE THIS ROOM...
...I'LL COMPLETELY BE CAIN HEEL...
...EVEN WHEN DEALING WITH YOU.
SO...
...PLEASE...
...ERASE THE FACT THAT I'M REN TSURUGA FROM YOUR MIND.

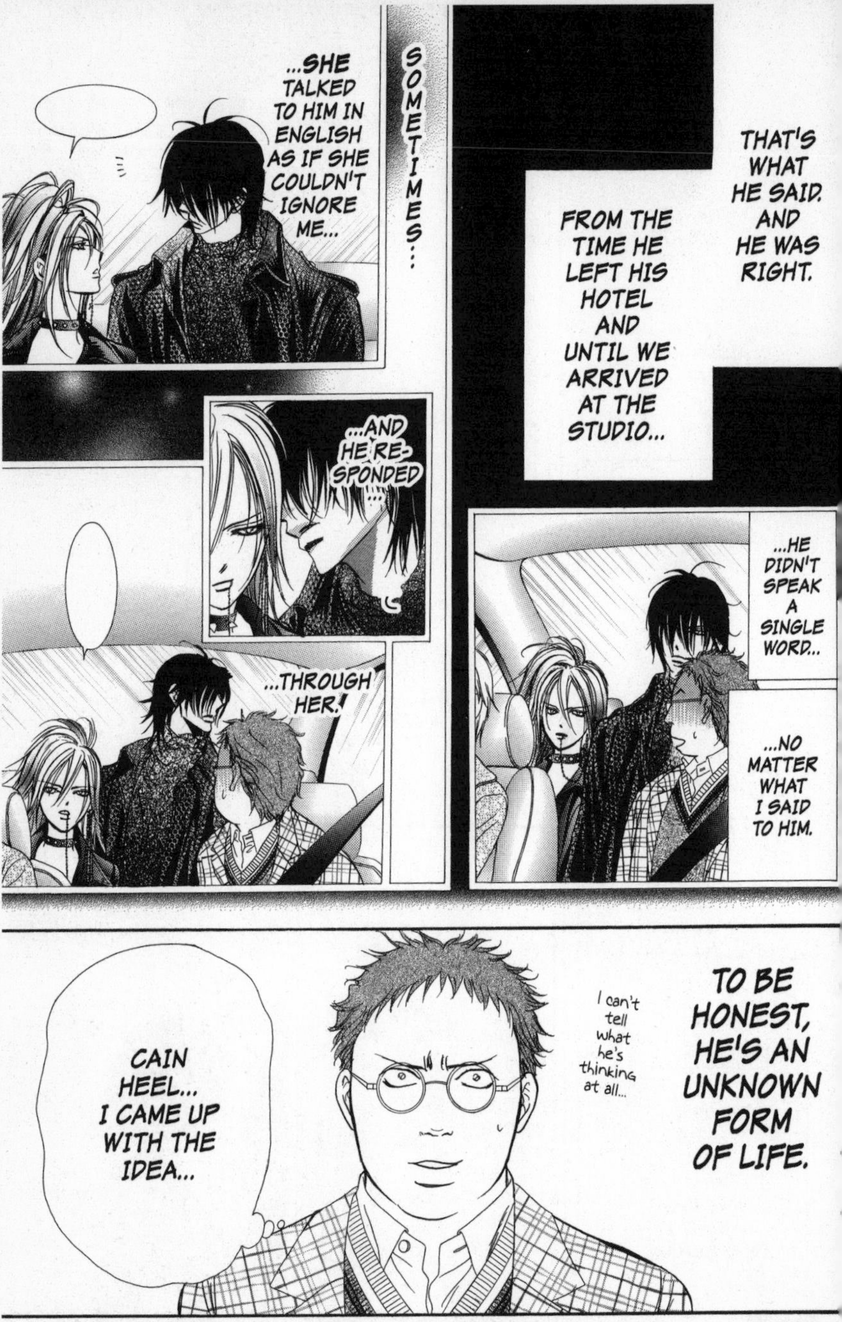
THAT'S WHAT HE SAID. AND HE WAS RIGHT.
FROM THE TIME HE LEFT HIS HOTEL AND UNTIL WE ARRIVED AT THE STUDIO...
...HE DIDN'T SPEAK A SINGLE WORD...
...NO MATTER WHAT I SAID TO HIM.
SOMETIMES...
...SHE TALKED TO HIM IN ENGLISH AS IF SHE COULDN'T IGNORE ME...
...AND HE RE-SPONDED...
...THROUGH HER.
TO BE HONEST, HE'S AN UNKNOWN FORM OF LIFE.
I can't tell what he's thinking at all...
CAIN HEEL... I CAME UP WITH THE IDEA...

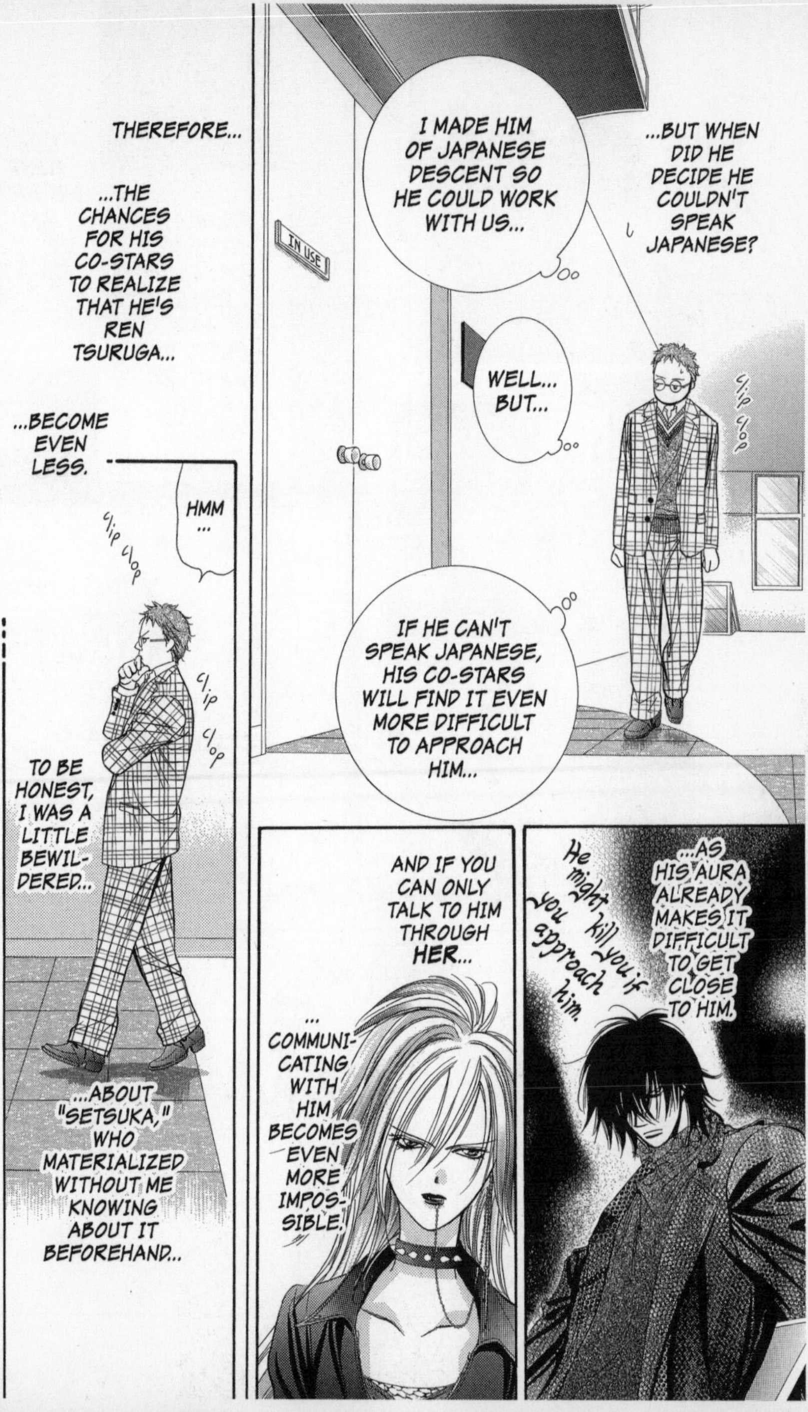

...BUT WHEN DID HE DECIDE HE COULDN'T SPEAK JAPANESE?
I MADE HIM OF JAPANESE DESCENT SO HE COULD WORK WITH US...
IN USE
WELL... BUT...
clip clop
IF HE CAN'T SPEAK JAPANESE, HIS CO-STARS WILL FIND IT EVEN MORE DIFFICULT TO APPROACH HIM...
...AS HIS AURA ALREADY MAKES IT DIFFICULT TO GET CLOSE TO HIM.
He might kill you if you approach him.
AND IF YOU CAN ONLY TALK TO HIM THROUGH HER...
...COMMUNICATING WITH HIM BECOMES EVEN MORE IMPOSSIBLE.
THEREFORE...
...THE CHANCES FOR HIS CO-STARS TO REALIZE THAT HE'S REN TSURUGA...
...BECOME EVEN LESS.
HMM...
clip clop
clip clop
TO BE HONEST, I WAS A LITTLE BEWILDERED...
...ABOUT "SETSUKA," WHO MATERIALIZED WITHOUT ME KNOWING ABOUT IT BEFOREHAND...

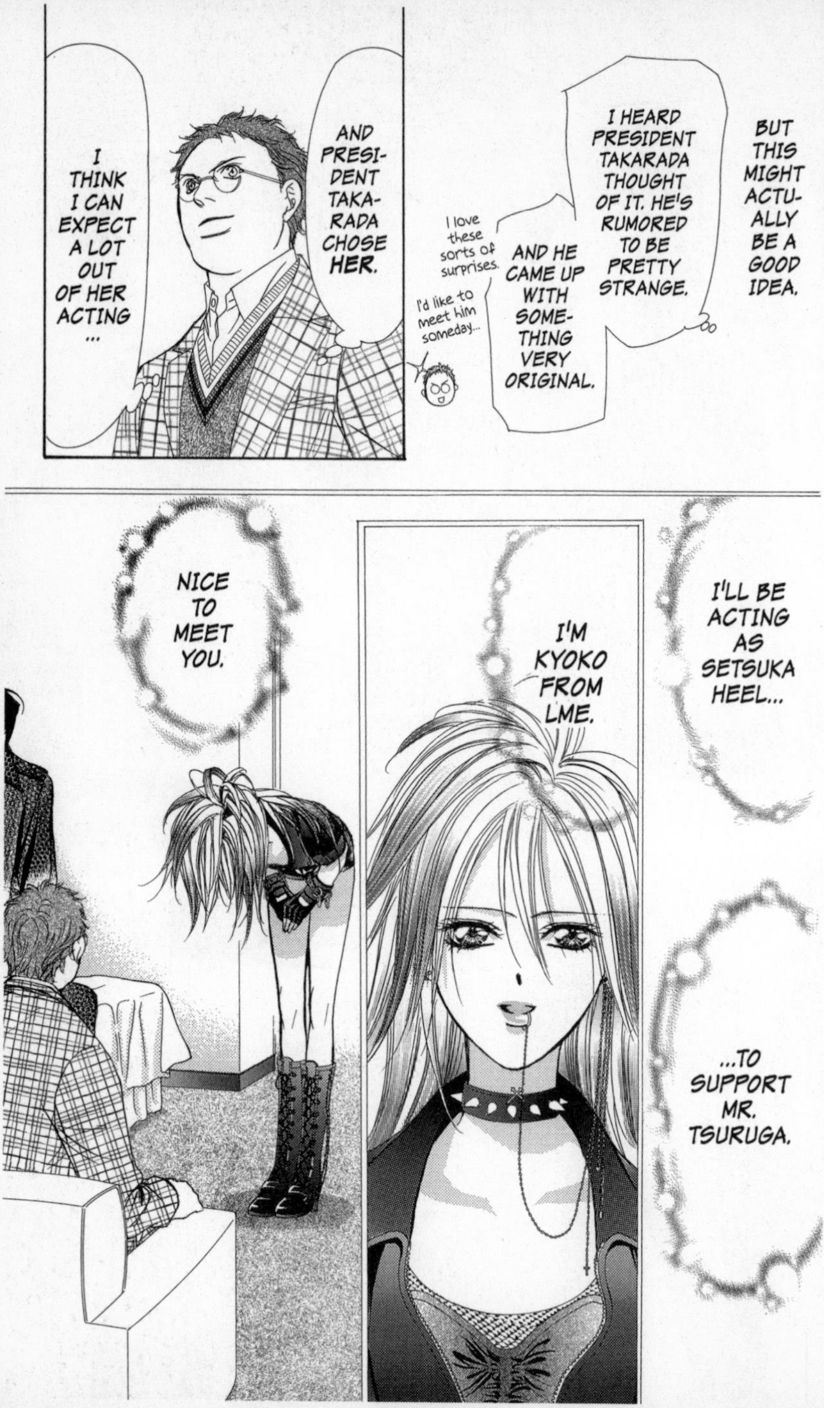
BUT THIS MIGHT ACTUALLY BE A GOOD IDEA.
I HEARD PRESIDENT TAKARADA THOUGHT OF IT. HE'S RUMORED TO BE PRETTY STRANGE.
AND HE CAME UP WITH SOMETHING VERY ORIGINAL.
I love these sorts of surprises.
I'd like to meet him someday...
AND PRESIDENT TAKARADA CHOSE HER.
I THINK I CAN EXPECT A LOT OUT OF HER ACTING...
I'LL BE ACTING AS SETSUKA HEEL...
I'M KYOKO FROM LME.
...TO SUPPORT MR. TSURUGA.
NICE TO MEET YOU.

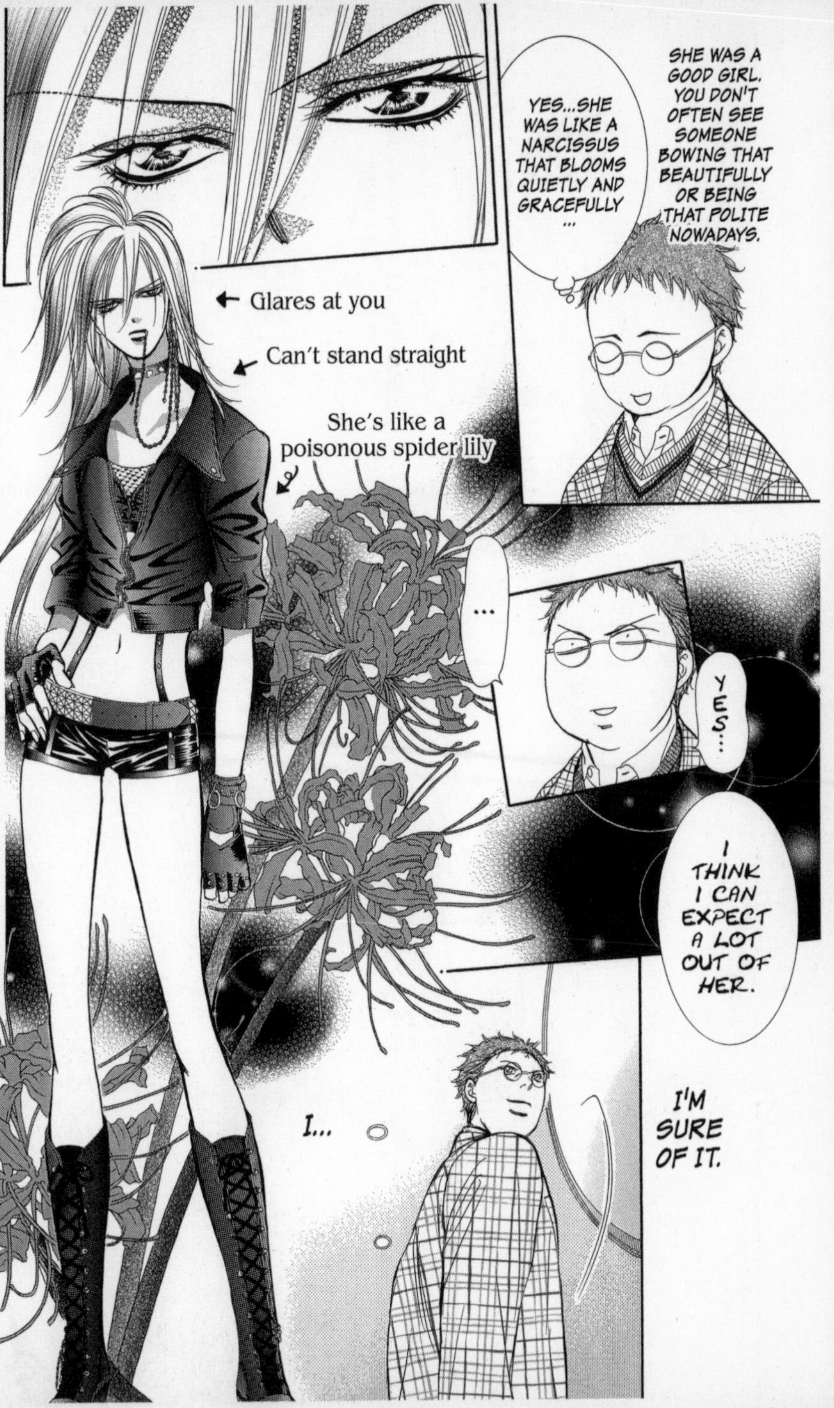
SHE WAS A GOOD GIRL. YOU DON'T OFTEN SEE SOMEONE BOWING THAT BEAUTIFULLY OR BEING THAT POLITE NOWADAYS.
YES...SHE WAS LIKE A NARCISSUS THAT BLOOMS QUIETLY AND GRACEFULLY ...
Glares at you
Can't stand straight
She's like a poisonous spider lily
...
YES...
I THINK I CAN EXPECT A LOT OUT OF HER.
I'M SURE OF IT.
I...

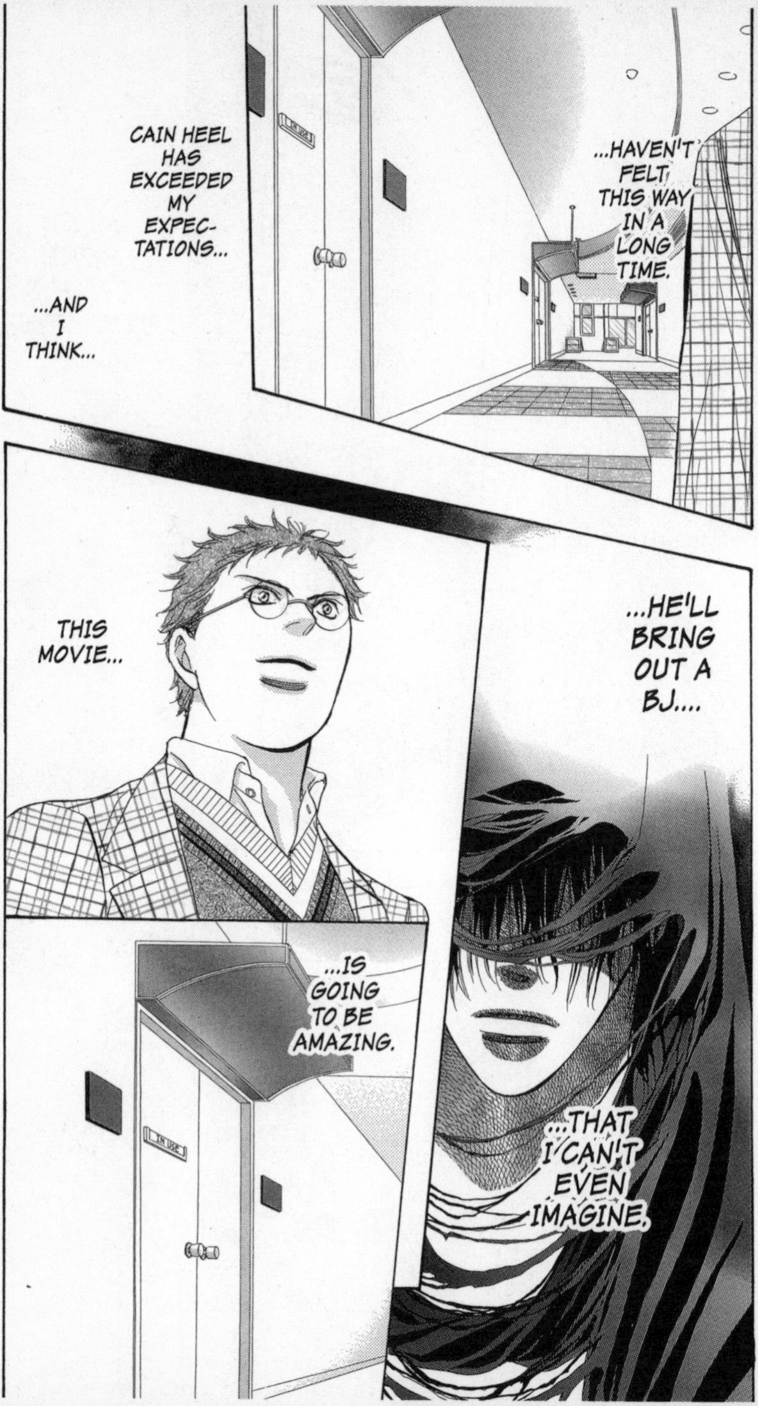
...HAVEN'T FELT THIS WAY IN A LONG TIME.
CAIN HEEL HAS EXCEEDED MY EXPECTATIONS...
...AND I THINK...
...HE'LL BRING OUT A BJ....
...THAT I CAN'T EVEN IMAGINE.
THIS MOVIE...
...IS GOING TO BE AMAZING.

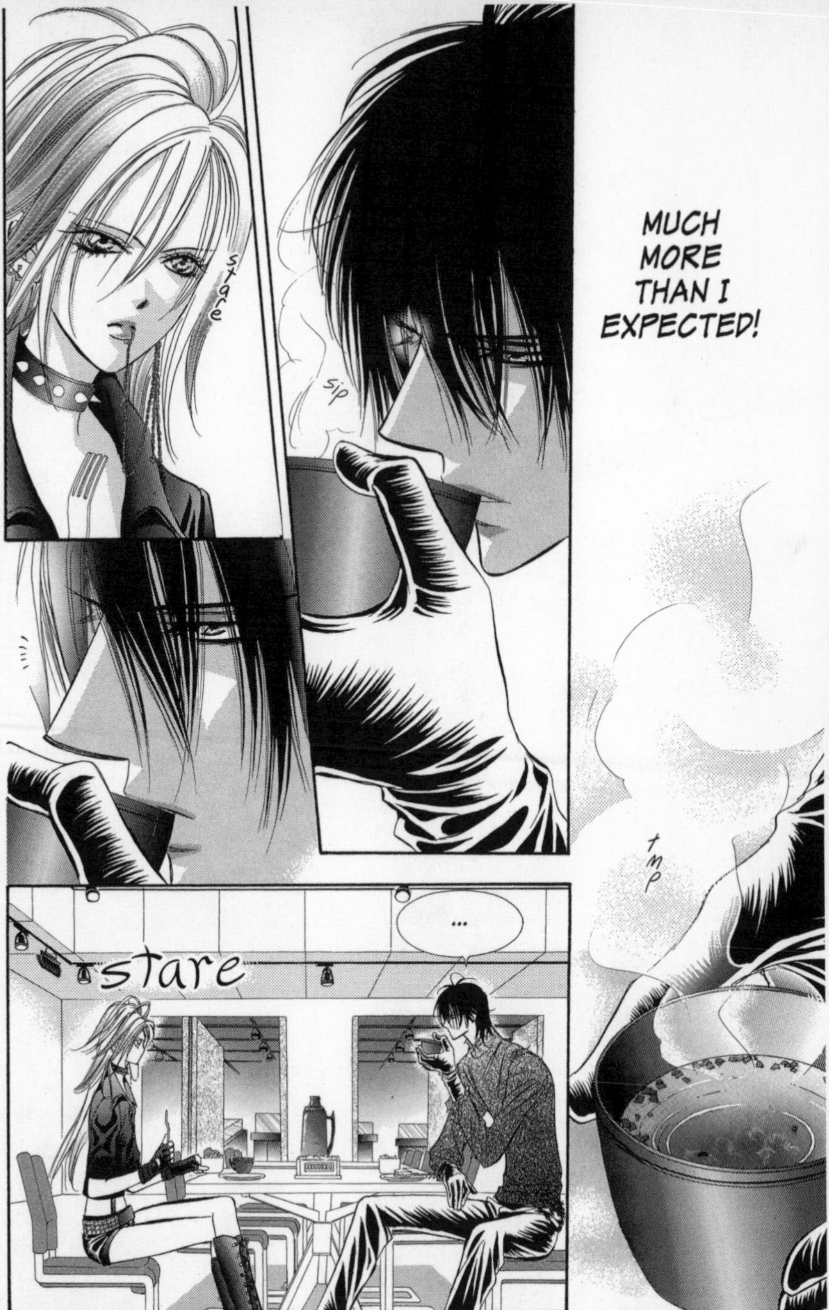
MUCH MORE THAN I EXPECTED!
sip
stare
stare
...
tmp

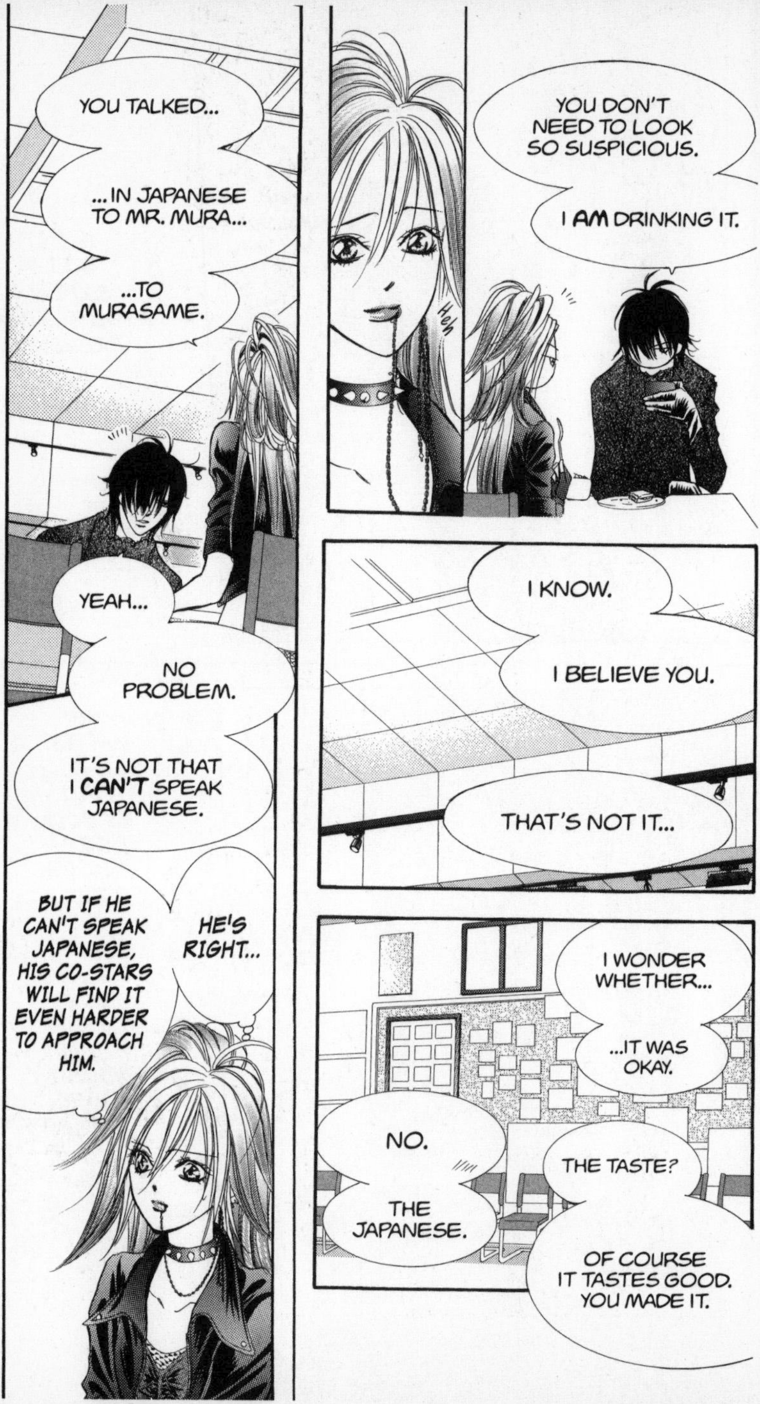
YOU DON'T NEED TO LOOK SO SUSPICIOUS.
I **AM** DRINKING IT.
Heh
I KNOW.
I BELIEVE YOU.
THAT'S NOT IT...
I WONDER WHETHER...
...IT WAS OKAY.
THE TASTE?
OF COURSE IT TASTES GOOD. YOU MADE IT.
NO.
THE JAPANESE.
YOU TALKED...
...IN JAPANESE TO MR. MURA...
...TO MURASAME.
YEAH...
NO PROBLEM.
IT'S NOT THAT I **CAN'T** SPEAK JAPANESE.
HE'S RIGHT...
BUT IF HE CAN'T SPEAK JAPANESE, HIS CO-STARS WILL FIND IT EVEN HARDER TO APPROACH HIM.

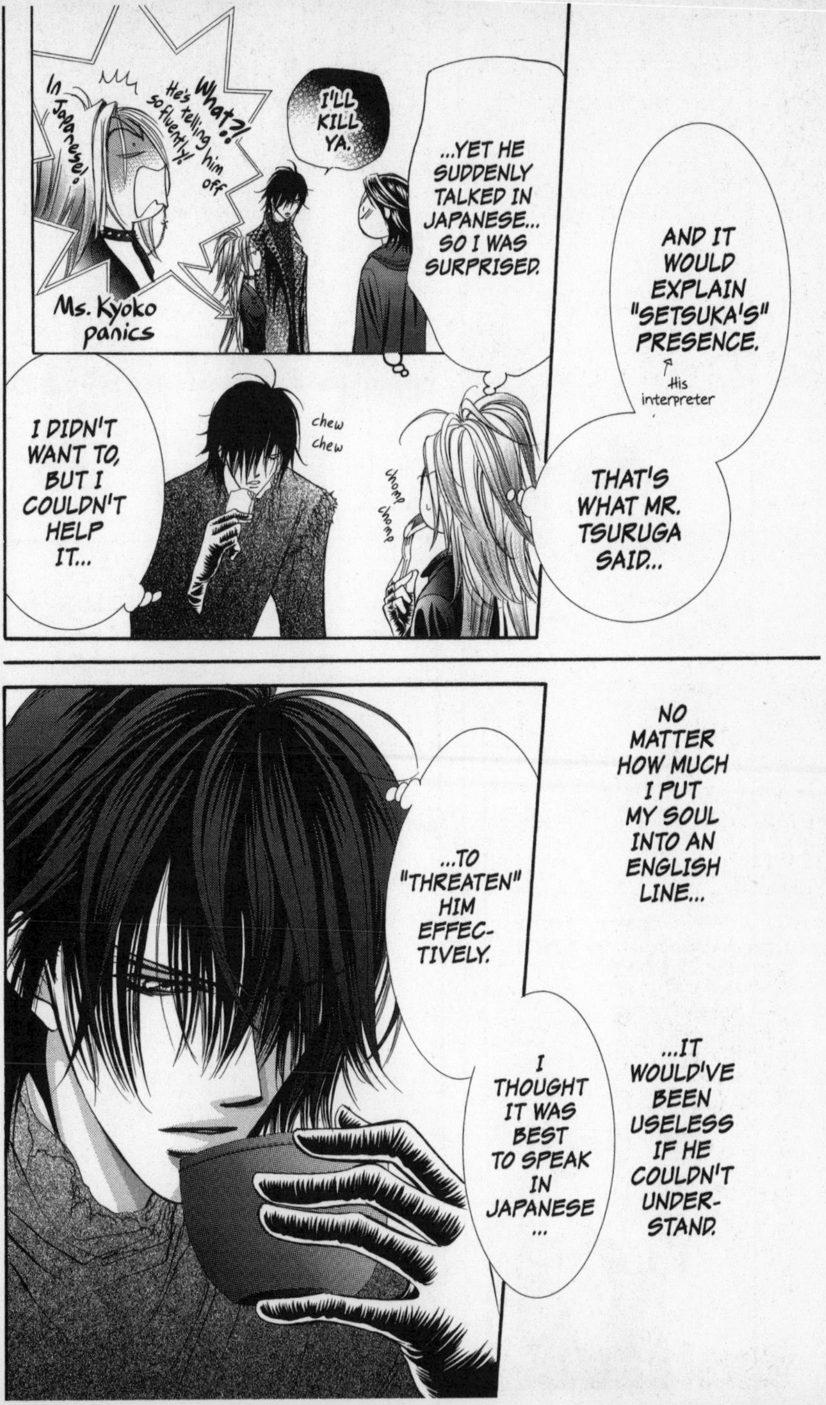
AND IT WOULD EXPLAIN "SETSUKA'S" PRESENCE.
His interpreter
THAT'S WHAT MR. TSURUGA SAID...
...YET HE SUDDENLY TALKED IN JAPANESE... SO I WAS SURPRISED.
I'LL KILL YA.
What?!
He's telling him off so fluently!
In Japanese!
Ms. Kyoko panics
chomp chomp
chew chew
I DIDN'T WANT TO, BUT I COULDN'T HELP IT...
NO MATTER HOW MUCH I PUT MY SOUL INTO AN ENGLISH LINE...
...IT WOULD'VE BEEN USELESS IF HE COULDN'T UNDER-STAND.
...TO "THREATEN" HIM EFFEC-TIVELY.
I THOUGHT IT WAS BEST TO SPEAK IN JAPANESE ...

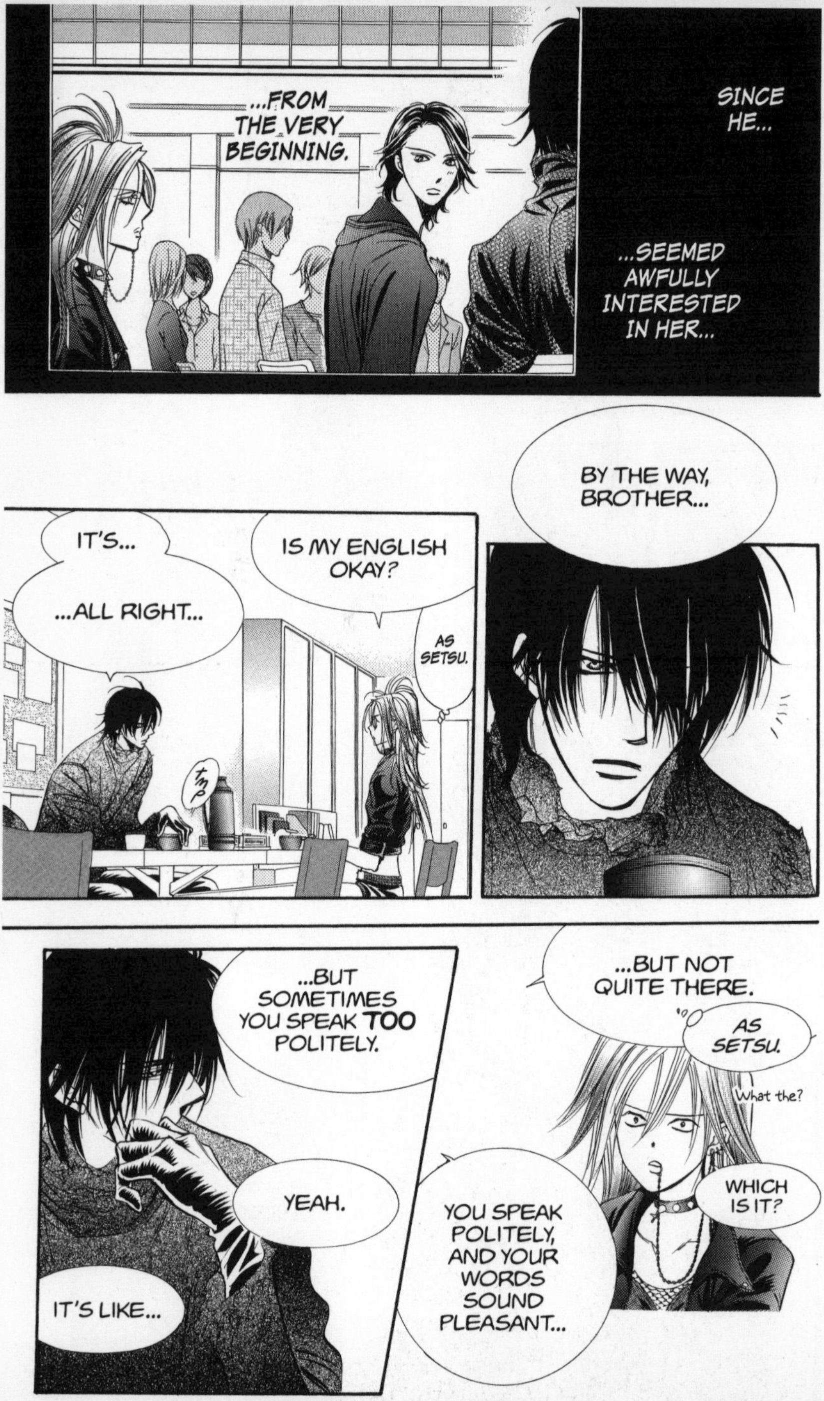
SINCE HE...
...SEEMED AWFULLY INTERESTED IN HER...
...FROM THE VERY BEGINNING.
BY THE WAY, BROTHER...
IS MY ENGLISH OKAY?
AS SETSU.
IT'S...
...ALL RIGHT...
tmp
...BUT NOT QUITE THERE.
AS SETSU.
What the?
WHICH IS IT?
YOU SPEAK POLITELY, AND YOUR WORDS SOUND PLEASANT...
...BUT SOMETIMES YOU SPEAK TOO POLITELY.
YEAH.
IT'S LIKE...

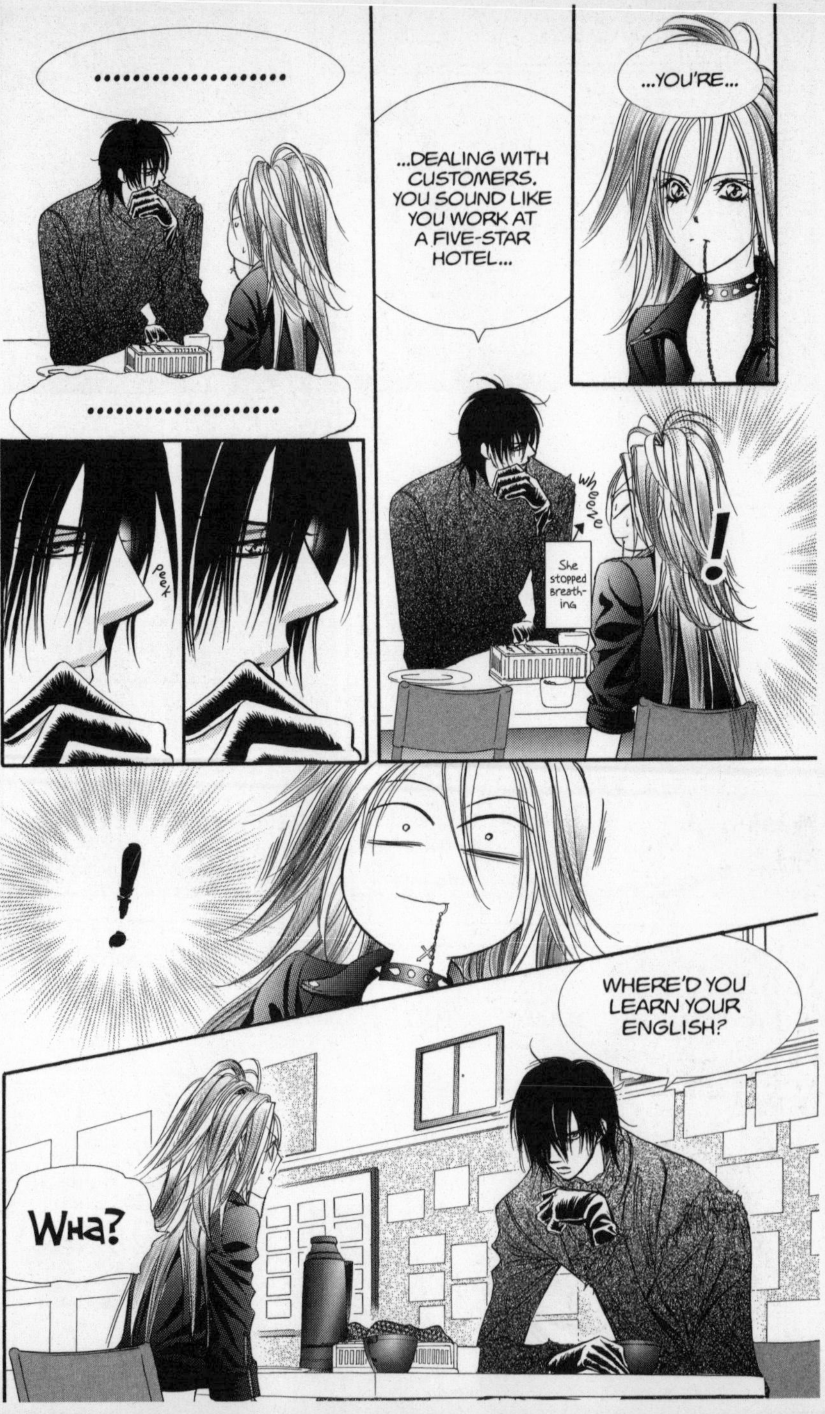
...YOU'RE...
...DEALING WITH CUSTOMERS. YOU SOUND LIKE YOU WORK AT A FIVE-STAR HOTEL...
....
....
!
wheeze
She stopped breath-ing
peek
!
WHERE'D YOU LEARN YOUR ENGLISH?
WHa?

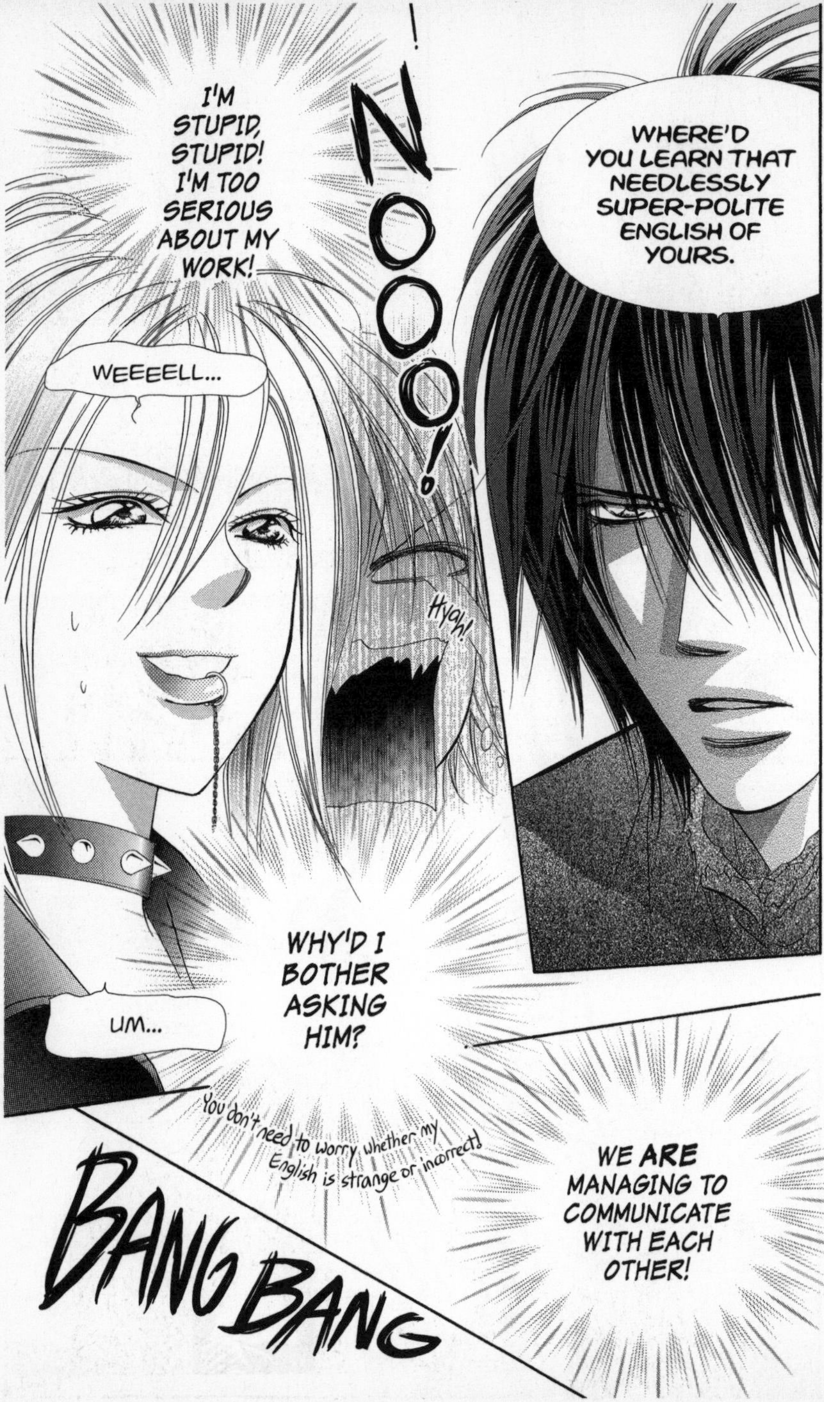
WHERE'D YOU LEARN THAT NEEDLESSLY SUPER-POLITE ENGLISH OF YOURS.
!
NOOO!
I'M STUPID, STUPID! I'M TOO SERIOUS ABOUT MY WORK!
WEEEELL...
Hyah!
WHY'D I BOTHER ASKING HIM?
UM...
WE ARE MANAGING TO COMMUNICATE WITH EACH OTHER!
You don't need to worry whether my English is strange or incorrect!
BANG BANG

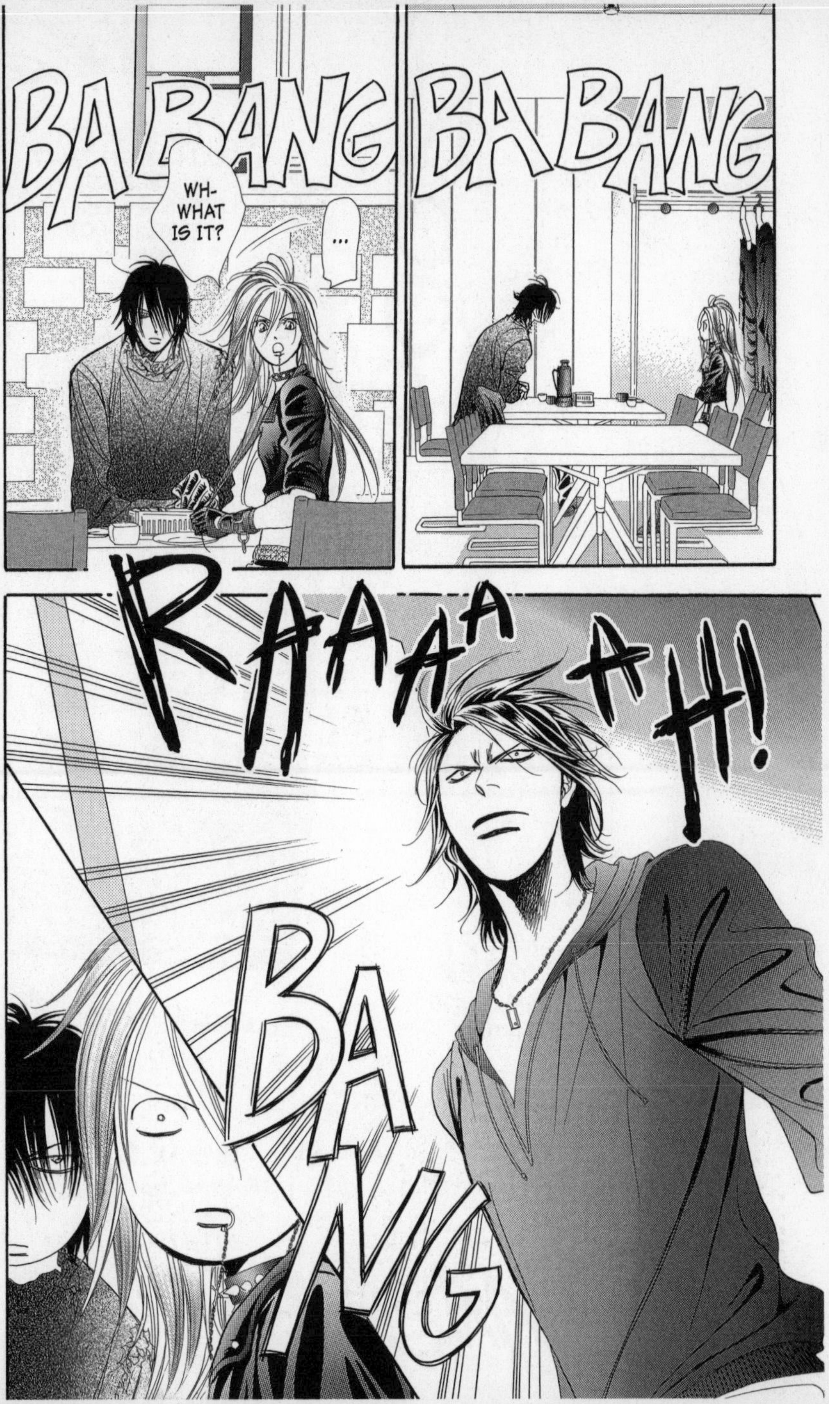
BA BANG
BA BANG
WH- WHAT IS IT?
...
RAAAAH!
BA BANG

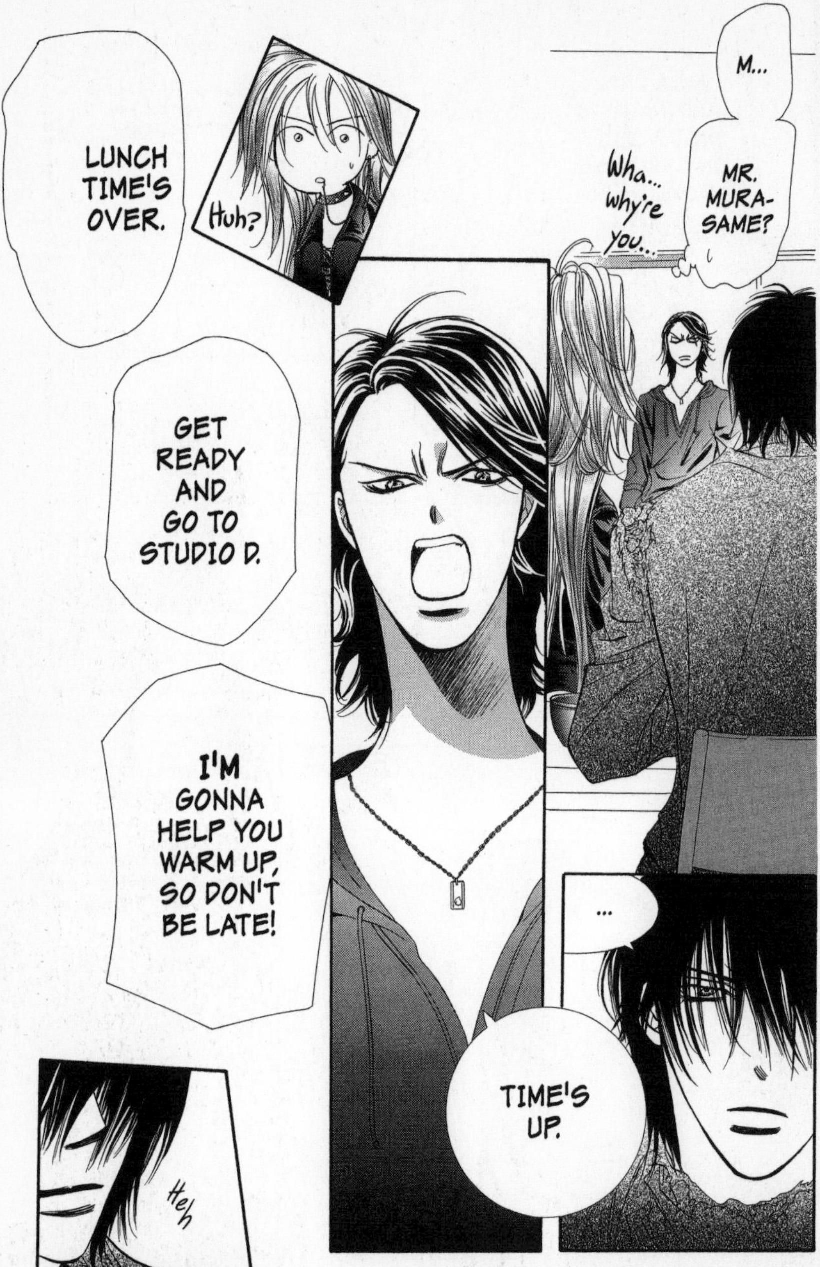
M...
MR. MURA-SAME?
Wha... why're you...
Huh?
LUNCH TIME'S OVER.
GET READY AND GO TO STUDIO D.
I'M GONNA HELP YOU WARM UP, SO DON'T BE LATE!
...
TIME'S UP.
Heh

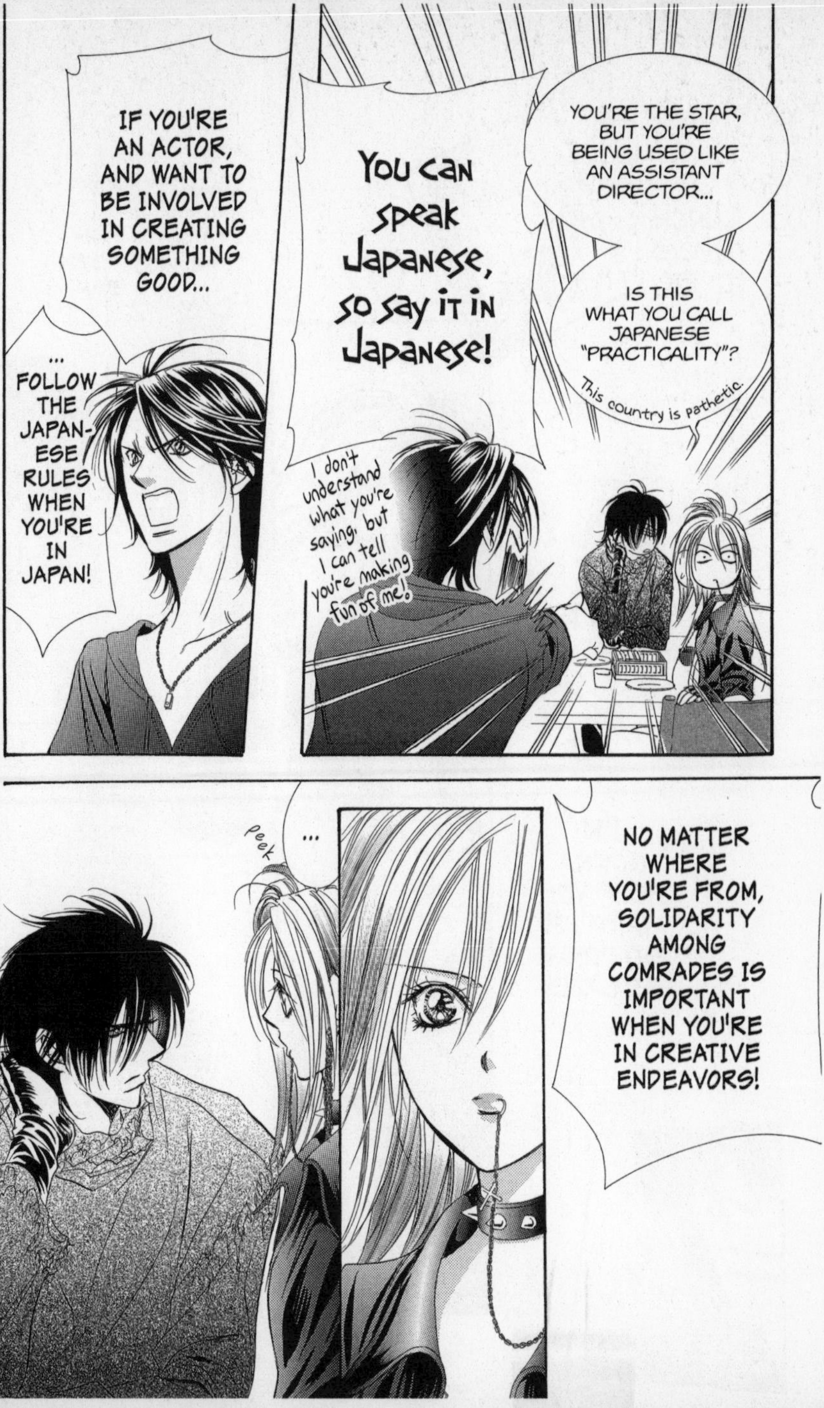
YOU'RE THE STAR, BUT YOU'RE BEING USED LIKE AN ASSISTANT DIRECTOR...
IS THIS WHAT YOU CALL JAPANESE "PRACTICALITY"?
This country is pathetic.
You can speak Japanese, so say it in Japanese!
I don't understand what you're saying, but I can tell you're making fun of me!
IF YOU'RE AN ACTOR, AND WANT TO BE INVOLVED IN CREATING SOMETHING GOOD...
...FOLLOW THE JAPANESE RULES WHEN YOU'RE IN JAPAN!
NO MATTER WHERE YOU'RE FROM, SOLIDARITY AMONG COMRADES IS IMPORTANT WHEN YOU'RE IN CREATIVE ENDEAVORS!
...
Peek

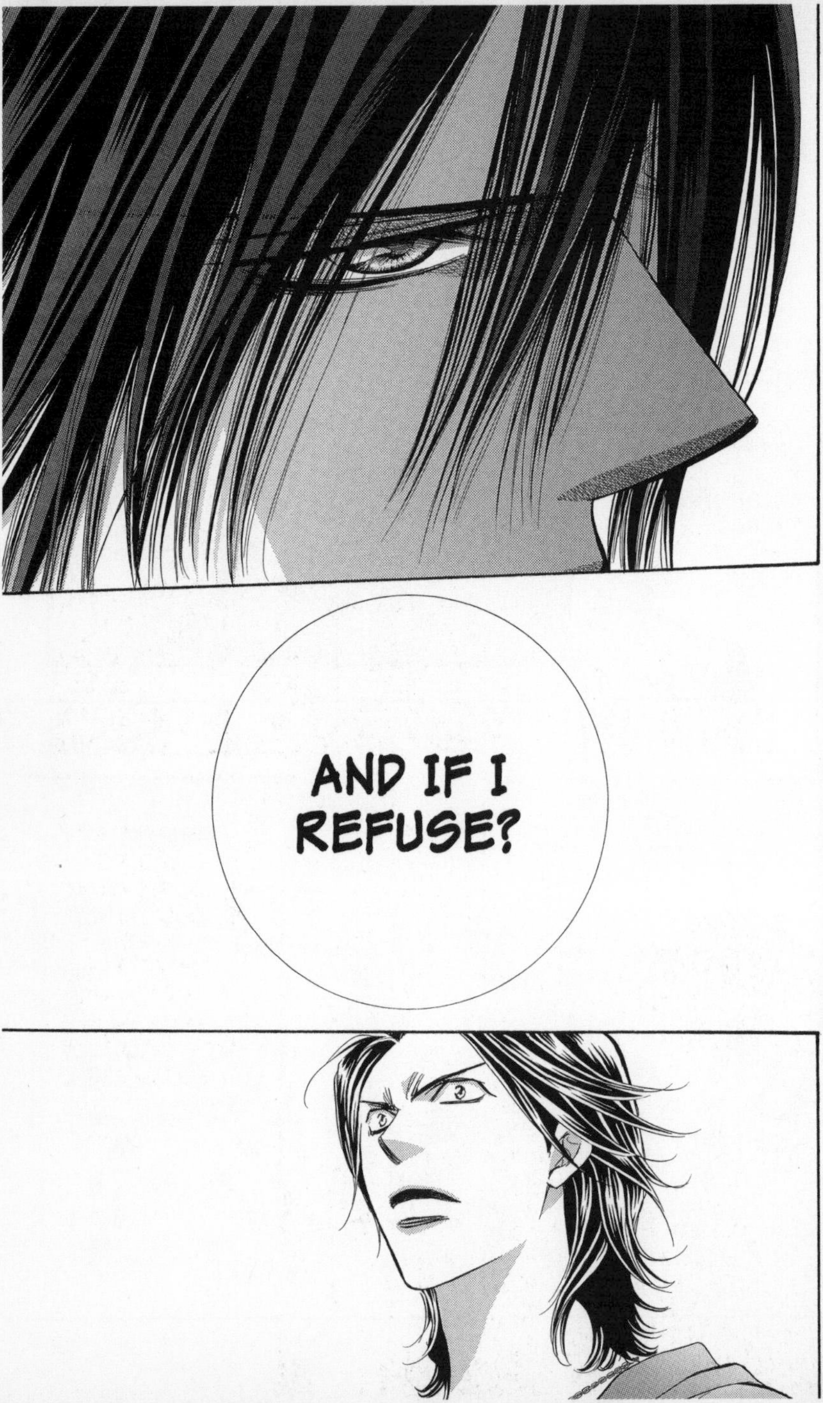
AND IF I REFUSE?

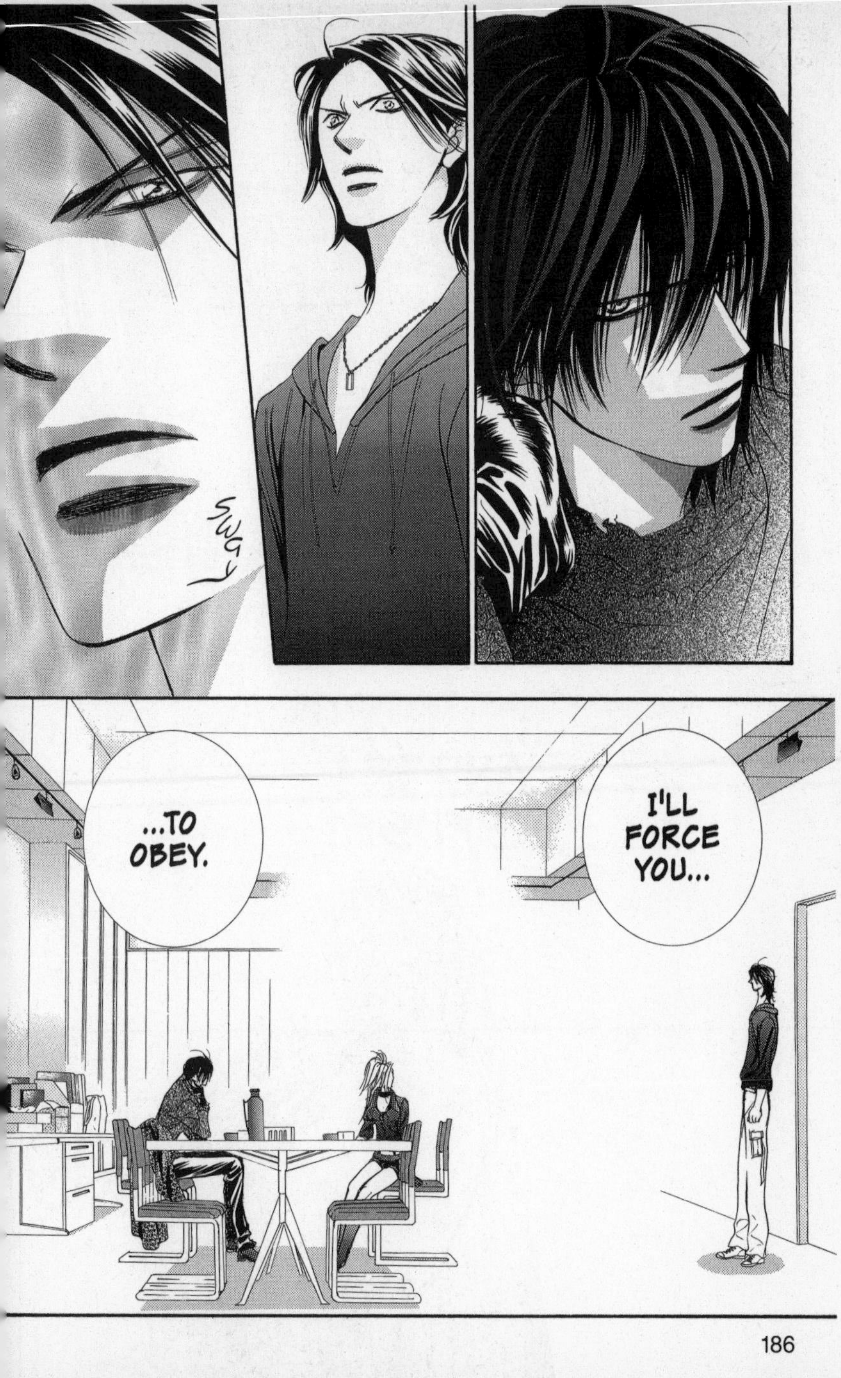
SWAY
I'LL FORCE YOU...
...TO OBEY.

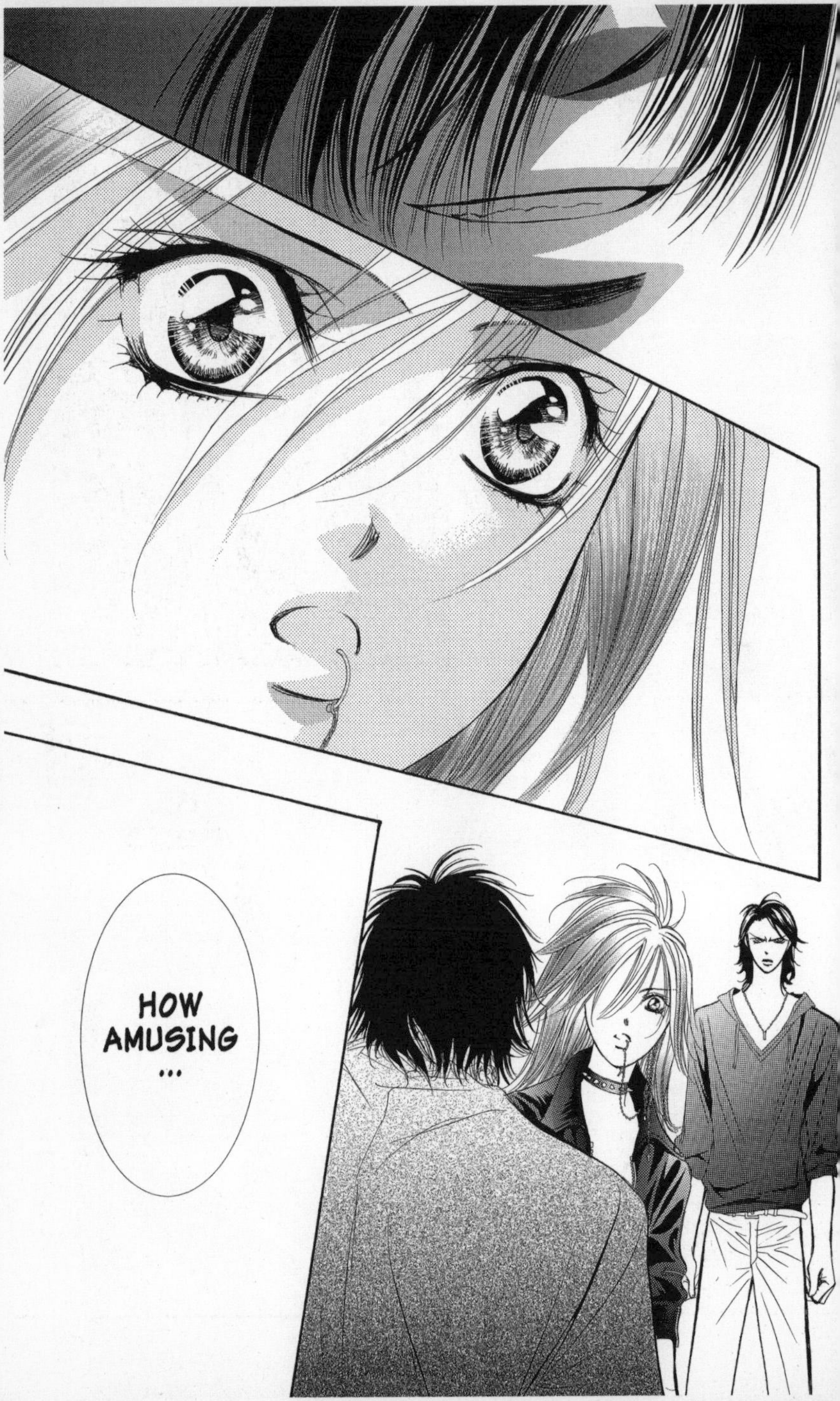
HOW AMUSING ...

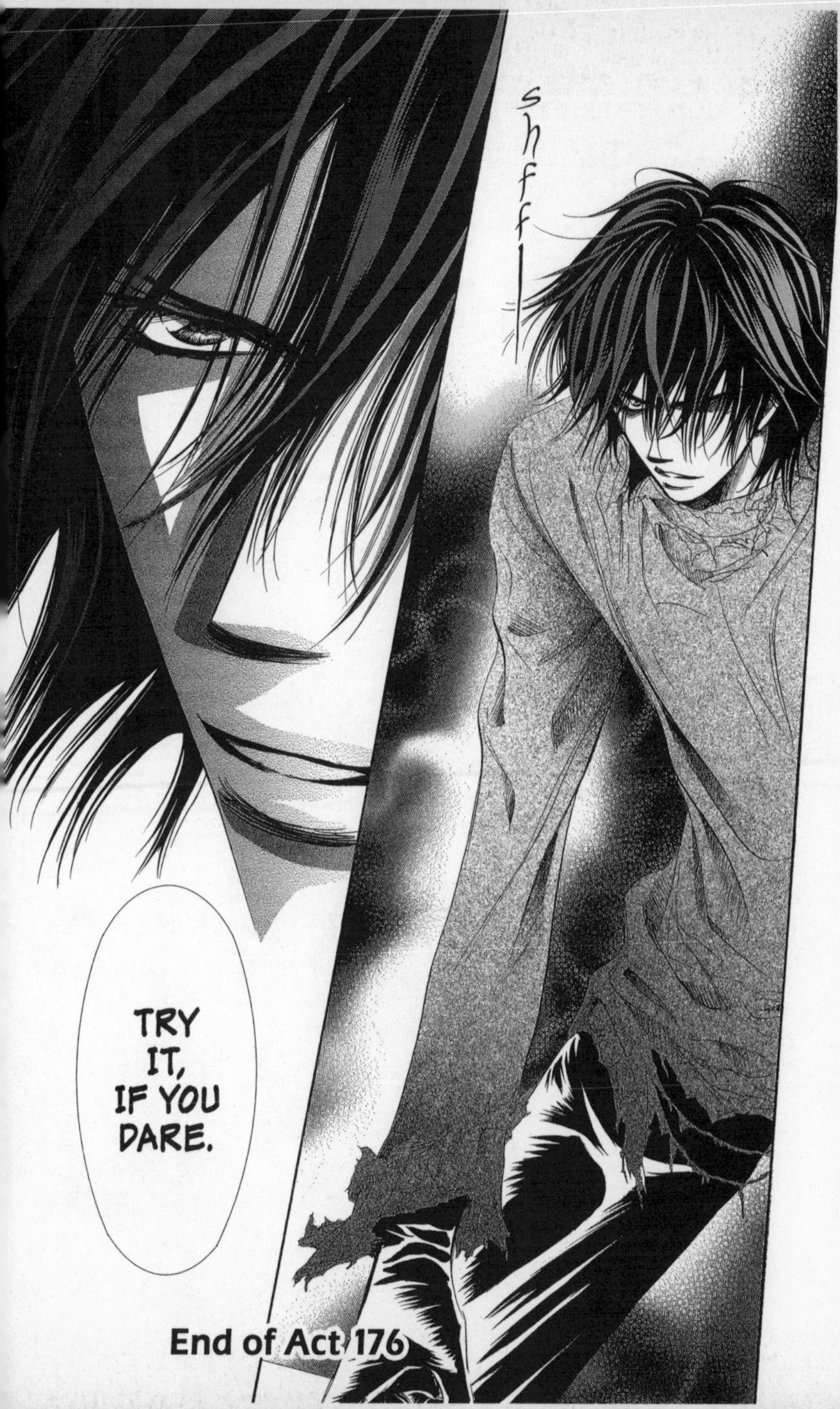
shff
TRY IT, IF YOU DARE.
End of Act 176

Skip·Beat! End Notes
Everyone knows how to be a fan, but sometimes cool things from other cultures need a little help crossing the language barrier.

Pg 167, panel 1: Like a Japanese bike gang
It is common for members of Japanese biker gangs to change the kanji spellings of their names, often picking more dangerous or tough sounding kanji than the originals.

Page 167, panel 1: Cain Heel kanji
The kanji Murasame imagines Cain Heel using are:
渦 (ka) means "whirlpool"
院 (in) means "shadow"
氷 (hi) means "ice"
屡 (ru) means "again and again"

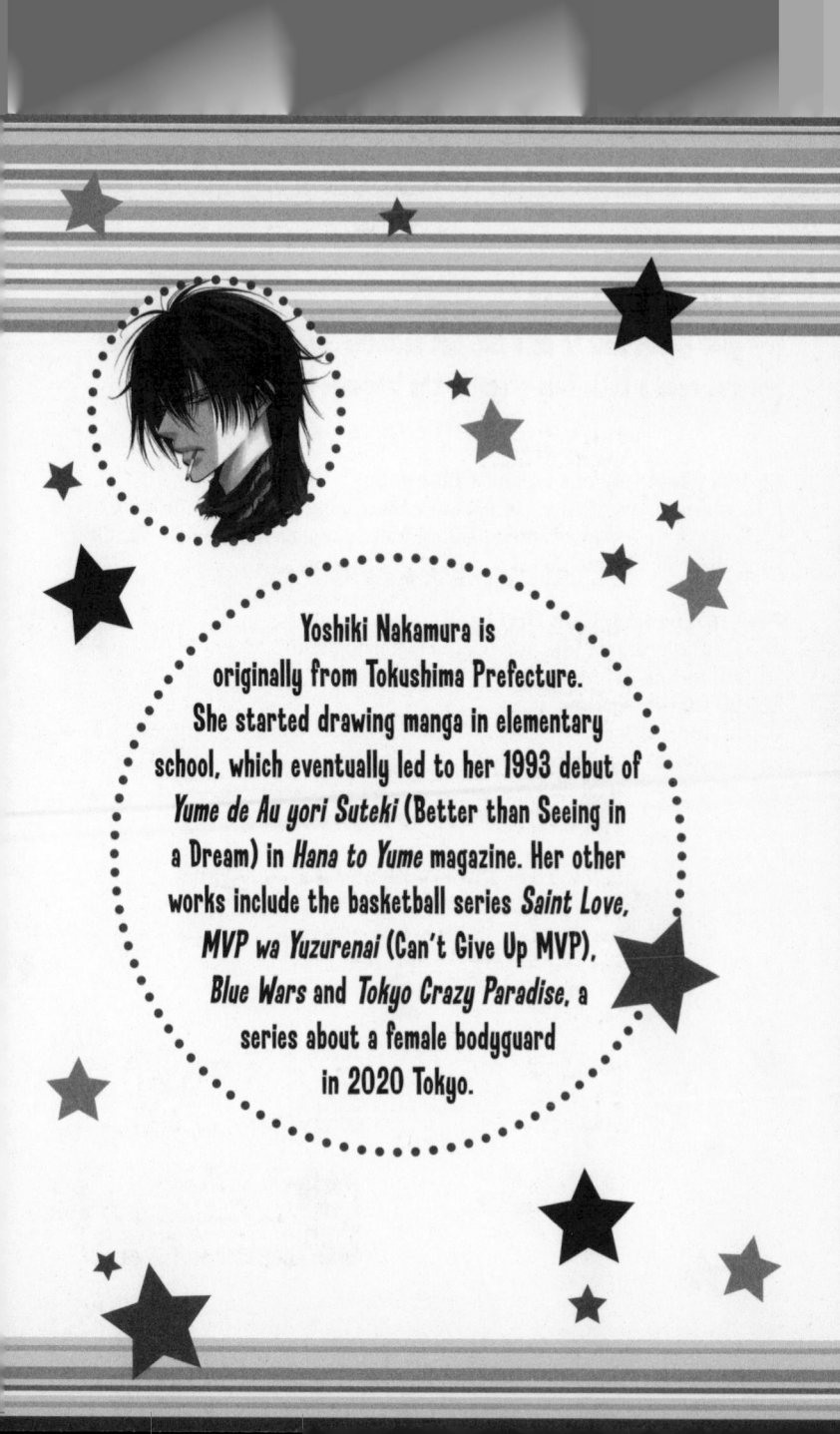

Yoshiki Nakamura is originally from Tokushima Prefecture. She started drawing manga in elementary school, which eventually led to her 1993 debut of *Yume de Au yori Suteki* (Better than Seeing in a Dream) in *Hana to Yume* magazine. Her other works include the basketball series *Saint Love*, *MVP wa Yuzurenai* (Can't Give Up MVP), *Blue Wars* and *Tokyo Crazy Paradise*, a series about a female bodyguard in 2020 Tokyo.

SKIP·BEAT!
Vol. 29
Shojo Beat Edition

STORY AND ART BY YOSHIKI NAKAMURA

English Translation & Adaptation/Tomo Kimura
Touch-up Art & Lettering/Sabrina Heep
Design/Ronnie Casson
Editor/Pancha Diaz

Skip·Beat! by Yoshiki Nakamura © Yoshiki Nakamura 2011.
All rights reserved. First published in Japan in 2011 by HAKUSENSHA, Inc., Tokyo.
English language translation rights arranged with HAKUSENSHA, Inc., Tokyo.

Printed in the U.S.A.

Published by VIZ Media, LLC
P.O. Box 77010
San Francisco, CA 94107

10 9 8 7 6 5 4 3 2 1
First printing, October 2012

www.viz.com

www.shojobeat.com

SURPRISE!

You may be reading the wrong way!

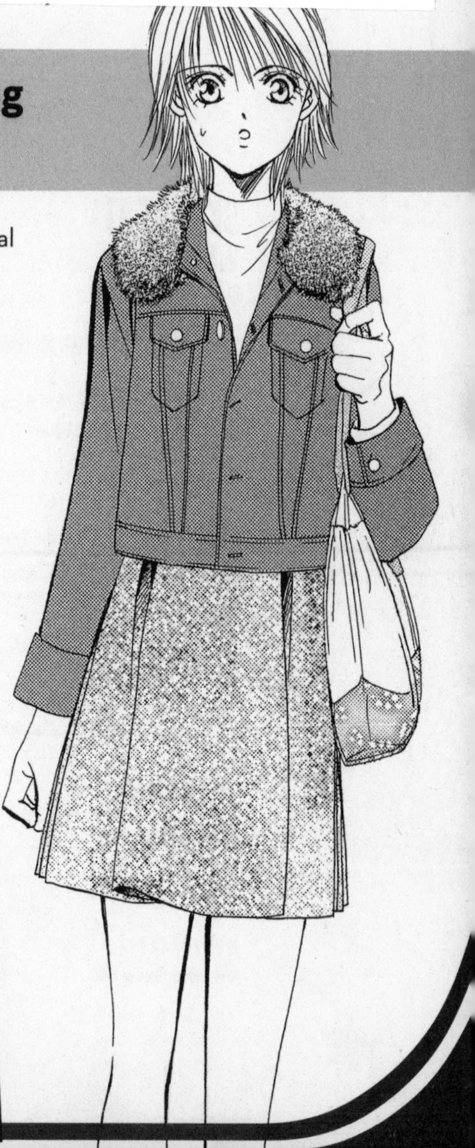

It's true: In keeping with the original Japanese comic format, this book reads from right to left—so action, sound effects, and word balloons are completely reversed. This preserves the orientation of the original artwork—plus, it's fun! Check out the diagram shown here to get the hang of things, and then turn to the other side of the book to get started!

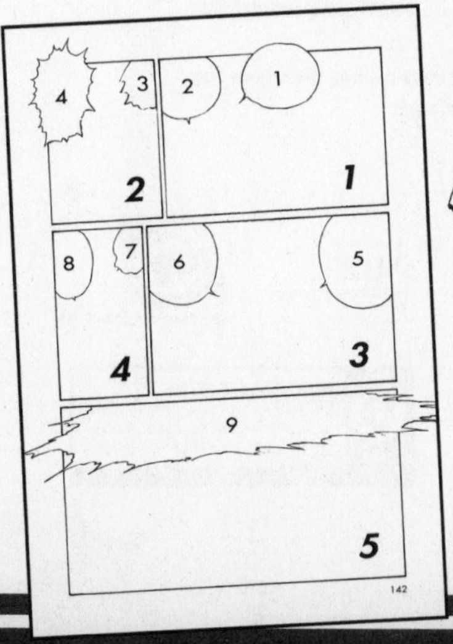
1
2
3
4
1
2
5
6
7
8
3
4
9
5
142